CRIMSON FALLS DUET

DANI RENÉ

BITTER VOWS

CRIMSON FALLS DUET BOOK ONE

*To the girls who prefer the Big Bad Wolf because
he's an expert when it comes to eating you.*

LYCAN

Life doesn't afford us many chances to make right what we've done wrong.

It also doesn't allow us to apologize to those who have passed—no longer walking this earth. When I was younger, the guilt ate away at me. Inch by inch, my soul was consumed by the incessant culpability taking hold of me, but then I realized—if I allow myself to *feel*, I'll never survive. Instead of allowing sentiment to burrow its way inside me, I've buried what most would call *human emotions*. And all I'm left with is the ice-cold ruthlessness that grips me.

Especially growing up with the family I did. The Shaw name was synonymous with violence and bloodshed, and even though I should walk away, change it, I don't. I'm proud of the fact that we're known as people you do not cross. My brother decided to walk away from it all. It hurt at first, but now, I realize family isn't always blood.

Choices are what guide us, taking us through the darkness that's been holding us hostage for so long that when we look up into the light, we don't recognize it. Over the years, I've become accustomed to the shadows, and I've basked in them. I no longer want an escape.

Strolling through my club, Heaven, I stop when I reach the immaculate mahogany bar. I cast a glance over the large, dimly lit space, taking in each patron who has already entered my domain. When I opened this place, it was meant for those who wanted to play, to indulge in fantasies that aren't *normal,* and even though my tastes are eclectic, I didn't realize just how dark some tendencies go. I've learned, though, and I've reveled in the shadows.

Black suede booths curl around silver-legged tables, which seats four people. Each one private as they snake against the far wall. To the left of the bar is the entrance to the club, which is where we've just come from, and I notice how it's hidden by the sleek, black, silken curtains that keep this space private.

Stools line the bar area, and to the right is the hallway, which leads to rooms where the games begin. Once the couples or groups have acquainted themselves and agreed to an evening's festivities, they move to one of the private rooms.

Some like to be watched, so I've ensured that there is space for them as well. Every person who walks into Heaven finds solace, pleasure, and satisfaction. When they leave, it's as if all that happened within these walls are a memory, a happy one, but nothing more than an escape from their harsh reality.

I take in the customers who are settled with drinks. The men in expensive, tailored suits and the beautiful women draped over their arms—eye candy. Most of the politicians and businessmen who frequent Heaven are corrupt, married, or owned by the mafia.

My club offers them a cover for the activities which Heaven is famed for. With Masters and slaves, Dominants and their submissives, along with single women who crave the degradation and humiliation that's usually frowned upon, I've given them somewhere to enjoy their desires.

But everything comes with a price.

Everything.

Membership is not cheap, but there are rules that govern every person who walks in the door, and even after they leave, they know that confidentiality is key. Isaac, the barman who's worked for me for years, slides over a tumbler with deep amber liquid.

"Thanks."

"Busy night?" he asks, knowing that I'll have the headcount before the doors open. I only allow so many people in the club at a time, and each night, I limit the number of patrons who enter Heaven.

"Yes, we have a special party tonight," I tell him before I take a sip of my drink, watching the couples slowly forming as they get to know each other. Each woman who walks in here has signed an agreement that she understands what happens in here stays here. And each man knows that he will immediately cease all play if he is told to stop.

My cell phone buzzes in my pocket, and when I pull it out, I notice a familiar name—Alexei Carnevali. One of the Mafia princes I've known since I was a kid. We grew up together, did shit while studying at university, and now that we each have our own companies, we've become closer than I anticipated.

"Alex," I greet after pressing the phone to my ear. "To what do I owe this honor?"

"I was wondering if you can help me," he starts. "I have a job coming up which I'm certain would interest you." I can hear the excitement in his tone, and I have to admit, my interest is piqued.

"Oh? I'm always open to working with you. Especially if it means bloodshed." I signal for another drink as he chuckles at my response, my gaze landing on the door as two patrons saunter in. One is an influential politician, the other, someone I've been keeping my eye on. His money has been his downfall, and his wife has no fucking clue about his proclivities.

"There's a convent about two hours outside of Los Angeles, which I need your men to check up on, and since you have connections over there, I figured you'd be the best person to ask. I've heard rumors of the Cartel moving illegal goods into the States, trading them up from the border to the City of Angels."

My ears perk up at his words. "Illegal goods?" I've had connections all over the country, all over the world, but if Alex is coming to me, then this must be big. Even though he must have people down there, I have a feeling this goes deeper than just the Cartel.

"Girls." The one word has me on my feet. My target for the evening is moving toward the booths, a woman on his arm that isn't his wife, and even though my blood is boiling with the need to take him down, what Alex just confessed is more important.

"Send me the info. I'll have them shut down within a few hours. Blood will spill."

"If I were closer, I would ask you to wait for me, but I'm in Italy; a job that needed my attention," he informs me. The lowering of his tone tells me he's not alone.

If he's in Europe, then I wonder where his *familia* is. "What about your cousins?" I know the Moretti brothers are based in LA. I've never met them personally, but I've spent enough time with Alex to know they're not men you mess around with.

"They're... indisposed. Miami needed their attention." His voice tinged with mystery has me pondering what they're up to, but I know better than to ask. I don't get into their business, and they don't get into mine.

Nodding to myself, I tell him, "I'll sort this out." The

promise is there as I move into my spacious office, drink in one hand, my phone in the other. Kicking the door shut behind me, I settle behind my cherry wood desk. The sleek leather chair molds to my form, and I relax against it before waking my computer with a nudge to the mouse. When the screen lights up, Alex's encrypted email is waiting. "I've got the info; just leave it with me. I'll confirm once the job is done."

"Talk soon." He hangs up before I can say anything more, but there's nothing else I can tell him. I hit dial on Kahn's number. The one man I know will have a vested interest in this.

It takes him two rings before answering. "Mr. Shaw."

"Kahn, I have a job for you and the team. I know you're out on the East Coast right now, but before you dive into training, I'd like you to check out a convent," I tell him, leaning back in my chair, casting my gaze down at the club below.

Silence greets me for a long moment before he responds, "A convent?"

"Alexei Carnevali just called," I inform my best man. "He has it on good authority that illegal goods are being moved from New York to Mexico. The Cartel is involved, but we can't walk into their territory without proof, or we will start a war."

"Goods? As in...?" He allows his words to filter into the silence between us, and each time I think about what Alex told me, the more my blood boils at the thought of what's happening to innocent women.

"Yes."

"I'm on it," Kahn tells me, raw honesty in his tone, but also a hint of the hunter I know him to be. That's why I hired him when he first walked into my club. A man with the desire of a predator and the skill of a trained assassin. *What more could I want?*

"Good. Keep me updated." I hang up, my glare still on the thieving asshole downstairs. Mr. Bardot is nothing more than a cheating scumbag, but he doesn't realize just how he's about to pay me back for walking in when I had to.

A fucking Bardot coming in and ruining shit in my life once more. It's not the first time I've had to learn about their family. The name is synonymous with secrets. The Bardot family come from old money, and with the help of his mother, Grace Bardot, they stole more from us than just a few million.

But then I learned more about Horatio. He's got problems, some than money won't fix. I only found out because I looked into why he spent far too much time in my club. It was then I realized something was amiss.

At first, I thought it was my good for nothing brother, but Darius had no access to funds, not mine anyway. Not Shaw money. But there's more to the story than just the money. The problem is that Horatio has lost a lot more than his livelihood. He's about to lose something far more precious to him.

With a sardonic grin on my face, I push to my feet,

button my suit jacket, and make my way down to the main area of the club. Time to speak to Mr. Bardot and ensure that his signature is on the contract before he even thinks of playing in one of my rooms tonight.

Only, he doesn't know just how expensive his *needs* have become.

SCARLETT

The sleek, silver dress that drapes over my curves is beautiful, but even as I stare at myself in the mirror, I'm torn between going to this party or staying home. My mother, Marinda Bardot, is one of the most publicized socialites, while my father, Horatio Bardot, is working hard to get into the senator's office.

Wealth comes at a steep price, and they don't realize it. Since I was a child, I knew what I wanted to do, and it wasn't to be the pretty arm candy my mother would like me to be. I have goals, dreams, and they don't involve a man putting a diamond on my finger and knocking me up while he goes to his pristine office to run a Fortune 500 company.

I want to be the CEO of my own life, but with the Bardot name comes responsibility I'm not ready for. Granted, my gran, who I look up to, will understand if I told her my plans. Because of her, I was able to get an internship in New York in a few months.

My folks were not happy about that, but they acquiesced because Gran wanted it. Slipping my feet into the four-inch heeled sandals, I take in my outfit, my long, red hair plaited in a thick braid down to the middle of my back. Stray curls have already come loose, but I don't tie them back. My wide, dark eyes are lined with black, my lashes darkened by mascara, and my lips are shimmering from the gloss painted over the deep red lipstick.

Perfectly poised.

I silently make my way out to the hallway, listening for my parents arguing, but find silence. Thankfully, they haven't already started fighting, but the night is still young. By the time I reach the foyer, my mother appears from the dining room, a flute of champagne already in hand, her eyes sparkling as she takes me in.

"Oh, Scarlett," she coos. "You look beautiful. There'll be so many men wanting to dance with you this evening. I hope you're ready." Her excitement about finding me a man makes me want to run back upstairs and hide in my room. At my age, I should've moved out of the house already, but I stayed. Mainly to keep an eye on my folks, but also, I've always felt safe in my childhood home.

"Well, they'll have to form a line," I tell her with a fake

smile plastered on my lips. If there's one thing she's taught me to do well, that's pretending. It's not that I wouldn't like to be with someone, but the fact that she wants to marry me off to the most eligible bachelor leaves a bad taste in my mouth.

Laughter bounces from her lips, sounding like a tinkling coin against the expensive tiles as my father saunters toward us, a tight smile on his face and a gaze that flickers with apprehension. I notice the tension taut in his shoulders as he takes us in. "Are you ready?" he asks, his focus on me, and I nod. It doesn't take my mother long to swallow down her drink, and soon enough, we're in the town car as it weaves down our long driveway.

My phone buzzes in my purse, and I find a message from my best friend, Aelin. The moment I walked into class and settled beside her, I knew I'd found a connection. She looked over at me, her silver eyes shimmering as she took me in. Her smile was genuine, nothing like girls and women from the social circles I've been used to growing up. It was refreshing.

"I hope you're not going to sit on your phone all night, Scarlett," my mother admonishes, which I was expecting. The fact that I do have friends outside the people she knows doesn't sit well with my mother. It never has.

"Leave the girl, Marinda," Dad tells her, his gaze meeting hers. Something passes between them unspoken, which has ice trickling down my spine. My father turns his attention on me, offering me a smile that doesn't reach his eyes. He's never lied to me. I know this because when Dad would tell me something serious, he would always meet my gaze, but his next words are uttered with his stare on the seat behind me. "It's nice that you have friends. Your future might change in an instant, and who knows when you'll need someone to talk to."

"What do you mean?" There's a twisting in my gut, a coiling serpent tightening with every silent second that passes. My father's expression is one of guilt when he looks to my mother, then me.

"Just that Aelin is a nice girl. You should keep in contact with her." He waves his hand as if dismissing the topic, and I know if I ask anything more, he'll only ignore me. When my father decides to keep things to himself, there's no way of getting him to open up.

I don't respond, merely nod and continue with my reply to Aelin, letting her know I'm on my way and I'll see her soon. The charity ball is being held in town in a lavish, five-star hotel with only celebrities and politicians in attendance. The guestlist is filled with names that most would be excited to rub shoulders with, including Aelin's dad, who's one of the most well-known names across the world, a famous rock star with a penchant for causing women to drop to their knees. And soon, my best friend will be on tour with the band, leaving me to a lonely summer with my grandmother in Crimson Falls.

Thankfully, I enjoy spending time at the manor house, or I would be depressed having to spend time at home. Grace

Bardot is a woman who no longer needs anything — no man, no friends, and certainly not the number of staff who work for her. She spends her days sipping gin and tonics in the sunshine while reading her favorite romance novels. The Bardot money is what they call *old money*. Because of Gran's parents, she's always lived a comfortable life, which afforded me one as well.

The car comes to a stop, and the back door whooshes open where we're met with the flashes of cameras, shouting press, and fans scream as my mother and father exit the vehicle. Stepping foot onto the plush red carpet, I attempt to ignore the shouts of my parents' names as we make our way through the crowd, stopping a few times to allow the cameras to capture us.

Finally, inside the enormous, gilded ballroom, my gaze flits around, hoping to find my best friend. It doesn't take long for me to spot the sleek, raven hair in the crowd. The only woman here with her hair not pinned with diamonds and pearls.

Leaving my folks to mingle, I make my way over to Aelin, who's already giggling up a storm with some dashing man in a three-piece suit. A dark tie leads up to a smooth, angular jaw, pale skin, and full, pink lips.

A squeal from beside me catches my attention before I meet his stare, and Aelin pulls me into a hug. "This is my best friend," she gushes, and I finally find the eyes of the man, no, actually, the boy she's talking to. He looks like he's younger than us.

"Nice to meet you," he tells me, offering a hand which I accept before side-eyeing Aelin.

"Can I talk to you?" I hiss at her. Glancing at the cute guy, I smile. "We'll catch you later." Pulling her through the crowd, we find the bar where I grab a flute of champagne for myself and one for her. "Are you crazy?"

"What?" Her wide, golden-brown orbs shimmer with amusement.

My gaze finds her boy-toy before I look at her again. "That guy isn't even old enough to drink yet." Rolling my eyes, I can't help but laugh when she giggles playfully.

"Oh come on, like you are? Also, I was having fun. His older brother is a hottie, so I did have a plan," she tells me conspiratorially. I sip my drink, allowing my gaze to rove the room, taking in the faces of the men and women who are all draped in designer clothes and exquisite jewels. Aelin's hand lands on my arm, her fingers wrapping around my wrist before she whisper-hisses, "Who is that?"

"Who?" I turn to where she's staring to be met with a man who looks like he's just stepped off the film set of some rough motorcycle club movie. He doesn't look like he fits in here with his leather jacket and black tee. His boots are dusty, his jeans fit too tight, hugging muscled thighs as he saunters deeper into the room. His midnight-black hair reminds me of my best friend's, and his tanned skin speaks of someone who's been outdoors in the full sun all day, every day.

Dangerous. That's the word to describe him.

"Now that is a man," Aelin murmurs more to herself than to me because I can't drag my gaze away. Menace emanates from him as if he were wearing it like a cologne. But then he makes a beeline for my father, which has my mouth dropping open in shock. The two men seem to know each other, but Dad pales when his gaze lands on the stranger. "Uhm..." My best friend's voice filters into nothing when my father disappears with said stranger into the hallway, talking heatedly as they go.

"Uhm, is right," I tell her, my attention now torn between catching up with Aelin or following Dad to find out what's going on. My gaze snaps back to where my mother seems completely oblivious to everything as she laughs and flirts with someone in a suit who looks like he's got one foot in the grave.

The emcee announces that dinner will soon be served and requests everyone to take their seats. All the while through dinner, Dad's face is a picture of pure dread. I lean over and whisper in his ear, "Are you okay?"

He chuckles. "Of course I am." The fake smile is back, lying to me directly to my face. It's the second time in my life he's done it, and my gut churns with unease. "Why don't you enjoy your dinner, sweetheart?" he tells me, nudging my chin with his knuckles in a gesture that usually would calm me down. But after what I've witnessed, it leaves a sinking feeling in my stomach.

LYCAN

The paperwork is in place. There's nowhere to run now because tonight, I'll be meeting *her*. I've been flicking through her social media for a few days now, taking in every photo I can. I've devoured her with my hungry ogling, and my predatory fangs are ready to sink into the sweet, supple flesh of Scarlett Bardot.

The one photo I've saved is of her in a beautiful red dress, the color of blood. The sleek, silky material hugs her curves like a second skin. Her long hair is draped over one shoulder in a thick, auburn braid. The thought of her with those flowing locks over her voluptuous tits makes my dick hard. She's not skinny, with curves enough to grip and manhandle, but even so, I'm certain she'll be able to bear children. All I need is one son.

Horatio didn't know what he was setting his daughter up for when he walked into my world and wanted to play with the big boys. The dollar signs in his eyes flashed as he learned about everything that Heaven could gift him, a place to delve into the darkest fantasy, but also a place you could lose your soul to the devil. To me.

When Kahn arrived back from the gala, he told me exactly what Bardot had said; he gave Horatio the ultimatum. The payment will be his daughter's hand in marriage.

And then Kahn informed Horatio Bardot I will be bringing the contract to him personally. While we dine with the beauty, I'll assess her to ensure she's completely oblivious to who I am and why I'm there.

I should have been at the gala to hammer the final nail in the coffin, but having my right-hand man do it, allowing me time to prepare the contract, was necessary. And I wanted to meet Scarlett in her home for the first time. Not at some fancy party that had nothing to do with me.

Picking up the phone, I dial Alex's number. Two rings later, I hear his voice. "Do you have news for me?" The eagerness in his tone is the only giveaway that he's been waiting on me. It's only been a few days since he called, but Kahn and the team moved quickly.

"They walked into the convent, found a basement of fifteen girls, all new to the church. My men are looking into a chain of convents they'd been moved through posing as real churches. The nuns have young women join, all the while training them for more sinister futures. I have a few names. One, in particular, stands out."

"Lorenzo?" Alex asks, naming the person in question, no surprise in his tone. He knew we'd find it. He knew I would send Kahn to do this job, and that's why he called me.

"You realize this is going to blow up before the month is at its end?" I lean back in my chair, ignoring the paperwork I need to get through before dinner tonight. I have a couple of hours, but I'm intrigued to know why Alex really allowed me to take the lead with this.

"That's the idea. Once the Cartel knows we're onto them, we'll have started a blood war. Something I'm looking forward to because I want that man's life in my hands, and when I finally get it, I'll ensure to snuff it out."

And there it is, the underlying promise. There's nothing I've ever done for the mafia that didn't come with another hidden agenda, and this time it's no different. I should feel used, but I enjoy when justice is found.

"My man taking the lead on this won't stop until he's found Lorenzo," I tell Alex. "If he does..."

"I know. It's not Lorenzo I want. Tell your team they have permission to take what they need, a pound of flesh, or more, but I want the leader."

Chuckling, I shake my head at his passion. Once, long ago, that was me. When they took my father's life, and my brother sided with them instead of his blood. That's why

Darius and I no longer see eye to eye. He believed their lies about our father, and I, being the eldest son, took on the responsibility left to me. "You'll get him. My men won't step on any toes. I can assure you of that, Carnevali."

"Good. I'm flying home tonight. I may have to visit Heaven for an evening of decadent play before I get back to LA." I can hear the smile in his voice. The temptation of spending a few hours in my club's exclusive back rooms has become a staple to most Made Men in this city.

"I'm not in New York for another few days, but when you're at JFK, let me know. I'll have one of my cars collect you and bring you straight to the club. You can have a quiet evening, or you can choose any one of the women who are regulars."

"Only one?" He laughs, and I realize he's always been one to partake in a ménage scene, or even three women, with him enjoying the spoils.

"Well, you know you're welcome to anything in any one of my clubs." Pushing to my feet, I grab my jacket, realizing the time. "I have to head out. Important meeting tonight, and I can't be late."

"Of course. See you soon," Alex tells me before hanging up, leaving me to my thoughts of this evening's festivities. Pocketing my cell phone, I grab my keys and wallet before leaving the office, locking the door behind me. When I reach the club floor, I find Sawyer, one of the men working with Kahn.

The tall, ex-marine has been with me for almost five

years, learning the ins and outs of the underground export business the Shaw name runs. When I took over from my father, I knew I needed men I could trust.

"Mr. Shaw," he greets when I near him as he settles himself on a stool at the bar. The club isn't busy, a handful of clients have made themselves comfortable in the booths, and the sleek, silver bar, which curves like a horseshoe, is empty but for Sawyer.

"I'm heading back to Crimson Falls," I tell him. "Can you stay to close up?"

He nods. "Of course." There's a rigidness to him, cold, closed off, and I wonder briefly if he's ever had the love of a woman. He doesn't play in the club, he's never mentioned coming home from Iraq to anyone, and when we've spent time together in meetings with the team, his focus has been laser sharp no matter which of the women I employ would stroll in, needing something from me.

"Good." I move past him, making my way to the garage where my shiny, raven-colored Cadillac Escalade waits. I settle back in the driver's seat as I start the engine, and the speakers play a soft melody. The gentle voice of Ruelle comes through as she sings "Find You" and I can't help but smile.

It's time to meet my future wife. Only, she doesn't know about me. She doesn't realize her life is about to change.

The streets are busy for this late, but I glide through the city as I take the highway out to Seattle's northern suburbs, where Bardot lives with his family. A man with the means to live anywhere in the world, but he chooses *my* city. As much as I love the Big Apple, it's only one of many venues I consider elite. Seattle has taken my heart and allowed me to play when I need to without having to form long-term connections with women.

But Horatio is one of the reasons I haven't left Seattle yet. He knew what he was doing when he bought the house just outside the bustling metropolis. The fact that my father trusted him angers me. The fact that he took from me only infuriates me further. The money he took hardly made a dent in my fortune; however, when someone takes something of mine, I believe it's only fair to claim something of theirs in repayment.

I'm pulling up to the Bardot mansion's wrought iron gates when my phone rings through the speakers. "Yes?" I answer, knowing it's Kahn calling with news, and by the time the car winds up the long, paved driveway leading to a three-story house, my focus is on my eagerness to meet Scarlett Bardot.

"I stumbled upon something you might want to know before you walk into the Bardot house tonight," he tells me, his voice tense, the clipped tone of his words warning me that I'm not going to like the outcome of his investigations.

Hitting the brakes, I say, "Tell me everything."

SCARLETT

I haven't been able to talk to Dad since the night of the charity gala. He's been gone for a few days, and tonight is the first time he's been home. The man he was talking to still has me on edge because I have no idea who he was. The stranger didn't fit in, and he never returned when Dad did, which means the stranger was sent away.

Only, I'm not sure if it was a friendly parting or not.

Classical music drifts from the dining room as I make my way down the stairs. My parents must have guests over because I hear glasses clinking together and my mother's laughter at something someone said. Whenever we have guests, it's always like this. She puts on a show in front of them, but by the time they leave, she and Dad are at each other's throats.

The moment my sneakers hit the expensive Italian tiles, my mother's voice rings out to me. "Scarlett, come in here for a moment, darling." The fake tone of her voice has me rolling my eyes.

My twenty-first birthday is coming up, and I told her I wanted to spend my summer with Gran before I fly to New York to start my internship. The excitement at finally moving out on my own has taken over, and I've been counting down the days until I'm free. Spending my life behind the opulent walls of the Bardot mansion has been stifling, and I'm more than ready to find my independence.

It's been difficult to accept that my future had been planned for me, even before I could walk. Just last year, my mother was convinced I would be married by the time I'm twenty-one, but she soon learned my desire was to work hard, build a company from the ground up, and not depend on a man to pay for everything.

I reach our lavish entertainment area, which leads into the dining room and take it in. Decked in furniture which cost more than most people make in a year and dripping with a gilded chandelier, I find my parents both dressed to the nines, along with a man I've never met before.

The moment I enter the room, his gaze snaps to mine, stealing the breath from my lungs at the luminosity of the jade color. A seemingly nonchalant glimpse lands on me, locking on mine, reminding me of the vacations Dad used to take me on to British Columbia. The lake house we had overlooked a thick forest, which was as dangerous as this man's stare. The stranger's dark hair matches his charcoal suit. The danger that he seems to exude fills the room with menace, but I tip my chin up, showing him an act of defiance. My mother and father may cower to the wealthy assholes who walk in here, but I won't. My gaze tracks his silver button-up shirt because I need a reprieve from his intensity, but it doesn't help distract me because his body is immaculate in form.

Everything about this man seems put together for a reason. He doesn't wear something for the sake of covering up. It's been chosen specifically for him to lord over the people he's around. His presence screams wealth, and when he looks at me, the corner of his mouth quirks slightly as if I amuse him.

The heat in his gaze burns me from head to toe as he regards my outfit—sneakers, a black lace tank top, along with a pair of frayed denim shorts. My long, red hair has been straightened to the middle of my back, and my makeup is nonexistent since I didn't expect us to have company.

"There you are," my mother says, a smile plastered on her face as she takes in my appearance with a slight scowl before she pastes on the fake smile. "Come here." Her hand waves toward me, gesturing for me to close the distance, but with every step I take, the more I *feel* the stranger's eyes raking over me. It's almost as if he's touching me.

"Scarlett, this is Mr. Shaw," Dad says, introducing the

stranger to me. "He's having dinner with us this evening." There's a hint of tension in my father's voice, but he offers me a smile, which sets me at ease for the moment, but something else niggles at me. My dad is formidable, but the air in the room is thick with foreboding.

The man in question, Mr. Shaw, locks his cool gaze on me and offers me a smile. His hand extends toward me. The moment I slip my fingers along his palm, electric currents shoot through my arm, but I can't pull away because his hold is like solid steel.

"It's lovely to meet you, Scarlett," he says, allowing my name to roll off his tongue like the smooth whiskey he's drinking. His deep baritone and slight accent I can't quite put my finger on, send tingles of awareness right through me—from the top of my head to the tips of my toes.

"Same here," I answer in a whisper before he releases my hand and allows me to step back. The scent of him hangs in the air—cigars, and cinnamon. It is a strange combination, nothing like anyone I've come across before, especially since my dad and none of the men he considers friends have ever smoked in this house.

"Shall we?" Mom breaks the silence with a nervous grin, and we all follow her to the dining room table, where I notice four places have been set. I didn't plan on sitting with them, but it seems my presence is needed.

I settle in beside Mom as she slides her chair forward. The two men take their seats, Dad, at the head of the table, while Mr. Shaw settles in opposite me. Even though I'm not usually a nervous person, this man sets my stomach tumbling as he takes me in. It's almost as if he's assessing me for something.

Dinner is served moments later. The fragrance of spicy tomato soup and fresh, warm bread fills my nostrils, but even that can't wash away the scent of Mr. Shaw.

"Tell me, Scarlett," he speaks as I lift the spoon, scooping up the red liquid. "What is it you would like to accomplish in life, or better yet, what is your career choice?" Intrigue glints in his eye. Assessing me, he smiles, tipping his head to the side, and I wonder if he does it so he doesn't look as scary. But it only makes him seem more sinister in his appraisal of me. He reminds me of a dangerous animal, watching its prey, stalking until it's time to strike.

My gaze holds his for a moment before I focus on his mouth as he takes the spoon to his lips. The wetness from the soup causes a gentle glisten to capture and hold my attention. The deep red color reminds me of blood and just how predatorily he looks as he swallows, his tongue darting out to savor the taste of his kill. His throat works, the Adam's apple under smooth, tanned skin has my body doing strange things. I've never really watched a man like I'm doing with him, and I'm not sure why.

"Scarlett?" Mother's cool tone brings me back to the present, and I clear my throat, casting her a quick glance.

"Yes, sorry. I'd like to hopefully open my own media agency," I tell him with confidence brimming in my tone. "The need for honest reporting is something that has become somewhat of a passion of mine. What do you do?" My inquiry causes him to chuckle, the sound low, rumbling through his chest, and I wonder what's so funny.

"I don't think little girls should be so curious," he tells me, then sips another mouthful of his soup, but each movement he makes sends heat through me, and I can't explain why. His use of the term *little girl* rankles me, but I don't bite because he's trying to annoy me. I can tell with how he's watching, waiting for me to take the bait.

He's handsome, classically so, with sharp features and a jawbone free of stubble, but there is a dark shadow over the otherwise olive skin, which tells me if he doesn't shave, there'd be a beautifully thick beard. His lips form a tempting cupid's bow, with the lower lip fatter than the top. A mouth I'm sure could do sinful things if given a chance.

I'm not overly experienced, but I know enough to recognize a man who can make women swoon with a mere glance. His dark brow arches, and I realize I'm staring again. Shaking my head, I drop my gaze and eat my soup in silence, unsure of how to take him. Or even why I'm here in the first place.

"And you're planning on running it all by yourself?" he asks, and I *feel* his stare on me once more. The heat of it captures me, and I nod. "Words, little girl."

"I'm not a little girl," I bite out through gritted teeth, shoving my bowl away in frustration. "I'm twenty. I'm an adult."

This causes him to chuckle, his head angled as he

regards me with amusement. "Oh?"

"Scarlett!" My mother's tone turns my name into a curse word. Her heated glare is scorching me, but I don't look at her. I'm staring at the man before me.

"Yes," I answer back, causing him to laugh once more. "It's not funny. I'll be twenty-one in a month, and when I complete my internship, I'll have the necessary experience to start my own business. And I'll be able to do anything a man can do, possibly even better." Folding my arms across my chest, I don't turn my attention away from Mr. Shaw.

He sits back, and I don't miss the way his gaze flicks to my chest before meeting my stare as he regards me, the corners of his mouth upturned. His hands rest on the table, fingers tangled in between each other, and a thought of just how they'd feel touching me sparks through me for a split second before he speaks. "I like your fire, little red." His tone holds what I can only deem respect with fire blazing in his eyes. "It's refreshing. Most women cower in my presence," he continues, pushing to his feet, which has both my folks standing as well.

But I don't. Instead, I sit in my chair, my arms crossed as I watch his next move.

"Thank you for dinner, folks," he says in a bright tone, which belies the darkness swirling in those forest depths because his gaze never strays from me. "I'll have to get going if I'm going to catch the early flight to New York."

"Of course, I'm so sorry you have to leave so soon," Mom coos as if she's about to kiss his shoes as he leaves our house. "Let us walk you out. I have to apologize for Scarlett. She's feeling anxious about her future."

"There's no need for that," Shaw says before stopping at my chair, his hand landing on the back of it, but I feel the brush of his knuckles against my skin. He leans in, his lips a hair's breadth away from my cheek, and he whispers, "The big bad wolf won't eat you if you don't veer off the path."

I turn my head, branding him with my stare. "That's a fairy tale told to little girls to scare them."

Those deep, jade gemstones take in my sleek strands before he shrugs. "Perhaps. But little girls should always be wary of predators hunting for sweet, supple flesh," he says. "Especially when they go visit Grandma." He straightens as I shoot to my feet, but he's walking off before I have time to focus on what he's just said.

"Wait," I call, but all he does is offer me a wave as he makes his way to the exit where my parents are cowing to him as if he were the fucking King of England, and they were mere peasants.

I don't know who he is, but his attempt to scare me won't work.

I'm not a little girl afraid of the big bad wolf.

At least, that's what I tell myself.

LYCAN

The plane touches down on the East Coast, and I'm already anxious to get back and see *her*. The private hangar is empty apart from my men, who seem to have taken it upon themselves to ensure I have two cars waiting for me. When I built *my* empire from the ground up, there was only one thing I knew I needed to do, and that was to ensure my brother never came near me again. Being in New York sets me on edge because I know he's not far.

Our father left me with the export business, but I created Shaw Industries and made it what it is today—a sought-after conglomerate that would make the wealthiest men weep. With hotels and nightclubs, exclusive BDSM venues, and even a security company that would seed out the most hidden secrets, men come to me to *fix* what they broke. Kahn and his team have ensured I can vouch for them without blinking, and that's what I wanted, something to be proud of. With my plans to open a string of BDSM clubs across the country and then the world, I knew I needed to come to the New York branch to ensure everything is running smoothly.

But the thought of Darius on the loose sets me on edge. My brother isn't someone I can rely on or trust. With me being someone who runs his business with an iron fist, I don't doubt some of the men I've let go over the past few months have found him and ensured he knows my every move. But I'm not afraid. I've never been scared of him, and he knows it.

I should be back in Washington, where *she* is, but I needed to face the team here in person. Once I'm done, I'll fly back and find my little red when she visits grandma in Crimson Falls and claim what is rightfully mine. The fire she exuded certainly left me hard for her all night. I didn't want to walk away from her and come out here, but offering her a false sense of security will ensure she won't see me coming.

They've always called me the hunter and my brother the wolf, but I became both somewhere down the line. When the Bardots fucked me over with Horatio stealing money from me, I showed them I'm not some pushover they could fuck with. And now, their beautiful yet feisty daughter's hand in marriage is my payment.

After meeting her last night, I'm certainly intrigued by the young woman. She may be young, but she's exquisite. The way she carries herself captured my attention and every inch of her sweet curves tempted me enough to keep me interested.

What she doesn't know is that her life has already been planned out. It's sweet she thinks she'll be opening her own business. When I'm done with her, she'll be in my bed, pregnant with my heirs. At thirty-nine, I know I have to get started on a family who will be there one day when I'm gone. That's why I wanted someone younger, someone supple and sweet.

As I make my way to the car and slip onto the bench seat, my driver takes his place and starts the engine. His gaze meets mine in the rearview mirror, awaiting my command.

"I'll be going to Hawthorne first," I tell him, and he nods as we pull out of the parking area. I reach for my phone in my breast pocket and find it buzzing wildly. "What?"

"We've spotted Darius. He's on a bike heading out of Miami."

"Keep a tail on him. I don't need him disappearing again." I hang up before they can give me any excuses. My brother thinks he can outsmart me, but I have more money than god, which is what he walked away from, and it also gives me the upper hand.

Flicking open my app list, I scroll down to the one I need and open her profile—no new photos or posts. The last one she put up was of her in that god-awful black and denim ensemble she wore to dinner. The top itself wasn't bad, the lace offering a hint of what's beneath, but other than that, I'm going to have to get her to dress appropriately since she'll be on my arm at all the events I attend.

When I told her to be wary of the big bad wolf, I wasn't joking. She didn't need to know the finer details just yet. I can't wait to get my new bride to my home. The house in Crimson Falls, my father's stately property, will be ready for her.

The fact that her new home will not be far from her grandmother's house is convenient. Since it's right next door to the Bardot mansion is a testament to just how far I'll go to get her and keep her. I thought about buying somewhere else, a new city or town, but I know throwing money around isn't going to be the way to ensure her compliance.

I want her submission in every way possible, and there's no doubt in my mind she's going to be a challenge.

When we pull up to the building, I glance out of the window, taking note of the bustling streets. The door opens, and I step out, offering my driver a nod before I button my suit jacket and head into the awaiting, gleaming foyer.

Gold shimmers from the chandelier hanging from the center of the ceiling, offering a glittering entrance as you walk into the apartment block. An upmarket position within the city, wealthy patrons dripping from head to toe in designer labels pricing that most would balk at. Well, when I say most, I mean anyone who isn't me.

"Good evening, sir." The receptionist grins. I run this place like a hotel. You can't rent an apartment long-term, and most of the clientele only need a month or two.

"Is everything ready?"

A soft blush turns her cheeks pink, but the dark-haired beauty doesn't capture my attention like Scarlett. There's no fire. She's far too submissive and compliant. Which has me wondering if that's what my little red would be once I've broken her in. That won't do. I like fire. I love to be burned by my choices. It makes the challenge that much more exciting.

"Yes, sir," she responds and leans over her desk to offer me a glimpse of her cleavage, which looks like it's about to spill from the dress. "It's nice to see you again."

"I'm sure it is." I turn on my heel and head to the private elevator that will take me up to the rooftop club. It's an exclusive, well-known slice of heaven, and when the car deposits me outside the sleek, black doors, I twist the silver handle and step into every Dominant's fantasy.

Women kneel beside their Masters, and some even have two submissives who obediently await their next orders. Some have male submissives; others have a mix of male and female. When I first opened Heaven, I planned for it to be exclusively for my staff, for those who lived the lifestyle, but over time, it became something of a gem that people paid an extortionate amount of money for.

People like Bardot and his wife. Only, she no longer wanted this life, and he, on the other hand, took it upon himself to partake in the festivities when she didn't know. The more money he needed to pay his membership fees, the more money he stole from me.

Now, he'd do anything to ensure my silence. Hence the reason I have a new bride to take care of when I get back. But for now, I move through the space, heading toward the viewing rooms.

"Mr. Shaw," a voice drifts over the soft, classical music that plays in the background, and I turn to find Kahn. The businesses I run are varied, and he's one of the soldiers I send in to extricate information when needed.

"How are you doing?" I glance over my shoulder, taking him in. He's worked for me for several years after leaving the marines, but I know there's more to him than meets the eye. His file told me so, even if he didn't. It took him a while to admit his reasons for wanting this job. One being the income, but the other, focus. He knows about my resources and connections. His sister was taken just after he returned home, and he's been looking for her ever since. I don't mind him using my resources for it, but I wish he'd tell me.

I'm not a complete monster. I hope he finds her.

"I'm good. There's been some talk about the priest moving down to NOLA after we cleared the girls from the one Carnevali mentioned," he tells me as we stand side by side, watching a scene play out before us. A submissive getting her face fucked roughly, spit running down her chin as tears stream down her flushed cheeks. Her body merely a plaything for the man using her.

Pleasure is written all over his face, and I imagine having Scarlett in that exact position. I turn away, needing to calm down before I jump on the plane and head back to see her. Meeting Kahn's gaze, I inquire, "And you'd like to sort that out for me?"

"I would." It's his way of telling me he needs this. There's something more going down at the church with Father Lorenzo and his flock. "He's been on my radar for a long time, and there's someone there I'd like to ensure is safe."

I'll gladly allow him to fly out tonight to kill Lorenzo before the good Father steals more girls off the streets.

"Tell me something, Kahn," I speak. "Does this have anything to do with the real reason you agreed to work for me?"

His gaze snaps to mine, and he nods. He knows that I know. If he were someone I didn't respect, I would kill him right here, in front of everyone, and make sure people fear me. But for now, I'll allow him to do what he needs to.

"Go. When you get back, I need to know everything."

"Yes, sir." He offers a salute before disappearing. Now that I've sorted him out, I make my way to the private room where I have a redhead waiting for me. She's not Scarlett, but she'll have to do.

SCARLETT

By the time I reach my grandmother's estate, I'm exhausted. The small town she lives in, Crimson Falls, Washington, is nothing more than a vast forested area with a few exclusive homes dotted within the trees. Hidden like a rare jewel, it sits amongst the tall pine trees, usually in clouds, with a light drizzle that can continue for days on end.

As the car draws nearer to the large estate, anticipation trickles down my spine like a snake slithering across the ground. The memory of Mr. Shaw's words sends a cold shiver through me, which shakes me to the bone.

It's been so long since I visited, but I knew it was time

to see the old lady and spend time with her. She's getting on in age, and from what Mom says, she's not doing all that great. I'm also here to help her with the annual Bardot Ball that raises money for children abandoned by their parents or orphaned. The event sees guests drive up just for the evening, but there's another worry that's twisting my gut. *Would Mr. Shaw be in attendance?*

After he left, my parents told me he's going to be around a lot more. I'm not sure why, or in what capacity, but they both seemed afraid of the prospect, which doesn't sit well with me. As handsome as I find him, there is something sinister that sparks in his gaze.

We come to a stop just outside the mansion. The building is three floors of pure opulence. Wealth drips from every corner of my grandmother's house, and as much as I'd rather be at home, it's a reprieve from sitting and listening to my mother telling me what a disappointment I am.

The driver opens my door before offering me his hand, which I accept. The moment I step foot on the soft soil, awareness of being watched slithers over me. It feels as if there are eyes on me, waiting in the shadows. But as I turn to look out at the long driveway, taking in the trees surrounding the estate, I don't see anything in the darkness. It's late, nearing nine in the evening, and after the long day, I'm exhausted.

"Miss Bardot," Ellington, my driver, calls to get my attention. "I'll get the bags," he tells me. "Please wait at the door for me."

Nodding, I offer him a smile before making my way toward the large, ornate entrance that beckons. With a wrought iron handle and knocker, the dark wooden door sends more cold awareness through me.

This will be my home for the next four weeks. As much as I wanted space from my parent's constant bickering, the ghostly feel of the property makes the hairs on the back of my neck stand on end.

The rumors of Gran's deteriorating mental capacity have been whispers I grew up with, and I have a feeling that's why my parents agreed to me visiting her. Perhaps they want this stupid ball to go off without a hitch, so the Bardot name isn't tarnished. That's all they care about anyway, and that's the reason they sent me instead of coming themselves.

With my last name, I'm known throughout the country as the most eligible bachelorette, but even though my reputation precedes me, I'm still single—much to my mother's disgrace.

By the time I turn twenty-one, I should be married with children, at least according to my mother. The traditions that run in my family are archaic. Even though we're in the twenty-first century, they seem to think we're still living in the middle ages.

"Here you are." Ellington's voice causes me to jump as he walks up behind me. "I'm sorry, miss," he apologizes with a tepid smile. I watch as he pushes the door open, and a loud creak of annoyance comes from the hinges as it gapes, welcoming me inside.

Shockingly, the house is warmer than I expected when I enter. The marble tiles underfoot echo with the click of my heels. The long, deep-red-and-brown rug that lies in a straight line leading up to a sweeping spiral staircase gifts the enormous space with a hint of balminess.

I wonder if there's a heating system of sorts, but my grandmother would never pay for this place to be kept heated if I had to guess correctly. A heavy chandelier hangs above me, with crystals glinting in the dim light.

"Hello." A voice comes from my right, forcing me to turn toward a doorway that leads off from the foyer. "Welcome to Bardot Manor." A woman who looks to be in her mid-forties smiles at me brightly.

"Thank you," I respond. "I'm—"

"Scarlett Bardot," she says, interrupting me. "We've been so excited to have you visit. I hope you had a lovely trip?"

"Yes, it was acceptable," I tell her before glancing around once more.

Ellington offers me a nod before tipping his black driver's hat at us and exiting, shutting the heavy door behind him. And that's the final nail in my proverbial coffin. Once the car leaves, I'm stuck here.

"Let me show you to your room," the woman, who I still don't know, says.

I place a hand on her arm, needing her to look at me before I ask, "What is your name?"

She gushes, holding her hand to her chest. "I'm so

sorry. How rude of me. I'm Estelle," she informs me before curtsying as if I were the queen and she a mere servant. It seems Gran has taught the staff to bow down to her. I'm not surprised.

"No need for formality. I'm not my grandmother." Before Estelle can respond, I head toward the staircase and take a few steps up before turning to see the woman following without my bags.

"I'll have Gray bring those up shortly."

"Thank you." I face the staircase, and when Estelle reaches me, she turns left, and I follow. The hallway is carpeted with thick, dark brown material that allows us to move silently, the plushness quieting our footsteps as she takes me all the way to the end and pushes open a dark wooden door. The bedroom ahead is prepared with fresh flowers in a vase on the vanity made of dark, rich oak, sitting looking over the enormous four-poster bed, draped in what looks like fresh bed linens. The pillows are the color of deep merlot, and the comforter a similar dark red.

"This will be your wing of the house. Your grandmother is on the other end. You're welcome to explore on your own, but just be wary of going out into the garden after dark." Her voice is tainted with a dark threat that has me snapping my gaze toward her.

"Why?" I question, waiting for her response. For a moment, I wonder if she's going to reply, and I turn away, allowing her privacy rather than gawking at her. I open the curtain to look out over the lawn's lush greenery and flowerbeds with bright leaves shimmering with water droplets under spotlights that illuminate the beauty that awaits me tomorrow morning.

The bright colors of the petals—reds, yellows, oranges, and even purple—are so pronounced under the glow I can make them out easily. A pathway leads toward thick forests that further extends to a mountain that looks like a large, black mound. The forest ahead reminds me of those I read as a girl in dark fairy tales. "There aren't any big bad wolves out there."

"Oh, no, not at all. We just have the gardener working at night. He sets the traps for the foxes who attempt to make a play for the chickens in the coop. It can be dangerous if you don't know where they are."

"And he does this at night?" I spin on my heel, looking at the older woman. *Why would someone want to do that at night?* It's rather strange.

"Yes, he feels it's better than doing it in the day; that way, we can explore the gardens safely while the sun is up," Estelle says as she waves her hand in the air as if she thinks it's as silly as I do.

"I see. And how old is he?" My curiosity piques at the thought of someone wandering alone at night in the shadows, lurking outside my window.

Her gaze snaps to mine at the question, her eyes wide as she regards me. "Oh, he's not for you, sweet Scarlett. You stay clear of him."

Her words have me laughing out loud. "I'm not at all

interested in a man who works in a garden setting traps, I can assure you of that." I shake my head with a grin. Knowing that when I get home, I'll have a multitude of bachelors waiting for me, and it will all be my mother's doing.

Her brows furrow at my words, but she doesn't respond. Estelle only offers a curt nod before she heads for the door. Her reaction to me is strange, and I wonder if I've offended her by what I said.

"Good night, Miss Bardot. I trust you'll sleep well," she greets before walking out of the room, leaving me staring at the empty space. I want to close it, but only moments later, an older gentleman brings my suitcases, and I guess it's Gray.

"Good evening, Miss. Bardot," he says, as he pulls the suitcases through the door and sets them down on a stool near the closet.

I watch him for a moment, before enquiring, "You're Gray?"

"Yes, ma'am." He nods with a gentlemanly bow.

"Tell me something, Gray." I turn to face him fully, watching as he straightens to full height. "The gardener who works for Gran. Is there something I should know about him?"

The old man's eyes widen as he regards me. "I... I think perhaps you should meet him yourself, ma'am," he tells me, his voice shaking as he speaks, which only sets my curiosity alight.

He doesn't say anything more, pulling the door shut

behind him, leaving me with even more questions than I had before. The house is large, and I'm excited to explore. It's been a long time since I've been here, and with the multitude of rooms, I wonder just what could be hiding within the walls, or more so, outside the walls of Bardot House.

I cast my glance out of the window once more, taking in the darkness, and as a shadow passes across the lawn, my heart leaps against my rib cage, and I can't drag my gaze away from the large figure.

When he stops, I notice his head twist, eyes landing on me, as if he can see me in the darkness. I can't make out what he looks like, but he seems more beast than man as he watches me. The whites of his eyes burn through the darkness, and I have to move away from the window, my breath coming in short spurts of nervous air.

There's something very peculiar about him. About the shadow in the garden, but perhaps it's my mind playing tricks on me. Sighing, I move to the suitcases and promise to get ready for bed. Exhaustion takes over, and I know tomorrow, in the light of the sun, I'll be able to explore better.

SCARLETT

When my eyes open, there's no sunshine streaming through the window. Instead, I'm met with the dire grayness of clouds hanging heavily in the sky. The house seems more haunted, with the weather turning somber than it would if the golden glow of the day were shimmering inside.

I quickly dress in a skirt with a sweater that warms me. Even though the heating is on, there's still a chill in the air when I open my bedroom door. The moment I step foot in the kitchen, the chef and Estelle stop speaking and turn to regard me.

"Good morning, sweet Scarlett." The old lady grins happily. "This is Jean-Pierre; he's the full-time chef at Bardot

House."

"Nice to meet you," I tell the older gentleman who's dressed in a proper chef's uniform.

His face crinkles when he smiles. "Ma cherie," he says with a tip of his head before turning his attention back to the stove.

"Are you hungry?" Estelle asks, moving swiftly toward me. "I've set out breakfast for you in the dining room. Your grandmother said she'll be back in a few days. She had business in the city, so she'll be gone for a little while."

"Oh." Disappointment squeezes in my chest, stealing the words from my lips. I was hoping to see her, spend some time with her before the ball. It's been a few years since my gran and I were able to sit and talk, to catch up on the news of what I've been doing.

"Don't worry," Estelle mumbles as she leads me through the dining room entrance, and I find myself in a familiar room. When I was much younger, I recall being in here for lunch with the rest of the family. Sitting at the long, twelve-seater table always felt as if we were royals. "She'll be back soon enough."

I'm seated at the head of the table, gifting me a view of the room, and then I'm left alone with what looks like a buffet set out for a princess. Fruits that shine as if they'd been polished, freshly made toast, eggs, and sausages, along with juice and a French Press of steaming coffee. I start with that, pouring myself a mug full and heading toward the window to take in the view.

With the weather being so dismal, I think I'll have to stay indoors and read. If I recall correctly, my grandmother's library is filled with classics as well as some intriguing volumes of the ancestors who first moved to Crimson Falls.

Sipping my drink, I watch two staff heading to what looks like a vegetable patch at the far side of the kitchen. They both carry baskets, and begin filling them with greens, which I'm sure will be used for dinner tonight.

I settle in the chair and fill my plate with delicious smelling food. The silence of the house is startling, the clinking of the cutlery is the only sound, and I wonder if spending a month here was a mistake because I do like to have someone to talk to or music to listen to. I'm sure Gran won't mind me using her music room, but it's going to be lonely all by myself.

With the ball a week away, I'm sure she'll be in attendance, but with her running Bardot Industries, she may not stick around if she didn't even want to greet me before leaving this morning.

Loneliness seeps through me like a rabid poison.

Growing up with my folks who were more interested in spending time with their friends, I've learned to be alone, but there are times it becomes too much. Perhaps I can call Aelin to come to visit for a few days. She'd love it here.

Once I've finished eating, I head toward the kitchen only to find it empty. Furrowing my brow, I turn and make my way through the house, taking a long hallway toward the library, which I remember as a girl. The room hasn't changed much. The walls are lined with shelves of uncracked spines, calling to me to explore. An enormous open-brick fireplace sits against one wall, which has a large grandfather clock above the mantle.

A three-seater couch with matching armchairs furnish the middle of the room, surrounding a thick brown throw rug and a knee-height coffee table. On the smooth surface, I spy a few magazines, mostly home improvement ones, which don't interest me.

I allow my gaze to take in the bookshelves, tracing my finger over the smooth spines. Some are old, first editions, others are newer, with sleek glossy covers, and I can't help but giggle at some of the romances she's collected over the years. I find an old copy of fairy tales. The one of Red Riding Hood piques my interest, and I slide it out.

The cover doesn't have an image; instead, the title is engraved in gold on the dark green jacket. I flick it open and find a handwritten note, which I scan with furrowed brows.

My darling, Grace,
As the wolf loves his damsel, so I love you.
Yours always,

C.S.

I'm not sure who C.S. is, but I must ask my gran when she returns. My grandad died before I met him, but his name was Randolf Thurston. I recall Gran telling me she would never take another man's name, and that's why she was always Grace Bardot.

It must be an old friend. It's a beautiful gift. She's

always loved the old stories by the Grimm Brothers instead of the newer, less scary retellings.

Settling in one of the amber leather armchairs, I curl my legs under my butt and open the book.

A sound startles me, causing the book I'd fallen asleep holding to tumble to the floor. Another heavy crunch sends my mind reeling. The room is now drenched in black, and I glance at the fireplace where a clock hangs above the mantle. I'm not sure if the hands are correct, but if they are, I've slept most of the day away.

It's almost six, which means dinner will probably be served soon. Pushing to my feet, I move to the window, wanting to find the sound that woke me, but all I see are shadows in the garden ahead. A shiver takes hold of me, and I force my sleepy body up the stairs to my bedroom to find a hoodie. Perhaps some fresh air will help me wake up.

I still can't believe I spent my first day in Crimson Falls asleep. In my room, I discard the sweater I'd been wearing and grab the red hoodie and pull it on over my T-shirt. Donning the hood to cover my hair, I race down the stairs and out the patio doors onto the stoop, which is hard beneath my sneakers.

Light streams from the spotlights, illuminating the garden just like they did last night. A howl from somewhere in the forest has a gasp falling from my lips. There isn't any staff outside, but I should be safe since Estelle told me there are traps for any foxes wanting to get onto the property.

I take one step off the stoop onto the lush grass, which feels as if I'm walking on a cloud.

A sound to the left of where I'm standing startles me, and I wonder if the gardener is outside doing work. "Hello?" I call out, but there isn't any response. Shrugging, I move farther into the garden, to where I recall two of the staff picking vegetables this morning. The patch is dimly lit, and I can make out a few types of lettuce and some carrots which have been pulled out. I don't recognize a few other plants, and I make a mental note to ask Jean-Pierre about them.

A branch cracking has me whipping my head behind me, but I don't see anyone there. The hair on the back of my neck stands on end when I hear another scrape of what I can only guess is a shoe against concrete. My gaze snaps to the stoop, but there's nobody there either.

"If you're trying to scare me, it's not working!" I call out to who I can only guess is the gardener attempting to freak me out. Shaking my head, I move toward the house, and that's when I see a large figure at the door. A scream is stuck in my throat when he moves slowly, predatorially toward me.

I can't see his face properly, but from the shadows, I can tell he must be at least six-five with broad shoulders, and he's wearing a dark hoodie that covers his face. Then

I notice the glint of a blade in his hand. And that's when I race through the garden.

LYCAN

Being back in Crimson Falls is intriguing, but also, I'm anxious to get this contract in motion. The home I grew up in, the one where my memories now lie, is where I'll bring her. Even though I haven't been here in a long time, I know it will be the perfect place for me to ensure my little red is safe while she comes to terms with her new life.

The flight back from New York was quick, and the drive up here was refreshing. A change from the city. The furnishings my decorator chose are exquisite—all dark woods, glass and steel in the kitchen, and claret carpets overlying the expensive marble tiles.

I head up the sweeping staircase and turn left down the

hall to the room I've had set up for Scarlett. Upon pushing open the door, I find the ornate four-poster bed, a myriad of cushions, and a deep red comforter.

On the opposite side of the bed is a vanity with a beautifully intricate mirror. Carved from the finest oak, the frame shows a little girl with a red hood and the wolf right behind her. They've painted the hood perfectly, her long hair hanging over her shoulders as the predator makes his way toward her.

Reaching for the sculpted scene, I trace my finger over the hood, the memory of Scarlett's sleek, red hair flickering in my mind. The length perfect for fisting around my hand, her eyes wide and bright as she regarded me with fire and defiance. My cock jolts with the memory, and I can't help but grin. How perfectly delicious it will be to break her down and watch her submit to my whims.

When I planned to bring her here, I wanted the room to feel like home. Even though she's going to hate me for a while, I figure at least she can hate in comfort. The contract I signed with her father ensures she's mine and no longer a Bardot. She will be a Shaw as soon as the ceremony is complete.

A man relinquishing his hold on his daughter because he fucked up is a sad state of affairs. But he did it to ensure I never divulged what he did behind his wife's back. Yes, she knew about the money, the club, but she I'm certain has no clue her husband has a much larger secret, one that would most certainly break the perfect family unit he's managed to build.

Power has been my drug for a long time. I've reveled in it. Knowing I have the command to take down anyone who steps in my path is a heady feeling. Dominance goes hand in hand with the emotion, and I can't wait to see Scarlett on the other end of my control.

A smile slowly moves along my face, one that isn't filled with humor, but a sinister need to have her here right now. I have time, but I'd like it sooner rather than later. When the Bardot ball takes place, she will be on my arm. And if she tries to escape, I'll lock her up in this palace until she submits fully, in every way possible. Another grin graces my lips at the thought, this one filled with dark humor.

"Mr. Shaw," the voice of the man I put in the Bardot home to keep an eye on my new possession calls to me, causing me to return to the present. "I've met her," he says as he enters her bedroom, where I'm still standing over the vanity.

"And?" I turn, facing him as he moves deeper into the room. I've known Gray since I was a child. From the moment I realized I would never have a normal life, he was there for me. He's been good to me, obeying my commands without question.

He nods slowly, a small beam of happiness on his face, and for a moment, I think he's going to tell me not to do this, but then he says, "She's beautiful, I have to admit. You will make a wonderful couple. But there's something you do need to know."

"What is it, Gray?" The frustration in my tone has him wincing, and I have a feeling whatever it is he has to tell me, I'm not going to like.

"Your brother is here," he informs me, and he was right in being wary of telling me. My hands fist at my sides as I focus on trying not to smash my knuckles into the brand-new mirror. I can't break anything I've set up for her.

"Where is he?" The words are gritted through my clenched teeth. I knew he'd come back to haunt me, but I didn't think he would be so close by.

"Uh... he's working for Mrs. Bardot. She hired him to do the garden, set the fox traps." Gray looks up at me, and I can tell he's more fearful of my wrath than my brother's stupidity. He was around when my brother decided to fuck over the family to join a fucking motorcycle gang. He took the word of murderers instead of his own flesh and blood.

He became someone different. Someone I didn't know, and the more time he spent with his new family, the more he'd forgotten about his lineage. I never forgot, though, and if he thinks he's going to steal *my* payment, he has another thing coming.

"Make sure the girl is safe and stays indoors," I tell Gray. "And if my brother goes near her, I'll kill him myself." I have a feeling my sweet little red isn't someone who'll obey the order to stay indoors. Only, she doesn't know just how feral the predators on the outside are.

"Yes, sir." Gray turns to leave, and I face the mirror once more. I know Darius will do something. I have a feeling the asshole is here to fuck with me. But what he doesn't know is I have ways and means to ensure he can't go near her.

My phone buzzes in my pocket, and when I pull it out to find an unknown number, I'm sure it's my brother. Swiping the screen, I press the device to my ear.

"You know, she's quite the looker," he tells me, the familiar voice ringing in my ears. As much as I hate him, I love him. There's a fine line between the two emotions, a *very* fragile line.

"She's mine, Darius," I inform him, attempting to keep myself calm but failing when my fingers tighten around the cell phone. I only earn myself a chuckle in response.

"And you think the Bardots are just going to let you take her? She's quite curious, isn't she?" He's testing me to see what I'll do, what I'll say. The thing about it is, my brother no longer knows who I am, but I know exactly who he is. I've seen him over the years, had people watching him, and I saw him turn into a monster. My intel has been wrong. He must've known I had eyes on him. The moment I'm done here, I'll have my team fired for fucking this up. They should have known he was in Crimson Falls.

"Darius." His name is a threat on my lips, the tone of my voice giving away just what I'm feeling right this second—pure rage. "I'm not your little brother anymore. I've welcomed the violence that you told me I couldn't find within myself. And as a Shaw, I don't give a shit about family anymore. I will kill you if you go near her."

"From the garden, I can see into her bedroom," he

informs me coolly, as if he's telling me about the fucking weather, which certainly doesn't help my anger. My feet carry me out of her room into the hallway. I'm already pulling the gun from my shoulder holster when I reach the ground floor of my house. "She looks so beautiful in her little tank top." His taunts continue with amusement tainting every mumble. My blood boils with every word he utters. "I wonder just how she'd feel squirming under me."

"You'll never find out," I grit, my jaw ticking with feral rage as I pull open my back door and head out into the garden.

"Oh? Perhaps I should lure her outdoors with a pretty flower. And when I do, I'll open her with my blade, just like a blossom being cut from the stem. Do you think she'll bleed red or blue? I can wait to taste."

"Over my dead body." The words are out of my mouth before I have time to focus on the fact that he's so close by that I can practically smell the violence he emanates. My feet move swiftly across the thick lawn.

What I loved about this property is it connects to the Bardot Manor. Our gardens overlook each other, and I can be on their land in about ten minutes. There is a thick outcropping of trees before reaching it, but I'll get to him, and I'll kill him once and for all.

"Perhaps I'll find out sooner," he tells me. "As you know, curiosity kills the kitten." A scream pierces the speaker before the line dies. *Asshole.* I can't hear anything from where I am, but I quickly make my way down the garden toward the forest that backs up against my property.

I'll find her. I'll find him. And when I do, I'm putting a fucking bullet in his head.

SCARLETT

My throat burns from the scream as I race away from the scary-looking, inked man who stepped out of the shadows. I'm not sure who he is, but I can only guess it's the gardener, the one I was told to stay away from.

"Come on, pretty girl, come out and play," he coos from behind me, his deep voice sending sparks of fear through me, and I push forward, trying to get away from him. "I can smell that sweet fear of yours." His deep voice drips with malice, causing my heart to skitter wildly against my chest.

My long, flowing red hair tangles behind me as thickets and branches snag in my wavy locks. The cool ground beneath my feet causes me to shiver as I race toward the enormous, looming mansion on the other side of the forest.

Footsteps are closing in behind me. I can hear his heavy footfalls, which only have my lungs squeezing, and breathing becomes difficult. I attempt to swallow, but a thick ball of dread threatens to choke me and give me over to the beast behind me.

A howl in the distance forces a squeal of surprise to tumble from my lips. My mother always told me not to go into the woods when I was a kid, but I need to get away from the stranger behind me right now. Another screeching howl comes from somewhere in the darkness, and my heart leaps into my throat.

My lungs burn, and my legs ache.

In, out. In, out.

Breathe, Scarlett.

My heart bangs violently as my lungs slowly start giving out. My breaths are harsh, shallow, and quick. But I push forward, forcing my legs to move quicker, even though I'm ready to pass out. I hit a patch of trees, and then they slowly open as if welcoming me into another world. A house illuminates the darkened world before me with golden light streaming from a few windows.

I'm so close.

The neighbors will help me.

I'm sure they will.

I'm not sure if Estelle or Gray heard me screaming, but someone will figure out I'm gone soon enough. A crack of a branch behind me has another squeal pealing from my lips as I race through the darkness. My skin scrapes and scratches as fearful tears slowly drip from my lashes, making the path blur before me.

I can smell something akin to candle wax, which is strange. And as much as I want to stop, to take a breath because my stomach aches and my chest is tight with exertion, I don't. My feet hit the edge of the forest, and suddenly, I'm ripped backward, my feet flying into the air as strong, thick arms wrap around my waist and haul me back into the gloom of the trees.

"No!" My scream is silenced by a heavy hand covering my mouth, and the more I fight, the tighter the arms hold on to me. My muffled shouts dissipate into the dense trees behind me as I'm dragged through the murkiness.

"If you keep fighting, little red, you'll make my cock hard. I like it when little girls squirm," a deep voice barrels through me, sending ice through my veins, and I still all movement. The man carries me as if I'm weightless, and soon I see a clearing up ahead.

It's not the same voice from earlier, and I wonder who's caught me. The nickname *little red* is what Mr. Shaw called me the night we met at my parent's house, but I know it can't be him. He's not anywhere near Crimson Falls.

The house I saw in the distance becomes clearer, and my captor allows me to my feet, but his hold on me stays strong as his arm snakes around my waist, and when I finally get a glimpse of his face, a gasp tumbles from my mouth.

"What are you doing here?" The shock is clear in my

tone, but Mr. Shaw just offers me a sly grin that has dread sluicing through my veins.

"I'm here to keep you safe from the predators out there," he informs me, gesturing with his head toward the forest we just exited. And that's when I take in the house before me. Three floors of pure opulence similar to Gran's mansion, but this one is even bigger, with old brick that looks like it's from a scary movie, rather than modern-day real life.

The windows are lit up, just like I saw from the woods. "Why am I here?"

"Because it's not safe for you to be out there," Mr. Shaw tells me as he leads me into the house via the kitchen door. A similar layout to Gran's with all modern appliances, along with a shiny gas stove that looks like it's never been used.

A table is sprawled along the window, overlooking the garden, and when I glance out toward the property line, I see the dark shadow of my hunter standing there, watching.

"There..." I point, but by the time Shaw looks out, it's gone. "He was right there." My gaze snaps to his, and I see something flickering in those depths of green. "How did you—"

"Don't ask questions you don't want the answers to," he warns before turning on his heel. I watch him move to the fridge before he pulls open the heavy metal door and asks, "Do you want something to drink?"

"I—I... No, I mean, I need to get home."

"You'll stay here tonight." His tone is no-nonsense as he

grabs a bottle of wine and finds a corkscrew in one of the drawers. When he sets two glasses on the breakfast bar, he meets my inquisitive gaze. "I don't want you out there while he's looking for you."

"How do you know he's looking for me?" My curiosity has piqued, and I wonder if Mr. Shaw will offer me the answers I need. I doubt it from the look on his face. He opens the bottle with a pop and pours two generous glasses of white wine before handing me one and taking the other for himself.

"I know things that will cause you to be sick, little red," he tells me. "Now, drink up, and I'll show you to the guest room." My stare is locked on his movements, how he brings the glass to his lips and sips the alcohol. Once again, I'm stunned by just how handsome he is. For someone who was racing through the forest moments ago, he doesn't seem at all perturbed. He hasn't shaved, and like I imagined when we first met, there's a dark dusting of stubble lining his perfectly angular jaw.

"Fine, if you won't tell me how you know, at least tell me your name." I set my glass down, meeting his stare.

His mouth crooks into a wolfish grin as he regards me. "Lycan Shaw," he says, holding out his free hand to mine. "It's lovely to meet you again, Scarlett Bardot."

My gaze falls to his strong hand, and I finally accept it after being at war between wanting to touch him and wanting to run in the opposite direction. We shake, and his thumb circles my skin, sending goose bumps dancing across every inch of me.

"Well, it's a pleasure to meet you too, Lycan." His name tastes like sin on my tongue and poison on my lips. "Why am I here?" I want answers, even though he seems adamant about not giving them to me. But he has to offer an inkling at least.

"Everything will be answered when you get to your room, Scarlett," he informs me before setting his empty glass down and turning for the door. "Follow me."

My mouth gapes then shuts quickly as my feet move behind him, leaving my untouched wine on the counter. "What do you mean, *my* room?"

He doesn't respond. His steps are long strides, showing off his tall frame and how his slacks and shirt fit him perfectly. There's no doubt this man is breathtakingly gorgeous, but my fight-or-flight instinct has taken over, and I glance at the front door as we pass it.

But Lycan anticipates my thoughts and says, "You can try to run, but there are only two evils you have to deal with, the hunter outside or me." He takes the stairs slowly, waiting for me to make my decision. "But make no mistake, little red," he says, stopping to glance at me from over his shoulder. "I will find you. No matter where you go. The big bad wolf always finds the girl."

The threat is clear. I can't escape, not now. I'm not sure which is worse, being murdered by some crazy person in the forest, or being imprisoned for the evening in a beautiful home with a wolf who seems as lethal as he is beautiful.

When we reach a door on the second floor of the house, Lycan pushes it open and steps aside to allow me to enter the room. It's furnished with a dark wood four-poster bed, an elegantly carved vanity, and two enormous doors that I'm guessing lead to a bathroom and closet.

Spinning on my heel, I take in Lycan as he leans against the doorframe. His shoulders relaxed, arms folded, as he focuses on me. Those deep, luminous, green depths expose my fear as he stares at me from top to bottom and up again.

I ask once more, "Why am I here?"

LYCAN

Her gaze is burning as she regards me, perusing every inch of me. Those full lips purse into a pout, frustrated at not knowing what's happening. It's evident that she's angry, and I smile.

"What the fuck is going on?" Her arms cross over her chest, causing her tits to perk up as she storms toward me. I expect her to touch me, punch me, or slap me, but she doesn't. And I find that I *want* her to put her hands on me.

She's close—inches from where I'm leaning against the doorframe to her bedroom. The scent of her perfume invades my nostrils, and it takes over my senses as she pins her glare on mine. Her lips purse as her nose scrunches.

"If you don't tell me—"

Tipping my head to the side, I narrow my gaze on hers. "What? You'll what?" The challenge in my tone is clear. I quirk my lips at the corner, a smile ready to dance along my mouth as I focus on her.

"I don't know," she backs down. "I just need to know why I'm here, what you want with me, and who that man was chasing me. You clearly know him since you were there to *save* me."

"That's a lot of information for a little girl to take in. Isn't it?" My brow lifts at her in question, and the blaze of her stare sizzles as she narrows her eyes.

"I'm not a little girl. I'm a woman. And I need to know what's going on. Or I'll walk home." In her attempt to walk past me, my hand shoots out, gripping her wrist, tugging it closer to me. "Let me go, Lycan."

I want nothing more than to pin her down and spank her ass until she's begging for mercy, I will not show. Keeping my voice calm, I command, "You'll stay here, Scarlett."

"No. I don't want to." She sounds like a petulant teenager, but I can't deny her voice is like an aphrodisiac to me.

Chuckling, I push off the doorframe and grip both her shoulders, lifting her off her feet. I walk toward the bed dumping her on the mattress, causing her to bounce on the softness of the bed. "Stay." When I turn, I expect her next move as she tries to make her escape, but I'm fast, much faster than her.

My arms wrap around her, bringing her back to the bed and pushing her onto her back. Her legs and arms attempt to attack me, but she's not strong enough, and seconds later, I have her wrists bound to the wooden poles of the headboard and her ankles tied to the foot end.

"What the fuck are you doing?" Her rage bounces off the walls. The poison she shoots at me from her gaze should hurt, but I closed myself off to emotions a long time ago. There are instances in my life I allow myself to feel, and that's when I'm dominating a woman in a scene.

Other than that, I'm cold, heartless, and unfeeling.

"Let me go!"

"Your screaming won't earn you your freedom," I tell her, keeping my tone calm, neutral, which only has her tugging at the restraints that will never let her loose. I've bound her too tight, and the sight of her lying there, ready for me, has an effect I knew to expect.

Her vulnerability in this moment has my cock throbbing against my zipper.

I'd love nothing more than to strip her bare and feast on her, but I have things to do. I have a brother to kill.

"Please," she pleads, her voice turning soft, but the heat in her eyes still dances with a threat of death if she were to wield a weapon. Thankfully, it doesn't faze me. If I were stupid, if I were years younger, I would've wilted for her, but I'm no longer weak.

"You'll stay. Once I'm done with my business, I'll return for you." I make my way to the door. Twisting the handle,

I tug it open and step out into the hallway to her screams. Once I shut her inside, her voice gets muffled by the thick wood.

Leaning my head against the cool surface, I close my eyes and listen to her for a while longer before I lock her in and head down to my study. I promised Kahn he would be able to go to the church to seek out the priest who may have news about his sister, but I need him and his team here.

My brother has gone rogue, and I'm done playing games. Picking up my cell phone, I hit dial on Kahn's number. Four rings and he finally answers—out of breath and gravelly.

"Are you busy fucking?" I ask my tone taking on a gruff rumble.

Kahn chuckles. "No, Mr. Shaw, I was working out. Late night in the gym," he tells me. "What can I do for you?"

"Are you leaving for the convent soon? Or are you still in New York?" I settle back in the expensive leather chair and close my eyes. My head is pounding from today's shitshow, and even with Scarlett upstairs, safe, I'm not at ease. If Darius is so adamant about stealing her, he could walk in here at any moment. Not that I won't see him approach, but the thought of a fight tonight doesn't bode well for the state I'm in.

"I'm still around. Did you need me?"

"I'll make sure the jet is ready when you get to the airstrip. I need you in Crimson Falls before sunrise," I inform him. "Bring the team. I have a feeling this could be a tough job."

"What's happening?" Usually, I wouldn't tell the men until they were all in the room with me, but this is a special case. I've never asked them to do something so personal before. Killing my brother is not something I planned to do for a while yet, but when someone threatens my life, livelihood, and possessions, I fight back.

"Darius is here, and he needs to be taken care of as soon as possible."

Silence greets me. I'm certain Kahn is in shock at my response. If I had to be honest, I am too. Holding someone's life in your hands is a powerful feeling. Something that takes hold and doesn't let go. Not easily anyway.

"I'll make sure the guys are on the flight."

"Thank you." I hang up before tapping out a message to the pilot. Once my men get here, we can map out a plan. There's a lot to do with only a week to go before the ball and at least a month before my marriage to Scarlett. Especially getting her ready and onboard.

That's going to be my toughest challenge yet.

SCARLETT

When I open my eyes, I shoot up from the comfortable, form-hugging mattress to find I'm no longer bound. Instinctively, I glance at my wrists to find a hint of the bindings that kept me prisoner. I'm not sure how much time has passed. I must've been exhausted that I fell asleep while bound to the goddamned bed.

Lycan Shaw is a monster, but I need answers. I push off the bed, feeling the softness of the carpet underfoot, and for a moment, my toes dig into the thick wool. The curtains hang open, and I notice it's still dark out. Surely the sun is coming up soon.

Pacing the room, I stop when I hear a sound outside

in the garden a story down, and I notice Lycan stalking from the house toward the property line. The shadow I saw earlier is gone, but it doesn't make sense that he's out there when he didn't want me going home. I wonder if the staff knows I'm missing, or if Gran has called the house and they've informed her I'm not there.

I didn't see Estelle or Gray when I walked out last night. They must know I'm no longer in the house. The staff must've heard me scream. Surely, they'll come to find me.

A shot rings in the air, causing me to jump back from the window. I suck in a shocked breath and hold it, listening for more volatile sounds, but silence greets me. I exhale and find my lungs struggle to pull in more air as my heart thumps at my ribs.

I should've run when I could, when he released me, but there's something about Lycan Shaw that intrigues me. *Why would he save me and then keep me prisoner?*

I turn back to the bed to find something lying on the nightstand I didn't see earlier. Lycan's earlier words ring in my mind as I pick up the creamy, thick paper folded into a rectangle. *"Everything will be answered when you get to your room."* Ripping open the envelope, I pull out the letter that's been folded three times over. The handwriting is familiar, and I recognize it instantly. It's my father's scrawl, signed at the bottom of what looks like a contract.

I scan the pages of the terms and conditions. Every word, each sentence, sends ice through my veins. My father signed my life, my hand in marriage, over to Lycan Shaw.

There's no reasoning behind it, just that he thinks it's better for me in the long run. The words *safe and secure* are underlined a few times in thick black ink.

I read it and reread it, but nothing makes sense.

Dad wants me to marry a man who's possibly twice my age. Someone I have only ever met once at dinner a few nights ago—a man who stole me from the forest and brought me to a gilded prison.

When I glance up at the room once more, I take in each detail, every corner, each item. Every inch of this bedroom has been created especially for me, from the mirror with the carving of Little Red Riding Hood and the wolf, to the bedding that is in my favorite color.

The door flies open, and standing on the threshold is the man who *bought* me from my father. His expression is calm, but his tense posture has the hair on the back of my neck prickling.

"What is this?" I ask him, throwing the contract onto the bed before making my way toward him. Anger surges through me as his mouth tips slightly. "I asked you a fucking question, Mr. Shaw," I mutter, spitting his name with as much venom as I can conjure. "I'm not a fucking possession you can barter with like that. I'm a woman, a *person*. What kind of man buys a woman from her father?"

He doesn't react; he merely watches me, intrigue dancing in his gaze. His nonreaction only sends my rage into a spiral. My gut twists as he regards me with cold indifference, the smirk on his handsome face turning upward.

"Talk to me!" My fists pound against his chest, but I only get one hit in before his hands grip my wrists. A deep rumble vibrates through his chest as he pushes me back until my ass hits the edge of the mattress.

Lycan leans in, his tall frame cocooning me as he stops inches from where I'm bending backward painfully. I know if I were to lean back further, I'd end up pinned between him and the mattress where I slept last night, my hands still in his hold as he pushes them to my sides. He takes this opportunity to kick my feet apart before stepping in between my legs, causing me to tumble onto the soft comforter. The hardness of his desire presses against my core, forcing heat to sizzle between my legs at the contact.

"If you ever lift your hands at me again," he speaks, calm, clear, and threatening, "I will bend you over and whip you with my belt until you're bleeding all over my pristine carpets. Am I understood?"

There's not a hint of anger in his voice, but his eyes, they're expressive, burning like open flames as they pierce me. The depths steal me into their darkness the closer he gets. His lips brush along mine, and as angry as I am at him, I can't deny my body trembles under his.

The power he exudes sends heat blazing to my cheeks, and my stomach tumbles and twists with a need for him to move, for him to press harder against my center.

What the fuck is wrong with you, Scarlett?

I hiss when he tightens his hold on my wrists, the

harshness of his fingers pressing hard against my smooth skin, and I'm sure there'll be bruises, not from the bindings, but from his touch.

"Get the fuck off me." My words are meant to sting, but instead, Lycan chuckles at my outburst. "I'm serious." He doesn't move, and even though my rage is burning a blaze through me, I can't stop my body from responding to him.

"So am I." There is no doubt in my mind that he will whip me, and he will enjoy every moment of my torture. He pushes away from me, and an unwarranted whimper of agony escapes my lips. "Are you hungry?"

"What?" The query pops out of my mouth with shock drenching the word. My mouth gapes at him, my eyes wide, confusion settling in my chest.

"I don't like repeating myself," he throws back easily, his grin making him seem younger than what I can only guess is about forty years.

"No. I'm not. I want answers." I don't want to sound like a petulant child, but I know I do. I can hear it in my voice. It annoys me that he does this to me. I'm not *this* girl. One who acts like an immature teenager, but something about Lycan Shaw makes me feel young.

Lycan stays silent for a long while before he sighs. "Your father fucked up," he speaks, turning his back on me as he moves to the vanity. His fingers trail over the smooth surface before he glances at the window as if seeing something in the murkiness outside. "He did things that were..." He pauses for a long moment, and my mind whirs with something Dad would've done, and I want to scream. "Illegal." He doesn't look at me as he tells me this, and I wonder what my father could've done that was so bad. He's always been a good man. At least to me, he's been a good father. "He has secrets only I know, and that's why he'll repay me with your hand."

"I don't understand. Why not arrest him?" I push to my feet, needing to stand for this, or at least I think I need to be. "Lycan?" Lycan's steps fall softly on the carpet as he takes two strides toward the window while keeping his back to me. For a moment, he stands there silently, and I wonder if he'll answer.

His hand threads through his dark hair, a lock falling into a shimmering eye as he gazes at me over his shoulder. "Your father is a smart man, but I'm smarter. He wanted more than he could hold onto, including your mother. He thought secrets would remain hidden forever, but he fucked with the wrong person."

My curiosity wins out as he trickles information to me, and I lap it up like a puppy needing sustenance. I take a couple of tentative steps toward him. "What do you mean?"

"He stole from me," Lycan says, his profile half shadowed as he regards the window, his focus on the outside instead of me. "And now I've taken from him." That's when he turns to look at me. His one hand landing on the edge of the wooden vanity, his knuckles turning white, and I wonder briefly if he's reigning in his desire to be near me.

"You can't *steal* me. This isn't some archaic eye for an

eye belief," I bite out, forgetting that this man holds all the power. But then again, I have control as well. He can't do anything to me if I don't want him to. He wouldn't force me. He can't.

"Those questions racing through your pretty little head right now, they're pointless," he tells me in his smooth baritone, a hint of an accent brightening his words, making them seem lyrical. "Because I can do anything I want, to anyone I want, at any time I want." This time, he turns toward me fully, showing off his height, broadness, and dominance. The control and power that follow him like perfume grip my chest squeeze the breath from my lungs, and I can't find the response I need and crave.

"Don't treat me like a child."

He chuckles before stepping away from the soft, silver illumination streaming into the bedroom from the moon outside. "Then don't act like one," Lycan counters seriously. He leans against the vanity, and for a moment, I see him as the wolf, but something internally, my gut, tells me he's not. "I'm not the bad guy here."

"You *bought* me from my father. I think that makes you the asshole."

"If you continue to curse like that, I'm going to be forced to take you under hand and show you how naughty girls are treated," he bites out, those jade orbs flaring with danger as he pins me in place with a stare.

"Oh?" I challenge. "What? Are you going to spank me, *asshole*?" I have no clue what I'm doing, why I'm taunting him like this, but a second later, before I have time to apologize, his body is looming over me, his one hand gripping both of mine as he spins us around, shoving me against the smooth wooden surface he was just leaning against. My butt sticks out toward him, which only makes me blush. Thankfully, I'm still wearing shorts, and I'm not naked in front of a man who *bought* me.

His hand comes down in a loud, harsh swat against one cheek of my bottom, and then the other. Alternating between the two, he spanks me hard, painfully, causing the sting to trickle its way over my skin.

Embarrassment floods my mind.

My cheeks hot and red, and my panties... those are soaked from the assault.

LYCAN

Her body trembles under my hold. The gentle curves of her frame have my erection thickening with the need to slide into her heat. To hear her cry out. Soft whimpers free themselves from her pouted lips, and I can't help but smile at her. Our reflection in the mirror shows my dominance, but it's her submission in this moment that has my cock rock-hard.

"Are you going to act like a petulant child, or can I release you now?" I ask, trailing my fingertips over her spine, reveling in her reaction to me. A moan of deep pleasure escapes her when I reach the juncture between her thighs. Heat spills easily from the apex of her figure as I taunt her pussy over the thin layers of the soft, cotton shorts that hide what I crave.

"Please," Scarlett pleads, but I'm not sure what she's asking for. More of the same or for me to release her from my hold. "Please, Lycan."

Leaning in, I engulf her with my body, keeping her in place, allowing my lips to trail over the shell of her ear before I ask, "What, little red? Tell me what this pretty pussy craves." The command is gentle, a caress of words along her smooth, porcelain flesh.

"I... I can't marry you," she whimpers as my finger continues to taunt her. "I—I don't want to be arm candy for an asshole who doesn't love me." A tear slips free from her long lashes, and as it trickles down her flushed cheek, I lap it up, tasting the salty emotion as it spills from her eyes.

"You're not arm candy," I tell her because it's the truth. She's so much more than that. "If you think for one moment I'm going to let you go, to walk out of my life..." I inhale a deep breath to keep calm. "Then you're sorely mistaken. You are mine. I own you now, and you will submit to me. Perhaps not tonight, but soon." I press down on her clit, sending her over the edge, and her keening cry is music to my ears.

I watch her ride the wave of her release for a long while before I step back, finally releasing her from the confines of my body. Scarlett straightens, her glassy eyes flicking to mine. Heat, confusion, and a hint of anger swirl in her gaze. But the shame that colors her cheeks has me wanting to see more of it in her expression.

"Why did you do that?" Her words are croaky, her body still shivering from the intensity of what just happened. My cock, on the other hand, feels like steel against my zipper. "Why?"

"Because I like to make pretty girls cry," I respond. "And because you are mine. My little red. And nobody is going to take you away from me."

She straightens her shoulders, tilting her chin in challenge as her eyes narrow. "What if I want to walk away from you?"

"Learn about your father's transgressions before you make your choice. There are always a lesser of two evils in this world." I shrug, shoving my hands in my pockets before I continue. "And your choice should come from knowing all the information."

"Then tell me," she pleads, tears filling her lashes, threatening to fall. She looks so beautiful on the verge of breaking down, and I want so badly to pin her to the wooden vanity and claim her, mark her as mine.

"Give me a week," I request. "Should you feel the need to leave after, I'll rethink the terms of the contract."

Her eyes widen farther, those glossy orbs holding me hostage, and for a moment, I allow her to ponder what I've just said. Then she mouths, "A whole week?"

Nodding slowly, I focus on keeping my expression calm, collected, and not allowing the desire that's burning its way through every inch of my body to show. She doesn't need to know I'm on the verge of fucking her until she's screaming the roof down. "While you're in my house, you will not touch yourself. Every orgasm you have while you're here, and trust me, there will be many, are mine to give you. I own you, Scarlett; it's written on that contract."

"You can't own someone. If I'm not willing to give you something, you can't take it," she sasses, crossing her arms, but I don't miss the tremble in her hands.

A smirk curls my lips, and I raise a dark brow at her in a challenge. If she thinks I'm a good man who won't take what I want, then she's mistaken.

"Right? You wouldn't..." Her words filter into nothing, the silence deafening when she realizes I'm no gentleman.

Taking a step toward her, I notice her attempt at moving away, but she's now pinned between me and the smooth wood of the vanity. She's small, only reaching my chest, so she has to tip her head back to look me in the eye.

There's a hint of fear, but it's mingled with curiosity. When I close the distance between my mouth and hers, I notice desire dancing in her eyes, but the moment she blinks, it's gone.

"Don't underestimate me." I keep my voice calm. My composure is hanging by a thread when her tongue darts out, wetting her plump lips. "When I sign a contract, when I agree to anything, I don't break that promise. You will say your vows in a month, and when you sign your name, it will be Shaw, not Bardot. On your twenty-first birthday, you will be my wife."

Another emotion dances across her expression before she asks, "And if I refuse?"

"There is no choice in the matter. Whatever you do, wherever you go, you are mine. And I take care of my belongings. Now, I want you to sleep. When the sun has risen on this day, we'll talk more." I step back, needing the space because I'm so close to ripping her clothes off and seeing what I now own. Turning on my heel, I make it to the door before I hear a soft whimper. She's crying, but tears don't afford her mercy. They only make my dick hard.

"Will I ever see my family again?" Her question has me stalling, the door ajar, and my one foot over the threshold. When I glance over my shoulder, I see her, the girl under the strong façade she tries to portray, and it only makes me want her more.

"We'll talk in the morning." I shut the door behind me, knowing that if I were to have stayed in that room for a moment longer, I would've taken everything that belongs to me. Twisting the golden key in the lock, I leave her to mull over her situation.

I have things to do.

A brother to kill.

And a priest to call.

SCARLETT

I spent the night tossing and turning. Dreams of a big bad wolf invaded my mind and took hold of me. All I saw behind my lids was a large predator following me through the woods as I tried to get home.

At one point, I actually believed I was out in the cold with the enormous gray wolf following me, but when my eyes snap open in shock, I shiver but find myself alone in the immaculate room that Lycan confirmed is mine.

The rising sun is slowly brightening the deep purple sky beyond the curtains, which in turn illuminates my bedroom. I have to be honest; the bed was comfortable even though I didn't get a lot of sleep. I'm sure I would have had a great evening if I wasn't being kept captive in a mansion owned by the man who's convinced he's going to marry me.

My mind still cannot fathom how my father could have signed over my life to someone like this. *Did he know Lycan long before he agreed to this preposterous contract?* I wonder how long the two men who clearly want to rule my life knew each other before Lycan requested this bullshit. I'm not marrying him. And he doesn't realize how much I'll fight back, because if he thinks otherwise, he is misleading himself.

I need to talk to my dad or even my mother because the idea of being with a man like Lycan Shaw forever doesn't leave me all warm and fuzzy. But then the memory of what he did to me last night assaults every sense. My skin prickles as the phantom touch of him teases me. I can't stop the ache that slowly tightens in my stomach when I recall how his fingers brought me pleasure, even as anger rolled through me.

He's an expert.

He clearly knows my body and can manipulate me like a musical instrument, but that's only an indication of how many women he's been with, and that's not a man I want to spend my life with. When I do decide to give myself to someone, to take their name, it will be because I'm the only one they're with. I don't share, and I certainly will not be a wife forced to bear children while he goes fucking everything in a skirt.

When the bedroom door opens again, I'm met with a

gentle smile from an older woman I haven't seen before. She moves into the room and sets down a tray that has a plate covered with a silver dome, along with coffee, which I can smell from my bed, and a glass of orange juice.

"Mr. Shaw will be with you soon," she says before heading out, leaving me alone to ponder just what *Mr. Shaw* wants to do today. Perhaps he'd like to kick a puppy. Rolling my eyes at the childish thought, I push off the bed and make my way to the tray. I reach for the coffee first, which is rich and dark, and I add a splash of milk from a small porcelain jug and a spoon of sugar, which I slowly stir into the liquid.

"Didn't take you for having a sweet tooth." His deep baritone comes from behind me, and I almost drop the mug, but I set it down before I face him. I take him in, allowing my gaze to rove over him from head to toe. Dressed casually in a pair of dark blue jeans and a Henley, which matches the color of emeralds, I can't help but admire just how handsome he is.

His tanned skin, with the dark dusting of stubble now closer to being a beard than not, makes my thighs involuntarily squeeze together. He doesn't come inside; he lurks on the threshold of the bedroom, and I wonder if he's staying far from me to hold onto some form of restraint.

"What was that gunshot last night?" I ask, remembering seeing him in the darkness, hearing the loud echo ringing in my ears. His expression turns dark as if he's shutting down the hatches, keeping all the secrets inside. Those emeralds simmer with rage for a split second, but with a blink, it's gone.

I expect an answer, but when he opens his mouth, he changes the topic. "The priest will be here this evening to meet with us. I want us to write our own vows," he says nonchalantly as he crosses his arms and leans against the wall not far from the door.

He knows what he's doing. Keeping the escape route blocked. Even if I could get past his looming frame, I have a feeling I wouldn't get very far. He'll catch me without putting in any effort.

"You want me to write vows?" Incredulity laces my tone, causing Lycan to chuckle. "I'm not marrying you." I'm adamant, squaring my shoulders after stepping away from the vanity, leaving my coffee behind. I'm almost certain I'm going to need two hands for this interaction.

"Of course you are," he says. "It's in the contract. You have no choice in this, Scarlett." He straightens, pushing his hands into his pockets, forcing my attention to drop to his crotch, which has my stomach fluttering wildly at the thought of what he's hiding in there.

Snapping my eyes to his, I shake my head. "No. What you're suggesting is archaic, just something my parents would do to piss me off. To rule my life as if I were still a child."

"Oh?" His dark brows arch as he watches me inquisitively. "If you force my hand, Scarlett, I will happily bind you to me and carry you down that fucking aisle." His tone is a crash of no-nonsense whiplash—commanding and domineering.

"And what? You expect me to wear a pretty white dress as well?" My sneer is evident.

His smirk is unmistakable. "Let me make something clear," Lycan says, taking two long strides closer to me, eating up the distance before he continues. "You will be Mrs. Shaw by the time this month is over. On your birthday, you will be mine." And that's when it hits me — I turn twenty-one in a few weeks, and he wants us to exchange our vows. I never once thought I'd be married so young.

Narrowing my gaze, I tip my head to the side as I watch his reaction to my next question. "What do you want? Why me?"

This time, he moves closer, swallowing the inches that keep us apart, wedging me between his muscled thighs and the furniture. "I want a queen, little red," he speaks softly, his voice merely a taunting whisper as his breath wafts warmly over me. "I want a woman I can proudly walk beside in public. To watch every man's eyes on her while they slobber for a chance to take her, but knowing she is mine. In her elegant beauty, she'll shine amongst the fake, plastic smiles while I introduce her to my world."

He stays silent for a moment, probably waiting for what he just said to sink in. When he doesn't continue, I prompt, "What else?"

"I also want that same woman to come home with me every evening and allow me to fuck her until she can't think straight. I want to wear her out, make her cry and scream, make her come, and then I want her to take my seed. I want her porcelain flesh to be marred by my mark. The bruises I'll bestow on her skin will be my ownership of her, and when my cock isn't inside her, she'll feel the emptiness. The craving to have me will be her addiction, and her heart will be my ultimate prize."

My heart catapults into my throat at the elicit promise of what he wants and needs from me. And deep down, I wonder if I can give that to him. I'm not some sweet, submissive doll he can dress and play with. Folding my arms in front of me, I meet those deep, jade depths. "You want arm candy and a fuck toy." I shake my head as realization takes hold of me, and the picture becomes clear.

"If you want to put it so callously." He shrugs before a small, wolfish grin tilts his perfectly pink mouth. "But..." Lycan reaches for my hair, tangling a lock of my long, red strands around his finger before tugging. The smaller smile from seconds ago turns dangerous as the corners of his mouth tilt upward, and he continues, "I want someone with intelligence who can stand beside me while running my business. A woman with strength and fire."

My mouth falls open, gaping at his admission. I never expected him to give me so much honesty. "And that's why you chose me?"

"Oh, little red, no." He shakes his head. A somewhat hungry stare burns through me as he offers me a slight chuckle. His tongue teases his lower lip before his perfectly pearly whites bite down on the flesh, forcing my eyes to lock on the full, pinkish mouth I'm tempted to taste. "I was given you as a payment. I didn't know I would *want* you until the night we met."

"That makes no sense."

He tugs my hair once more before gripping my chin between his thumb and forefinger. "When you spoke back to me, when that fire burned in your eyes, that's when I decided I'll take you, and your father agreed." A flash of satisfaction dances in his darkening gaze before he leans in, his mouth teasing its way over my cheek to my ear. "And that makes you mine."

The heat of his breath and the promise in his tone has my skin bursting with goose bumps, the tightening in my gut twisting with a need for more pain as he tugs at my hair. My thighs instinctively squeeze together even though I try to fight the desire that's burning through every inch of me. My stomach somersaults with a flurry of nerves when Lycan's teeth graze the supple flesh of my ear lobe.

I don't know what I'm supposed to do here.

I want to hate Lycan, and I think I do, but also, anger at my parents takes precedence.

But even under all that, there's the need for him that's coursing through my veins like a drug. It's as if I've been shot up with something strong and volatile, something I'm not sure I can fight. Even though I know, I should.

Pulling away, I lock my glare on him before I voice, "I won't marry you." But the hoarsely whispered words aren't as strong as they were earlier.

"We'll see," Lycan responds before stepping back, leaving me cold and shivering at his absence. "Eat. Enjoy your coffee. I'll see you later." He heads to the door and stops on the threshold, glancing at me from over his shoulder before winking.

And then he's gone, and I'm left angry and frustrated.

SCARLETT

Unconvinced.

That's the emotion coursing through me when I wake up in the darkened bedroom. When I think about marrying Lycan, I'm unsure of myself, of his intentions, which he seemed to make clear last night, but there's a hint of doubt plaguing me.

Pushing off the bed, I pad barefoot to the window, pulling open the heavy, lined curtains to find what looks like a chilly morning, the grass shimmering with drops of dew settled on the green blades. The forest beyond seems to swallow up the light, offering only a warning—don't enter here.

I move to the vanity, taking in the beautifully carved wood, the smooth surface where Lycan had pinned me down before spanking my ass. The memory is still fresh in my mind, replaying when I need it least. I don't want to remember how his hands felt on me, but every interaction so far has been intense. And if I had to be honest, it's left me frustrated—more at the fact that he has such an effect on me.

I shouldn't *want* him, but my body betrays me each time. The man is an Adonis, and when he's around me, I'm merely a mortal girl, one with needs that flare like wildfire at his touch. Shaking my head, I go into the bathroom to freshen up before dressing in a pair of leggings, and a large sweater that falls just below my butt. Slipping on a pair of ballet flats, I pull my hair into a messy bun before I open my bedroom door.

He hasn't given me an order not to explore the house. Instead of sitting in the room, I'm going to try to learn more about the man who's stolen me. If I can find a phone, perhaps I can call my grandmother. She'll know what to do.

At the thought of her, I wonder if she knows Lycan. Surely, being neighbors, she would need to know the person living next door to her. The fact that he knows my father is also jarring. A connection that is still confusing me. Growing up, I never heard the Shaw or even about Lycan himself. *Why has he only now appeared in my life?*

My feet carry me down the long hallway, silently over the carpets which line the floor, leading me from door to door. Each one I push open is another bedroom. By the time I reach the far end, the last door is locked, and I can't for the life of me figure out if it's another bedroom or if on the other side is something far more sinister.

A giggle bubbles in my chest at the thought. I've been reading far too many romance novels. My mind is clearly playing tricks on me. But I wouldn't put it past Lycan to have a *red room* where he would torture women into submission.

Heat sizzles over my skin, leaving goosebumps in the wake of the thoughts that take hold of me. *I don't want Lycan.* And even as I tell myself silently that it's true, my mind and body are at war.

Ignoring the niggling at what's behind the black, wooden door, I turn and head for the staircase, leading me down to the ground floor. The house is silent. There's not even a clink of cutlery or crockery from the kitchen.

The smooth, marble tiles muffle my steps as I head into the living room to find it empty. The house is immaculate with furnishings that ooze wealth and beauty, something I've grown up with, and so I'm accustomed to the stench of money. It reeks. As thankful as I am that I didn't have to get a student loan for my studies, I also know just how much responsibility comes from having family money.

I wonder briefly about Lycan. He's much older than I am, but I'm sure he must feel some heaviness from always having to be flawless. When you're thrown into social circles all your life, it comes with the expectation that you're perfect. But nobody can be, and that's something my mother never understood.

Every inch of the house has been decorated with the utmost care, from the color of the fabrics to the paint against the walls. The floor underfoot is warm, and I wonder if there's a heating system hidden from sight.

"Oh," a soft voice of shock comes from behind me, causing me to spin on my heel. A woman, who looks to be about my age, stands before me, a silver tray in hand.

"Hello."

"Hi," she greets. Her eyes are wide, her mouth tilting upwards at the corners. "Are you...?" Her voice falters, her cheeks turning a soft pink as she regards me. "Are you here for Mr. Shaw?" The way she's looking at me makes me feel as if she's assessing me.

"I..." Honestly, I have no clue how to answer her. *Am I here for him? Or am I a prisoner in his house?* A bit of both. I'm not sure why Lycan wants me of all people. Surely there are a million women out there who would be better suited to him. "I'm not sure," I finally tell her.

"Oh," she whispers, setting the tray down gently. She moves quietly as she places the cup, small teapot, and plate on the setting at the head of a long, wooden dining table. The silver cutlery shimmers as the sunlight that's now streaming through the patio doors brighten the space. Once she's readied everything, she steps away.

"What is your name?"

The young woman glances at me with uncertainty on her pretty features. With long, chestnut hair tied into a ponytail at the back of her head and porcelain features, I wonder if Lycan finds her attractive.

Shaking my head to clear the stupidly jealous thoughts away, I focus on her. "I'm Scarlett. My family lives next door. Well, my grandmother does."

"You're the Bardot?" Her gasp is loud, her eyes even wider than before, the blue tinkling like sparkles in the sunlight. "I… I didn't realize you'd be here."

Confusion settles in my gut, my brows furrowed before I ask, "What do you mean?"

Her mouth opens as if to respond, but a moment later, she shakes her head and makes to leave me alone in the room with more questions than I have answers.

"Wait, please. I didn't mean to upset you."

She glances at me from over her shoulder, her expression void of emotion as she looks at me. "My name is Aliana," she tells me. "Please, don't ever speak to me again. It's best that way." Before I can ask something more, she's gone. The door to where I'm guessing the kitchen is hidden swings shut, and I'm alone.

What have I done to her to make her so angry?

The door I entered through opens, and there on the threshold is the man who brought me here. Dressed in a gray suit and black button-up, he looks like he's ready for board meetings, and I wonder what work he does. I don't recall him telling me, and I don't remember if my father mentioned it at the dinner when we first met.

"Now, this is a sight I could get used to every morning,"

Lycan says with a wolfish smirk, making his handsome face light up with amusement. "What are you doing here, little red?" He moves through the room as if floating on air. When he finally reaches me, I take in the dark stubble on his jaw, and for a moment, my hand tingles with the need to touch it.

"I... I was just exploring the house and found my way in here," I tell him, omitting the fact that I met Aliana. The pretty girl seemed to not want me around, and to be completely honest, I wouldn't want to be around here, but I know if I tried to leave, Lycan would find me before I made it next door.

"Well, sit," he tells me before pulling out one of the chairs, which I slide into. Perhaps Lycan will give me answers. I can only hope and pray. "I'll call your grandmother later," he informs me, which has me straightening my back.

"Let me talk to her. I need to understand—"

"You don't need to do anything." His dark green gaze lands on me, holding me hostage, stealing the breath from my lungs with the dark promise of something I truly don't want to fathom. He is danger wrapped up in a tailored suit. That's all it is. Undeniably handsome, but also unpredictable in his demeanor.

"I need to speak to my family. You cannot hold me here for no reason. I'm not your property, even though my father signed that godforsaken agreement." My voice is brittle with frustration, my throat feels dry as if sandpaper has lodged itself in my esophagus, and with each word I utter, it only seems to hurt more and more.

"If you'd like to talk to someone, it can be your friend, Aelin. Other than that, you're not to talk to anyone else." His voice comes out with a warning that if I were to try anything, he'd know, and he would hurt me.

"Then let me speak to her," I plead because if I can talk to her, then she can get help. She can call my father and get him to sort this mess out. Fix what he did.

Lycan ignores me for a moment as he pours the hot tea into a cup. I watch as he drops a small spoon of sugar into the liquid and stirs a few times. Once he sets the teaspoon down, he shoves the cup toward me. "Drink this. It will calm that fire so we can talk like adults."

"Don't treat me—"

"Scarlett," he growls, my name a warning on his lips, his eyes blazing with fury when he looks at me again. "If you don't want to obey me, I'll happily tie you to the St Andrew's cross in my dungeon and leave you there, naked and crying, until you realize I'm the one in charge here."

My mouth falls open in shock, but my body responds to his threat with heat sizzling in my veins. The apex of my thighs pulsing with unrelenting need, and I can't stop myself from squirming in the seat. I don't want him to have this hold over me, this effect that sends me rabid with hunger for him to do just what he's promising. But I can't help it. My traitorous desires take hold when Lycan throws his dark promises at me.

"You may be in charge in this house, but you don't own

me."

"Yet," he adds, knowing he has me because my father has agreed to allow Lycan to marry me. "Are you joining me for breakfast, or are you going to your room to sit alone?" Lycan asks so gently I snap my gaze to his, finding in those emerald orbs genuine concern.

"Do you want me to eat with you?" I'm not sure why, but after I voice my query, my heart gallops like a wild horse in a field, enjoying its freedom. But it won't last long because that stupid muscle that beats wants him to say yes. Even though my mind is convinced he must say no, that I should *want* him to say no. I don't.

For a long moment, Lycan watches me, taking in my hair, my face. When his gaze lands on my mouth, his tongue darts out to wet his full lips. "Yes, stay. Perhaps you'll enjoy my company and realize I'm not as bad as you think," he tells me as a satisfied grin forms on his perfectly handsome face.

"I doubt that," I bite out, taunting the wolf while sitting in his den. I must be stupid, but this man brings out the childlike qualities I've always had. "What could you possibly tell me to make me change my mind about marrying you?"

"Besides the fact that I saved your life... That would be my brother. And he isn't a man you want to be caught in the dark with. He's a hunter. He enjoys making pretty girls his toys."

My eyes widen in surprise at his confession, but quickly recover before testing, "Just like you?" I realize he could get angry. He could lock me in my room and never let me out, but I can't find it in myself to sit quietly.

"The women I take are willing accomplices to the pleasures I bestow on their bodies. I didn't hear you complaining while you drenched my fingers." Lycan picks up his mug, sipping his coffee as he regards me.

The door behind us opens, and the girl from earlier appears once more, this time with two plates of breakfast, including a mound of delicious-looking scrambled eggs, two rashers of bacon, and what I can only guess is dark rye toast.

Once we're alone, I look at Lycan before speaking. "I'm a woman. A touch from someone handsome, someone who's just saved my life is—"

"That's bullshit, and you know it," Lycan throws back. "You like the danger," he tells me with the confidence of someone who's known me all my life. "There are women out there who crave it, who ache for the need to be taken, owned, to be submissive under a man who knows how to make them feel something."

"I feel—"

My throat constricts when his eyes land on me, and I can't find words because I've never seen such unadulterated desire like I find in Lycan's stare. He leans back, his fork dropping on his plate with a loud clatter that echoes in the silence hanging heavily in the room around us.

"Look me in the eye. Tell me honestly that you don't enjoy the feeling of being helpless," he requests with a dark undertone to his voice, one that's gritted in gravel and drenched in desire.

My mouth opens to retort some form of denial, something to tell Lycan Shaw he's wrong about me, but I can't. Not because I'm scared, but because he's right. My stomach twists with the memory of what he did to me, how he touched me while holding me down on the cool surface of the vanity. And every moment of that only confirmed what I already knew—I'm broken.

"You don't have to be ashamed," he says before forking eggs into his mouth. His jaw works as he chews, and it's the sexiest thing I've ever seen. His chiseled face has the makings of a perfect sculpture, and I wonder just how many women have fallen prey to the man who's sitting at the head of the long table.

"I'm not ashamed about anything," I tell him. "There are things that aren't spoken about in my friend circles. In the society I grew up in, sex was something that happened behind closed doors." It's true. There weren't any women who opened up about their personal lives. There were no confessions about husbands and boyfriends who were good or bad in bed and certainly no conversations about their own pleasure.

Even my best friend, as open-minded as she is, is not one for oversharing. Sometimes that's a good thing, but other times, it's lonely. Not to have anyone to confide in. So, I kept my secrets to myself.

"That's the trouble with the old money society," Lycan

says as he breaks through my thoughts. "They're far too conservative, only to do the darkest, dirtiest things in secret." A glint of knowing sparkles in his gem-like eyes.

"Oh?" I want to know. Curiosity has always been my downfall, and right now, I want Lycan to tell me just what his desires are, what he's capable of, but something tells me he won't.

"I don't think you're ready for that conversation, little red," he chuckles before he continues eating, and I realize the talk is over. I focus on my plate and attempt to enjoy the meal, which is delicious, but the churning in my gut has my thighs squeezing together with memories.

I recall my ex-boyfriend, a good guy for all intents and purposes, but he was also someone who never could understand how my mind worked when it came to sex. I wanted him to grip me harshly, to spank me, to make me cry out, but his sweet nature had made him soft. Nothing wrong with that, I cared about him, but he wasn't a man who could get me off. After our dates, I would race to my bedroom to grab a vibrator to find pleasure with the dark fantasies that ran through my mind.

And now, I may have found my match, only, he *bought* me from my father. That's not how I wanted to meet the man I'm going to marry. I promised him the week, which I can do. There's no reason I shouldn't give him a chance to prove his worth.

But I just don't know if I'll survive a lifetime.

LYCAN

When breakfast ended, Scarlett disappeared upstairs. I wanted to confess everything to her. Tell her about my proclivities, and even though I'm certain she'll be able to handle them, I didn't. The more I open up to her, the more likely she is to use something against me.

I can't trust her.

I shouldn't trust her.

My office door swings open, and Kahn saunters in dressed all in black. His heavy boots thud against the wooden floorboards as he nears my desk. I watch him silently as he slips into the high, wingback chair that faces me.

"Darius is in New York. He's been meeting with the

Capo of the Moretti *familia*. There's something odd going on. Why would he be talking to Alex's cousins?"

That's a good fucking question. I don't respond to Kahn; instead, I pick up my mobile and hit dial on Alexei's number. I'll get the truth, one way or another.

"What can I do for you, Shaw?" Alex's thick accent comes across the speaker after one ring.

Leaning back in my chair, I tell him, "My brother and your cousin seem to be buddies. Any reason why?" I'm not afraid of Alex. I've known him far too long to fear him, but I wouldn't want to get on the wrong side of him.

"Interesting. I'm not sure." Papers shuffle on the other side of the line before he speaks again. "Looks like Franco has him running a job down to Miami. I can get the details on it if you'd like."

"I would. Darius is volatile. I don't trust him. He may be blood, but he hasn't been family for a long time." With the job Kahn's doing for Alex, looking into the church and convent, I don't want anything to come between my relationship with the mafia, but I can't have them working with the one man I *don't* trust.

"I understand. Give me an hour. I'll speak with the cousins and see what is happening on their end. I haven't been in the Big Apple for long enough to have met with them yet. Perhaps it's time I pay my *familia* a visit." Amusement laces his tone, but I'm too fucking wired to join him.

"Thank you. I'm with Kahn now. I'll have an update on the convent in your email soon."

"A pleasure as always," Alex says before hanging up. My gaze is locked on my right-hand man, needing some form of distraction from my thoughts of breakfast with Scarlett.

"I want to go in, undercover." Kahn's deadly serious expression is the only clue that he's ready to kill. Everything else about him seems calm, laid back. If I didn't know him, I would've said he's sitting with a friend, chatting about drinks tonight or the woman he fucked this morning.

"Give me a couple of days." I pick up the folder and slide it over to the edge of the desk nearest to him. "The contract is signed. All I need is our little princess to agree, put her signature on the dotted line, and I'll happily have you go do anything you need to. But she's still a flight risk."

"You think she'll run?"

"I do. All the way back to grandmother's house." The link to an old fairytale isn't lost on me. This, however, isn't fiction. This is real life, and Scarlett Bardot now belongs to the big bad wolf.

"I'll stay in the cottage until you're ready. The team is waiting on my order," Kahn informs me as he flicks through the information I got for him. "It seems Lorenzo has taken up residence in the convent. He's playing the good priest while he uses the women who come to him for help as toys in a much bigger game."

My blood runs hot through my veins. I can't imagine what Kahn is going through. His sister was taken when she was sixteen, stolen as she was walking home from school, and we haven't had a link to finding her for years. But it seems we've made a breakthrough.

"I want to be there when you take him down," I tell him. I'm not someone who has friends, have never been, but if I did call someone a friend, it would be Kahn. "I want to watch as he pays the price for his indiscretions."

A small, yet sadistic smile curls Kahn's lips. Fire blazes in his dark eyes as he regards me, excitement painting his expression like the goddamned Joker. He may not have bright green hair or clown makeup on, but there's something dark in the way his gaze brightens with dangerous intent.

"Of course," he agrees with a quick nod. "I wouldn't have it any other way. Unless you're on your honeymoon by then, enjoying the spoils of a long-awaited victory," he tells me, leaning his elbows on his knees. "I have to be honest; if you didn't claim her, I wouldn't mind taking her just to see the look on her father's face."

"I think perhaps I should have her visit Heaven," I ponder out loud. "Maybe she'll get a glimpse of what her father is really like. She'll finally know the truth about just how far he'll go to get his kicks." *And how far I'll go to have her bound in my playroom.*

"I think that sounds like a brilliant idea." Kahn pushes to his feet. "I better get going. Have a few things to do before I meet up with some of the guys tonight. I can't persuade you to join us. Can I?"

I shake my head. As much as I would like to let loose, have a few bourbons before coming home to Scarlett, I think it's time I showed her what she would be giving up if she walked away. "No. I need to spend time with her, to get her to trust me before the gala."

"Are you sure taking her there is a good idea?" Kahn's brows furrow with worry, and I want to say no, I don't think it's a good idea, but I can't keep her away from her grandmother, not forever. Because she needs to learn the truth, and I want it to come from the one person who is guilty of the domino effect that's plagued both families for years.

"I'll ensure she behaves."

He nods before leaving me to think about my plans for tonight. I pick up my mobile and hit dial on another number, one I haven't called in a very long time. I wait for the rings, counting them when they sound.

Once.

Two.

Three.

"Mr. Shaw," comes the voice that sends anger scouring through every vein in my body.

"Grace Bardot," I utter her name, hoping the contempt is clear to her. "Your granddaughter is quite the spitfire," I tell her. She knows where Scarlett is. She knew the moment I brought her into the house. Horatio would have told Grace about the contract because his *mommy* always fixes his fuck ups, but this time, she has no way of remedying her son's mistake.

"She will never marry you. Not because I forbid it, but my granddaughter is not stupid to fall for the likes of you." Venom laces every word she spews. She's trying to come across as formidable, but she's nothing more than a wounded animal trying to throw me off the scent.

"Like you did with my father?" I challenge easily, earning me a gasp in response. I knew she'd tell me I'm bad news, even though she knows I've never denied it. The woman is a viper, one that can easily strike, but she has nothing on me. Whereas I know what kind of man her son is, and I can take him down without blinking.

"The past is in the past," she warns. "But the curse still lies in wait. For years we've fought it, and when Conall died, I thought it would die with him."

"A curse is a way for the elders attempting to stop us from ever loving, but you have no reason to fear. I'm not capable of love." And it's true. I may find Scarlett attractive, alluring even, but my heart has been solidified, and nothing will ever change that.

"Don't ever discount the strength of a family curse."

Anger takes over as her words ring in my ears. I've always wanted the truth, wanted her to admit what she did. But she never has. In all our altercations in New York, she's never once allowed me the freedom from pain by revealing the truth. But now that I have her on the phone, just us, I ask, "Is that what you told my father when you had him killed?"

The silence on the other end of the line is deafening. There's no denying it, and there's no admitting it. But one day, and one day soon, I'll find out the truth.

"Make no mistake, Grace, I will marry your granddaughter. She'll take my name, and once that's done, the Bardot line will be nothing more than a distant memory."

"Scarlett will attend the gala, as planned." The hint of pain in her voice is unmistakable. If there's one thing I've learned over the years, it's that someone like Grace Bardot, who comes from old money, is filled with far too much pride to ever allow anything to get to her. To break her down. But she knows I'm a formidable match. And I'll happily step into the ring and fight her to the death.

Not mine.

But hers.

"She will." I nod to myself. "But if you even think of saying anything about our agreement, there will be consequences. And trust me when I say I always get what I want."

"You're just like him, you know," she tells me, her voice lowering to nothing more than a whisper. "Charming. Handsome. And yet, you're still trying to prove yourself."

My chest tightens at her words. The reminder that I lost my father is a steel blade in my chest. I know what was taken from me because I was old enough to know the man who raised me, who taught me everything I know, and then the Bardots took that.

"Don't ever speak of him," I sneer, my free hand tightening into a fist at the thought of finding my father's body, lifeless, blood dripping from fatal wounds. "You have no reason to even think about him. If I could remove him from your mind, I would."

This time, she offers a sigh before speaking. "I'm sure you're capable of it, but you wouldn't hurt the family of the woman you're about to marry."

"Is that a challenge, Grace?" I can't help but chuckle. She knows I won't back down. And she knows I'm capable of far worse than her mind can even ponder.

"She won't forgive you." This is true. There's no doubt in my mind.

"And I'll never forgive you."

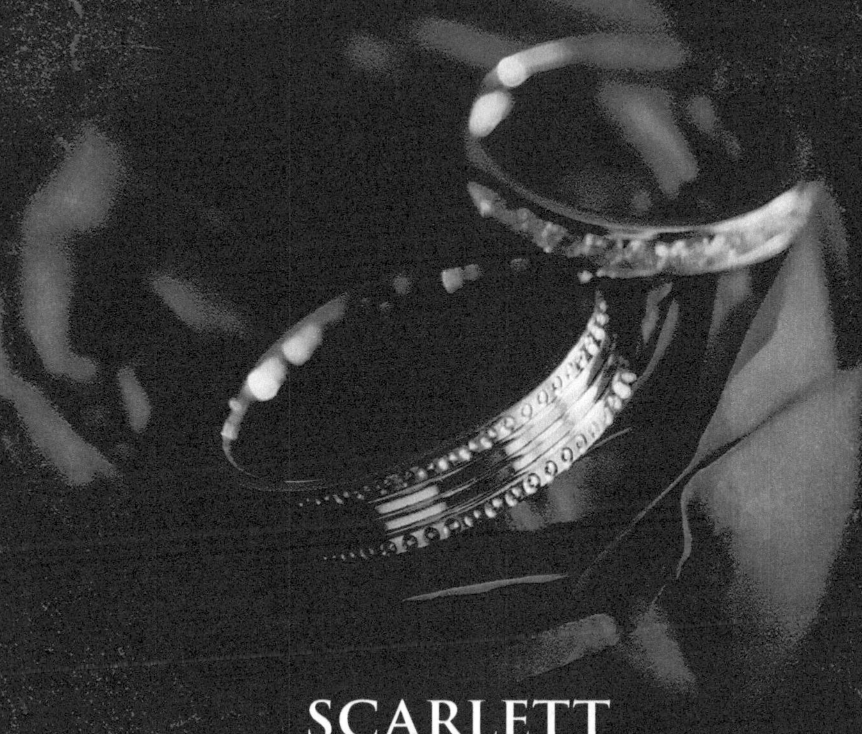

SCARLETT

When a knock comes on my bedroom door at six in the evening, I pad to it and pull it open before I have time to rethink it. On the threshold is Lycan in a pair of dark jeans and a light-blue button-up. The cuffs have been rolled up to his elbows while the top three buttons are undone, offering me a glimpse of smooth, tanned skin.

"Hi." Those perfectly-formed lips curl into a friendly smile before he continues, "I have dinner ready and was wondering if you'd like to join me."

"Is that an order or an invite?" I test, offering him a glimpse of a grin before I school my features. He could just pick me up and walk down to the dining room with me, but he doesn't.

"It's an invite to join your fiancé for a meal. We'll sit on the patio. It's a lovely evening with the fire blazing," he informs me. "Meet me in fifteen minutes. Choose something pretty from the closet." He gives me a slight nod before making his way down the hall, leaving me staring at the empty doorway.

Once I shut myself in the bedroom again, I race to the closet to find something to wear. Thankfully, I had time to shower earlier and wash my long, wavy, red hair. The length almost hitting the base of my spine.

Flicking through the hangers, I find simple black pants with a matching long-sleeved, red blouse. It's as if the whole wardrobe has been designed in outfits rather than items. I dress quickly before adding a dab of pink gloss to my lips. I line my eyes with black kohl and run the brush through my unruly hair.

I'm not sure why I'm nervous, but the flurry of wings in my belly is enough to have me giggling like a teenager about to head on her first date. I wish for a moment I could talk to Aelin and tell her what's happened. Perhaps tonight I can ask Lycan if I could get my phone. I'm almost certain she's sent out a search party for me. But then again, she might be partying in the city with enough guys to keep her busy for months.

Once I've breathed deeply to calm my nerves, I leave my bedroom and head downstairs to the hall to the dining room, where we spent breakfast together. The meal was tense but seeing Lycan do something so *normal* was eye-opening.

When I promised to give him a week to allow him to prove he's not a monster, I didn't think it would be possible. Yet each interaction with him has been filled with sexual tension rather than animosity. He's been polite, almost gentlemanly.

But even so, I'm not about to go tripping over myself because he's nice to me. It doesn't change the fact that he only has me here because of my father. And that's also something I need to learn more about. I have to know what's happened between the two men in my life.

Why did my father force Lycan's hand?

Did he know what would happen to me?

By the time I reach the glass doors that have been opened, allowing the cool evening breeze to sweep through the dining room, I have more questions than ever before. But what I find waiting for me takes my breath away.

The pillars that form a picturesque frame to the garden have been strung with white fairy lights. The table set for two has four tealight candles dancing in the gentle breeze. And the two place settings are perfect, waiting for us to take our seats.

Lycan picks up a wine glass from the cotton tablecloth and hands it to me. The red liquid shimmers under the soft illumination. If I were ever to tell someone about my dream date, this would be it. It's as if Lycan has burrowed himself in my mind and stolen every thought I've had about spending an evening with someone I care about and made it real.

"Welcome," he says as I take the glass from him. With a sip of my drink, I allow the warmth of the fruity, yet spicy alcohol to soothe the bird's wings that have taken flight in my stomach.

"This is beautiful," I remark as I slip into the waiting chair Lycan's pulled out for me. He helps me with the seat before taking his own. Lifting his glass, he holds it up over the dancing flames, and I mimic his action.

"To a new beginning," he says before clinking his glass against mine. The crystal tinkling while his gemstone eyes twinkle with mischief.

"Is this your way of attempting to soften me to the idea of marrying you?" I challenge before taking another mouthful of wine, hoping it will keep me calm through the dinner. Before Lycan can answer, we're joined by his staff, who bring out plates with steaming food, waiting to be devoured. I notice the girl from this morning isn't one of our servers, and I want to ask about her, but I don't.

It's not my place. Not yet anyway. Once we're alone, I take in the meal in front of me—a bed of lettuce with small, bright red tomatoes, cucumber, and herbs. There are roasted cubes of pumpkin and steamed potatoes surrounding a beautifully prepared piece of chicken. My stomach growls in response, and a chuckle has me lifting my gaze to find Lycan watching me intently.

"I hope you enjoy dinner," he tells me. "I didn't think

to ask if you're allergic to anything. Forgive me." He tips his head to the side in apology, and I can't help but take in the shadows that dance across his face from the flames.

"Oh, no, I'm not. I pretty much eat anything." We settle in after that, eating in comfortable silence, and for the first time since I was brought here, I feel *normal.* Perhaps it's a mistake to allow myself the liberty of not being scared or worried about what's going to happen, but knowing we're right next door to Gran's house also sets me at ease.

"Your grandmother is looking forward to the gala," Lycan says as we're halfway through our meals. This causes me to snap my focus on him.

"You spoke to her?" Disbelief laces my tone because she hasn't even bothered to talk to me or even ask after me. Surely, she's concerned about me being here.

"I did. I gave her a call earlier to let her know you're well." I'm staring at Lycan, mouth gaped in shock at his cavalier attitude. "I've known her a long time," he continues in between bites of his dinner. "She's a formidable woman."

"Why did you not allow me to speak to her?"

"You'll see her soon enough," he tells me before popping a forkful into his mouth. His jaw works as he chews, his shrewd gaze locked on me. Suddenly, my appetite has dissipated into a swirl of anger, not at Lycan this time, but at my grandmother.

Instead of finishing my half-eaten meal, I pick up my wine and gulp down what's left before glancing at Lycan, who's holding the bottle ready to fill up my glass. I allow him to before drinking down half of what he poured. Anger sluices through me at how my family can just allow me to be taken.

"I'm sorry," Lycan says suddenly, causing me to focus on him instead of swirling the crimson liquid in my glass. "Sometimes family isn't always what you expect them to be."

"Like with your brother?" I throw out, remembering how he warned me against the man who chased me through the woods. *The hunter who wanted to steal me.* The thought has a cold shiver skittering down my spine.

"Yes." It's only one word, but it's drenched in agony and rage. Lycan doesn't look at me as he finishes his meal before lifting the white napkin to wipe his mouth. Once he's done, he sits back, drink in hand, to stare out at the dark garden beyond our idyllic setting. "There were times when I was younger, after my father died, that I believed Darius would come home."

"I'm sorry you had to lose two people you loved." For a moment, he looks human. Almost. I guess grief makes people seem more real because it's only then they allow you to see inside them. The pain takes hold, and the walls they build come crashing down, even if only for a short moment. And that's what I glimpse in Lycan now. The heartbroken young man, not the wolf who could devour me whole.

"Love is merely an empty promise," he murmurs before sipping his drink. The wine staining his lips blood-red. "It's a word people throw around when there's nothing more to say or when they feel as if they're losing the game of life."

"That's not a way to look at it."

This time, he pins me with those emerald orbs. "Isn't it?" His dark brow arches, his jaw ticking as he regards me, and those beautiful eyes glimmer with a challenge.

"No. Because love makes you strong, it makes you fight for what's right." Even as I say it, I feel like a martyr because I've never been in love. I've only read about it in romance novels, which, to be fair, are all fiction. I don't know the depth of passion in my own right, only what I've come to learn from the heroes within the pages of a book.

"You're one of those girls who wants the knight in shining armor to save you," Lycan remarks. "I'm not that. I never will be." Darkness crosses over his face. His eyes hold danger, and even though I should be scared, I'm not.

"I don't need a knight to save me," I bite out, frustration at being called out, lancing my chest, causing my cheeks to heat, and I pray he can't see my embarrassment stained on my face.

"Next time you're in danger, and you're thinking about what you can do to get out of it, I want you to recall this moment. Remember the words you uttered because I may not be a knight, but if anything happens to you, I'll be there," Lycan informs me. "And only when you finally admit you're mine will I kill everyone in my path to keep you safe." He tips his glass toward me in a cheer before he swallows back the last of his drink. His throat works as he swallows, and I can't help but watch him with anger and desire fueling my blood.

I'm not sure how to respond to his promise. Instead of speaking, I nod and finish my drink. The staff appears again as if on cue, removing the plates and replacing them with small bowls of gelato and a bottle of bubbly, which Lycan proceeds in popping open.

He silently fills two flutes before setting the bottle in the ice bucket brought out with our dessert. Everything has been thought out tonight; he planned this, and even though I'm a whirlwind of emotion, I allow myself to enjoy the moment.

I pick up my spoon and scoop some of the cool ice cream into my mouth. Flavors of candy burst on my tongue—vanilla and strawberries—and a moan of pleasure vibrates in my throat. When my lashes flutter open once more, Lycan is beside me, on his knee, holding out a small, black velvet box. I don't need to open it to know there's a ring inside. And the way those green eyes are locked on me, holding out a hope of want and desire, I realize this isn't just *any* dinner — this is a proposal.

"I didn't think of doing this until this afternoon when I was sitting in my office alone," he tells me. "I wasn't going to because our marriage isn't what you would call traditional."

"No, it's not at all."

"But I would like you to wear this ring," Lycan says, popping the lid on the box. The silky pillow that holds a gold ring topped with a heart-shaped ruby sits waiting for me. It's beautiful, simple, yet elegant in every way. It's perfect.

"It's like you've read my mind," I blurt before thinking it through. My admission makes Lycan smile as he pulls out the ring, holding it out to me. I could refuse him right now, I could tell him to go to hell and try to run, but until I've spoken with my grandmother and my father, I don't know what my future holds.

With a slow nod, I allow Lycan to slip the ring on my finger. It's heavy, weighting my hand down as the sparkling jewel now confirms I'm going to be his. *A week.* That's what I promised.

"If in a week you want to take it off, you're welcome to. I always keep my word," he tells me, once more making me think he can read my mind. If he can, he'll know how at war I am with myself over this situation. Lycan picks up the champagne glasses, offering me one, which I accept. "Here's to a future which neither of us expected." He sips his drink as I do mine, and our gazes never falter. And for a moment, he allows me in to see the man inside. The one who lost a father, who has an estranged brother. A man who's as unsure of his place with me as I am of my place with him.

In this moment, my heart stutters.

He seems human.

But as quickly as it flickers in his eyes, it's gone in the next second. And I wonder if he'll ever allow me in fully.

LYCAN

I wanted nothing more than to spend the night with her. Seeing her wearing my ring, I was overcome with pride that I have her on my side. Perhaps not fully—yet. But soon, she'll come to realize I'm not a man who takes no for an answer. And I will whittle away at her defenses until she submits.

As much as I would like to join her for breakfast, I need to talk to the team. Kahn called late last night, informing me that Darius is back. For some reason, he's returned to Crimson Falls, but we can't find the bastard.

Stalking into my office, which is filled with men all dressed in black, I glance around, taking in each one. They're anxious, just like I am. The air in the room is twisted with the need for violence.

We should've been locked in a meeting all night, but even after Kahn's call, I couldn't bring myself to sit around talking about my brother. But we need to figure out the best way to lure Darius out.

The night I brought Scarlett here, I knew he would linger, and when the two security guards I keep onsite slinked into the night, through the forest and into the Bardot garden, they found the cottage beside the house empty. A note waited for me on the wooden table, one that caused my blood to heat.

He'd disappeared once again.

I can't afford to waste time looking for him while I have a girl upstairs who could either stand by my side or end up running. The wedding needs to go ahead, but I also need her to be on my side when the gala happens in a few days. Even though she's now wearing my ring, there is no guarantee she'll trust me when I haven't given her a reason to.

There's so much more to the story than she can fathom.

But it's not entirely my story to tell.

Kahn's gaze locks on mine the moment I slide into my chair. "He's close, and I have a feeling he'll make an appearance at the gala. I can go hunt him down," Kahn says, his stare on mine, waiting for the response he knows is coming. This is what he was trained to do. It's something he loves. There's no doubt in my mind, if I were to nod, he would be out there in an instant, his predatorial instincts kicking in, and his team right behind him.

My memory leaps back to Scarlett questioning me in her bedroom about the shot she heard the night he chased her through the forest. When I walked out into the garden that night, gun in hand, I didn't expect Darius to be hanging around, but then I noticed him hidden amongst the trees, waiting. I took a chance. I pulled the fucking trigger but missed.

He isn't back at the Bardot mansion. We now know that. What still doesn't sit right with me is how Grace hired him in the first place. She must know he's a Shaw. There is no denying he is my father's son, and she had to realize who he was when he got the job on her property.

Which begs the question—*what the fuck is Grace Bardot hiding?*

Kahn's watching me, waiting for a response to his comment. If my brother were to die today, I'm not sure I'll feel the pain. Actually, I don't feel anything, not anymore. *Except desire for the girl upstairs.*

My life has been a series of unemotional ties—one-night stands, contractual obligations—all offering nothing more than satisfaction for a moment. I never allowed myself to grow close to someone, to open what's left of my heart, and to have someone burrow themselves into my soul.

Scarlett is merely a means to an end.

She's part of the plan for revenge I will finally claim over her family. There wasn't another way to do this, to make them pay. I push my chair away from the desk and stand. Buttoning my suit jacket, I round my desk after picking up the folder.

"I want to question my brother. A niggling in my gut tells me there's more to this story than I know. He's working with the mafia, but he's also in Grace Bardot's pocket." I glance at each man in the room, all focused on me as I speak. "He's hiding something, or she is. One way or another, I will find out what it is. "I want you to search every fucking corner of this town. Find him, but bring him back alive." The order is clear, and Kahn offers a nod.

The sound of chairs scraping along the wooden floorboards fills the room as each man rises and takes his leave. I don't think it will take long for them to do a sweep of Crimson Falls, and it won't take them long to find him, wherever he's hiding.

Once I'm alone, I head to the patio doors that overlook the garden. The spot where I breached the trees with Scarlett in my arms is right in front of me, and I wonder if she'll ever come to terms with being my wife. Wearing my ring, she may have given me an inch into her thoughts, but there's so much more to break through.

In a few weeks, she'll take my name, and there's nothing she can do about it. I may have given her an out after the week is up, and I'll allow her to think she has a choice, but in actual effect, she's in this to the end.

If she refuses, her father will go to jail, and something tells me it's not what she'd want. Her life has been a series of events planned by her parents who wanted to rule her future. I'm not them. I may have failed to mention she's also here to give me an heir, but if she truly wants her own company, I'll give that to her. Call it repayment because this is a business transaction.

Nothing she's done in her life has been of her own will, and now I'll take the last remaining choice away from her by making her a Shaw.

I should feel bad.

But I don't.

I turn and stalk out into the hallway. The sound of the front door opening alerts me to visitors. Gray steps aside for me to see the tall brunette who's entering my home. The wedding dress designer, Opal, or something like that. Behind her are two younger girls pushing a brass railing with black clothing bags lined up for Scarlett to choose from.

When I selected the options from the website, I had her in mind. As I flicked through the choices, I couldn't help but picture her wearing each one, and that had my dick hard. But what had me stroking myself was the thought of ripping the material from her body on our wedding night and claiming her.

"Mr. Shaw, I'm Opal," the designer greets with a smile and an offered hand as I near them. "I trust you're well." Her dark eyes are filled with excitement, only because I told her money is no limit.

"I am. Thank you for making the trip on such short

notice. My bride is rather stressed about the wedding, and I'd like to take as much off her plate as possible." I gesture for her to follow me down to the dining room. With the curtains open, the sunshine streams through, offering a bright space to revel in the elegant gowns. I've ensured the staff have moved furniture around for this very reason. The room is large enough for Scarlett to try on the dresses, and the full-length mirror I had brought in from one of the guest rooms is ready and waiting.

"Thank you," Opal says. "I'll get ready if you'd like to bring her down."

Nodding, I make my way up to my fiancée's bedroom, knowing that this will end up in a fight. Scarlett hasn't warmed to the idea of marrying me yet, and even though I understand why she needs to submit, or I will be forced to *make* her bend to my will.

I push open the door to find her at the window seat. Her head snaps toward me, her eyes wide. I take in her outfit, the knee-length white socks hiding her beautiful calves, along with a pair of light blue sleep shorts which tease at a glimpse of her panties underneath.

Her top is floppy, hiding her tits from view, but I know what's under the material. I've glimpsed her bikini photos on social media. When I was doing my research, I made sure to study each and every picture, so I'll know my bride inside and out.

I raise a hand toward her. "Come."

Her brows furrow in confusion before she asks,

"Where?"

Running my fingers through my hair, I lift my gaze to hers and regard her for a long while. "You're trying on wedding dresses."

"No."

"Scarlett, if you continue acting like this, I can just bind you to the wall and have them dress you while I watch." The thought of her bound to a St. Andrew's cross flits through my mind, and I have to stifle the groan of pleasure that rumbles in my chest.

"You're insufferable." Her huff is nothing more than a taunting grumble, but the sound of frustration that escapes her lips makes me want nothing more than to bend her over and spank the insolence from her.

"And you're mine. Now come, I don't have all day to stand here arguing with you."

Scarlett rolls her chocolate-brown eyes in annoyance as she pushes off the window seat and pads barefoot toward me. She's tiny without shoes on, and I can't help but want to pick her up, haul her over my shoulder, and lock her in my bedroom. But that has to wait for our wedding night.

She follows me down the hallway to the staircase, and we silently make our way into the dining room, where the dresses are now hanging freely. All I see is white lace and satin, along with jeweled tiaras I know will look exquisite on Scarlett.

Only the best for my future wife.

"This is..." Her voice is tinged with awe, her pouty lips

parted with shock as she takes in the set up. Her lashes flutter, and those dark-rimmed irises are wide as she looks at every inch of the space before turning her wide gaze to me.

The designer rushes forward with a bright smile on her face. "Welcome, Miss Bardot. I'm Opal. Such a pleasure to meet you. I trust we'll have something to your liking." When Opal glances at me, I nod, taking my leave as I pull the doors shut. But before I disappear, I lock my gaze on Scarlett's and give her a warning glare. *Behave.*

Back in my office, I'm nervous. I've never felt like this before. Usually, I'm calm, relaxed, even when taking down my opposition. But Scarlett does something to me.

She makes me want.

She makes me crave.

She makes me *human.*

And that can never be a good thing.

SCARLETT

The first dress didn't have much material to it, and I have a feeling that Lycan had something to do with that. The second one was pretty, but it wasn't something I would be caught dead in with the almost nonexistent front and back. My cleavage was prominent, far too exposed if he intends to make me walk into a church.

I grew up in the church, going to catechism, learning passages from the Bible until they were ingrained into my mind, never leaving, and even though I don't go every Sunday, there is no way I'll be standing in front of a priest wearing that.

If that's what Lycan wants, he can find someone else

to marry.

"Let's try this one," Opal says after I've undressed for the third time today. She's pretty, and for a split second, I wonder if Lycan's dated her, or if he's been intimate with her. A spike of jealousy crashes through me before I pull myself together and offer her a smile.

"So, how long have you known Mr. Shaw?" I query as I take the slip she's holding out to me. Her gaze lands on mine, but there's no guilt or jealousy in her pretty eyes.

"A few months. He was at one of my fashion shows," she remembers with a smile. "He even offered to donate toward my charity. I have to say, you're very lucky."

My mouth opens, but no words come out. I'm not sure if I am lucky or if my luck had run out, and I was left with a man who *bought* me. "What charity is it?" I ask instead of talking more about my future husband.

Her gaze drops to the floor, and I can tell she's nervous from the way her hands twist in front of her. "I...Uhm... I've always wanted to support women, to show them they're strong, not because they're a wife or mother, but because they're warriors. So, I started up a charity to help women coming from abused homes." This time when she looks up at me, my heart stutters.

"That's amazing." It's the truth. I've heard about women living in fear daily. Women who aren't strong enough to fight back but also feel stuck. "You know," I start, turning to face her fully. "I'd love to interview you. I'm a media relations student, and I'll be interning in New York next month. It would be an incredible story to take to the company."

Opal's eyes widen. Her smile is bright, lighting up her face with excitement. "That is something I would definitely love to do." She grins, and we move back to the mirror, where I look at what I'm wearing.

The material of the sleek, floor-length, satin dress hugs my curves. For some reason, looking at myself in the mirror makes this all too real. As the girls flurry around me like excited hummingbirds, ready to flit into the clear, blue sky, I turn my gaze away from my reflection and out to the garden. I don't want to admit that this feels like some strange and twisted fairy tale.

Every girl dreams of her wedding day. I, for one, never thought I'd marry someone of my own choice. And it's as if those thoughts brought Lycan to me. Because I didn't choose him, and yet here I am, donning a princess dress which looks like it's straight from the pages of a book.

My prince isn't a knight in shining armor but a commanding wolf in an expensive, tailored suit. Once everyone steps back, I realize I was lost in thought, and when I glance at Opal, she's grinning as if she's just won the lottery.

"This is it," she coos as she claps her hands together excitedly. I want to turn, but in the same vein, I want to run and hide. I want them to remove the mirror, so I don't look at just how perfectly this dress fits.

"Are you sure?" I ask, still nervous, keeping my eyes from landing on the glass to my left. She grins wider, nodding quickly as she takes the veil and gestures toward me. I offer her a small smile and tip my head so she can place the bejeweled crown with sheer lace over my hair. It hangs low behind me; the weight of it is astounding.

"Yes. A picture of perfection." She offers me a chef's kiss before stepping back and allowing me space. As much as I don't want to be excited to see the result, I do turn and face the mirror finally. My breath is stolen for a long moment as I look at the woman staring back at me.

Atop the satin shift is a gown made purely of lace. Now I see why I had to put the silky material on first. If I didn't, this would be see-through. The lace covers my chest to my neck. It cinches at my waist before exploding into a wide circle all the way to the shiny marble tiles.

I twist and turn, taking in every angle. The back is completely bare, with thin lace twisting from my shoulders down to the base of my spine, creating a delicate V-shape. The veil hanging down my back looks like it's been made from the most fragile snowflakes with a delicate pattern of unique shapes.

The crown on my head sparkles in the light coming in from the floor-to-ceiling doors to my right. Doors that could lead to my freedom if I ran right now. But I wouldn't get far because I know my captor will not let me go.

Opal picks up a box that was sitting on a chair behind her and brings it to me. "This is for you. I think it will suit the dress." She hands me the gift, a rectangular, merlot-colored box with a red ribbon. When I tug at the bow, it falls away easily, and I lift the lid to find a gold bracelet. When I lift it from the suede cushion, a small charm dangles, and I have to set the box down to get a better look.

"This is gorgeous," I tell her, but my eyes are focused on the charm between my thumb and forefinger. A small, intricately designed wolf with a deep-set green eye, watching me. "This is..."

"Mr. Shaw said that I should give this to you, to wear on the wedding day," Opal tells me. "He left it here with a note." She points to the chair before looking at my shocked face. "Are you okay?"

"Yes, yes, sorry. I think I'm just overwhelmed." I take a step back and slowly move toward the mirror, where I finally allow myself to look, to really look at the woman there. The one staring back at me with her cheeks flushed, her lips pouty, and her eyes sparkling with emotion.

The dress is perfect.

"This is it," I tell myself, but Opal claps excitedly behind me. As much as I want to tell her to save me, to call my father and tell him what's happened, I don't. Instead, I smile. If Lycan wants arm candy, I can be that. If he wants someone who'll run his businesses with him, I can even do that. But if he thinks for one moment he's going to get me to change my name at the end of the month, he's wrong, and I'll show him that.

He may not have *wanted* me before we met, and he may only want this wedding to happen because of some archaic contract, but I'll make him fall in love with me, and then I'll run. I'll escape into the darkness of the forest, and he won't ever find me.

Four weeks until my birthday. It's a long time to let someone in, to feel something for someone, and the moment I see the humanity in his gaze, I'll be the one to strike. I'll end him and this godforsaken agreement my father has allowed.

I'm not a toy.

I'm not a possession.

But I can play the part just as well as anyone.

SCARLETT

By the time I've had a shower, and I'm sitting on my window seat, I'm exhausted. The dress I chose is perfect. It's absolutely breathtaking, and I'm sure Lycan will agree. I catch myself sighing as I wonder why I'm even going ahead with this, even wondering what he'll think. It's not like me to give in, to submit to a man, especially after what he's done to keep me here. But if I'm going to play into his game, get him to love me, and then end this farce, I need to make sure he trusts me, which is why I accepted his ring.

My bedroom door opens with a silent murmur against the plush carpets, and I'm met with one of the maids. Dressed in black and white, she looks to be about my age, or perhaps a few years older. She offers a small smile as she sets down a silver tray with a glass of red wine, along with a white envelope. My name is scrawled in elegant handwriting on the front.

"What's this?"

"Mr. Shaw has requested you have some wine, and also, he's left you a note." Of course, he did. The young woman nods before she leaves me in the room, pulling the door closed behind her. I want to run after the girl and ask her more questions. But I focus on the note instead.

I pick up the envelope, slowly unfolding the flap to pull out the note my fiancé wrote. The immaculate script is beautiful, and I allow my gaze to rove over the perfectly formed letters.

Tonight, you'll dine with me, and perhaps we can take this a step further.

L.

Direct and no-nonsense.

Just like the man himself.

I realize he's someone who doesn't like the word no, and he's also someone who always gets what he wants. If I were to tell him I'm not hungry, or I'd rather eat alone, he'd march up here and lift me over his shoulder, kicking and screaming. And he'd enjoy it too. I'll then be carried down to the dining room. So instead of fighting, I'll follow his rules.

Padding over the carpet, I make my way to the closet to find something to wear. I have an inkling that this isn't going to be a "burger and fries" type of dinner after last night, so I need to ensure I'm elegant, yet sexy. If I want the man to fall in love with me, I should appear to be ready to take the next step with him.

Which brings a thought to my mind—if he wants me as his wife, he'll want sex. Heat coils through me, settling low in my gut as I recall his fingers, how they taunted and teased, how I fell apart as he touched me. His perfectly timed strokes sent me reeling, and I don't doubt he would and could do it again and again.

Flicking through the hangers, I find an emerald satin cocktail dress the same color as Lycan's eyes. The garment is far too exquisite to wear in the house, but I can't help the need coursing through me to impress him, to show him I'm not some stupid girl he can boss around.

I'm a woman.

I take the item into the bedroom and lay it on the bed. Next, I choose lingerie which has been packed in a glass cabinet in the walk-in closet. There's everything from white cotton panties to black and red lace. Picking out a charcoal set, I smile for a moment, wondering if he'll even see this tonight. The bra and panty are made of sheer lace, with thin straps that feel like heaven across my skin.

I find a pair of silver heels I slip on after I've donned the dress. At the vanity, which steals my breath each time I take in the scene of the wolf chasing Red, I settle on the stool and start applying some lip gloss over a nude shade I found in one of the drawers. As I line my eyes with black, I allow my mind to develop a plan of action.

The mascara makes my lashes seem even longer and curled. And when I'm done, I sit back for a moment to summon the courage to face him again. I haven't seen Lycan since he left me in the dining room with Opal. Nervously, I get to my feet and head for the door, which I find still unlocked. In the hallway, it's deathly silent, and I'm thankful for the peace before I have to make conversation with the man who wants to marry me.

I move toward the staircase with ease, taking in the tapestries hanging high against the walls. The home is enormous, just like my grandmother's. I have to ask Lycan if I can talk to her, to see her. With the Bardot Gala coming up quickly, I'm sure she's worried about where I've disappeared to unless Lycan has fed her some story about how I'm spending time with him.

The thought coils in my stomach, anger flaring as I reach the steps and take them slowly, wanting to prolong my alone time. But I can't put this off forever, so when I reach the double doors of the dining room, I stop, inhale a deep, cleansing breath, and release it before I push my way into the vast space.

Everything has been returned to normal. The furniture—table, and chairs—fill the center of the room, allowing the cabinets against the walls to frame the place settings where I spot Lycan at the head of the table.

He's dressed impeccably, just like I knew he would be. His suit jacket is unbuttoned, allowing me a view of his button-up, which is a dark gray, reminding me of storm clouds on a cool winter's day. The color pops against the pitch black of his pants and jacket. I don't miss the fact that he's not wearing a tie, and the top few buttons of his shirt are undone. A glimpse of tanned skin has my mind wandering alone into territory I'd rather steer clear from.

"My soon-to-be wife," he voices, his tone filled with arrogant confidence. His lips quirk as his eyes hungrily rove over me. He takes in my long, red waves, then his heated stare burns its way over my face, to my lips, and down, finding my cleavage just peeking out from the neckline of the dress.

When he reaches my legs, he lifts his fist to his mouth and stifles a cough before coming toward me. His long strides swallow up the distance instantly, and seconds later, he's looming over me like a starving predator ready to devour its prey.

"You look rather breathtaking this evening," Lycan murmurs in a low, seductive baritone, which has my spine tingling with awareness of just how close he is. His eyes, those gemstones, shine with a ferocious need that heats me from head to toe.

"Thank you," is all I manage before he steps back and offers me his hand. I accept with trembling fingers, and he leads me to a chair to the left of him. He pulls it out, allowing me to settle before pushing it in. Everything is shimmering under the dim yellow bulbs from the chandelier, and even Lycan looks like a dark angel sent from the depths of hell to dine with me tonight.

"How was the dress fitting?" he asks as he waves his hand toward the staff who bring out plates they set down in front of us. The presentation is gorgeous with finely chopped herbs around the edge of the porcelain, and in the center is a miniature bruschetta with smoked salmon and cream cheese. Adorning this beautiful appetizer is a dollop of caviar. I've only ever tried it once but am looking forward to tasting it again.

"It was good," I tell him, meeting those eyes that seem to pierce right through me, searching for something deep within. Something I'm not willing to give him, not yet. But the moment I think it, I realize I need to offer him more, because if my plan is going to work, Lycan needs to believe this is becoming real. "I found a dress. It's perfect."

"I'm sure it is. Opal informed me she gave you the gift?" I watch him lift his wine glass, press it to his full, pink mouth, and take a long, languid sip. I can't deny he's handsome, more than I could ever have imagined a man to be, but he's the bad guy.

"Yes. Thank you." I turn my focus onto my food and lift the starter to my mouth to take a bite. As my teeth sink in, the flavors burst on my tongue. An involuntary moan vibrates in my throat, and when my gaze finds Lycan's, heat burns in those gemstones.

"I've always enjoyed watching a woman feast. There's

something so erotic about it," he murmurs. A small quirk at the corner of his mouth makes him look like a starving beast rather than a man.

"Oh?" I ask after swallowing the last bite. "Is that a line you use on all your women?" I taunt, causing fire to blaze in his stare. My stomach coils with both anxiety at taunting the wolf and desire at wanting him. Confusion twists its way through me like a coiling serpent about to strike. I can't allow myself to fall into his trap.

"*All* my women don't dine with me," Lycan offers. "Yes, there are some who have accompanied me to parties, but none have seen the inside of my personal space. My home is mine."

"So, you've never brought a woman home?" Incredulity thrums through the words, vibrating each syllable with confusion. He's a handsome, wealthy bachelor, one who must have women falling over themselves to be with him.

"I'm not into relationships. I prefer..." He lifts his fingers to his lips, tapping on them gently as he considers what to tell me. And I find myself leaning forward, intrigued by how he's about to explain his confession. "Women who aren't around for very long."

"So, you prefer escorts who leave after the deed is done?" Once again, I sound like I'm judging him, and perhaps I am in some way. I don't have any right to, but the anxiety that took hold of me earlier turns to an emotion I cannot admit I'm feeling.

A chuckle falls free from Lycan's mouth, his lips parted

in a way that allows me a glimpse of pearly whites, while his face lights up in amusement. "No, little red," he says. "I don't pay women to fuck me." His voice turns to lava, burning through every inch of my body, causing goosebumps to flare over my skin. "They beg, they plead, and they find bliss while I taunt and tease." His gaze, locks on mine, and I'm caught in his web. I can't turn away. "Would you like that, little red?"

My mouth pops open, but I can't find the words. I'm saved when the staff returns, clearing our plates and bringing in the main course. I'm pleasantly surprised to find a bed of couscous covered with stir-fried vegetables. To the side is a thick, juicy steak, along with a salad made of lettuce, tomato, more herbs, and olives.

Once we're alone, I feel his eyes on me, watching my reaction to dinner. Instead of looking at him, I focus on the plate and say, "This looks delicious."

"It certainly does." His response is low, gravelly, but I don't have to lift my head to know he's watching me. And his words have nothing to do with the meal before us. Lycan leans back in his chair but doesn't deter his gaze from me. It's as if flames of desire lick at my skin, traveling from my hand, teasing their way up to my wrist, forearm, and bicep. By the time they reach my shoulder, I shiver at the heat.

I'm not sure I can play this game with him. He's far more experienced. There's no way in hell I could ever win if he does this to me if I allow him to affect me in such a way. My lashes flutter when I feel his nearness reach for me. His hand lands on mine in a commanding gesture, and I realize why. I'd been trembling, holding the fork as it tinkled against the fine porcelain.

"You were rather calm walking in here, little red," he says, his voice taking on the tone of a commanding officer speaking to a soldier readying himself for the front line. "And for a moment, I thought you were finally coming to terms with the wedding. I thought" — he pauses for a moment before continuing — "that you were willing to be my wife, allowing me to finally claim you."

His words incite anger through me. A spark igniting the kindling in my gut, causing me to tug away from him, shoving my chair back against the cool, marble tiles. The clatter of cutlery on the table bounces against the walls, echoing in a poignant warning.

"You're the rogue in this story, Lycan Shaw," I point out. "Being kidnapped by a man doesn't make me want to fall in love with him. It doesn't even make me want to try." My plan is in the gutter. I should've ignored his jeer, but my stubbornness wouldn't allow it.

"I never said anything about love," he comments, folding his arms across his chest, making his shoulders seem even larger with bunched-up muscles. Strength and dominance are what this man wears, like a goddamned cologne. "Sit."

"No."

Lycan's hand's fist on the table. His jaw ticks with frustration as his usually jade irises turn almost black as he regards me. "Scarlett, you must mistake me for a man who doesn't mind the word *no*," he speaks slowly, clearly, and every word is drenched in barely constrained anger. "When I give you an order, you will obey me without question, without sass, and most certainly without that stubborn demeanor you insist on portraying."

He doesn't rise. He sits, still, very fucking still. He reminds me of a predator, lying in wait for the prey to run, because a man like Lycan Shaw enjoys the chase. I can see it glimmer in his stare. The way he's taking in my posture, my stance, he can tell I'm about to bolt out of this room.

"Run." Lycan jerks his chin toward the door just as his lashes flutter with excitement dancing in those dark depths. "I like the chase." His tone drops to almost a whisper, one that's heavy with desire and laced with a threat. One that tells me he will catch me, and I may not like what he does then.

Without another thought, my feet move, and I'm racing toward the patio door, which is ajar, instead of the door leading into the rest of the house. The night breeze hits me as I step out onto the cobbled patio, and my heels click onto the stone, but I focus on the garden. My mind flits through my options, and I quickly make my way deeper into the darkness and away from the house.

"I know this property very well, little red," Lycan warns in amusement and condescension. For a moment, I hate him with a fiery passion, and I want nothing more than to turn around and slam my fist into his face. But I know that won't do anything but hurt me.

My legs carry me out onto the lawn, and I'm thankful my heels aren't sinking into the ground. It's firm, allowing me to run faster than I anticipated. Instinct has me wanting to turn around, but I don't. Instead, I wonder how I can get off his property. Going into the woods isn't an option, so perhaps I can find somewhere to hide.

Heavy footfalls follow me. Even though I'm not faster than he is, he doesn't come near me yet. My heart catapults into my throat when I hear a howl from deep in the woods. There's nothing but darkness ahead, so I turn to my left and race toward the pool house. If I can get around it, perhaps I can hide somewhere. Maybe there's a shed hidden in the shadows.

But by the time I slink behind the large structure, my lungs are struggling to pull in air. My hands are shaking as I feel my way around the wall, smooth concrete against my palm. With every minuscule step I take, tension radiates through me. Leaning against the wall, I close my eyes and attempt to focus my hearing on the man following me.

Even though I don't hear him running or even walking, it doesn't mean he's not near me. I'm almost certain he's close, and that means I have to find somewhere to disappear. Straight ahead leads to more of the backyard, with what looks like wooden poles sticking up from the ground. I should've explored outside earlier, but stupidly, I thought I could do this.

I thought I was strong.

My heart cracks at the thought of me losing my life because of my immature thoughts. A scraping sound startles me, and I almost scream into the night, but my hand shoots out to cover my mouth, and I shut my eyes so tight, hoping that it was all just my imagination. Even though I know it wasn't.

Quickly, I slip off my heels and take a tentative step toward the grass that leads out to where I'm guessing the kitchen door would be. I move silently onto the softer, mushier lawn, finding my feet in soggy soil. Either they've just watered here, or I'm about to sink into quicksand. The thought makes me giggle inwardly as I note how far I have to go before I reach what looks like a shed in the distance.

Another step.

And another.

But the moment I reach the first wooden pole, I'm slammed into the soft, wet ground by a heavy, warm body. A scream pierces the night, and Lycan's warm breath is at my ear.

LYCAN

Her body wriggles underneath me. My hand covering her mouth is warm from her short, nervous breaths, and her legs kick upward, but she's pinned beneath me, and she's not going anywhere. I can't help but smile when her ass wiggles against my crotch, causing my cock to harden with need. From the moment I first saw her in her parents' dining room, I knew she was going to fight this. I could tell. But now that I have her, I'm enjoying the taunt and tease we're doing.

"Are you going to behave?" I ask, even as she kicks at me. Her hands attempt to push herself up, but the ground is soft, muddy, and I'm sure the dress she's wearing is completely ruined. Not that I care because all I can think about right now is ripping it from her body and finally claiming her. I release my hold over her mouth, only to be met with a slew of curse words that have me chuckling.

Gripping her wrists, I pull them down to her sides, holding her steady as I push myself up on the slippery ground. Her face is dirty, her hair caked with mud, but she's never looked more beautiful to me.

"Let me go, you fucking monster!" Her voice is wrenched from her throat, so loud it echoes into the darkness. Thank fuck I let the gardener leave for the week to see his family. When the door to the small structure where he stays opens and Kahn steps out into the night, I can't help but laugh at his expression of shock.

"What do we have here?"

"Help me, please," Scarlett pleads as she looks up at him, walking toward us. I still have her pinned down, and filthy thoughts of having her bound to my bed infiltrate my mind.

"Oh, sweetheart," Kahn says. "My boss isn't a man I'd like to cross. As pretty as you are, I think it's best you obey him and not tempt him by playing a game of cat and mouse." Kahn drops to his haunches to take in the girl beneath me. A flicker of interest sparks in his gaze, but it's gone in the next second, and I'm thankful because I don't feel like killing my right-hand man.

Scarlett wriggles some more, attempting to tug her arms from my hold, but she's too small, too delicate to fight her way free. I lean in, my gaze on Kahn's when I whisper in her ear. "Would you like to play with us, little red?" I don't wait for her response before continuing. "I'm not usually one to share, but if you're feeling particularly *filthy*, I'm happy to oblige just this once."

"Fuck you!" Her words are spat with venom and malice, which get lost in the darkness because even though I should be hurt, I'm not. Emotions don't come into play with her, and I'm almost certain she knows it too.

That's what I tell myself. And that's the story I'll continue telling myself.

"If that's what you're offering, I'll bite," I inform her, keeping my gaze on Kahn. "Your bite first?" I ask him, nudging my cock against the crease of her ass. I know she can feel the hardness against her, and a small whimper of something between pleasure and pain tumbles from her plump lips.

"I think she wants to get dirty with us, boss," Kahn remarks while reaching for her hair, his fingers fisting into the matted strands, and I can't help but chuckle quietly. She feels it. She feels me. The vibration of my body rumbling through hers.

"Let me go, you monster," Scarlett announces, but she doesn't move. Instead, her body stills, almost as if she's giving up, but I'm not going to get played like a sap. She's waiting for me to lighten my hold on her, and then she'll strike. I'm not sure with what energy she'll do this, but knowing my little red, she'll find it within herself to pounce. And fuck, if that doesn't make me what to claim her even more.

When I finally let up, lifting my body from hers, I tug her from the filthy ground and pull her into my hold. Her gaze is locked on Kahn, probably waiting for him to say or do something, but all he offers is a mock salute before he gestures with a tip of his head toward us, leaving us in the darkness.

"Did you think you were having fun running from me, little red?" I question in her ear, my arms wrapped around her like a vise. She can't escape because she's mine.

"Don't think for one second you'll ever get me to submit to your games," Scarlett hisses, but she doesn't struggle against me like she was earlier. Instead, she's placated, her body lax, and for a moment, I enjoy her warmth.

Perhaps, with time, she'll come to love me. Even though I'm not capable of that kind of emotion with someone, I'll make sure she's safe, taken care of, and she will never want for anything when she's with me. I don't tell her this; instead, I slip my hand in hers, tangling our fingers together, and tug her along behind me.

I focus on the rage coursing through me instead of desire. Both emotions warring in my chest, in my mind. On the one hand, all I want to do is punish her with my hand, with my belt, and then my cock. On the other, I want to bind her to the bed until she finally submits. Until she realizes there is nowhere to run.

"Wait, please," Scarlett says as I step up onto the porch, where she stumbles behind me. I halt all movement, twisting around so I can face her. With the soft yellow glow of the lamps that illuminates the area, I'm awed at her beauty. I've known she was beautiful since the moment I laid my eyes on her, but seeing her messed, muddy, and broken like this is a new vision that makes my cock throb behind my zipper.

"Let me make something clear, Ms. Bardot," I bite out, allowing the anger to drench my words. "If you attempt that once more, I won't think twice about allowing Kahn to show you what he's capable of. He's been my right-hand man for many years now, and he knows my tastes vary, even though sharing may not be top of the list, but I'll gladly watch as he puts you through your paces."

"I'm not some horse you can train," she grits, her teeth clenching, and I realize she's trying not to lose her mind at me. "I just need to know the reasons. I have to."

"What you *have* to do is obey me when I speak. There are things that you don't know about yet, and I will allow you the knowledge when you're ready."

"I am ready now," she insists, her eyes sparking with curious need and ferocious interest. "Please?" This time, the word is a plea that turns my blood hot with need. How I haven't taken her to my bed yet is a mystery. It's only been a few days, but I have to admit, she's more alluring than I expected.

"I'll tell you when you're ready." Turning for the door, I tug her behind me, and I'm sure the trail of mud we're leaving in our wake will be gone by morning. The staircase will be caked with footprints, but all I can think about is locking her in the bedroom until she's had time to consider what she just did.

By the time we reach Scarlett's bedroom, she's practically vibrating beside me when I stop at the doorway and tug her until her back hits the smooth wooden panel. With my free hand, I tip her chin up, so those pretty eyes are on mine.

"I'm not the monster in your story, even though you've clearly made me out to be." I want to tell her about her father, but that would be going against the agreement we came to. Horatio requested that he be the one to tell her the sordid secrets he'd been keeping. And even though I didn't want him to, he's her father, and the fuck up he's made is his confession to spill.

I doubt she'll ever give him the redemption he seeks, but I'm sure he'll beg and plead, just to get back in his daughter's good graces. But I know for a fact, she'll never again see him the way she does now or did before he signed the contract, offering me her hand in marriage.

"Monsters all want us to believe they're nothing more than heroes. But what makes a man a villain in a story is how he conducts his business and how he treats a lady."

"Are you claiming to be a lady, little red?" I allow a smirk to curl my lips as Scarlett's muddy hand attempts to make contact with my face, but I'm faster. I'll always be quicker than her. And that's something my sweet girl needs to remember.

"You know, Lycan Shaw, just when I think you're

finally showing your true, gentlemanly colors, you go and say something like that which convinces me that you're nothing more than a monster." She sneers at me, her nose crinkling, and it's the cutest thing I've ever seen. Never once in my life have I thought of a woman being both cute and seductive, but Scarlett portrays both effortlessly.

"I never once claimed to be a gentleman, my sweet," I inform her. It's the truth. My tastes have darkened both my heart and soul and though I may be polite, there's nothing about me that would let a woman think I'm a gentleman. "Tell me something, Scarlett. If there was anything in this world that could be given to you, anything at all, what would you ask for?"

For a long moment, she considers this, her lashes fluttering against the apples of her cheeks, and even through the smears of mud, I notice her cheeks darken with a soft, pinkish hue. A flicker of something dances in her eyes, but before she answers, it's gone, and suddenly, she's no longer thinking of whatever had crossed her mind.

And her final response is a lie. "Just let me go." Her lips are parted on soft breaths as she shivers when I lean in to inhale her sweet perfume. It reminds me of a rainy morning on an overcast day—fresh, cool, and crisp—but also drenched in dirt. The contradiction is a strangely euphoric fragrance to my senses.

Tipping my head to the side, I grip her chin between my thumb and forefinger and pull her closer, so our lips are barely touching, but close enough for me to inhale as she exhales. Inadvertently connecting us for a moment before I respond, "That's not an option. Try again."

She tries to pull away, but there's nowhere to go. I've pinned her to the door. My body snug against hers. The soft curves allowing my hard ridges to fit perfectly to her body.

"Lycan." She murmurs my name like a parishioner calling out a prayer to the heavens above. It hits me right in the chest, in a place I didn't think still existed within me. Women I've been with have screamed my name, but never with such pained need. It's as if she's throwing it out there, allowing it to slither under my skin, snaking its way through my veins until it finds the one muscle I've refused to allow to beat since the night my brother left with the woman who scorned me.

SCARLETT

A shiver wracks through me as a lone tear escapes my lashes and trickles its way slowly, gently, down my cheek. Lycan's quick to react, the pad of his thumb tracing the salty emotion before he locks his gaze with mine as fire blazes in his green eyes.

Shock escapes me as a gasp stumbles over my lips at the action. He's so close, watching me, waiting for a reaction, but I'm too tired to say anything more. Fighting now will only anger him, and I'm not sure I can handle punishment under his hand right now.

"I'm tired," I whisper. More so that he'll leave me be, and I'll be able to think about what he said tonight. Not the promise of him and his friend Kahn taking me, making me pay for running, but that there's more at play than I can figure out.

"Tomorrow, little red, I'll come for you. Be ready at nine. Don't be late because I don't appreciate tardiness." His voice, a tone of deep, frustrated gravel forming the words, as if it's been kicked up from tires traveling too fast over the driveway. A reminder that everything about him is dangerous. Confirmation of just how unmatched we are, him being too dark, and me, well, I'm fragile under his hold. Not because I'm a woman, but because just a touch from Lycan as he trails my cheek with his knuckles, and I feel as if I'm about to buckle under the electric current coursing through me.

"Why?" I question in a whisper so soft I'm not sure he heard it. His mouth quirks, a slow, seductive smirk curling his perfect lips as he takes me in, from chin to hairline and down to my mouth where his heated gaze lingers for a long moment. With another movement, he is so close I'm almost certain he's about to claim my mouth with his, and in that few seconds, I want him to. I want to bend to him. I want to leap onto my tiptoes just to feel those full lips on mine.

But he doesn't. And my heart plummets, embarrassment at my thoughts coursing through me. Every inch of my body aches from the stupid escape which the man before me thwarted.

"Tell me, Lycan," I command, attempting to sound stronger, more formidable than just the girl he sees when he looks at me. Because I'm certain that's what I look like right now, dirty and muddy.

He shakes his head slowly, and I'm not sure if it's his answer, or if he's at war with himself trying to figure out what to say to me. He drops his hand from my chin, and I immediately miss the connection. It's stupid and immature to ache for a man who stole me, who had to have a contract just to get me to marry him. And perhaps I'll pay for the insane thoughts I have toward him, but just for now, I allow myself to consider what being his wife would be like.

When Lycan finally steps away, the cool breeze that sweeps away his warmth causes me to shiver. "Get cleaned up." More gravel rumbles in his throat. "Sleep and don't leave your room tonight, or I will be forced to lock you inside." The warning is clear. The mishap of my running from earlier will not happen again, and he'll make sure of it. "Tomorrow, we'll talk." Then he turns and walks away, leaving me staring at his broad back that tapers into a narrow waist. His shirt is filthy with mud, his dark slacks are probably caked in dirt, and his usually shiny shoes are no longer pristine.

When he reaches the far end of the hall, he stops and turns toward me. I expect him to say something, but he doesn't, he only opens the door and walks inside, and I'm left alone in the darkness.

I don't know what he could say to me tomorrow that would change my feelings about marrying him, but if I'm going to get out of this alive, I'll have to play by the rules. For now, I retreat into my bedroom where I shut the door and make a beeline for the bathroom.

Once the shower is heated and a haze of warmth billows around me, I strip down and step under the spray that has me hissing in pain at the scrapes and cuts from small stones where I had been pinned under Lycan's heavy frame.

The memory steals my thoughts, and an ache low in my gut twists and turns with the promise that the events of him chasing me, pinning me down, could happen again. It probably will. And I find myself squirming at the idea. *Would I want that?* The question hangs in the air, around me, dancing in the steam, and I realize with certainty that I had never felt more alive than when I was under Lycan, begging for him to stop.

Is it something that I would crave once more?

Yes. Yes, it is.

Grabbing the soap and loofah, I lather up to wash away the dirt stuck to my skin. But I know as I clean myself, there's no way I can wash away the touch of the man down the hall—the man who will soon be my husband.

After I wash my hair and rinse the strands, I turn off the taps and step out into the foggy room. Wiping my hand against the mirror to clear it of condensation, I stare at myself. The woman looking back at me is different somehow. More... confident.

I grab a towel and wrap myself in the fluffiness before heading back into the bedroom and opening the closet to find something to wear. When I was brought to the room for the first time, I didn't think I would find it comforting, but as I pull on the shorts and tank top, I'm at ease.

Even though it's late, I don't go straight to sleep. Instead, I settle on the window seat to look out into the blackest night. The garden below is empty, and I stare out at the darkness wondering why my grandmother hasn't even bothered to come here to see me.

Which begs the question—what has Lycan done to my family? My father is obviously not one of his favorite people, but what could my grandmother have done? Also, the book I found earlier addressed to her has me wondering if she knew the Shaws. Perhaps Lycan's father was C.S.? I think back to the note, speaking about a wolf loving his damsel.

Can history be repeating itself?

Is that why Lycan is trying to get me to marry him?

I need to know. There are so many questions and no answers. Even though Lycan promised we would talk tomorrow, something tells me there will always be more questions, and answers may not always fulfill my need for more information.

My bare feet pad down the hallway. The sun hasn't risen yet, and even though I'd love to open the door and step out onto the patio, I have a feeling I'd be caught red-handed. Silence hangs around me, like a thick, cloying cloud, as if he's already watching. Deep down, I have a feeling Lycan knows when I make the most insignificant move. As if my breathing is on his radar. When I reach the bottom of the staircase, I turn left instead of right. I should go to the kitchen, which was my plan when I shut my bedroom door, but now that I'm here, curiosity has piqued, and my feet move voluntarily toward the office door that's currently shut.

With a gentle twist of the handle, I push open the heavy wooden panel and find myself in a dimly lit room. Stepping into Lycan's personal space feels invasive but also exciting. My stomach twists with anxiety, with fear and elation at walking in and taking something that belongs to him, just like he's taken me.

Perhaps I can find answers about what my father is hiding. Lycan promised to talk to me, to tell me the truth, but something tells me he will most certainly be keeping things he deems inappropriate from me.

All my life I've been treated like a child.

And I'm done allowing it.

Settling in the expensive leather chair, I cross my legs under my butt and pull myself closer to the heavy, wooden table, which has two drawers on either side of where I'm seated. The first one I tug on is locked, causing frustration to trickle through me. The next one slides open with ease, but all I find is a case of cigars and a stainless-steel lighter engraved with an intricate design of a wolf's head. It looks like it's howling at the moon. Underneath the etching is curled script, *The Hunt.*

Confusion furrows my brows, and I flick it open, unsure of what I'll find under the cap, but it's empty. A few streaks of black, which I'm guessing have come from the flame, but nothing more.

I open the top drawer to my left and find a small stack of envelopes and a notepad. Two sleek, silver fountain pens and a bottle of black ink. A red sealer stamp sits to the side, and once again, when I lift it, I find an engraving of a wolf's head, but this time with the name Shaw under the collar of the beast.

I continue my search, opening the last of the drawers, and find this one filled with one thick folder. Black leather etched with Shaw on the front cover, and a zipper holding everything inside.

With trembling fingers, I lift it from its hiding place and set it on the desk. The hiss of the zipper echoes in my ears, causing me to wince, praying that the sound wasn't as loud as it seemed. In the darkness, a whisper can be amplified to sound like a scream. And Lycan's hearing must be as sharp as a trained hunter because I'm certain he could hear even the slightest noise.

Flicking open the folder, I pick up the page lying on top of the stack. It's been written on the Shaw branding letterhead—a letter to my father. It's the threat he sent to Dad to get him to sign over my hand in marriage.

But as my gaze scans the words, it doesn't come across as a threat. Instead, Lycan seems to want to *save* me.

She doesn't need to know the truth to go on living and enjoying her life. You're the fuck up, not her. And I trust you'll see things my way. If you or your wife come near me or try to break the contract, I'll see to it your daughter will never speak to you again. The moment she learns of your indiscretions, she'll walk away. Think very long and hard about it, Mr. Bardot. Do you really want to lose your daughter over a stupid mistake? Unless you think your stupidity isn't an error, then I'll take Scarlett and ensure she gets the life she deserves.

Don't mistake me for a patient man. Also, do not think for one second I'm doing this for you. This is all for the girl. She will be mine, and the moment we walk out of your house, we won't return.

"Have you read enough, *fiancée*?" Lycan's deep baritone skitters across the silence toward me, the darkness swallowing his form, but his penetrating gaze is laser-sharp, and it's on me. He doesn't move from where he's leaning against the doorframe, his thick, muscled arms folded across his broad, tanned, naked chest. Even in the dim light shining through the window, I can tell this man is more Adonis than human.

"I—I..." Words escape me. My throat clogs with guilt

and shame at being caught red-handed, just like all my fears coming true.

"When I promised to tell you everything in the morning, I meant it," he says, pushing away from the threshold and stepping into the room. My hungry gaze takes him in. He's only wearing a pair of red plaid sleep pants. Every other part of him is bare—feet, chest, stomach, and those arms. A memory of what happened last night trickles through my mind, and I can't stop from squirming in his chair.

He stops inches from the desk.

Dropping his hands to his sides, he pins me with a glare, and my intent stare eats up every other inch of him that was covered when he had his arms crossed. The dips and peaks of smooth skin taunt me, and the deep dip of his navel has a dark trail of hair sneaking down into the waistband of his pants.

"Are you enjoying the view, soon-to-be wife?" The amusement in his tone has me snapping my gaze to his face. Finding the corner of his mouth tipped, his green eyes blaze with intent, with malice, but also, with desire so hot it's as if a volcano has erupted behind those deep, orbs.

"I needed answers," I respond to his earlier question in an attempt not to talk about how attractive I do find him. I want to hate him right now. In this moment, I want to scream and shout, but I'd rather have him talk to me like an equal, and I know losing my shit will only have him shut down again.

"And I promised to give them to you." His expression is stern as if I'm a child who's about to get grounded for being bad. "But if you insist on acting like an insolent teenager, I'll happily lock you up and treat you accordingly."

"I just don't want to be in the dark anymore, and somehow, I don't..." Shaking my head, I push to my feet, and that's when I realize I'm wearing a tiny pair of shorts and a strappy top that fits tightly against me as if it were a second skin. Lycan's expression turns dark. His pupils widen, turning the normally green irises into black, but he doesn't smile.

"You don't?" A dark brow arches as he regards me with curious need.

"I don't trust you."

He considers this for a moment, and I almost expect him to admonish me for what I've just said, but instead, he smiles. "Good. You shouldn't."

"I'm supposed to marry you, but I can't trust you?"

Without responding, Lycan rounds the desk, stopping inches from where I'm standing. His hands land on my hips, and he holds me close, pulling me the last hairsbreadth until our bodies are flush. "I'm dangerous. I'm lethal. And I'm almost certain I will make you cry a lot more throughout this strange relationship." His brutal honesty scrapes against his throat, causing it to sound heavy, like tires on gravel.

For a long moment, I allow myself to stare at him. This close, even in the dark, he's utterly breathtaking. In such a way that I could forget how I came here. I could even push aside the fact that my father signed my life over to him. I'm still convinced he's a bastard, but he's right.

He is bad for me.

He will hurt me.

But even so, people I thought were keeping me safe all my life were clearly lying to me. The realization hits me suddenly—I'm alone. I don't have my parents to save me, which means I have to save myself.

My decision is made. I lock my gaze on his and nod. "Then allow me to learn more about the man I'm vowing to spend the rest of my life with."

LYCAN

Her request shouldn't be difficult for me, but it is. I can't deny the thought of someone knowing me inside and out scares the shit out of me because nobody has ever burrowed their way into my life, or my mind, for that matter. But those wide, cocoa irises seem to dig into me, and I allow her for a split second to see the fear bouncing around my mind before I shut down once more.

"I don't appreciate my wife snooping around my office."

"Soon-to-be wife," she throws back, a small glimmer of a smile taking hold of her plump, pink lips, which has me hungry to devour them. I could sit her on my desk. I could also spread those long, slender thighs and feast on her sweet cunt. Temptation to do just that runs rampant through me, and I wonder what she'd do if I were to take hold of her and pin her to the smooth wooden surface and have my way with her.

Would she fight?

I would want her to. I hunger for a woman with fire to show me just how strong she is against someone like me—a beast, a wolf in an expensive suit. I step into her, my feet touching hers, the warmth of her skin burning through me.

Scarlett gently reaches for my face, her palm cupping the scruff at my jaw, sending need coursing from her tender touch to my brain. Messages of wariness hit me in the chest, but this girl, this innocent woman, can't hurt me because she'll never be able to find the one muscle in my body that would crack if I allowed it to. It has been locked away for so long I doubt it works besides the fact of keeping me alive.

"What you'll find is not something you'll be able to handle, little red," I tell her earnestly. The truth scores my esophagus, the raw honesty reminding me of just how bad I am for her.

I wanted to save her.

I wanted to claim her innocence for my own.

When her father signed the contract, I convinced myself she'd be better off with the devil than a monster. Perhaps it's because I believed her sweet light would slowly snuff out my cloying darkness.

"You don't know me very well, Lycan Shaw," she tells me, both hands holding onto my face. Her thumbs circling my stubble. Her gaze drinks me in like a fine wine, but I'm nothing of the sort. I'm a smoky whiskey at best.

I can't stop the smirk that twists on my face. I lean in, slow and steady, keeping my stare locked on Scarlett's beautiful cocoa gaze. "Trust that I'll know you by the time you say I do," I tell her. "While we stand here, at an impasse, I have the urge to bend you over my desk and spank your ass until you're screaming for me to stop. Punishment for breaking into my office and looking through my private documents."

"Then punish me," she bites, stepping back out of my hold, and my hands already miss the feel of her soft curves. Scarlett crosses her arms, her tits teasing from the low neckline of her tight top. The smooth, creamy flesh taunting from only inches away, and for a moment, I picture them bound with rope, her nipples hard and clamped while I paddle her unruly ass.

"Drop your arms." My voice is stern. There is no debate in the order, and when her eyes flash with understanding, she obeys. "Open your legs, wide." Once again, my dominant voice takes hold, the words spearing into her as she slowly shifts her bare feet on the cool, hardwood floors.

"Is that what gets you off?" Scarlett grits, her teeth grinding as her jaw ticks in frustration. Fighting the urge to chuckle, I close the distance between us and grip her shoulder. My fingers dig into the soft skin before I trail my touch down her arm to find her hip once more.

The moment I circle her waist, my hand grabs the fleshy

globe of her ass, causing her to whimper when I squeeze. I know she likes the dominance. "It does. I love watching you obey me like a good little girl," I tell her.

"I'm not calling you Daddy." Her voice is cold, icy as it cools the heat between us for a second, and this time, I do laugh out loud.

"That's not my kink, sweetheart," I inform her. "But I do expect you to do as I say, in and out of the bedroom." Moving my free hand to her other hip, I hold her steady before I trace my fingers over the crack of her ass. "This is mine." My touch tickles its way over the curve of her outer thigh before I cup her between her legs. "This is mine as well."

"Lycan..." My name is a hoarse whisper that tumbles free from her lips, the usually sweet tone husky with need. "Please."

"Please?" My brow arches in question as I dip my fingers into the warm material, the wetness of her seeping through, and I feel like a god taking hold of his prize. "I like when you beg as well."

"I... I've..." Her words are mumbled, but she can't form sentences as I tease her pretty pussy with my fingers. Stroking her outside those tiny shorts, I send her reeling as her small hands grip my shoulders in a fierce hold. This is what we did in her bedroom, but this room, this space, is mine. My hand moves up, then dips under the waistband of her shorts.

"Tell me you don't want me," I order, needing her to

give me permission to dip into the tight heat I know is waiting for me. "Tell me I'm a bad man, and you hate me." Her mouth opens, and for a moment, I expect her to refuse my advance, but when she doesn't, I dip two fingers into her cunt, which is dripping wet. I pump once, twice, before I lean in and whisper my lips along her cheek. "Tell me how I don't make you crave the darkness," I murmur, the warmth of my breath feathering over her neck, and my teeth latch onto the soft, fleshy earlobe, and I bite down hard, causing a slew of whimpers and moans to fall free.

"I can't." Her admission has my cock throbbing, begging to be let loose to finally claim my fiancée. I walk her back until her ass hits the desk, and I gently push her down until she's leaning back on her elbows. My hands tug at her shorts, and then they're sliding down her legs.

This is too easy.

The thought comes to me quickly, and I have a feeling my soon-to-be wife has a plan to bring this contract to an end. Only, she doesn't realize I'm the one in charge. I'm in control. She may attempt to thwart my plans, but she won't win.

I drop to one knee and push her thighs apart. Looking up at her through my lashes, I grin. "Listen to me, and listen well," I tell her before my tongue darts out to swipe at the smooth lips that glisten with arousal. Her legs tremble on either side of my face. "You can never top me from the bottom."

Her lips open into an O when I dip two fingers inside

her body before I suck on her clit so hard her nails claw at the mahogany beneath her, but she can't find purchase.

"I'm in control. Always." I bite down on her clit, causing her to shake and scream out into the darkness as I devour her juices. "And when you eat, sleep, and breathe, I'll be the one making sure you do." I continue my ministrations as my mouth latches onto her smooth pussy lips, the soft hair that trails a teasing line over her mound tickles my nose. "And when this pretty little cunt comes and gushes, it will be for me, by me."

Adding a third finger, I pump faster and faster. Watching the pleasure break across her pretty face is like an adrenaline rush shooting through me. The power I have to either send her flying over the edge or keep her teetering is intoxicating.

"I wanted to save you," I admit, hoping she'll be too far gone to listen. "I wanted to make sure you weren't hurt by those closest to you, by those who promised to keep you safe, but in the end, only put you in harm's way."

Her body convulses around my fingers, and for a moment, I slow all movement, keeping her aching, trembling, and gasping for something. Her hips undulate, wanting friction against the nub of pleasure, but I hold her still.

"What are you talking about?" Scarlett breathes, her gaze glassy as she stares down at me. Her thighs still spread lewdly, her cunt dripping all over my palm. "I... Please," she pleads, realizing just how precarious her position is right now.

"I'm the one who owns you now," I tell her. "Am I understood?"

Her lips part on a squeal when I crook all three fingers, stroking the spot deep within her that has her toes curling and her fingers digging into the smooth, shiny surface beside her ass.

"I don't like to be kept waiting." The warning in my tone is gruff, darkness shrouding me as my vision turns blurry with the need to be inside her.

"Yes, sir," she mumbles before moving her hips once more to take the pleasure I'm not giving. "Please, just allow me to come."

In all my life, no other submissive I've had kneel for me has ever pleaded so beautifully. Yes, they've been on the brink, they've begged like good little sluts, but the way Scarlett intones her words has my cock leaking against my sleep pants.

Leaning in, I suck her clit into my mouth while finger-fucking her fast and hard until the cries of her orgasm bounce off the walls of my office, and her sweet, musky essence drenches my tongue and hand. The snug, pulsing walls of her cunt squeeze my fingers, tighter and tighter, and my only thought is how she would feel around my dick.

Through my lashes, I watch her come down from the high, and it's as if she's only now realized what I've done. Admitted to certain things while keeping her high on the need to come.

I slide my fingers from her body and bring them to my mouth, licking her taste. At the sight of this, her pupils dilate further, and soon, those pretty eyes are black with lust.

"Next time you come into my office without my permission, your punishment will not be so pleasurable, little red," I tell her before rising to full height, towering over her. I help her into her shorts before I settle in my chair. "Would you like me to tell you a story?"

A tale of darkness. That's what he told me, and it's been swirling in my mind even hours later as I slide under the bubbles. Warm water engulfs me, swallowing me whole, reminding me that I'm as fragile as a porcelain doll.

I listened to the story Lycan told, of how his father came to Crimson Falls all those years ago but was forced to leave. Everything he said sounded like a fairy tale gone wrong. And even though I can't imagine a little boy fleeing for his life, I realize my family isn't as innocent as I always believed.

There are secrets still hidden in Lycan's deep green eyes, and I know his admission had only been a pinch of salt in a myriad of truths. When I break the surface of the water, I open my eyes and find Lycan leaning against the doorframe, watching me.

"I have a meeting," he tells me, but his ravenous stare drinks in my naked form. Even though he can't see much under the multitude of bubbles, my nakedness is obvious.

"Okay." I don't know why I feel disappointed in that bit of news, but I am. "I thought you were staying to tell me more." My voice takes on a tone of sadness, of frustration, which only earns me a chuckle.

"I'll be back in a couple of hours," he informs me as he pushes to full height and fills the room with his large frame. "Be a good girl, and I might even reward you tonight."

"I'm not a submissive," I throw out quickly, causing his eyes to darken at the thought.

The corner of his mouth quirks. "I beg to differ, but that's a conversation for another time and place. You're welcome to explore the house, but don't go into my office." The warning is clear. But it only piques my curiosity even more. He must know this. "I'll know every move you make," he informs me easily as if reading my mind. I watch as Lycan turns and heads for the door, throwing a look over his suited shoulder before leaving me alone to ponder what I'm going to do today.

One room I will be exploring is the library. After confirming that his father knew my grandmother, I need to uncover more about their tryst, and I'm hoping his father had copies of the same fairy tale. I wonder if there are any more hidden notes or letters which will shed some light on their secret relationship.

Leaning back against the cool porcelain, I replay some of what Lycan told me.

"My father was a year older than your grandmother. At the time, the two names—Shaw and Bardot—were well known in Crimson Falls. They were considered royalty. And even when my dad left, there were still whispers of why and how."

Lycan's expression turns dark, and even as I snuggle into his hold, I shiver at the thought of my gran sending a man she loved away. My grandfather was strict in both personality and values, and I wonder briefly if he had forced her into marriage.

"My father loved deeply. I recall coming here when I was about five. My dad brought me here to say goodbye to the house. He told me things didn't work out but never explained why. He said there were too many ghosts, which didn't make sense to me at the time, but when I got older, when I learned the truth, I realized the ghosts weren't dead. They were very much alive."

"So, he loved my grandmother," I whisper, wondering if that's why Lycan chose to save me. "What about my father? Did you know him after your dad sold the house? answers "

Lycan stiffens under me. "Horatio Bardot was the reason I couldn't come back to Crimson Falls for a long time. But when he walked into my club in New York, he didn't recognize me. Only later did he learn the truth, but by then, it was too late. I knew too much about him for him to ever walk away."

"But my grandmother knows you, and she knows I'm here. Isn't she angry you've taken me? Or want me to marry you?" Confusion settles in my gut like a lead weight.

Lifting my gaze, I catch sight of his nod. "She does. But she knows if she tries to stop me, she'll only hurt her family, her son. Blood is everything to Grace Bardot."

"So, she doesn't care about me."

The dark, sinister grin that curls Lycan's lips sends cold dread shooting through me. "Your grandmother knows better than to hurt another Shaw."

His gaze locks on mine before I ask, "Hurt another Shaw? Did she hurt you in the past?"

He nods slowly, but a glimmer of rage sparkles in his eyes. "Something like that."

I push to my feet, my legs still wobbly from the orgasm he bestowed on me earlier. "I don't understand why you're treating me like a princess in your home when my family hurt yours. What did she do?"

The story seems credible. His dad loved my gran. They then went their separate ways before my dad was born. Lycan knew my father long before I ever came along. But why would he want to keep me happy, safe, if the Bardot family had broken the Shaws?

Unless they didn't.

Lycan doesn't respond, but pain etches itself on his face. An expression so agonizing it steals my breath. Realization hits me right in the chest, a confirmation of just what happened between our families.

"My father was the one who did something," I whisper,

He promised to finish the story when he got home from his meeting. Fear skitters through my veins at the thought of having to hear the truth about my family. Never did I think my father could be anything but the good person I thought he was. I grew up believing he was a hero.

And now, I'm not so sure.

In my bedroom, I get dressed quickly, wanting to explore before Lycan returns. By the time I reach the library, I'm anxious. Not sure what I'm looking for, I start at one end of the classics shelf, slowly sliding my fingers over each spine. The fairy tales are all first editions, and I pull out every one of them.

Carrying the stack to the desk, I settle in the wingback chair and get comfortable. I pick up the top book, the gold title sparkling in the low light of the lamp that sits to my right. Flicking open Cinderella, I'm astounded to find the same scrawled handwriting on the first page, just like I did in the copy of Red Riding Hood. Confusion takes hold of me because why would the books be in Lycan's house and not my grandmother's? Surely, she would have wanted to keep them safe.

My Princess,

The clock struck midnight, and I had to leave. There wasn't a moment I didn't watch you this evening, and it was magical knowing you're mine. The gala will forever be our place. Taking you to your father's office while people danced and laughed, was nothing short of intoxicating.

I'll forever be drunk on you, my darling Grace.

One day, I will put a ring on your finger. Until then, we will forever love from afar.

Your Prince
Conall

Shutting the book, I settle back, needing a breather before I flick open the next book, finding once again a note, much like the last two I've read. Each one speaks of their love, their tryst, and their want and need for each other.

My chest tightens at the last one, where he tells her that he's leaving. It's a goodbye letter, one that drips with agony from every inked word. By the time I shut the pages, they're blurry through my tear-stained lashes.

"I thought I would bring you something to drink, Miss Bardot," Gray says as he makes his way inside carrying a tray with a cup and pot of tea. When he sets it down, I wonder briefly if he knew about my grandmother and Lycan's father.

"Thank you, Gray. Are you no longer working at my grandmother's home?" I question when I realize he should be there, not here.

He smiles. "I do. She doesn't need me today, so I'm here with Mr. Shaw." Affection graces his tone when he speaks about Lycan. He hovers for a moment before continuing, "Mr. Shaw, Lycan." A grin creases his expression as he remembers something with a faraway look on his old, wrinkled face. "He's a good boy. He didn't deserve what happened to him. His brother..." Gray shakes his head, his thoughts taking over, but his admission sending my curious nature into a spiraling tornado, and soon enough, I'm about to burst with more questions.

"His brother?" I prompt, hoping the old man can offer some answers.

He's silent for such a long moment I'm almost certain he's not going to respond, but then he focuses on my face, taking me in. "You look just like her when she was younger," he remarks, his tone wistful in remembrance. "She loved Conall so much." The sadness in his voice makes my chest ache, my heart beating wildly against my ribs.

"Are you talking about Grace? My grandmother?" Once more, I urge with a gentle push of questions, and finally, Gray nods.

"She was one of the most beautiful women to grace this

home. For years, they spent time together, falling in love, and I was convinced the curse was coming to an end."

"The curse?" I want to shoot to my feet, to grab the old man by the shoulders and shake the information out of him, but I bite down on my tongue to keep my excitement at bay. I want to know more, to learn about the affair, the relationship they had.

"There is darkness once a Bardot and a Shaw come together," Gray tells me earnestly. His voice scrapes against his throat as he admits a truth I'm sure I'm not meant to know yet. "It may be an old wives' tale," he says. "But I believe that whenever love comes between your families, something bad happens."

"Something bad?" This time I straighten, making my way to where he's standing. As if the moment is lost to him, Gray shakes his head before turning to leave. "Wait, please? What happened with my grandmother and Mr. Shaw?"

He's about to answer when the deep, rumbling baritone of my fiancé breaks through the heavy silence. "Thank you, Gray, that will be all."

The older man moves quickly, leaving me with Lycan. He doesn't seem angry as he walks toward me, unbuttoning his suit jacket before shrugging out of the sleek, black material. Left in only his light grey shirt with dark pants, he looks slightly disheveled with a tie hanging from the pocket of his slacks.

"What have you been up to, little red?" Lycan asks, his gaze tracking the books, where I've been perched for the past hour, and a bit, and the tea Gray brought for me moments earlier.

"Reading."

A dark brow arches in question as he regards me with amusement. "You're a bad liar." He steps up closer to me. "I'm sure you've discovered the stupid little love notes my father left in the books," he says. "They're useless when the person you're writing them for doesn't give a shit."

"I don't believe she didn't give a shit. Romance isn't stupid." Tilting my chin in defiance, I lock my glare on Lycan's. "And you don't know what was felt by my grandmother. Have you ever spoken to her about it? Asked her why she didn't respond?"

He considers my question before shaking his head. "I didn't need to. My father ensured she was beside him throughout their relationship, even in secret. And what did she do? She walked out and never looked back."

"How, pray tell, do you know that?"

"She married your grandfather." His words are cold. Ice cold. "That's why love is something that we can never allow between us." There's no debating this with him. His walls have been pulled up, brick by brick. He's hiding behind his anger. Instead of allowing me in, instead of talking about it, Lycan's convinced he's right.

"I will not marry a man who regards love and emotion as nonessential in a marriage."

Lycan reaches his hand into my hair, tangling his fingers in the long, dark strands before tugging me closer. "Tell me something, little red," he commands. "Do you see yourself ever loving me?"

"I don't know you." My words are spat in anger and frustration because, honestly, I haven't learned who Lycan Shaw is. Yes, he's given me some insight into his family, but I don't know him. He's made me come, he's given me pleasure, but marriage, a partnership, is not only physical. It's mental, emotional.

He leans in, his lips whispering over mine when he responds, "That's not what I asked." I half expect him to kiss me, to claim my mouth with his, but his restraint is iron-clad. "You can't love me. I'm not a man who can return emotions."

"Then why marry me?" My mind whirs with possible answers to my question. Some I don't want to think about, others make my chest ache.

But when he finally responds, it's a dark promise. "Because once you take my name, you, Miss Bardot, will carry on the Shaw legacy as it was always meant to be."

Confusion settles in my gut. My mouth opens, but I can't find the words to reply. I want nothing more than to learn about him, his family and to better understand the reasoning behind his choices. But I'm sure no matter what he tells me, no matter how much we figure out, I'll always be the girl he bought. I'm the arranged marriage he sought by blackmailing my father.

"I'm tired." I pull away from him, putting space between us as I move backward, my ass hitting the high, wooden desk. He doesn't come for me; he doesn't grab at me. I make my way past Lycan before I stop, halting my retreat, and I'm closer to the door than to him. "If you focus solely on hurting others, an eye for an eye, your life will be a series of acts that will always leave you with guilt." I move to the exit and step out into the hallway before shutting the door.

My heart cracks slightly, a barely there fissure of pain at the thought of only being here to bring children into his life. And the idea of me stuck in a loveless marriage is not what I would have envisioned for myself, but now that I'm here, perhaps I can try to fix whatever my grandmother and my father broke.

Confusion settles like a heavy weight in my gut. I don't trust Dad, not after he signed my life away, but I also can't trust Lycan. Maybe I should talk to my grandmother. Perhaps she can offer some form of truth in the swirl of bullshit I've been told over the past few days.

Tomorrow is the Bardot ball, the gala where my grandmother and Lycan's dad used to meet. Maybe, just maybe, it's time for me to expose the ugly truths of our families.

LYCAN

Shrugging on the jacket of my charcoal tux, I fasten the two buttons before straightening my tie. Usually, I'd forgo the outfit, but tonight is special. Grace will be there, and I wonder if she's going to try and stop me from marrying Scarlett. Needless to say, it won't go down well, but then again, I don't give a shit.

My fiancée needs to speak with her grandmother, which I'll allow. But once that's over and done with, she will be coming home with me. For the moment, I'll allow her to believe the story of revenge against her father, but once she bears my name, I'll gift her with the truth.

I'm the monster in our story.

Never once have I denied it. But watching Scarlett come apart for me has made me feel like a man for the first time in a long while. She's made me *feel* something other than the need to dominate. Granted, I would devour her whole if she were to submit. And that's something I will be working on over the years we will spend together, but for now, I'm happy to play the gentleman just as long as it gets her to wear the ring, carry my name, and end her father.

With that thought in mind, I head out into the hallway, finding it silent and empty. I've become accustomed to the quiet, but I do prefer my apartment in New York, where I can keep a closer eye on Scarlett. Once this sham of a gala is over, I'll fly her out there and make sure she's under my watchful eye twenty-four seven.

When I reach Scarlett's bedroom, I push open the door without knocking. Her gasp echoes through the room, as I step into the space, taking in her slender frame in a bright red dress.

"You do realize knocking is considered polite," my feisty girl spits in frustration as she pins me with a glare so fierce it causes me to chuckle.

"This is my house, as you've learned. I make the rules." Ignoring her pursed lips, I close the distance between us. My thirsty gaze drinks her in from her perfectly painted toes to the top of her long, red hair. She doesn't flinch when I reach for her, my fingers tangling in the silky strands, and I gently tug her closer. The scent of her perfume invades my senses, and I can't stop myself from inhaling deeply, taking her fragrance in as if she were a drug, and I need to get high.

"This might be your house, and yes, you have your rules, but I still retain my privacy, as well as my need to have space from your overbearing nature," Scarlett hisses when I tighten my hold in her hair, causing glistening emotion to sparkle in her pretty eyes.

"Put your coat on. We're going to be late," I inform her, ignoring the rather arousing, yet petulant behavior of my little red. Perhaps after the gala, I'll show her exactly what my rules and her *space* entails. "I don't like to show tardiness when I'm the guest of honor."

"What?" Shock paints her pretty face, but I don't respond. Instead, I make my way to the door, leaning against the frame as I wait for her to pull on the crimson coat that matches her dress. There's a hood, which will come in handy since it's chilly outside.

She joins me with no more questions. Side by side, we look like a couple, and I know most of the guests tonight will want to know how the wedding plans are going. I'm almost certain her grandmother has warned the guests not to attend, but I have more pull around here, and I will make sure it's the event is the talk of the town.

The moment we reach the landing, my phone buzzes in my pocket. A call from Kahn. "Yes?"

"I have a problem." His icy tone is filled with frustration. I sent him and his team to look for my brother, but we also have Lorenzo to deal with. Everything is happening at the same time, and for a moment, I wonder if there's a connection. I'm not sure why I would even consider this, but the coincidence is too obvious.

"If it's my brother, kill him. If it's Lorenzo, let's call Alex and see if we can move in on the church," I respond, glancing at my fiancée to find her staring, wide-eyed at me.

"Lorenzo has gone underground. I have an inkling on where, but we raided the church and found nothing of consequence. That's not something you would want to tell Alexei." He's right. Going back to the mafia boss to tell him I lost the bastard he's looking for will only be a confirmation that we're not able to tackle a job so insignificant.

"Where was the last place he was spotted?"

"New Mexico," Kahn tells me, and I have a feeling we may need help from the Cartel, which means calling Victor Cordero, and that's not a man I want to be involved unless we need him.

"I'm headed to the gala right now. It's important." I don't need to explain. Kahn knows why I have to be there. "Get the jet ready. I'll fly out tonight and make sure the apartment is ready for Scarlett. She'll be joining me."

"Yes, boss."

Once I hang up, I turn to a stunned beauty who's glaring at me as if I've grown a second head in the time of my phone call. "I'll have the maid pack some clothes. We're leaving after the gala."

"Where? I can't just leave."

"New York. And you will do whatever I say. There are secrets in the city that may offer you the answers you're seeking." It's not entirely a lie, but it's also not the whole truth. Yes, there are answers in the Big Apple that Scarlett would need to learn about, but it may have to wait until after the wedding.

"This is ridiculous. I can stay with my grandmother. I don't need to follow you around like a lost puppy." Her adamant tone has anger surging through me. She doesn't realize just how much I'm doing for her, and perhaps that's the problem. Maybe I should offer her more answers, just to ensure she's on my side.

"Listen to me," I say, turning to face her fully. My hands cupping her smooth, tanned cheeks. "Your father has secrets in New York, things he's been hiding for years. I cannot tell you about them, or I'll break the contract—"

"You mean that if you were the one to divulge the secrets, I wouldn't have to marry you." Such an intelligent girl. "Is that why you want to keep me in the dark? I could just go to my grandmother and ask her about it. She'd tell me the truth."

"Would she?" I challenge easily, knowing that Grace Bardot would rather die than tell her sweet granddaughter about her past and present secrets.

For a long moment, Scarlett stares at me. Her lips part on a soft sigh before she shakes her head. "I don't know." There's a sadness to her face, an emotion I want to eradicate.

Stepping closer to her, eating up the distance between us, I allow my larger frame to loom over her. With my index finger under her chin, I tilt her head until she's looking directly at me. The silence hangs heavy with desire. As much as Scarlett doesn't *want* to feel something, she knows there's a magnetism between us, it's palpable.

"I want nothing more than to keep you here tonight, to sit with you on the couch, drink whisky, and talk about growing up as a Shaw." My admission is startling to both of us, but I don't stop. "I want you to know who I am. Even though I'm the monster in this story, the wolf seeking out his prey, I wouldn't hurt you. Not unless you want it."

"You'd just devour me whole until nothing is left," Scarlett responds, the confession true as it escapes her glossy lips.

Arching a brow at her, I challenge, "I didn't hear you complaining the last time I made you come."

The corner of her mouth quirks. "No, you're right. I want to hate you—"

"But you can't. It's not who you are." It's true. The woman before me may have anger toward me for what I did, but she doesn't hate. It's not in her vocabulary. Not in her personality. And as much as I wish I could remain cold-hearted where Scarlett is concerned, I can't deny the pull, the desire that warms my blood each time she's near.

Call it lust.

Call it stupidity.

But it's most definitely undeniable.

SCARLETT

I didn't think I would find myself intrigued by Lycan. Or grow to want to know more about him, but over the past couple of weeks, I have. It feels as if I've been here for months already. Instead, it's not been that long at all. As we near the Bardot house, Lycan offers me his arm, which I accept.

I wanted to bring him down. But I have a feeling there's so much more to this story than I wanted to admit. There are secrets he's keeping from me, and the more time I spend with him, I'm almost certain I can learn the truth about my family.

The admission Gray offered about the curse has also

been playing on my mind. I'll ask Grace what happened with Conall; she has to tell me. I'm her blood. Her family. She cannot refuse me answers when I'm about to walk down the aisle with the son of her first love.

The door stands open, golden light flowing from the entrance, and we're welcomed by one of the servants I recognize from when I arrived. Seconds after our coats are taken, we're escorted through the living room entrance where a few guests are already mingling.

"There she is." Grace's voice comes from behind me, and I turn to find my grandmother looking as elegant as ever. "Darling, you look beautiful." She leans in, gripping my shoulders and places a kiss on each of my cheeks. When her gaze lands on the man beside me, I notice a flicker of annoyance, but other than that, my grandmother is a steel mask of happiness. "Lycan," she grits but smiles as she does it. Shocking me, my grandmother takes his hands, leaving me to gawk at them. "I trust you're well. It's been far too long."

A cruel smirk curls Lycan's lips, and I'm sure he's about to insult her in some way, but he says, "Likewise, Mrs. Bardot." I realize my soon-to-be husband is playing a role. "I think once the party is underway, we should have a chat. There are a few things I need to go over with you." It's not a friendly request; it's an ice-cold command.

"I have company, Lycan." All my life, knowing my grandmother, I've never seen her falter, but right now, she's shaking as her throat works on a nervous swallow.

As much as I want Lycan to drop it, I have a feeling he's only going to continue on his quest until she agrees. And I'm not wrong, but also shocked when he says, "I'm hoping to take Scarlett to the Big Apple tomorrow, so what we need to talk about has to be tonight."

"Oh!" A gasp from my gran is the only expression of shock to his words. "Are you sure you should be traveling to the city this week?"

"There's no need to worry. I'll take care of her," he assures my grandmother, who seems even more uncomfortable now than she was moments ago.

Her gaze locks on mine, and she offers a grin. "You'll absolutely love it." My grandmother says before she's dragged away to other guests. I attempt to appear normal while my life feels like it's falling apart before my very eyes.

"Close your mouth, little red," Lycan whispers in my ear. "The only time I want that mouth parted in an O is when my dick is about to slide between those lips." His words are filled with amusement, but I don't laugh.

"What is happening? Why does she not want us traveling to New York? What are you not telling me? She seemed almost scared to refuse your request to talk to her. Why?" My questions are drenched in curiosity as a hiss of frustrated breath escapes my lips.

Lycan's green eyes sparkle with indignation as if he's angry that I'm even asking him about his relationship with my family, with my grandmother. His hand reaches for my arm. Taking me by the elbow, he leads me away from the crowd down a long, darkened hallway until we reach an office where he shoves me inside and kicks the door shut behind him.

"If you want to be punished, little red, I'll gladly oblige," he informs me as his hands grip the thick leather of his belt. Thoughts of him spanking me, whipping me until I'm begging for more, invade my mind, and I'm squirming on the spot.

"Don't change the subject," I bite out, crossing my arms in front of my chest after tugging myself free of his hold. "I want to know the truth. I'm done staying in the dark."

"I thought you liked the darkness, little red?" Lycan challenges as he moves closer to me, eating up the distance I've put between us in two long strides. As much as I want to run, I don't. I tilt my chin in defiance.

"We better get back to the party before my grandmother looks for us," I tell him, ignoring his question because if I had to be honest, I would say yes. I do enjoy the darkness. I want more of it, but right now, I want answers.

"You didn't answer my question. I don't like repeating myself," he informs me. "That calls for a harsh punishment." A fire blazes in his eyes as he steps into my personal space, his hands gripping my elbows as he holds me steady. There's no running from Lycan, not right now. "And tonight, I'll show you just what kind of punishment comes from you not answering me when I question you."

"Then do it," I bite out as frustration claws its way up my throat. "Why don't you do it right now?" I challenge, hoping he'll quell the ache that's started twisting in my gut. I may have denied the fact that I'm submissive to him, but it was a lie. Right now, all I want is for him to bend me over right here on the arm of the sofa and spank me.

I don't have to wait long before Lycan spins me around, hitches my dress over my hips, and one of his large hands comes down on my ass with a loud swat. A squeal of surprise tumbles from my lips, and another spank lands on the other cheek. He continues my punishment with grunts and growls rumbling in his chest. And my lips expel moans of pleasure with each smarting swat.

By the time I'm trembling, he stops. I don't know how many times his hand landed on my behind, but the sting is apparent. I'm certain my ass is bright red. Lycan's fierce grip in my long tresses tugs me to stand, and the hemline of my dress slinks down my thighs, hiding my panty-clad butt.

"Next time, it will be my belt," he promises along my neck before his teeth graze the lobe of my ear along with the threat. "Now, let's go out there and look like a happily engaged couple."

He takes my hand and leads me out into the throng of the party, where guests are drinking, chatting, and laughing. Music tinkles from the speakers as we move through the crowd and into the dining room, leading out onto the patio. Similar to Lycan's home, this one is illuminated with fairy lights that twinkle around pillars.

"It's scary how alike your house is to my grandmother's," I remark as we stop at the bar where Lycan orders me a white wine, and he gets himself a whiskey.

"It's the reason they built them, the ancestors of our families." A new tidbit of information I had no clue about. It seems every day with him, I'm learning something new. Lycan leans in his hot breath at my ear. "I bet that sweet cunt is soaked for me right now. Even with all these people around, you're needy for me to make you come again. Aren't you, little red?"

A gasp of surprise expels from my lungs at his salacious taunt, but I can't deny it, so instead of answering, I sip my drink. With our glasses in hand, we greet a few guests. Some I recognize as celebrities or famous politicians. Others are strangers to me. But it seems Lycan knows a lot more people here than I thought he would.

When the dinner bell rings, we move to the long table that's been set with the most expensive china and the shiniest cutlery. I slip into a seat near the far end of the table from where my grandmother sits, and Lycan settles in beside me.

The staff brings out plates of steaming food, but I can't concentrate when a looming figure slips into the chair to my right. Beside me, Lycan stills, his body turning rigid, and his knuckles turn white as he grips his knife so tight I'm half expecting it to shatter.

"What are you doing here?" His voice is laced with poison as if his words could kill the man beside me. When I turn my head, glancing up at the intruder, I'm shocked to see hazel eyes looking back at me.

"Brother," the man says, and that's when it hits me. This is Lycan's brother. The man who chased me through the woods, scaring me into his brother's arms, sealing my fate without knowing it. "I don't think you want to cause a scene," he says, glancing past me toward Lycan. "But I wanted to say hello to your pretty new fiancée."

"It's best that you walk out before I kill you."

"Always with the theatrics." A chuckle vibrates in his throat. With everyone's focus on dinner, nobody has noticed the interaction at this end of the table. But when I glance to my left, I find my grandmother watching intently, her knife and fork poised, waiting for a war I'm sure will soon be here.

"Darius." The name is a warning, causing my gaze to land back on Lycan. "If you even dare touch her, I will end you." There is no humor in his tone, and I don't doubt he's capable of killing someone. Something about his demeanor tells me he's done it before. And that sends an icy shrill of dread racing through me.

"Let's enjoy dinner," Darius says. "I'll be leaving shortly after. Also, I wanted to tell you face-to-face, call your bloodhounds off me, or I will *end them* one by one."

I feel like I'm watching a tennis match. Left to right, the threats are thrown, and I wonder who will give in first. I doubt it will be Lycan. He's a man who gets what he wants, and no doubt he will spill blood to do it.

"If I weren't convinced you are a threat, I would," Lycan responds before gulping down his drink and signaling for another. I take my own glass and swallow back the wine. I'm

caught between feuding brothers.
A dangerous place to be.

LYCAN

He's so close, yet so far.

If I did anything to him now, I'll fuck up my chances of business with every man in this room. As much as they may be corrupt, they won't allow first-hand violence into their lives.

And Darius knows it.

But what bothers me more is that he's seated beside Scarlett. Jealousy surges through me, along with rage and the need to kill. My brother was nothing more than a two-faced bastard who ran before he even realized what had happened to our father.

His beard is longer than I remember, his eyes darker,

filled with what I can only imagine are more sinister intentions. He glances at Scarlett, interest sparking in his gaze, and I wonder what he's really doing here.

He's not a fan of the Bardots either. Since we were little, we knew about the old woman who lived next door, but when we learned about her connection with our father, something in us changed. We knew we would never be close to the family.

And I'm sure now that I'm marrying Scarlett, Darius is fuming. As dinner is served, Scarlett's hand finds my thigh, causing me to clank my knife and fork against the fine china plate, ensuring every pair of eyes are on me.

Once the conversation starts up again, I glance at my girl, whose eyes are wide as she regards me. She leans in close, her lips inches from my ear, which doesn't help my need for her. "I think perhaps we should leave early," she tells me with a soft kiss to my earlobe, and my zipper is suddenly much tighter than it was moments ago.

"If you keep that up, you're going to have trouble on your hands," I tell her.

A soft giggle falls from her lips, and I want to steal every whimper she makes. But right now, we need to behave. There are people here I need to impress. Most times, I don't give a shit about who's watching; other times, I quite like an audience, but for now, I know Scarlett's reputation means more than me getting my rocks off.

"Eat your dinner, and when you're done, we'll leave." My voice is low, a whisper only Scarlett can hear. I pray to all that's holy she obeys.

With a slight nod, she eats, and I smile, watching her enjoy the dinner. My appetite is gone, or rather, it's shifted from my plate to the woman beside me. Lifting my gaze, I find Darius staring at me.

"Still in control," he remarks, but I don't respond because if I do, it will start a war. And that's not what I want or need right now. "You can hate me all you want," he tells me, talking over Scarlett who's between us. The only sweetness amongst the darkness that's lingering in the room. My brother and I are far too similar, and even though I don't consider him family, or at least close family anymore, he is blood.

Blood is a bitter vow to swallow. The lingering metallic flavor of guilt and deception hangs between us, and I know it will never be cleaned. It will never change.

I turn my attention to my drink, swallowing back the biting bourbon, allowing the burn to trickle down my throat until the fire has reached my stomach. My gut churns with the need to escape.

"You know, little one," Darius says, his voice loud enough for only me and Scarlett to hear. "He's never going to love you like you want. Marrying him may be your end." There's no joking in his tone, but I didn't expect there to be.

"I may one day grow old beside him, and maybe I don't love him yet, and he may not feel the same for me, but I'm not ever going to regret doing this. My life is my own. Even if I'm under contract, Lycan has given me a choice to walk away..." She glances at me before looking back at Darius. "But I don't want to." Her final words to him have my chest tightening as emotions I don't want or need take hold of me, and I'm soon lost in affection for the girl beside me, the same girl I bought from her father.

Affection is weakness, but I can't stop myself when it comes to her. Scarlett does something to me. She knocks down walls, breaks through steel doors, and burrows herself in the darkness I've long since buried.

Darius doesn't say anything, but the look he gives me tells me everything I need to know—he's impressed with Scarlett.

And that can never be a good thing.

SCARLETT

My nerves are shot. With Darius here, I know he's only trying to goad Lycan to act out, but the man who's now standing beside me is far too controlled, and I'm certain his brother knows that.

A stunning woman sidles up beside Lycan, so close I can smell her perfume. He stills beside me. His body turns rigid as he grips me tighter but doesn't say anything. She moves past us, and I notice the sway of her hips and the way her long hair hangs in silky waves down her back. She casts a quick glance over her shoulder at my fiancé before she disappears amongst the rest of the guests.

His arm snakes around my waist even tighter, and I find it difficult to breathe as we head toward my gran to say goodbye. I find her eyes on me, watching, intrigued by us. And I wonder if she'll tell my father about Lycan's display. Lycan grabs a flute of champagne, handing it to me before he orders a scotch from the waiter who scurries off to get the drink.

When I sip on the bubbly liquid, I pray the alcohol will calm the erratic thumping of my heart and the flurry in my belly. I want to come across as confident, calm, but with the man beside me who draws every woman's eye, I feel like a teenager beside him.

"Can I have your attention, please?" My grandmother calls out, clinking her glass with a silver knife. As the crowd falls silent, she continues, "Tonight is a very special one for the Bardot family. It's a night I didn't think would ever come to pass." Her eyes land on Lycan and me before she speaks, "But I'm so happy to finally say that my granddaughter, Scarlett Bardot, is engaged."

A flurry of murmurs fills the room after her announcement, and my cheeks heat as every set of eyes turn toward us. The strange, yet elegant woman who seems to focus on Lycan stares at him for a long moment before she turns her attention to me. Rage burns in the stare she pins on me, before she flicks her hair and rushes to the patio but doesn't walk outside. She lingers in the doorway, and I notice her opening her purse.

"Who is she?" I whisper as I attempt to smile at my grandmother who's embarrassing me more than I've ever been before.

"She's nobody," Lycan assures me under his breath, but I know it's a lie. Nobody can ever be nothing to another person when they act like that. The jealousy is clear. There's no doubt about it, that woman and Lycan were involved, and it was more serious than he's letting on.

"Let *me* make something clear," I hiss as my grandmother continues. "Never lie to me again." I step forward as my gran calls me over, and I make my way toward her, stopping beside her as she gifts me a show of affection.

LYCAN

Fire courses through my veins. The need to pin her down and whip her with my belt has taken over, but I can't do shit since her grandmother is standing a few feet away. As much as I don't mind an audience, that would be pushing my nonexistent limits.

When Scarlett joins me again after her grandmother allows her to, I wrap my arm around the slender waist of my pretty little red and tug her into my hold. The movement earns me a soft gasp of surprise. There are eyes on us, waiting to see what I'll do. With a slow smirk crawling along my lips, I turn to Scarlett, cupping her face in my free hand, and pull her closer, touching my lips to hers.

Every set of eyes that are watching us scorches my skin. I know there is one woman who is ready to kill, who will easily take Scarlett from me, but I can't let that happen, so when my beautiful bride-to-be opens her mouth, I allow my tongue to dive into her sweetness and put on the show everyone was waiting for.

A cheer surrounds us, clapping and shouting, a few pats on my back as I pull away from Scarlett, and I smile at the viper who's piercing me with her glare. I can't help but taunt her with a tip of my head, knowing that I'm goading her into making a fool of herself. She spins on her heel, leaving the room and heading outside, and I watch for a short moment as she lights up one of her long, menthol cigarettes. The shit used to stink up my bedroom, but when I let her go, I made sure to never come close to falling down that dark abyss again.

The guests congratulate us, but my mind is on getting out of here, making sure I can leave with Scarlett as soon as possible. The jet is ready, and I'm aching to be on it, with the woman in my arms, as we fly to New York. Heaven is waiting for me, and we'll leave the devils behind.

It should be easier to fake a smile. Especially with the assholes in this room, but deep down, I don't want to. I'm exhausted. Playing a game I know I'm no longer focused on. Each of the men at the party are clients of my club, and they all know what goes on in those private rooms.

Music tinkles from the band that's been set up in the corner of the large ballroom. People couple up around us, as the party properly gets underway. They dance and sway along the space that's been turned into a dance floor, and I decide it's time to escape.

"Let's go." I take Scarlett's hand and lead her to where Grace is standing, talking to guests I don't recognize. Her gaze turns to us as we near her, and the glint of annoyance in her expression makes me smile. "Thank you for a lovely evening, but Scarlett and I have to leave. I have business I need to finish up before we get to the jet."

"Oh," she gasps. "I'm sorry to see you go," she tells her granddaughter, not meeting my stare. "We'll need to talk. I hope you can give me a call soon. There are so many things I'd like to catch up with you on."

"We'll be back soon," Scarlett tells her grandmother. "I would like to talk to you about the books." I tense when Scarlett mentions those, and I notice her grandmother's mouth pinch in frustration before she looks at me. "I found them, I mean, those notes."

"We need to leave," I speak up, knowing that this is not the time and place to get into this fucking conversation. "Thank you again, Grace. It was lovely as usual." My hand in Scarlett's tightens, and I offer her a squeeze of warning as I take a step away.

"Darling, please," Grace pleads in a hushed whisper before we can escape. "Leave the past where it is," she informs Scarlett. "It's no longer relevant. Move on."

Tension bunches my muscles, holding tight as they twist. I know she'll never tell Scarlett the truth, that she walked away from the only man who loved her just to marry a piece of trash, gold-digging bastard. I'm sure there's more to the story, but because my father is dead and all his secrets buried with him, I doubt I'll ever find out.

"Why are you being this way?" Scarlett's plea hits me square in the chest. Her words so soft, whispered with such pained tenderness, even my breath is stolen from my lungs. I've never been aware of women, never allowed their tears to burden me. I quite enjoyed them crying, pleading for mercy. But there's something about the way my little red speaks to her grandmother that does shit to me. Shit, I don't need to be feeling.

It's dangerous.

When I came to the agreement with Horatio, I knew Scarlett would color my monochrome world, but never did I think she'd make me *feel*. Shaking my head, I step between the women.

"It's time to go, Scarlett." I pull her into the crook of my arm. "We'll be back to see Grace again soon." I allow the hint of warning to lace my words as I meet the old woman's gaze. The shimmering of guilt dances in her stare, but I don't want to question just what the fuck she's hiding. The sooner we can get out of here, the better.

I tug Scarlett beside me as we make our way to the exit. The large door carved from heavy, dark wood opens and allows us to leave the warmth of the house. But instead of turning for the car, which I note Gray is waiting inside the driver's seat, I veer off in the opposite direction.

"Where are we going? I thought we were going home?" Scarlett's use of the word home makes my mouth curl into pure satisfaction.

Could this be her acceptance of her position beside me?

Of our upcoming wedding?

"We're going to take the scenic route home," I tell her while leading her through the vast, manicured garden, which greets us with the dimly lit shadows that dance across the grass.

When we reach the entrance to the woods, Scarlett stops dead in her tracks, causing me to turn. Her eyes are wide, fear flitting through those pretty orbs, gems that sparkle with unbridled darkness.

"We're going through there?" Her question comes out in a soft, fearful whisper, her lips parting into a dick-hardening O. I want nothing more than to show her just how much I love that little expression on her face, but I'll wait until we're swallowed by the murkiness of the trees.

"Yes." It's one word, an order, no debating, and my little red sees it. She knows when I use my commanding, Dominant voice to never question me. With a slight nod, she steps up to me, and we slink in between the trees. I know the path like the back of my hand.

But she doesn't.

And that's what makes this so much fun.

A gentle tremble skitters through her, and my arm tightens around her small frame.

"I know you like the darkness," I say, knowing she can't

not hear me right now. It's as if we're the only two people in the world. We walk in relative silence as we move deeper into the woods.

Thick branches hide us from any prying eyes. I stop halfway to the house and tug her against me. Leaning back against the thick, wooden trunk of a tree, I stare down into her eyes that are glinting from the shards of silver peeking through the trees from the moon above.

"Would you like to please me?" I ask, lowering the commanding tone to a hushed whisper. But the bite of dominance still lingers.

For a moment, she considers her response. I watch as emotions dance across her pretty features. I'm almost certain she's about to say no, to refuse, when she shocks me and smiles. "I would like to please you," she whispers.

My hands land on her shoulders, and I push her down to her knees. The moment she hits the ground, my cock thickens, throbbing against my zipper as if trying to escape the confines. "Then you will have to learn to take me into that pretty little throat of yours, little red," I inform her with a low rumble.

Scarlett reaches for my belt with trembling hands, her fingers deftly moving to undo the buckle with a clinking echo. The hiss of my zipper is loud in the silence that surrounds us, and soon, her soft, gentle touch has me grinding my teeth, my eyes shut tight as I try not to come like a fucking teenager who's never been touched before.

Her movements are slow, almost unsure, but when I

open my eyes and watch her tongue dart out to lick the arousal at my tip, my balls tighten with the threat of spilling my seed all over her pretty face.

Fisting my hands at my sides, I stare down as Scarlett takes me into her mouth and her warmth envelops me, making every nerve in my body spark with desire and need to use her like a fuck doll for my pleasure.

Her plump lips slide down the shaft as she swallows me deeper into her heat, the tightness of her throat pulsing around the tip, and her gag reflex takes hold. A cough and splutter from her lips only wets my dick with her saliva, making the in-and-out slide easier.

With one hand, I grip her long, red tresses in my fist and control her movements, making sure to hit the back of her throat each time. And every time I do, she chokes on my cock.

"Breathe through your nose, little red," I tell her through gritted teeth as I slide out and thrust back in. The shimmering tears from her lashes sparkle in the dim light, making her look like a beautiful toy only made for my amusement and pleasure.

I'm sure her knees are protesting against the hard ground, but she doesn't fight it, she doesn't squirm. Without order, she binds her hands behind her back and allows me all the control I need to fuck her mouth like I would her pretty cunt.

The image of her bound in Shibari rope sparks in my mind, dancing like a movie scene, and my cock throbs at the picture. Using my hold on her, I pull her head back, then force it forward until I feel her throat constrict around my shaft, spit drips down her chin onto the elegant dress she wore tonight.

It's ruined.

And I know the moment I find my release, she'll be ruined too.

SCARLETT

Watching Lycan in control is like watching a king rule over his kingdom. I can't help but be in awe of just how much he possesses me when we're like this. If it's not his hands making me feel like I have to please him, making me wet and needy, it's his cock.

He thrusts into my mouth, making me gag. He smiles when the saliva soaks my dress. His thickness makes my jaw ache, but seeing the pleasure written on his face only seems to have an effect on me I never thought possible.

I'm turned on.

I'm pleased that I'm giving him pleasure.

Perhaps, underneath it all, I am submissive.

He uses me like I'm nothing more than a rag doll. His cock thickens, choking me as he pumps once, twice, and on the third and final thrust, his warm seed spills over my tongue, and I quickly swallow his flavor. And I find even though I want to hate it, hate him, I don't. The salty sweetness of his release is enjoyable.

Lycan slowly pulls from my mouth, and I watch, still on my knees, how he guides his cock into his pants and zips himself up. He silently helps me to my feet and brushes off my dress before straightening and meeting my gaze.

I don't have time to speak because his mouth crashes against mine, his tongue stealing itself inside my mouth as he devours me, and I'm certain tasting himself on my tongue. The kiss is breathtaking, possessive, and I find my hands twining around his neck as I pull him closer.

And to say my panties are now soaked would be a gross understatement. He's done something to me, broken through the walls, shattered the glass cage I'd built around me, and now amongst the shards, he's stolen me from the forest and captured more than just my body. He's taken my mind.

But he can't have my heart, I remind myself.

By the time we land in New York, I'm exhausted. I'm not sure what time it is, but I do know it's early morning because the sun hasn't risen yet. In the dark, we make our way to the waiting town car. Lycan slips into the back seat with me and orders the driver to take us to Hawthorne.

Lycan's hand is on my thigh, the confidence and demanding way he holds onto me confirms I'm his now. What we did in the woods still lingers in my mind, and it's as if his taste is now forever on my tongue. I've never found pleasure in doing that with a guy, not even the boys I dated before my life changed forever. But with Lycan, I felt like a queen, even though I was on my knees.

Lycan squeezes my thigh, causing me to turn my attention toward him. His gaze holds mine hostage with promises I can't fathom. I asked him to show me his world, and I have a feeling I'm about to walk into the wolf's den.

But I'm not afraid.

Not anymore.

I thought I would be. I figured the moment I'm alone with him, I would want to run and hide, but he makes me feel strong. It's strange, as if his strength and confidence courses through me as well.

"Stop thinking so much," Lycan tells me with a grin. "I can hear that pretty mind racing beside me." The amusement in his tone makes me blush. I don't want to feel child-like next to him, but there are times my inexperience shines like a beacon in the night.

"This world you're about to show me," I start, "it's new to me. So new, in fact, that I'm scared I won't fit in." My admission has his free hand reaching for one of mine.

"Trust me, little red," he tells me. "You fit in perfectly.

Your sweetness, that innocence that shines like a star in the night sky, and your delicious submission."

"But I never—"

"You did. What do you think happened in the woods? The fact that you happily kneeled before me and took my cock in your mouth, that's what I crave. Watching you douse your fire just a little bit to please me," he speaks, his voice laced with desire, before he leans in and brushes his lips along my cheek. "That was what a perfect submissive would do—anything to please her Dominant."

"So, I'm going to need a safe word?" The question is a mere whisper, one that makes my stomach twist and churn with nervous energy.

Lycan chuckles. "You will. Since you're to be my wife, I wanted to take this slowly. Most women I've been with were only there for a night. And most of them were used to this world already. With you, I needed to savor watching you slowly find your submission. I wanted you to discover it naturally, not by force."

"I thought—"

"When you're unsure, ask. Don't think about things you've never witnessed." Lycan assures me with a smile as he leans in closer, his mouth at my ear, the warm breath fanning over my cheek when he whispers, "But trust me, little red, when we play, I'll make sure the desires you have, those dark, twisted needs, will be fulfilled. And when I do pin you down and take your pussy for the first time, you'll scream."

The promise, the dark, lust-filled vow he offers me, sends heat coursing through my veins like fire through the woods. I want to speak, to respond, but I can't find the words. Thankfully, the car comes to a stop. My head whips to my left to find my new home for the next few days. Lycan's New York home is nothing like I expected.

I figured someone like him would have a bachelor pad in the city, but we're in the suburbs. The house before us is a three-story mansion with soft yellow lights that shimmer from only the lower windows.

"I thought we were going to your apartment in the city?" I ask as I take in the house through the window. The two large white pillars holding up the balcony on the second floor have vines snaking around them, and the open-brick façade is nothing short of magnificent. Lycan's driver opens my door and helps me out of the car. The gravel beneath my feet crunches when I step on it.

"I wanted you to see our future home on the West Coast," Lycan says when he joins me, his hand clasping mine as we head toward the double wooden doors that slide open as if knowing their master is home. The foyer is filled with soft light. Dark metal railings lead up a sweeping staircase, and large modern paintings hang on the walls as they disappear down the hallway toward the right.

The scent of food wafts toward us. "This is magnificent," I say as Lycan leads me toward the back of the house and into the enormous kitchen. Stainless steel and marble greet us as I take in the space. A countertop is filled with fresh bread and baked goods.

"Master Shaw," a man in chef's whites greets before his gaze lands on me. "Good evening, miss." The posh British accent is clear in his words, and a soft smile curls his lips. "It's lovely to have you both here."

"Thank you," I respond, a grin forming on my face.

"Marcel, this is Scarlett. She'll be spending some time here while I attend my meetings this week," Lycan informs the man whose smile widens as he regards me.

"It's lovely to meet you, Miss Scarlett," Marcel says. "I'll happily keep you company while you're visiting at Hawthorne."

"We'll see you in the morning," Lycan says before tugging me behind him before I have a moment to answer Marcel's kindness. I'm taken back into the foyer before we head up the stairs, my gaze flitting between artworks as we move down the hall. We stop outside a dark wooden door, and I watch as Lycan unlocks it with a brass key and twists the handle. He allows me to enter first.

The room is furnished in blacks, whites, and grays. There are no other colors anywhere in sight. The bed is draped in a black comforter, matching pillows, and the four posters are made of a dark wood.

The carpet underfoot is a soft, plush charcoal, and the curtains, in a slate hue, are lined, blocking out any threat of light. A shimmering softness beckons, and I walk over to touch the silky material.

"You'll sleep in here tonight. I haven't had your room

made up yet," Lycan speaks softly, causing me to turn and regard him, only to find him unbuttoning his shirt. The motion makes my cheeks heat, and my stomach somersaults at the thought of finally seeing him naked.

Shaking my head, I respond in an attempt to quell the need in my gut. "I don't need to have a room made up. I'm happy to just take any room."

"This isn't a debate, little red," Lycan tells me in a no-nonsense tone.

Folding my arms across my chest, I pin Lycan with a glare, but I only earn myself a chuckle of amusement in response. "I may have enjoyed what we did in the forest, but—"

He closes the distance between us in no time before he stops, looming over me. "What did we do in the forest, sweetheart?" he growls, the sound so feral it's as if the beast has come out to play. The flames dancing in his eyes send a shudder of warmth over me, making everything south of my belly button tingle with anticipation. When I don't respond immediately, he leans in. "I asked you a question."

"I... We... I mean, you know what we did," I bite out, frustration at my nervousness around him, causing me more annoyance than anything else.

"Oh? Why don't you remind me?" The challenge is evident in his voice, in his expression of interest, which he holds me hostage with. This close, Lycan is handsome, devilishly so with a wolfish smirk that makes my stomach flutter with excitement.

"Stop acting like a domineering asshole," I bite out through clenched teeth in an attempt to steer us off the conversation because as much I want to say it, I can't bring myself to talk dirty to him.

The corner of his mouth quirks. "Does my little red not like being a filthy girl for me?" he taunts as he reaches for my chin, holding it between his thumb and forefinger as he holds me steady so I can't look away from him. I can't turn my gaze from the man who's staring at me as if he's trying to see into my soul.

Swallowing the lump in my throat, I whisper, "I sucked your cock."

Fire blazes in Lycan's eyes, the color turning molten, sending heat scorching through me at my filthy words. I'm sure he's heard worse, heard dirtier, but for me, this is new. "Good girl," he praises. "And would you like me to pleasure you now?" He tips his head to the side while still holding onto my chin. "Would you like me to devour your pretty cunt until you're gushing all over my face and tongue, little red?"

"I..." Words fail me. I knew Lycan wouldn't be like any guy I've ever been with in the past, but his mouth is pure filth. "I'm not sure."

A rumble vibrates in his chest. "I think you do. I think your mind is whirling with images of my face between your legs. You do realize I've been hungry for you since the moment I saw you. I wanted to taste you since the moment you walked into your parents' dining room that night."

My mouth gapes at his confession. "You didn't even know me."

"I knew I wanted you; that was more than enough." There's no doubt in his words, no doubt in his eyes, and I have a feeling he knew I would eventually submit to this thing between us. Not the marriage, not the heavy ring on my finger, but the fact that my body craves his. Not only his touch, but so much more than that.

"Then do it."

Lycan moves swiftly, his free hand tangling in my long hair. He tugs my head back painfully, exposing my throat to his mouth. Lips and teeth attack me like a hungry beast as he kisses, sucks, and bites at my sensitive flesh.

"Once I'm inside you, little red, there is no running," Lycan warns in a low murmur along the column of my neck. "And when you come around my cock, my tongue, and my fingers, no other man will ever enter you. Are we clear?"

I nod because I can't find words. I'm lost to the pleasure rocketing through me as Lycan bites down on the smooth skin, and I know there'll be a bruise left after his attack. He releases me, allowing both hands to slide down my body until he's cupping my ass through the dress I'm still wearing. Lifting me against him, he walks us to the bed before throwing me to the soft mattress.

"Tonight, I'm going to have you, claim you, and when I'm done, that ring will forever be attached to your finger," he commands as he shifts the material of his shirt over his shoulders. The broad, muscled expanse of tanned flesh greets me with a taunt because I can't reach him. My fingertips tingle with the need to touch, to feel, to run along every dip and peak of his beautifully toned body.

A dark smattering of hair between the pecs of his chest makes me think about how it would feel against my breasts. Lowering my gaze to his stomach, I take in the dips of his abs, as well as the angled muscles that dip into the waistband of his dark slacks.

A trail of black hair sneaks down, trailing under the material toward his thickening erection. When my gaze snaps back to Lycan's, I find him smirking down at me.

"Enjoying the view, little red?" A dark brow arches in question, his challenge clear. He knows what he does to me. Confidence oozes from him like a cologne, and it engulfs me, holding me hostage in the masculine scent of him.

"Perhaps," I tease, my hands moving to my dress as I tug the hem up my legs to my thighs. I don't falter my movements or my stare on the man before me. By the time my panties are in view, the darkness in his eyes has turned molten with lust.

"Open your legs wide," he orders. Deft fingers toy with his belt, the thick leather whooshing through the loops of material, and a shiver trickles down my spine, ice and fire, burning me but leaving me cold, needy for him.

Obeying Lycan, I offer myself to him like a sacrifice, and the man before me, tall and foreboding, falls to his knees between my thighs. His large hands spreading me, opening my core to his heated stare.

He doesn't say anything for a long while, his thumbs slowly circling my smooth skin, sending goose bumps skittering in the wake of his touch. I watch in awe as he leans in, running his nose along the material of my panties as he inhales my scent. Even I can smell my arousal. Nobody has ever done this to me, taken me in like I was a fragrance to be savored.

His mouth presses down on me, my mound lifting against him as my needy whimper expels from my lips. "Please, Lycan," I plead, and I'm once again not sure of what I want from him. I'm unsure of what I need, but the man worshipping me like a deity knows. His thumb tugs at my panties, and I'm finally bared to his watchful stare.

Eyes burn with lust as he looks at my neatly trimmed pussy, and his mouth crashes down on me before his tongue laps at my folds. The sensation has my hips undulating against his ministrations as he teases and taunts with his lips. He fucks into me with his tongue, opening my body to him.

I try to move, to shift, but I can't. His hold on me keeps me steady. The mattress beneath me is soft, the material silky against my fevered skin. Lycan's gaze locks on mine, and the view of this strong, powerful man eating me like I am his final meal sends my mind to the abyss of pleasure as my head falls back and I cry out. My legs tremble on either side of his face as his stubble tickles my inner thighs.

"Look at me, little red," Lycan commands from his kneeling position, causing me to snap my gaze to his. "Good girl." Two words send pride through me, and I can't stop smiling down at him. "Are you ready to take my cock in this pretty little cunt?"

"Yes, please?" Another plea. Another poignant admission of just how much I do want him. "Please, Lycan."

"Good," he praises before rising to his feet. With his mouth wet from my arousal, he grips my hair, tugging me forward until my lips are on his. The taste of my pleasure coats my tongue as I dance it along his lower lip.

With a quick kiss, he releases me, and I watch as his slacks are shoved to the floor along with his boxer briefs. His cock, thick and angry, juts out toward me. A gasp tumbles from my mouth when he fists himself in one hand, causing the tip to weep with pleasure.

"Taste it," Lycan whispers, and I obey easily. No is fight left inside me because all I crave is him. My lips wrap around his shaft, the saltiness of his cum mingled with the taste of me has my body aching to be owned.

"Please fuck me," I beg shamelessly because there is no longer any room for being shy or playing innocent. Because around Lycan, I'm not. I'm his, and I want him to know that. The thought of running from him before our wedding has left my mind, and now all I can think of is him inside me.

He doesn't need me to ask him twice. Seconds later, he's hovering over me, my legs spread around his waist, and the wetness of his tip nudges my entrance. His gaze holds mine, waiting for the moment I'm filled, and I don't wait long.

His hips move as he thrusts inside my entrance, the thickness of him stretching me almost painfully, causing me to cry out as bliss fills my lungs, and electricity sparks my nerves. Every inch of me is alight with pure lust.

"Fuck," Lycan growls, lowering his forehead to my shoulder, his hands bunching the sheets beneath me as he grits his teeth. "You're so fucking tight, little red," he murmurs along the nakedness of my shoulder, the heat of his breath fanning along my skin. "My cock is going to be forever etched inside you."

"Yes," I hiss out my response as Lycan pulls out slowly, then slams back in. My back arches as euphoria slams into me like a tidal wave, sending me to the precipice. I'm on the edge, waiting to leap into the abyss. His movements are slow and controlled, but I dig my nails into his shoulder, dragging them down his back until I reach his hips. I grip them tight, pulling him deeper into me as I lift my ass from the mattress.

"Jesus fucking Christ, you're a bad fucking girl."

A giggle escapes me. Lycan's movements hasten. He pulls out and drives back in, his cock hitting so deep inside me it's almost painful. I crave more though, and when I arch once more, his one hand grips my throat so tight, I see stars. He doesn't choke me harshly, but as his fingers dig into either side of the slender column, I find pleasure, and my body awakens with newfound release as I soak his cock with my arousal.

"That's it," Lycan coos, still gripping my neck with a dangerous hold. His lips feather along my cheeks before he reaches my ear. "Come on my dick again while I choke the breath out of you." The command sends me over that cliff-edge, and I fly into the darkness as the bright lights behind my lids dance.

His cock thickens inside me. He opens me wider while I pulse around him. Lycan's hips slam me into the bed, fucking me with violent desire, and the bitter vows I promised him earlier are nothing more than a distant memory.

He doesn't relent as my orgasm shatters me like a splintered glass, leaving me in fragments on the soft comforter. His body owns me with every drive of his cock. The moment he finds his own pleasure, he growls into my mouth. "Give me your breath." I obey as he releases my neck, sending waves of ecstasy through every inch of my body. My lungs inhale passion and expel happiness as he swallows every lungful of air, and I can't stop the whimpers and mewls, but Lycan greedily breathes them in too.

LYCAN

Pacing the carpet of my office, I run my fingers through my hair, tugging at the strands. In the other hand, I have my mobile pressed against my ear. The silence that greets me is nothing new, but the breath that comes from the speaker is confirmation he's there.

"What the fuck do you want?" My voice is cold, filled with the rage I've built over the years, the same anger that has spurred me in my hatred of the man I was meant to love. The man I called brother. "I'm done playing games with you, Darius. There is nothing you can do to me that can make matters worse. You chose to leave. When you walked away, I was the one who kept the Shaw name going."

"Did you? Or were you just so fucking blind to our father's bullshit that you didn't see the truth? He cheated on Mom," Darius tells me. It's the same story he's been spewing for years, but there was never any proof. We're both the blood of our father, and there were never any other women.

"Don't give me that shit." I grit my teeth so hard my jaw ticks painfully. I'm certain I'm about to crack my teeth with the rage fueling me as I stare out the window each time I face it.

"The Shaw secrets will soon be revealed, brother," he tells me. I glance at Isaac, who is meant to be tracing the call. Only a few more moments, and I'll have him. I wait. "Do you really think I'm that stupid, Lycan?"

"I don't know what you mean."

He chuckles, the sound just like our father's. "Your pretty bride will wear your blood." His threat has me stilling all movement. I know he knows about Scarlett. "Her name will be the hue of her wedding gown." Isaac signals five seconds, and my heart rate spikes.

"You're a fool." Those are the last words I spew at my brother before the line goes dead. My gaze locks on the man I'm praying will give me good news, but instead, he shakes his head.

In a fit of rage, I fling my phone against the wall, watching it shatter into tiny pieces before it lies on the soft carpet of my office. The team Kahn had tagging Darius fucked up, and now Isaac wasn't able to trace the call.

My brother is clever.

And I'm fucking fuming.

"Isaac, go to the office and let Kahn know we've fucked up once again. Tell him I want this sorted. I want the whole team, not just two fucking imbeciles on the case. Darius needs to be found, and he needs to be found right fucking now."

"Yes, of course, Mr. Shaw," Isaac says as he quickly packs his laptop and tracing device away. The moment he's gone, I crack the knuckles of both my hands to stay calm, but the thought of my brother evading me once more only seems to make me angrier.

I spin around, facing the two ex-soldiers who are standing in my office. "This is why I asked you to keep tabs on him. How the fuck does he keep disappearing?" My fist slams against the wooden top of my desk, the thud loud and resounding in the office space. Anger surges through me as my men stand before me, shaking in their fucking combat boots.

"Sir," one of them says. He's been with us for a few months, and Kahn swore he's good. They knew each other while serving, but I'm not impressed with the bullshit they've fed me. The excuse is that they had taken a wrong turn, and the car Darius was in sped off in another direction. It's amateur, and I'll be talking to Kahn about it. "We fucked up, I understand, but we do have a location. We know he hasn't left the vicinity—"

I pin him with a glare which shuts him up quickly. "And how would you fucking know that?"

"The second team that was tagging him has scoured the roads. They picked up the SUV he's been driving." My rage eases slightly. Having my brother close by is dangerous because we're both volatile around each other.

"Then go back out there and find the fucker!"

They don't respond. Their answer is feet shuffling quickly out my office door. When I glance at the exit, I notice a pretty redhead staring at me with wide eyes. Last night, I took her once, and the second time, I tried to be gentle, but with those nails scraping down my back, I fucked her hard, and I'm certain she's still feeling the aftereffects.

"Come here," I command, allowing the anger to slowly dissipate because the sight of my soon-to-be wife walking toward me barefoot and dressed only in my shirt makes my dick take notice, and my mind focuses on her instead of the fuck up of my men.

"You sound angry," Scarlett observes, her gaze raking over my creased shirt and my slacks. I quickly pulled on this morning when Kahn called. When she reaches me, her hands cup my face, her thumbs circling my stubbled jaw. I had no time to shave this morning because I was too wrapped up in her naked body.

"I am. I was."

She tips her head to the side, her pretty lashes fluttering along her cheeks as she whispers her question. "Why?"

"My brother has evaded the tail I put on him."

"What is it about you two?" she questions, genuine curiosity dancing in her eyes as she watches my reaction, which is more than a wince, perhaps a grimace at the idea of retelling the story about my brother.

"Go and get dressed. I want to take you to Heaven," I tell her, ignoring the question but rather craving to have her in my club, in my private room where I can dominate her until I've had my fill.

Her mouth pops open as if she's about to ask why, but I pin her with a look that says don't ask questions. She moves effortlessly from my office, and I quickly tap out a message to Kahn to ensure it's all set up for when we arrive. Tonight, my little red will learn more about her future husband and just how he enjoys his games.

SCARLETT

When we walk into the club, the breath is knocked from my lungs. The dark yet decadent interior is drenched in pure elegance. This is not what I expected when Lycan told me it's a club where people come to act out their most salacious fantasies.

Black and silver.

Deep tones of red and purple.

Low lights that only offer hints of depravity.

My first impression of Heaven is that its name suits the club. Everything drips with lush opulence. Even though I imagined it being more of a dungeon, a play on the idea of heaven, it's not. The black leather sofas that line the circumference of the club look soft and inviting. The bar is steel and wood, giving off the allure of luxury. Women and men fill the dimly lit space, some on their knees, others on stage. A scene playing out at the moment is of a woman bent over and bound, the man behind her spanking her with a wooden paddle.

I'm out of my depth.

So much so that I can't stop my face from heating in embarrassment. But Lycan's gentle touch at the base of my spine grounds me, and I turn to look up into those forest eyes.

"Are you scared?" he asks while leaning in close. The music is a low, sensual drone of classical music—a soundtrack of the desire sparking through the room. The air thick with lust, and all I can feel is Lycan against me.

"No." I glance at the scene again, the man now fingering the woman, her legs spread lewdly for the audience as she screams with pleasure as his four fingers slip between her slick, glistening folds. Desire burns through me at the thought of being open like that for Lycan, feeling his fingers dip into my body as he takes me higher.

"Is that something you'd want to try?" he whispers in my ear, sending more heat traveling down my spine all the way to the apex of my thighs.

"I... I don't know if I can."

He chuckles, the sound vibrating through him and into me. "Trust me, little red, you'll be able to take it. That isn't something I'd do on the first go, but we can most certainly get you wet enough to take my hand."

The thought causes my nipples to harden against the soft lace material of my bra. My heartbeat thrumming between my thighs, and my panties are already wet with arousal.

"And I'd love to hear you scream, just like she is right now," he warns over the echo of the submissive coming hard all over the stage. Her body wracked with pleasure as she shakes and trembles. Her face is etched in ecstasy. There's no doubt she is in heaven right now.

"I need a drink," I tell Lycan who only smiles as he leads me to the main area of the club. There are waitresses and waiters dressed in black and white who expertly hold trays of drinks as they swish amongst the guests. Lycan pulls me into his hold, my back to his front as I look around. His body is large, cocooning me against him.

"Lycan," a soft purr comes from our left, and I glance over my shoulder to find a beautiful woman with long blonde hair standing beside us. She's draped in a sheer, black dress with lace underwear visible through the material. Her nipples are pierced with silver barbells, and a blush warms me from face to chest. I instantly recognize her, the same woman from the gala at Bardot Manor.

"Nice to see you, Lori," Lycan greets her, but his hold on me tightens. Her blue eyes find my hazel ones. "This is my fiancée, Scarlett," he informs her, his voice controlled, calm, but there's a hint of satisfaction that elicits a smile from me.

"Nice to meet you." My words are sweet, but they're not entirely friendly or free of jealousy either. I didn't for one moment think Lycan didn't have a past, but the thought of this woman coming near him at any point has envy coursing through me.

She doesn't respond, merely nods before walking off, leaving me glaring at her exposed back. The dress she's wearing is barely there, and I wonder why she bothered.

"Who is that?" I don't look at Lycan as I ask this, because if I had to be honest with myself, I don't want to see any desire in his gaze for someone else. The possessiveness is new to me, catching me off guard.

I've never been *that* girl, who would lose her shit over another woman. If a guy is easily swayed, then I'm not the one for him. And vice versa. But right now, with the ring Lycan gave me weighing heavily on my finger, I feel his grip tighten.

"That is nobody," he tells me. "She was someone I spent a few scenes with, and she meant nothing to me, not like you do."

Turning in his arms, I stare into his gaze. "I can't mean that much to you, not yet. I know we're getting married, and most times, it means you're in love with someone to walk down the aisle, but I don't want to fool myself into thinking I'm nothing more than a means to an end for you."

My acceptance of what Lycan and I are, came late last night. While I laid in bed alone, I thought about it. Knowing I will never have a marriage filled with love, I convinced myself I'd make myself happy. Perhaps if I had someone who could offer me what I lacked at home, with Lycan's agreement, of course, I could survive long enough to let Lycan have his vengeance.

It might sound stupid, but if I don't have another choice, I have to live with what life has thrown in my way. And that's something I learned from reading books. Where the heroine is forever looking out for herself, no matter what, I'll do the same.

"If you ever think you mean nothing to me, you're sorely mistaken," Lycan says, catching my attention, bringing it back to the here and now. "I may have signed a contract to marry you, but that doesn't mean you haven't slowly burrowed your way into my mind."

I note how he doesn't say, heart. He is convinced he cannot love. And even though my plan to make him fall for me has fallen by the wayside, his admission makes me think perhaps without trying, I could still accomplish it.

"Then show me your world," I whisper, allowing my lips to feather along his, earning myself a growl of need. The wolf that Lycan keeps locked away within him is hungry, and he bares his teeth when I bite down on his full lower lip.

Lycan's animalistic hiss is nothing short of feral and wild. Even though we're amongst guests only a few feet away, I want nothing more than for him to touch me again. Memories spark in my mind like fireworks on the Fourth of July. He takes a step toward me, eating up the few inches that were there before, and his hand grips my hip possessively.

"Every fucking man in this room right now wants you," he murmurs under his breath, reminding me that we're not alone. That's the problem when I'm near Lycan. All I can think about is him; all I see is him. He looms over me, like a giant, and I feel small and fragile.

"No, they don't."

A chuckle reverberates through him. "You're far too fucking sweet and innocent. It's a shame that I'm going to have to mar that beauty," he tells me earnestly. "I'll show you my world. I'll train you to be the perfect little submissive, but there's one thing I want from you."

"Besides the bitter vows, I'm meant to spew at our wedding?" I challenge, causing a predatory smirk to curl his lips which causes my stomach to twirl with nervous energy.

"Let me tell you one thing, little red," Lycan whispers along my cheek in a trail to find my earlobe, which he grazes with his teeth. "When you say your vows in a couple of weeks, they'll not be bitter but filled with want and need. Because when I'm done with you, you'll beg to be my wife."

His fingers dig into my hip, painfully reminding me of who's in charge. He steps back quickly, as if he wasn't there to begin with. And then, he's leading me with gentle fingertips at the base of my spine as we move through the crowd.

I'm utterly speechless, and that's how Lycan guides me to the curved bar where two young, handsome men are working. One of them sees Lycan and straightens, offering a curt nod, but he doesn't greet him verbally.

"Simon," Lycan says in a tone that underlies dominance. "My fiancée will have a white wine. I'll have the usual."

"Yes, sir." He moves quickly, grabbing glasses and setting them before us. The display of obedience is something I'm convinced Lycan enjoys. This is what he wants from me, no debating, no snarky comments, only obedience.

Once our drinks are poured with a flourish and a hint of a smile, Lycan hands me mine and picks up his tumbler, which shimmers with amber liquid. "I'd like you to take it all in." His gaze flits behind me, and I can tell there's annoyance where moments ago there was happiness and comfortable satisfaction—as if he were home.

When I turn, I find the woman, Lori, staring at us. She's perfected the vamp look, and her sights are set on the man who's right beside me. Tall, leggy, and someone I would picture Lycan beside rather than me.

"Are you going to lie to me again?" I question, but I don't turn to face him. I can't see the denial on his face when he tells me she's nothing to him.

"Let's go," he answers, pulling me toward the back of the club, where we disappear down the hallway into a room decked in black. The reminder of his bedroom comes to mind, and I have a feeling this isn't just a random room that can be used. This is Lycan's bedroom of choice.

"Who is she?"

"The woman who took everything from me and left me with nothing. Now can you stop asking questions and take off your clothes," he orders through gritted teeth. His free hand tangles in his dark hair, while his other brings the drink to his full lips as he swallows back the double shot of whiskey.

This is not the way I thought this evening would go.

Obeying him without debate, I slink off the black dress, and I stand before him in matching black panties and a bra that pushes my breasts together, giving me the illusion of cleavage.

His hot stare takes me in from my heels, which are a dark red. His gaze trails me gently, and it feels like his hands are all over me.

The straps of my shoes hold my feet as if it were Shibari rope binding my body. He stops his perusal briefly when he reaches the tie at the ankle, which is a silver clasp. My long, lean legs are bare, leading to my panties that are a delicate lace material, hiding what I know he wants to see.

My flat stomach tingles when he eases his stare upward, and it stops on my breasts, which are encased in the same lace material as my pussy. My nipples peak, hardening against the fabric until he finds my eyes.

"I want so much to hurt you," he murmurs before setting the glass down. "I want to see you cry, make you scream." His words instill fear, but the flurry of wings in my stomach confirm that I want it.

"Is that what would give you pleasure, Master?" I question, using the word I only know from reading romance novels to affect men like Lycan Shaw.

His smile is pure satisfaction. He didn't expect me to

say it, to gift him the title I've never before mentioned—
his title of my owner. I step toward him slowly, and for a
moment, I think he's going to get angry, but instead, he
watches like a predator.

When I'm inches from him, I lower myself to my knees.
The soft carpet under me is gentle against my skin, and I
bow my head in a show of submission I know will turn him
on. The thought has my pussy tingling, and I'm certain I'll
soon be wet with need.

"Put your hands behind your back and look me in the
eye." His order comes out gruff and husky. And once more,
I obey easily. Lycan steps back, taking in my kneeling form
before he walks over to a cabinet against the far wall.

A clinking of metal sends ice through my veins, but
when he turns to regard me, I notice they're only cuffs.
At least that won't hurt. When Lycan returns to me, he
crouches behind me, binding my hands together.

He helps me to my feet, and soon, I'm bent over the
edge of the mattress, my arms straining behind me. My
arms are bound with cuffs that fit around my wrists and
forearms, allowing my hands to rest on my lower back,
giving him access to my butt.

Another click of something echoes in the room.
Seconds later, I'm immobile because what I didn't realize
is Lycan had a spreader bar, which has now locked my feet
apart. I would be bare to him if he were to pull my panties
down.

"Choose a safe word," Lycan says. "Something you'll

remember, something unique. If you at any point say it, I'll stop." He crouches down, so we're eye to eye, and I don't recognize the man before me. The wolf has taken over. He's no longer Lycan but a beast in need of feeding.

The word comes to me easily, and with a smile, I say, "Wolf."

The corner of his mouth quirks, and he nods. Leaving me to stare at nothing but the wall on the far side of the bed.

I watch from my viewpoint, which doesn't allow me to see much. He moves across the room, fiddling with something in the corner, and when it sparks to life, I hear a stereo. Music drifts from the corners of the room, a familiar tune.

Sofia Karlberg sings "Lonely Together", and my heart aches in my chest when I listen to the lyrics as Lycan picks up a thick leather flogger. Nervous energy trickles through me when he nears me, and for a moment, I'm scared.

"Don't be afraid," he tells me as if sensing my fear. "I'll take it easy." The agony in his voice makes my chest tighten, and tears spring to my eyes. I want to know what's hurting him, why he's doing this, but I don't ask.

When the first lashing of leather kisses my skin, a hiss escapes me. He doesn't stop; he continues, another and another. With my arms behind me, the tips of the flogger touch my back in small spurts.

Lycan lowers his attack to my ass, sending heated tingles to my pussy, causing mewls of pained pleasure to escape my lips. I screw my eyes shut in an attempt to focus on not coming, because surprisingly, I'm close to the edge.

"If you come, I'll hurt you. I promise you that, little red."

"Please, Sir," I plead, the words coming to me easily because I'm not sure I can hold off. He continues his assault down to my calves and back up to my ass before he drops the flogger, and suddenly, an ice-cold item slides along my skin. When it slithers under the material of my panties, I realize it's a blade.

A gasp escapes me when Lycan cuts my panties from my body. The material falls to the floor, and I'm open to him now. My wetness is evident as he grips my ass cheeks, opening my body to his gaze.

"So pretty when you're wet and needy." His voice is dark and gruff with desire. Suddenly, his hand comes down on my pussy, causing a cry of pain to stumble free from my lips. His fingers taunt and tease as he opens me before slapping me once more.

My legs shake, my body trembles, and my mumbling pleas for him to allow me to come are a symphony alongside the sad song playing in the background. Lycan continues with his alternating torture of slapping and fingering, my arousal soaking down my thighs.

"I think my little red needs my cock," Lycan says from somewhere behind me, but I'm too far gone to even respond to him. With two more swats on my ass, he drives into me with one long thrust, causing me to scream as pleasure wracks through my body, and I fall over the edge into darkness.

"Bad girl," he coos, but he likes it, it's a good thing because I'm not punished for being bad. Instead, he fucks me hard. His hips slamming me into the bed, his body looming over me as he hisses in my ear, "This time, I'll be nice," and I can hear the amusement in his tone when he says the word nice. "But next time you come without my permission, I'll make you cry."

With that, he grips my throat, pulling me back, so our bodies are flush. His mouth on my cheek, his warm breath sending more heat skittering through my veins.

His thick cock opens me, driving in so deep I'm left breathless with every thrust. Sweat drips from my skin as he takes me brutally. But I can't stop the pleasure from taking me higher and higher until I'm screaming something incoherent because all I feel is him.

I'm nothing more than a ragdoll for him to use, and I'm not at all angry about it.

Lycan's free hand swats at the front of my pussy while his cock thickens inside me, and another orgasm breaks free from deep in my gut as he growls his release inside me. He stills behind me, still holding onto my throat while his other hand now gently massages my clit.

"My good girl," he coos finally before allowing me back to the mattress. He uncuffs me before unlocking the spreader bar. Once he drops the items to the floor, he pulls me into his arms, and we settle on the bed, Lycan's arms around me, holding me tightly against him, and I've never been happier.

My lashes flutter closed, and I realize I'm falling deeper with every moment I spend with him. He's opened my eyes to something more, and I don't think I could ever return to the girl I was before.

And that thought scares me as I fall into a dreamless sleep.

LYCAN

The sun hasn't even risen yet, and I'm planning something I'm not sure Scarlett will approve of, but my gut has been churning with worry for days, and this is the only way I know my plan will work.

When I spoke with Kahn, he told me I should go ahead with this, so we're about to do it. A knock at my office door has me glancing up to find the devil himself walking in. Kahn looks happy with himself as he settles in a chair opposite my desk.

"Priest is ready," he tells me.

"And Simon?"

He nods. "He's willing to be a second witness. We have

everything. We just need a bride," he informs me.

"I need to talk to her. She's still asleep," I inform him. "Give me some time. Tell him to be here at eight. I'll make sure Scarlett is ready."

"Are you sure this is the way to go about it?"

I know his concerns about the very public wedding on Saturday, but if Darius is going to attack, it's going to be there. I need her to have my name, my protection by then. "If something happens, get her to the convent. Stay with her. Don't let that fucker near her."

Even though I'm ready for my brother, I have to have a plan in place if all goes to shit. Knowing my life, it's most definitely going to go to shit the moment I'm standing at the end of the aisle as I wait for her to reach me.

Pushing to my feet, I head to the door with Kahn following. "I trust you," I tell him. "I know you'll make sure she's safe until I can get to her."

"She will be safe. I'll put my life on the line for her. The same goes for you." I know he's telling the truth because that's what this man has always done for me.

He leaves me as I walk down the hall to the bedroom where I left her earlier. Upon entering, I find my sweet bride sitting amongst the black silk sheets with her skin bare and beautiful.

"Good morning," I greet as I make my way toward her.

"Hi," she says. "Where were you?"

I lean in to press a kiss to her forehead. "I needed to do some business. I have something I need to talk to you about." When I settle on the mattress, I can read the fear in her expression.

"What's wrong?"

Sighing, I take her hand with the ring on her third finger in mine and meet her questioning stare. Better to rip the Band-Aid off quickly. "I want us to get married today."

"What? Why?"

"Our wedding on Saturday will go ahead, but I want you to have my name and protection before that day comes." I keep my gaze on hers. "I just want you to be safe if anything were to happen."

She watches me for a long while before saying, "You're worried about your brother." I nod, and she continues. "Do you think he'll do something at the wedding? I mean, there'll be guests, and your team will be there."

"I don't put anything past my brother." It's true. I don't trust him. And I most certainly wouldn't trust him not to hurt Scarlett, and I find fear choking me at the thought of something happening to her.

I look into those pretty eyes and find affection. Love. My lungs struggle to pull in air when I realize those emotions are reciprocated. All the fights, debates, and arguments have brought us both here.

It was about revenge.

It was about her father.

But right now, it's no longer about those things.

"This is us," I tell her. "Bitter vows aside," I tease with a grin. "I want you, little red. I crave and hunger for you constantly. You're mine, and you always will be. I just... I need you to know that before we walk down the aisle. And the only way I can do that is to say my vows today."

A small smile graces her pretty face. "Okay. Then we'll get married today."

Seeing Scarlett walk out of the bedroom in a bright red dress that hugs every curve of her frame has me coughing into my hand to keep the growl from escaping my lips. She looks like pure seduction, a beautiful vixen walking to her death as she takes my hand.

"Are you ready?" I ask before pressing a kiss to her knuckles.

"As ready as I'll ever be." She notices the men standing to the side waiting for us. Kahn, Simon, and the priest I had Kahn find last minute. I woke up this morning with the thought of marrying her today, and I needed to make it happen.

"Shall I start?" the priest asks, who I recall is named Arthur.

"Yes." I nod, taking both Scarlett's hands in mine.

With a nod, he begins. "We have gathered here today to lawfully bind Scarlett Bardot and Lycan Shaw in holy matrimony. Since they will be saying their own vows, I'll ask Scarlett to speak first."

My girl inhales a deep breath before smiling up at

me. Her light shines through her expression, her eyes are shimmering with emotion, and I ache to steal every moment of this day and commit it to memory. I'm not sure what's going to happen tomorrow, but for today, I'm basking in happiness I never thought I would feel.

"For weeks, I was convinced when I finally said my vows they'd be filled with bitterness and rage," Scarlett says with a soft smile. "But I no longer find those emotions in my words." She holds my hands as if I were a lifeline. "This isn't how we were going to do this, but I, Scarlett Bardot, take you Lycan Shaw in happiness and sadness. I'll walk through heaven and hell beside you, as long as you're the one ruling over the kingdoms. Our path ahead may not be paved with ease, but I cannot wait to see what lies before us."

My chest tightens considerably, and I realize for the first time in my life, I'm falling. I've fallen. I've never expected to find happiness with someone, not with a woman who is filled with so much innocence and light.

But here she is.

"The darkness inside me has eased because of you," I tell her. "We may not be standing before hundreds of people, and you aren't wearing a pretty white dress, but even as we do this in my club, I know our future will be filled with happiness. I vow, bitter or not, to keep you, hold you, cherish you, and ensure you're forever smiling."

A tear escapes her lashes, trickling down her cheek, but I don't steal it because I love to see how those pretty eyes glisten with emotion just for me.

"I'm not the prince, I'm the wolf, but I'll forever keep you safe from the hunter who aims to steal you from me." I lean in, my lips brushing along her. "From today and forever more."

"I love you," Scarlett says suddenly, causing my heart to still in my chest for a second before thumping wildly against my ribs. "I didn't think it was possible." She smiles, shaking her head slowly. "But somehow, you've battered down my walls."

Cupping her face, I run my thumbs along the apples of her cheeks, and I can't stop the grin that cracks along my face. "I love you too, little red," I admit honestly. "I really do. Fuck the arrangement with your father. This" — I pull her closer — "this is real."

Scarlett giggles playfully, and she kisses me as the priest sighs that we've completely fucked his ceremony. "I now pronounce you husband and wife," he says as I pull my wife into my arms. Even though our wedding will still go ahead for the guests, today is for us.

SCARLETT

My grandmother looks over at us, watching from afar, but peering in so closely she may as well be standing beside us. I've enjoyed my time in New York while learning more about Lycan's world, the dark and twisted cravings of a man whose beast lies in wait for when I kneel for him.

I didn't think I would.

But the wolf who appears when Lycan hungers for me is nothing like I've ever experienced. He's like a bomb waiting to explode, and I want nothing more than to be right beside the destruction he leaves in his wake.

Time has passed, making me more aware of how easily I've fallen into a life with him. Fallen in love with a man who bought me. It sounds like the makings of a romance novel. But it's my real life. And I couldn't be happier.

The buildings we've visited in the hopes of me finding one for my company have given me pause. When I was first taken to the Shaw mansion in Crimson Falls, I was convinced I would be free of him within the week. But now, I find myself more enthralled with him.

The wedding is fast approaching, and with more plans being confirmed—venue, food, guests—I'm no longer nervous. I don't necessarily want to walk down the aisle so soon, but I no longer hate the man who's currently speaking to Kahn while pacing the living room carpet.

We head back to Crimson Falls tomorrow to finalize the last details for the big day, but something has been bothering Lycan for a couple of days. And I have a feeling it's because of whatever Kahn is currently telling him.

And I'm sure it has something to do with his brother.

I approach my grandmother, wanting to talk to her without Lycan listening. By the time I reach her, she's finished her wine and asking for another. I'm not sure why she came when she doesn't seem happy about the engagement.

Even though this party was meant to celebrate our union, Lycan and I are aware of her animosity toward the upcoming nuptials.

"I thought you'd be happy," I say when I step beside my grandmother. I can't tell her I'm already married to him, so I play along as if nothing has changed since she last saw us.

She doesn't answer for a beat, but then says, "Nothing about a Shaw and Bardot together should bring about happiness."

"Is that because your heart was broken by a Shaw?" I challenge, because she knows that I know about her and Conall. Perhaps I shouldn't goad her, but I need to know about the curse that has been whispered about.

"The past needs to stay buried, but your man keeps dredging it up," she whispers, nudging her chin toward where Lycan is now talking to a couple of guests, his call ended, and I wonder what the outcome was.

"I don't understand what the problem is about learning something that happened to our families." I don't look at her this time. Instead, my focus is on the way Lycan's fake smile is plastered on as he watches us. He's not listening to what the man beside him is saying.

"There are some secrets that should never be brought to light. I made mistakes, I admit that, but when I walked away from my past, from Conall, I promised him to never allow our families to unite. It's wrong."

This time, I spin on my heel to regard her. "What's wrong about it?"

Her gaze glints on mine. "Do you love him?" she asks, a challenge in her words.

Do I?

Yes. I do.

Am I attracted to him?

Do I lust after him?

Yes, and yes.

There's no doubt in my mind Lycan is my other half, a match I didn't expect. Love wasn't something I expected to feel, but it's there now, and I'm not letting it pass me by. I didn't expect him to say it, to tell me those three words, but he did. At least, he didn't seem anywhere near emotions that strong. But his heart is beating for me now, and I've got a grasp on it.

"If you don't love him, tell him. Stop this farce of a wedding," my grandmother says softly, but the urgency of her tone is clear. She doesn't want this wedding to go ahead.

I grin because I know what she's trying to do. Mom said she did this at their wedding as well. When my mother and father were to wed, Gran thought she could stop it, or control it. Instead of answering, I challenge, "And if I don't?"

This time she looks directly at me, her gaze lingering on my face as if she's taking in every inch of me to memory. "Nothing good will come of it." She swallows back her drink before making her way for the door, and I watch as my grandmother disappears without looking back.

A cold shiver races down my spine.

Awareness that her warning will come with dire consequences.

The dress is stunning, just like I knew it would be. I

wanted today to be perfect. Over the weeks of getting to know Lycan, seeing his pain about how his father died and how his brother didn't believe a word of what had happened, I understand why he is so closed off.

But he did open up to me.

He gave me parts of himself I'm certain not many people were privy to. And it means a lot to me to have moved forward, to have overcome what I believed about him before. He's not a monster at all. Perhaps a beast, yes, but he's all man.

I didn't think I could ever find it in myself to love him like I should—as a husband. But I do. And I would like to try to find my path alongside him, to walk forward today down the aisle and know that my future is safe. To know the man I'm saying "I do" to is someone capable of love. Deep down, I know Lycan is.

There's no longer any doubt in my mind.

The sleek, white dress hugs my curves, and the lace train lays behind me along the carpet. As the two maids Lycan hired to dress me fix the tiara to my head along with the veil, I glance at myself in the mirror, taking in the elegance.

My bedroom door swoops open, and Aelin rushes in. "Oh my god," she gushes when she sees me. "You look incredible." Her voice bounces off the walls as she stops in front of me, her hands on my shoulders as she holds me at arm's length.

"I'm so glad you're here," I tell her honestly. When I

asked Lycan if she could be my maid of honor, he agreed. When his humanity shines through the cold exterior, I can't help but smile because as much as he tries to hide it, I know he cares deeply for me.

"I cannot believe you're getting married."

Once the women are done with my hair, they leave us, and I settle onto the stool provided, so I don't crease my dress. Even though I'm not yet in my heels, I need to sit because my knees are shaking. I don't want to admit how nervous I am, so I paste on a smile and look at my one and only friend.

"Trust me, if you had asked me a month ago if I would be here, getting ready to walk down the aisle, I would've told you you're crazy," I admit easily.

"This man must be all that because the Scarlett I know would never allow a man to dictate anything about her life," she says. "Or is it *because* he has a big dick?" Her teasing has me laughing, and for a moment, I enjoy the lighthearted banter between us. It's been so long since I've seen her, going from talking to someone every day to not seeing them for weeks is strange.

"I am not talking about his dick," I throw back, knowing my best friend will be asking more about Lycan, as well as any dirty details about our sex life. Aelin was more provocative than I was, even when we came of age, she would go out to parties, meet boys when I would be the wallflower. I couldn't find the courage to tell her about my tastes. Not the ones I hid in the dark for so long.

Those same fantasies Lycan brought to life.

I should've spoken to her more. Over the past few weeks of me being here, I should have reached out. Even though Lycan didn't forbid me from calling, I didn't. Perhaps it was because I couldn't really explain my situation. My father put me here, he forced my hand without my permission, and as much as I wanted to hate him, I'm thankful he showed me his true colors.

"Are you okay?" Aelin asks then, her hands holding mine, pulling them close as she regards me with earnest curiosity.

"Yes, I am." It's the truth. If she had asked me when I first arrived here, I would've said no. But I truly am okay. "It's been eye-opening."

"Oh, I'm sure it has." She wiggles her eyebrows, amusement brightening her face as she takes me in. I can feel the heat on my cheeks. But she doesn't press me for more information. Thankfully. "So, where's my dress?"

"Over in the garment bag hanging on the back of the door," I tell her, pointing to where she came in. Now that we're shut in, she can see the item. Aelin rushes to it, unzipping it quickly to find the dark crimson dress that reminds me of a rich, red wine.

I didn't want pinks or blues, or any pastel color, and the red just fit so perfectly with what I had envisioned when we decided to have the wedding at the house. With vast gardens, and the beautiful scenery that overlooks the woods, I envisioned a fairytale wedding.

"This is epic," Aelin remarks as she strips down to her underwear and slowly slides the satin over her frame. It fits perfectly, like I knew it would. And when the straps are draped over her shoulders, I can't help but grin.

"I knew you'd pull that off," I tell her quickly as I push to my feet and rush to her side. Her long, blonde hair hangs to the middle of her back in waves of silk. "This is perfect. I wanted something different."

"I must say, the color scheme is totally you," she tells me with a giggle. "But I love it. I just want this day to be perfect for you." Once again, she takes my hands in hers, and emotion pricks at my eyes. I was so convinced I would walk away from Lycan before I got to this day. I wanted to escape, but right now, all I want to do is walk down the aisle.

"It's perfect because you're here, and you get to share it with me," I tell her honestly. "But don't make me cry. They spent hours on my makeup," I tease, offering a smile as I try to keep the tears at bay.

"Well, let's not keep your future husband waiting."

"I'll be there in a moment." I watch her go after a quick hug. Once alone, I take a few deep breaths before I pick up my phone. There's one person I need to talk to before I do this, one person I need to ask one simple question before I say, "I do."

DARIUS

For years I've waited. Needed proof before I walked into my brother's home and told him the truth about our family. About our father. As much as I loved him, I knew he was bad news. I learned a long time ago the Shaw name wasn't all it was cracked up to be. There were things hidden in closets, secrets, things he didn't want to have come to light.

And even then, I knew I couldn't be the man my father wanted. Yes, he was good to us as kids, but the older we got, the more I learned about who he truly was. Our mother, a woman who had loved him unconditionally, wasn't only just a pawn in his game, but she was a stand-in for the person he truly loved.

Lycan may have believed otherwise, and I allowed him to, but now as he takes a wife, he needs to learn the truth about the pretty redhead he'll share a bed with. Today is the wedding, and it amuses me that I've chosen a suit and tie to wear to the event. The black jacket hugs my rather large frame, with slacks that just fit.

A white button-up is not my choice of clothing, but for my brother, I'll do it. I need to blend into the crowd until I have my opportunity to stand and tell him the truth. I didn't want to do it this way, but I don't have a choice.

When I called my mother, I asked her to do it, to admit the shitshow she'd brought upon our family, but she refused. Which only leaves me with one option. I don't feel bad about it. The anger, the rage I've lived with knowing I was cast aside because I wasn't willing to fall into line, has made me hate everyone.

Lycan.

Scarlett.

Even Grace.

Picking up my weapon of choice, I screw on the silencer and smile down at the black metal that lies heavily in my hand. I found a family, and they gave me a gift I could never thank them enough for. Knowing I'm a killer is one thing but realizing the next person I'm about to murder in cold blood is my brother, well, that's another thing altogether.

Being a biker outlaw, I've seen my fair share of dead bodies. It doesn't faze me anymore. I doubt it ever will again. Lycan doesn't realize the first kill I ever made wasn't our father. He may believe it, and when I tried to tell him the truth, he didn't want to listen, so it's time I righted the wrongs of my brother and I.

Making sure my gun is strapped to my shoulder holster, I shrug on the jacket and pick up my keys. My mobile phone is off. My wallet in my pocket, I head out to the car. It's only a few blocks away, but I will need to get away from the mansion as quickly as possible.

In the driver's seat, I start the engine and pull out onto the road toward the house. When I reach the spot I marked out days ago, I come to a stop and sit watching the guests make their way inside.

Excitement churns in my gut, a reminder that soon I'll be reunited with the memories, the truth, and the admission that comes with what I'm about to say. A limo pulls up, and as the back door opens, *she* gets out. Her black dress is evidence that she's not happy about the union.

I knew she wouldn't be. And she would've made it known.

I exit my own car and make my way around the house. I blend in as I move through the crowd of guests and up the stairs. Lycan would be in his office by now, talking to Kahn about security.

Nobody would seek me out.

Nobody would even bother asking who I am.

There are so many strangers here today. I'm just one of the many faces. I've ensured my hair has been cropped short from the ponytail I usually sport. My beard has been shaved, and my hazel eyes are now dark brown from the contacts. I look nothing like Darius Shaw.

I hear them usher the guests to the garden, but I quickly race up the steps onto the landing and take a right toward her room—my brother's fiancée. The door opens, and out comes her best friend, Aelin.

I've had to learn all about the pretty blonde when I was doing my research. The moment she sees me, her eyes widen. "Who are you?"

"Who are you?" I throw back, offering her a smirk which seems to have the effect I need.

She grins. "I'm the bride's best friend, Aelin." She holds out a dainty hand, which I accept, bringing her knuckles to my lips and pressing a kiss to the smooth skin.

"Well, it's lovely to meet you," I tell her before releasing her. I keep her stare, holding her hostage with a mere glance. "I trust you'll enjoy the show." I straighten and leave her staring at my back as I step into the bathroom not far from Scarlett's bedroom.

I wait inside listening to the music change, and when they play the bridal march, I step out of the bathroom and find Scarlett in the hallway. The darkness enveloping her from the dim light of the interior of the house.

She spins on her heel when she hears the door click, and her gaze widens when she takes me in. I can see the wheels spinning in her head. She's trying to place me, but she won't recognize me. I know she won't.

"Scarlett," I greet with a bow. "It's so lovely to see you."

Confusion creases her brows. "I'm sorry. I don't think we've met."

Nodding, I gift her a lie. "I'm one of Lycan's acquaintances. An old friend, so to speak." For a moment, I'm almost certain she's going to scream, but I would happily shut her up with a hand to her throat, but when she nods, I ease the tension in my shoulders.

"It would be an honor to escort the bride to the aisle," I tell her with a charming grin plastered on my face. I offer her my elbow, and she slowly but gratefully accepts with a smile.

"Thank you. I can't find anyone," she tells me with a soft, gentle tone that makes the blood in my veins boil with anger.

I shouldn't hate her.

It's not her fault.

We walk out onto the landing and take the steps down to the foyer. Turning left, I lead her toward the patio doors. The moment we step out onto the soft grass, I glance up and grin at Lycan, who looks like he's ready to kill.

Walking down the aisle is surreal as I hold onto Scarlett's hand. The gun in my shoulder holster feeling heavier with every step. We're almost at the end of our march when I reach into my jacket, flashing the metal at my brother, whose eyes widen.

A gasp of guests from behind me doesn't deter me. That's when I hear feet shuffling and a few of the women screaming. I don't turn. My focus is laser sharp. He puts his body between the gun and Scarlett, but he doesn't need to worry. I won't hurt her.

When I first heard he'd signed the agreement for her hand, I thought it was a lie. I figured he was doing it merely for revenge. But now I see he does have feelings for her because he steps forward, taking her hand in his. He tugs her toward him, and he leans in. The whisper he gifts her with causes her to flick her gaze toward me, which is evidence that he's just told her who I am.

He pushes Scarlett behind him. "Hello, brother," I mutter. "Call your pack of hounds off."

He offers a nod, and I hear the clicking of weapons from behind me. "What are you doing here?"

"I came to give you the truth." I hand him the paper I had folded up in my pocket for the past two weeks. The proof that I'm not my mother's son. I'm not Lycan's full-blood brother.

He takes the page, and Scarlett tries to read from over his shoulder. She's a tiny thing. Fragile. Something I can break only to get revenge on the man before me.

"This is fucking ridiculous," he spits, throwing the proof to the floor like I knew he would. He thought I was lying all these years. When I glance to the left, I find my mother staring at me in horror. All the guests have gone. It's only her. She waited for me to show my face. She didn't think I would.

"Hello, Mother." I smile at her, causing Scarlett to gasp

in shock. And that's when I pull the gun from my holster and aim it at my brother. "I'm here to do the job you asked me to do."

Grace pushes to her feet elegantly. That's one thing about her — she always had an air of grace about her. I suppose her name suits her.

"Put the gun down," she says, but I smile, ignoring her. "This is not needed."

I turn back to Lycan. "This is what she asked for," I tell him, nudging my head to the side. "With you gone, Grace will gain everything. Why do you think she didn't want you marrying Scarlett?"

"What?" This comes from the pretty redhead. Her confusion is clear as she steps forward, but Lycan's arm comes out, blocking her from being in my line of fire. "Is this true, Gran?"

"I had Darius when I was young and stupid. I thought I was in love with Conall. It was a stupid fairy tale that could never work."

Scarlett's mouth pops open in shock and anger. "I... But how?"

"Family time is over," I say, tired of the revelations. I came here with one job in mind, and I'm going to finish it. Grace promised me what is due to me, and I'm here to collect. "Grace, say goodbye to your granddaughter."

Lycan grips Scarlett, his gaze locked on mine as I cock the gun and take aim. The last word he utters to her is, "Go." And that's when I pull the trigger and hit him right in the chest.

"Lycan," Scarlett yells.

"I said fucking go!" His voice booms as he drops to his knees, and Scarlett moves, but she doesn't know the woods like I do.

She runs, and I smile. She knows I will follow. I will always follow her, even if it means I will be walking into the middle of a blood bath.

A war of my own making.

But what Scarlett doesn't know is that Lycan made sure she was bait for the hunter.

THE END... *for now*

BITTER TRUTHS

CRIMSON FALLS DUET BOOK TWO

Hearts break. Tears fall.
The future is dimmed without his light.
But I'll be strong...
The Hunter may have me, but I won't stop believing
the Wolf will find me.

DARIUS

Revenge is a dish best served with a side of vengeance.

I spent my life in the shadows, wanting to hide from the truth that I was nothing more than a product of my father's indiscretions. And even in the darkness, I knew the truth—nothing can mend what my father had broken.

Now I'm here, waiting, racing through the woods after a pretty little girl I learned is my niece. Her grandmother, my biological mother, had me when she was young and abandoned me. She left me with my father, then went off and married someone else. Anger surges as I recall the day she told me her story. When I asked for proof, she gave me the test results.

Darkness shrouds my actions as I near her running form, her white dress torn and dirty from her escape, but I'm almost there. I'm so close I can smell her fear as it emanates from her supple skin. I can hear her short breaths, and I can't stop my cock from jolting. Perhaps I shouldn't think about her sweetness in that way, maybe I'm broken, but seeing her run from me makes me hungry to have a taste.

Just a bite.

It couldn't hurt.

The woods are dense, but through the dark brown of the trunks, I focus on the white, the slight frame of the beauty that's running for her life. But what she doesn't know is I'm a hunter, one that can so easily capture her, but the chase is a part of who I am. It runs through my veins. Shaw blood burns hot when we're chasing our prey. Even Lycan knows this, and perhaps that's why he told her to run. He knew I'd enjoy this. He must've.

The last thing she heard was my brother shouting for her to run from me. And now, as I howl out into the darkness, I inhale her fear along with that sweet nectar of her perfume.

When she reaches the breach in the trees, a scream catapults from her lips when she realizes my family is waiting. The bikers who took me in as a young rebel are there, their arms wrap around her, and the moment she's bound, I stop behind her, knowing my breath is hot in her ear.

"Your wolf is dead," I tell her while fisting my hands

at my sides. I want to hurt her, but that will come. And when it does, she'll wish she was dead. A sob of pure agony tumbles free from her mouth, and I can't help but smile.

Slade throws her into his truck, which had been waiting as I chased her through the woods. The SUV I hired is still parked near the house where Lycan's men will find it. I made sure of that. When they do, they'll see exactly what I want my brother to find.

I shot him. Twice.

Leaving him for dead was part of my plan, but a part of me wonders if he'll ever survive the wounds I inflicted. And I wonder if he'll get the gift which I left for him before he takes his last breath.

Bear pulls up beside me on his bike. The truck behind us keeps a safe distance, but I can practically feel Scarlett's rage from the backseat. I didn't plan on taking her. I wanted her dead, along with my brother, but stealing her is definitely a bonus.

Call it collateral. Grace will never want her granddaughter hurt, which means she'll ensure I don't take my anger out on the girl. Without my emotions, I can easily make Scarlett bleed for being born, but I'll keep her alive to ensure I get my money.

Hatred is the only thing I feel. Guilt no longer rules my life. When Grace told me what had happened in the past, she gave no inkling that I was even loved, so why should I care about her, or her little granddaughter?

I thought for a moment that Lycan would see the

truth, that he'd finally stand beside me, but the moment affection flashed in his eyes for the girl, I knew I had lost him for good.

I waited, craved even, just to see my brother again, the boy I grew up with. But he was long gone.

For years we'd been at war, and now that war has ended by my hand. I focus on the road ahead, which will soon be riddled with teams of men who will seek vengeance for Lycan. But I'll be long gone.

My brother tracked me for years, but never caught me. I had to walk into his home for him to finally see me, but even then, I was in control. As always.

We head out onto the highway which will take us far from Crimson Falls, and with every mile I put between me and that shit hole, I feel the tension in my muscles ease.

Time and again I've wanted Lycan to see the truth behind all those old books and open those brick walls he loves to hide behind. I wanted him to realize things aren't always as they seem. I loved Crimson Falls once. I didn't want to leave. However, my home, everything I knew, was a lie.

When we reach the compound five hours later, it's dark, but I'm eager to see her, talk to her. Swinging my leg over my bike, I turn to see Bear and Slade pulling the little minx out of the backseat. Her screaming and kicking are no match for the two burly men.

Bear grips her around the middle, lifting her as if she weighs nothing.

"Take her to the basement," I instruct him. "It's time for us to have a little family meeting."

He nods, moving to the back of the house where we have a shed with a basement. This is where we take the assholes who try to fuck with us. And it's where I interrogate them, ensuring they spill the beans about everything and everyone.

The staircase is gritty under my boots. The suit I'm still wearing doesn't fit in with the dirty room I enter. "There's my little niece," I grin as I near her. Bear has her bound to a chair, blood dripping from her mouth. "What happened?"

"Bit down on my fucking hand," he growls, showing me the teeth marks Scarlett left on the flesh between his thumb and forefinger.

I can't help but chuckle. "Feisty little thing. Aren't you?" I question, looking into eyes that remind me of her mother's. So many secrets, so little time.

"Fuck you!" Fire blazes in her glare, and I can't help but remind myself that she's not her mother. She's definitely not Marinda, the woman I fucked hard against their kitchen counter while Horatio was sitting in Heaven with young women on his lap. But Scarlett doesn't know that. She reminds me so much of her mother, beautiful, filled with anger, and yet I can't stop my dick from throbbing behind my zipper.

"Such a filthy mouth," I observe. "Is that why Lycan was so enraptured by you?" Arching my brow, I don't wait for her to answer before I pull out my phone. I quickly find what I'm looking for and hit dial, tapping the speaker icon so Scarlett can hear.

"Hello?"

"Dad! Help me!" She screeches at the top of her lungs Even though hearing her beg should ensure the need for revenge is satiated, it's only anger that seems to surge through me and I backhand her across her face so hard, the chair topples over, taking Scarlett to the ground with it.

"What the fuck? Scarlett, is that you? What's happening?" The panicked tone of Horatio Bardot is like music to my ears.

"So many questions, Horatio," I finally respond after a moment. "I think your little girl needs a daddy," I tell him, my smirk curling as the pretty redhead glares up at me from the floor. Bear moves to pick her up, but I raise a hand to stop him.

"If you hurt my—"

"Do you care?" I challenge, cutting him off. "Because weren't you the one who signed her life over to Lycan Shaw?"

His response is guilty silence.

Tears glimmer in his daughter's eyes. Horatio doesn't know who I am. His mother never told him about his half-brother. But now isn't the time for a family reunion.

"What do you want?" The resignation in his tone makes me smile. First this bastard, and then his mother. I'll make sure they both pay for what they did to me, to my father, and to Lycan. As much as I hate my brother, he is blood.

"Fifty million in an account which cannot be traced. I'll

send you the details." My gaze fixes on Scarlett. "I don't need any negotiations on this. It's the money for your daughter. Or will you sell her out again?" I hang up before the asshole can answer me or question why I'm doing this.

"Cut," a voice calls from behind me, calling me by my club name, which causes me to turn. "Ambulance arrived at the Shaw mansion, Lycan is in ICU, doesn't look good." Kai, our enforcer looks at me before his gaze lands on Scarlett. The flicker of desire in his eyes dance like a flame as he takes her in. The torn dress, which is gritty with dirt, her face has a couple of scratches along with my large handprint, the blood caked on her mouth, and the way her eyes flash with pure venom makes her every fucker's wet dream.

"Good. Keep me updated."

He nods but doesn't leave immediately. "If you need a hand..." He allows the sentence to hang heavy with promise. There is no doubt in my mind that every man who's sitting in the clubhouse would love to be left alone with Scarlett. And I doubt she'd survive.

"Leave," I order, keeping my tone level. I don't need them to know she's something to me. All they know is that she's collateral.

I don't trust people with information they don't need. This job has been in the making for years. And now that it's finally here, I can't have anyone fucking it up. I glance at Bear, who's awaiting his orders. The man is an animal, but he's tame compared to Kai.

"I've got it from here," I grit, needing to be alone with

her for a moment.

"Sure, boss. Let me know if you need me down here." He glances once more at Scarlett before leaving us. The heavy thud of his steps echoes as he reaches the first floor and shuts the door behind him.

Once we're alone, I turn to her. "Would you like to sit up?"

"Fuck you!" She spits blood and saliva on the floor, which will only mix with the rest of the crimson from our evenings down here questioning criminals.

"You know, we can do this the hard way," I taunt. "I quite like it like that. I'm sure my brother trained you for the darkness that comes with a good hard beating."

Shock paints her pretty face like a mask as she regards me. I may not be able to fuck her violently, but I can make her scream. And I'm certain it would be a beautiful symphony to listen to.

"Why are you doing this?" Her plea is quieter than her curse. Tears trickle down her face, falling to the floor where her head is leaning on the cold concrete.

Tipping my head to the side, I regard her for a long while, contemplating if I should admit my pain to her. "Do you know what it's like to be sent away by your own parents?"

Scarlett's gaze lingers on my face before she nods. "Yes, yes, I happen to know what that's like. From the outside, my life might seem perfect. It might look like I have everything, but my father *sold* me to Lycan. He signed my life away."

"Did he? I mean, you didn't seem all too bothered to walk down the aisle to marry my brother." Rage simmers through me. Her words only seem to turn up the heat on my already volatile emotions. Perhaps that's why Lycan was so taken with her. She does something to a man. Her sweet innocence mingled with the seductiveness of a vixen.

"No, I wanted to marry him because I learned to love him," she spits out, a sneer curling her pretty face, and I want nothing more than to grip her by the neck and haul her up to my level where we're eye to eye. I want to see the fear in her eyes, not the goddamned fire. Because that shit makes me hard as fuck.

"And you think he loves you too?" I challenge. I've known my brother all my life. He isn't capable of love. Even when *she* left him all those years ago, I knew he didn't love Yasmine. She was nothing more than a slave he could find pleasure with. She enjoyed the darkness he exuded.

"Yes." Comes Scarlett's response. It's a mere whisper. And if it weren't so quiet down here, I wouldn't have heard it. "You killed him."

"Not yet," I answer quickly. It seems the shots weren't fatal. There's always time to right my wrongs. "But I'm sure when I see him again, I'll finish the job." Shrugging, I turn to grab a chair and drag it along the cold concrete, making sure that the noise is loud enough to cause Scarlett pain.

"Why do you hate him so much? Why do you hate me?"

I settle in my seat while considering her questions. When people are in danger, or when they're hurting, that's the question they always throw out. *Why?*

I ponder my response for a while, wondering if I should tell her more about myself. If I should offer her honesty. "I wanted nothing more than a family to care for, but what I got instead was shame for being who and what I was."

She shifts, tilting her head so she can truly look at me. But it's when she finally speaks, do I realize she's really concerned. "I don't understand."

It's not a plastered-on worry that's creasing her brows. She truly has no clue what her family is like.

SCARLETT

He looks at me with an expression much like his brother's. I didn't realize it was him when I walked out of my bedroom, but now that I'm really looking at him, I notice the similarity to Lycan.

"When I was born, my mother gave me up because I wasn't the son of the man she was marrying. She didn't want me." I want to shrug it off, to act as if it didn't hurt me. Back then, it cut like a mother fucking blade, straight to the heart. Now though, I've learned to hone my pain into anger.

Scarlett shakes her head. "You can't know that."

"I do, because she told me." His expression, drenched

Bardot mansion, she gave me a job, not realizing who I was. I spent months with her, learning about who she was. When I realized my mother was a cold-hearted bitch, I knew I could never find happiness or family with her."

There's breathtaking agony in Darius's tone, which has me wanting to comfort him, but this is a man who stole me and shot my husband. His fucking brother. I have to remind myself there's nothing human about him. He's nothing more than a criminal.

Then what was Lycan?

My chest tightens when I think about him. All I can do is hope and pray he pulls through, and I can convince Darius to let me see him. Once Darius gets the money from my father, I'm sure he'll release me. Hurting me won't do him any good. He must know that.

"Can you please help me up?" I whisper, trying to break through the fog of rage that's so clear in his eyes. He moves slowly, and my gaze trails his movements. He pulls out contact lenses, turning his eyes to a similar green as Lycan's.

Now, without the eye color differentiating them, I realize Darius looks just like his brother. Their father must have some very strong genes because when I look at Darius, I don't see any resemblance to my grandmother.

Darius rises then, as if he forgot I was here for a moment, pushing the chair which I'm bound to upright. The pain radiating through my arms eases slightly. He leans over, fixing me with a glare so harsh, my lungs struggle to pull in air. Darius can't be a Bardot, or half Bardot, because he's all Shaw. Which begs the question, *where did he get those maternity results?*

"Who told you my grandmother was your birth mother?" I ask, knowing he might get angry and slap me, or hurt me, but I need to know. I have to figure out how he would believe her over his father.

"Your grandmother graciously provided a test." His voice is pure grit and gravel, once again sounding just like his brother's. But something doesn't make sense. Why would she agree to a test or provide one when she knew he would want to hurt me, or Lycan for that matter?

My grandmother is strong-willed, and she's not someone who would give in so easily. Not even for her own son. My father had to beg and plead for any and everything he wanted, and he'd have to work his ass off before she even considered his request.

"What if she lied to you?" My voice is a low whisper, praying he doesn't lose control in the small space of the basement. "I don't think Grace is your mother. I've known her my whole life, and something doesn't make sense."

"Oh?" Darius arches a brow. "And what is that, *princess?*" he sneers, using the moniker in a condescending tone which ripples through me.

"My grandmother isn't someone who would offer information about herself without a price attached to it." I keep my gaze on his, hoping he can see the truth in my eyes. I can't afford for him to get angry right now, because if he can trust me, perhaps he'll let me go.

At least, I hope so.

"She will always want something in return. I doubt she told you to hurt me, or to kill Lycan." Guilt flickers in his gaze, and I wonder if I hit the nail on the head.

Darius pushes away from me, the chair rocking on its legs, and I pray it doesn't fall over again. Thankfully it doesn't. Cold seeps through me from my feet on the icy floor, and the chilly air that surrounds me has me shivering.

"I'm done with this bullshit," Darius says suddenly. "You'll stay here until I figure out what's going on." He spins on his heel, his gaze landing on me. For a moment, he says nothing, but then he shrugs off the suit jacket he's wearing and settles it over my shoulders.

"Thank you," I say, grateful for the bit of tenderness he's offering. "If... If you hear anything..." I'm unsure how to ask him what I need to, but I hope he'll know what I mean.

His gaze lingers on me, taking in my face as he moves up the stairs without responding. I want to scream, to beg him to tell me the moment he hears news about Lycan's condition, but I don't. Pleading doesn't work with him.

But the moment I let out my breath, Darius surprises me by slowly turning to regard me from the threshold, then nodding. "I'll tell you if I hear anything." He turns to leave, and I watch him walk up the steps until he reaches the door. He stops, glances at me once more before he says, "I've never seen him in love before. No other woman has ever affected him like you do." And then he's gone, leaving my heart bleeding for more news on Lycan's condition.

When Lycan told me to run, he promised me he'd be okay, that he would come for me, but if he's in the hospital, I don't know how he'll ever find me. Perhaps he'll have Kahn and his team come for me. Maybe, just maybe, I'll survive this.

I have to.

Glancing around the room, I take in the shelves on either wall. There's a small window beside the top shelf to my left, but I could never fit through it, even if I could get loose. A metal table sits to my right, and on it are tools—a spanner, a hammer, a few screwdrivers—but I have a feeling they're used for anything but fixing things.

The stench of blood is rife through the small, stuffy space. A thought comes to me and I quickly shimmy the chair over to the table. If I can stand, I can reach for something on the surface, untie my hands, and perhaps I can free myself and get out of here.

I'm not sure how many men are in the house or even on the property, but I can't sit here and wait for Darius to return.

By the time I've shifted toward the table, the door creaks open, and soon enough, I'm staring at a young, tattooed guy who looks at me as if I am his next meal. He takes the stairs one at a time, slowly, predatory, and I realize I'm in trouble if he gets a hold of me.

"Boss man says you're off limits," he says, his accent thick, but I can't quite place it. When he reaches the last stair, he jumps to the ground with both feet landing hard.

"But I enjoy breaking rules." His lips curl, and his eyes flash with dangerous hunger as he regards me.

"I think you should listen to *boss man*," I whisper the moniker given to Darius, because I can only imagine what he would do to this boy if something happened to me. I'm the reason he'll get paid, and if I'm hurt, my father won't give these bastards a cent.

The young man closes the distance between us. The threat of him being so close sends ice racing through my veins, a shiver wracks my body as he stops inches from me. I'm not in the best position to fight back. But I want nothing more than to hurt him if he touches me.

I'm married.

Those two words steal the air from my lungs. And the thought of Lycan in hospital hits me right in the chest. I double over, a sob breaking through my fear as I realize I am married. I'm Mrs. Scarlett Shaw, and my husband is in ICU because his brother shot him.

"What the fuck's your problem?" The boy asks, and I wonder briefly if he'll think I've lost my ever-loving mind. Perhaps my reaction will send him running. I can only hope. His hand reaches for me, grips my neck, and brings me closer to his face as he practically lifts me with one arm. He holds me hostage with a look of pure, filthy desire. "I wonder if you'll bite my dick off when I shove it down your throat." His words are filled with venom.

I look into his eyes, a bright blue resembling that of a tropical ocean as it shimmers with dappled sunlight. But there's nothing good about this boy. He must be eighteen at the most. I wonder how he came into this life.

"Leave me the fuck alone," I bite out before I spit in his face, only to earn myself a slap so hard the thick taste of metal coats my tongue. Grinning manically, I spit the crimson liquid to the ground before glancing up at the boy. Because that's what he is, a boy. "You can hurt me as much as you like, I'm not going down without a fight."

"Nam." A heavy voice bounces against the walls, warning clear in the tone as the young boy pales. When he spins around, a fist slams into his jaw, and I hear the crack which causes me to wince even though I haven't been struck.

"Boss man," Nam whimpers, clutching his jaw. "I-I... I didn't—"

"Aye, you fucking didn't do shit. Get your ass back upstairs and clean the fucking kitchen, you sack of shit." Darius's deep growl even has me cowering. I watch as Nam races up the stairs. As soon as the door shut, Darius crouches down as he pulls out a piece of cloth from his pocket and dabs at my mouth. "I'm sorry."

"Why? Didn't you want me to pay?" I shouldn't poke the bear, he's just saved me from some little bastard, but I can't stop myself.

"No. You weren't meant to get hurt. I'm not one for spilling blood unnecessarily." He looks at me, locking his gaze with mine, and I can tell he's not lying.

"What about Lycan's?" It's a challenge I'm not sure I'll win, but I have to try.

DARIUS

She's right.

Fuck, she's so fucking right.

"Yeah," I respond in a whisper of regret and guilt. "That was... That was my anger that took a hold of me, it got the better of me and I allowed it." As much as I hate admitting I was wrong, I have to because it's true. I wanted my brother to pay for staying in that house, for being the favorite son, but all this time, all I did was rob myself of a family I could've had with him. And now, he's in fucking ICU because of me.

The rage which fueled my actions as it burned through me has simmered into almost nothing. It's still warm in my veins, but as I consider her words, and my response, my chest tightens. Lycan is still my brother. It doesn't help that his wife keeps needling away at my anger, getting in my head with her words.

"I need to know if he's okay," Scarlett pleads, her eyes shining with pain and worry.

I realize I've done this to her. Not just her, but Lycan too. I've taken so much, and yet, I'm the one who's lost everything.

I want to be angry at how much she loves him. I also want to tell her he's not capable of love, but I saw the way he looked at her. After seeing how he shoved her out of the way, standing in the line of fire to save her, I'd be lying if I denied my brother's love for this woman.

"I will tell you as soon as there's an update." I turn away, not wanting to see her cry because her tears don't fill me with happiness anymore. The emotions twisting inside me feel like a fucking tornado ripping through a town, leaving nothing in its wake. I'll be nothing.

The thought consumes me, and as I run my fingers through my hair, I tug fiercely at the strands. The sting grounding me to the moment. I need the pain to remind myself of what's real. For a long time, I would get lost in memories, in things people have said, stories I've heard, and I found that pain was the only way to remain grounded.

Agony reveals truth.

No matter how bitter it tastes.

"Darius," Scarlett calls to me, her voice like silk along

my skin. "There's no reason for you to hate me, or Lycan. We would be here for you no matter what."

My blood simmers, and I have to swallow down the rage that's slowly fueling itself through me. The need to cause pain overwhelms me, and before I have time to think, I spin on my heel. My hand latches onto the thick red waves that feel like satin in my fist. A gasp of surprise falls from Scarlett's lips, and I find myself wanting to steal the sound with my mouth.

How the fuck am I so attracted to her? Lured in like a fish in a net.

She's a siren.

"Don't talk to me like I'm nothing more than a wayward child you're attempting to placate." My voice is gruff, the thickness in my throat choking the words from me. "You're here, taken from my brother as revenge. I couldn't steal the house, his money, or the fucking club from him. But you, he feels something for you, and this will hurt him more than any worldly possession. Emotion is weakness," I inform her, something I'd learned a long time ago. "Never mistake the war raging within me, for goodness. There is nothing good inside me. Not anymore."

Her gaze burns with frustration. "You're a lost fucking cause," Scarlett bites out. "I wasn't trying to placate you," she grits. "I'm someone who offers kindness when I see it's needed. I'm human. I grew up without love in my life. My family planned my future since I was a kid, and I can see pain when I look at you. The same pain Lycan lives with, and the exact agony that I have long since learned to master."

Her words shock me. I didn't think my brother felt anything. He never did when we were younger. When our mother died, or rather, when *his* mother died, he didn't shed a tear. There were times I wondered if he even realized she wasn't coming back.

Emotions are weakness.

At least that's what our father told us. It was something we feared because if we had any feelings at all, he would slam it right out of us.

"Any affection you hold for someone is something they can use against you," Dad says, his cigar sitting between his lips. He lost mom, but there's a darkness that resides in him now, and I can't put it down to mourning. "Never allow anyone to have that power over you," he warns before taking a long drag on the fat Cuban which billows smoke from the red-tipped cherry.

"I can't miss mom?" I ask, knowing Lycan won't even bother questioning him. The black sheep, that's who I am. I don't obey, I don't follow the rules, I may as well be the outcast because that what it feels like.

Instead of responding, he lifts the paperweight in his hand, and for some reason, I flinch. Usually, I'm not scared of anything, of anyone, but with my father, he's like a bomb waiting to explode, and the moment he detonates is the day we'll all be left in pieces on the ground.

"This symbolizes emotions," he tells me before lobbing the heavy glass ball at me, which I quickly dive to catch because I'm

sure if it had fallen and shattered, he would take a belt to my ass. "See how they weigh you down?" He chuckles at this.

It's as if he's made one of the best jokes in the world, but as he laughs, he wheezes, and I wonder when that cigar is going to kill him.

One day.

I hope.

It may not be good to wish death on your father, but I do. Every fucking day. At sixteen, you'd think I'm stronger, that I can handle his bullshit, but each moment I spend with him, my anger seems to grow. It's an entity on its own now.

"Dad, I think we get it," Lycan offers, his voice placating, but there's no doubt in my mind Conall won't get angry at him. He'll merely grin as if Lycan's words are soothing.

"Good, now go off and have fun. You're teenagers!"

As if that's going to change anything.

I set the paperweight on his desk, but Conall grabs my hand in his fist and holds me hostage. "Be careful of who you trust," he warns in a low growl. I consider his words for a long moment before it dawns on me. He means because he's seen me with the boy next door.

Dad hasn't told me why, but each time he's seen the young boy here, he's given me a warning, a threat to keep me in line. I'm not sure what it is about him, or them, but my father hates the Bardots. The boy lives with his parents, but I don't see much of his dad, only the mother. We may not be best friends, but he seems to be a cool kid.

"Yes, sir," I answer in an attempt to get free, and for a

When I focus back on Scarlett, she's watching me intently. I move toward her, my hands extending to untie the rope, and the moment she's free, she sighs. "Thank you."

My gaze latches onto her wrists as she massages them, her thumbs circling the smooth, delicate skin. The door to the basement opens, and I'm met with Howler. He's our tech genius. I put him on the case to find out if the records Grace Bardot gave me were legit.

Working for her under the ruse of another name was something I did to get access to her home, to possibly learn what happened to my father. I knew it was the Bardots who killed him, I just needed to prove it. Then one day I finally admitted to Grace who I was, she was shocked. She hadn't seen me in years, so she didn't recognize the man before her from the boy she must have remembered being the son of the man she once loved.

When Grace offered me the folder, I read the results and my heart hurt. For the first time in years, I allowed that useless fucking organ to do its thing, to experience pain. I let fucking weakness in.

It's been almost eight months since I found out the truth. Even though I was on her property, on the grounds of the Bardot Manor, she never once came to me. There wasn't even an inkling that she wanted to know who I was, and as time passed, I learned little tidbits about her.

When Lycan's plan caught my attention, the contract he signed to marry Scarlett, I realized I had to make a move. And thankfully, the little one walked right into my clutches the night she wandered into the garden. In a way, I helped my brother capture her, but now she's here, and I'm not letting her get away until I get what I want.

"Got something for me?" I ask Howler when he reaches me. His face giving nothing away. The man has one expression—stoic. Even if he's in a good mood, you can never tell.

He hands me a printout, which I scan slowly. The details on the page tell me that Grace Bardot is a lying bitch. One that I need to put an end to. The test results she gave me were nothing more than fabricated lies. But that doesn't make sense.

Why lie about a child you never had?

"Was I right?" Scarlett says, still not standing. She looks up at me with those soulful eyes, and I want nothing more than to see just why my brother was so intrigued by her. I wonder briefly what she'd feel like. Now that the truth has been revealed, Scarlett is not my family, she's fair game.

Would she fall for me like she did Lycan? We are brothers, after all.

"Yes," I admit, keeping the gruffness out of my voice. I offer her the printout before turning to Howler. "Find everything on Grace. I want to know all about her, even things she's had sealed. The Bardot family are keeping secrets, and I want them all uncovered and brought to light."

He nods quickly. "Sure thing." His gaze falls on Scarlett, before he looks at me and the corner of his mouth ticks so infinitesimally, if I wasn't staring at him, I would've missed it. But the knowledge is in his eyes. She's gorgeous, and she's ours now.

Howler leaves, shutting the door behind him, and I turn my attention back to the pretty redhead. "You'll come upstairs with me. Any fucking games, I will kill you. Make no mistake, you might be owned by Lycan Shaw, but right now, you are property of Darius Shaw, and around here, that means a hell of a lot more."

Scarlett looks at me, and for a moment, I think she's going to fight me on what I just said, but she doesn't. "Okay." Is all she says before she rises, and I'm once again met with just how beautiful she is close up.

"Good girl," I murmur, knowing what my brother would've taught her. And the thought of that only serves to make my dick jolt with appreciation.

SCARLETT

"Good girl." The two words have emotions coiling within me. I want nothing more than to hear the praise coming from Lycan, but I have to remind myself that the man beside me is the reason I can't.

Darius leads me up the steps, and out into the backyard of a large estate. I'm not sure where we are in the country, but there doesn't seem to be anything for miles. I wonder if Kahn and his team could find me.

They've been following Darius for years, keeping tabs on him. The only reason I even have an inkling of this is because Lycan told me, but would they find this place, and even if they did, would they be able to free me?

When we reach the large two-story house, I note the women who hang around, some sitting on the laps of guys in leather, and others merely leaning against the wall smoking.

The sun is setting on the horizon behind the house, and the sky is a deep orange hue, with shades of pink and purple slowly taking over as night swallows the light. Music blares from the speakers attached to the outer wall of the house, and there's an enormous fire pit with dancing flames where a metal pole twirls around, roasting a whole pig. The sight has my stomach roiling, and I have to swallow down the acid to keep from puking.

Darius tugs me behind him, and soon, we're inside a kitchen which looks like it belongs in a farmhouse with wooden surfaces and thick beams of oak holding up the ceiling.

Against one wall is a stove big enough to cook for a family of, I can only guess, about fifty people. It's warm inside, and as we move deeper into the house, I take in the country-style furnishings. Darius leads me up the stairs, down the hall, and into a bedroom which matches the rest of the house.

A four-poster bed with heavy wooden beams on each corner. The bedspread is a dark brown, with white sheets underneath. The pillows match the blanket. Everything is rustic which gives the space a homely feel, and even though this isn't my home, I can tell the people who live here love it.

"You'll sleep in here." Darius points at the king-sized bed. "I'll be over there," he tells me as his finger points to the sofa in the corner of the room.

"In the same room?" I spin on my heel, my gaze catching his. "I can't do that."

"Why? Scared you'll want me between those pretty thighs?" he challenges, as his eyes spark to life. Desire clear in them. Now that he's aware we're not related by blood, he wouldn't stop himself from taking me. But would he force himself on me? I don't know.

"I'm married."

He guffaws at my words. "Oh, I don't doubt it, sweetheart," he tells me. "But my brother and I have shared women before. We've even fucked them at the same time." Fire dances in his eyes, the shade of green so similar to that of my husband's as he peruses me. The color blazing like a gemstone in the sunshine.

My brows furrow in confusion, and shock. "You know I'm married?"

"I can have Howler find out anything I want. And you'd be surprised at how much I have learned about you, little one," he tells me before eating up the distance between us in a few small steps.

He reaches for my face, his fingers tugging a strand of my red hair as he brings it to his nose to inhale the scent. The motion causing me to tremble, with fear, and with intrigue. This man has violence emanating from him like a cologne, but there's something softer about him.

"All those dirty little secrets you hold, I can find out about them with a snap of my fingers." He leans in further, his lips at my ear. "I can even find out how wet your pretty cunt gets when my brother pins you down, when he holds you to the ground and shoves his cock inside you. I bet it makes you scream."

His words send heat and shame racing through me and my cheeks warm with embarrassment as I try to shove him away, but Darius is huge, and he's far stronger than I am. He laughs when he sees my expression. He's enjoying my discomfort. Perhaps it's turning him on to see my fear as well.

"How would you know what he did to me?" I spit, furious at the thought of him seeing me like that. Of anyone but Lycan seeing me like that.

"Those woods offer darkness and shadows, where evil men can hide," Darius muses as he steps back, allowing me space to breathe. "I used to love seeing you fight back; it made my dick hard." At this, he grips himself through his jeans, and I gasp at the bulge.

"Just let me go, please," I plead with him, hoping he'll realize this is wrong.

"I love a woman who begs. I even enjoy tears. Did you cry the first time my brother fucked you?" he questions, and the words only seem to heat my blood with both rage and desire. Confusion twists in my gut. *How am I getting turned on by this?* "I see he's trained you well. But he doesn't know about your humiliation fetish. Does he?"

My gaze snaps to his. "My what?"

The corner of Darius's mouth curls, the smirk making

him look so much like his brother, it's scary. How did he ever think they aren't blood? Granted, I've never seen their father, so perhaps they look more like him than their mother.

"You're still so new to this world. So innocent in what you want to admit," he speaks, before turning to the chair which sits at a desk in the opposite corner of the room, while I'm pressed against the cool wooden beam.

"What world? You mean the fact that your brother enjoys tying me up?" I challenge, causing Darius's stare to flash with heated desire. That's exactly what he means.

"I'm certain he's spanked you," he says, and I don't want to respond, but I nod anyway. "And has he shown you what it's like to have your pretty, delicate throat fucked?" Another challenge, one which makes my cheeks heat.

"I'm not talking to you about this." Folding my arms across my chest, I settle on the mattress because I'm scared my knees are about to give out. Nerves have gotten a hold of me, and I'm not sure I'm going to be able to talk to Darius for much longer. As much as I want to admit things with confidence, I can't because I'm still... like he said, *new to this world.*

"Why?" When he regards me, I notice the interest he pins me with. I'm not like other women, certainly not ones that Lycan and Darius are used to. Perhaps he'll be able to tell me about the woman at the club, the one who Lycan didn't want to talk about.

"The woman you shared," I start, hoping he'll offer

some answers. "Is she someone still in his life?" My heart constricts, my chest tightens when he narrows his eyes, and I think I've made a mistake in asking him.

"Why, little one? Are you jealous?" He waggles his dark brows at me, and I can't stop myself from rolling my eyes. "There are ways to make Lycan jealous," he offers with a salacious wink.

"I'm not going to sleep with you," I tell him. "I want to go back to him, please."

"No can do. I'm waiting on your daddy to send me my payment," Darius informs me. "Once that's done, I'll decide what to do with you." His words hold a dark threat.

Before I have time to think, I push to my feet and race for the door, but Darius is fast, and his hand slams against the wood before I can pull it open and slip out. His large, looming body pins me against the hard surface, and the thickness I feel against my ass causes a shudder to race through me, and a whimper of surprise stumbles from my lips.

"That's all for you, little one," Darius promises, grinding his hips against me. "Would you like us both inside your fragile body?" he asks, his words a warm hiss of pleasure when I push back against him in an attempt to free myself, but all I only succeed in turning him on further.

"You don't want to do this," I warn him, shutting my eyes so tight, attempting to focus, to calm my erratic breaths. My hands shove at his chest, but he's more than double my size. Memories assault me, but even with those come shame, so I shake my head to clear my thoughts. "If you hurt me, there is no going back from that, Darius."

He stills.

It's true. And he knows it.

If something happened to me, Lycan would kill his brother.

"Stay here," he says finally, stepping away from me. His hand grips my arm, and he tugs me away from the door before he opens it and steps out into the hallway. "And if you try anything, and I do mean anything, I won't think twice about binding you to my bed." He shuts the heavy wooden door and leaves me glaring at the grain. The lock clicks, and I realize I'm in this for the long haul. There is no escape. The same way I was a prisoner of Lycan's for so long, I'm now stuck with his brother.

Sighing, I move to the window. The heavy curtains are open, and I can see far beyond the high walls that surround the house. In the distance is a city, but I can't really tell from here where I am. There isn't many houses close by, and when I open the window, breathing in the fresh air, I can't smell the ocean, so at least I'm sure we're not on the coast.

Leaving the window, I pad over to the wardrobe which I find is a large walk in, and inside are rows of denim and leather. Heavy biker boots sit in tidy rows on the carpet, and in the center of the space is a countertop with drawers. I try each one, finding them locked, and instinct tells me there could be weapons inside.

Abandoning my search, I head back into the bedroom

and to the door opposite the closet. Inside is a bathroom which is smaller than I expect, with only a shower above the corner tub, and a single wash basin which has a mirror hanging above it.

When I glance at my reflection, I gasp. My hair is a mess, and tears have distorted my perfectly made-up face. I quickly open the tap and splash my face. I grab the bar of soap sitting in its dish and lather up my hands before scrubbing my palms over my cheeks and my closed eyes.

By the time I'm done, I look refreshed, and my hair looks partly normal with just using my fingers to run through the unruly strands. I step back and consider changing my clothes. Maybe even showering. But I'm not sure when Darius is going to come back, and if he does, I don't want him to find me naked.

The thought of him knowing about my needs, my desires, and knowing about what Lycan and I have done makes me nervous. Yes, I've found solace in the way Lycan would pin me down, in the way he'd push inside me, force himself on top of me, it made me come harder than I ever have. Even just the memory seems to cause the burn on my cheeks and my stomach to twist with need.

I recall the first time I read about it. I'd picked up a novel, wanting to get lost in the wispy romance, but in the end, it was the darkness that enveloped me, and I was lost to the depraved acts. Reading about how the woman enjoyed being out of control, how she loved having the heaviness of her partner pinning her down, I found myself entranced.

When I did finally have sex, it wasn't even close to what I'd fantasized about. I thought I was broken, that I couldn't orgasm, no matter how many times I had been with Bryden, my ex from college. He was sweet, gentle, and as much as I wanted to enjoy it, my needs ran darker.

My mind played out the scenarios I read about. And only then could I find my release. And now Darius knows about those cravings as well.

Back in the bedroom, I settle on the mattress and curl up, leaning my head on the soft pillows. The comfortable mattress makes me sigh. My eyes flutter as weariness overtakes me.

"Don't go into the garden at night." A warning. A threat.

Eyes follow me as I meander through the house. I can feel them, but I can't see them. Someone is out there. Perhaps that's why my father told me not to go out at night when I was little. This house has been haunted for a long time. I read stories about the old Bardot mansion, but I never truly realized just how eerie it is.

As a little girl, I was convinced nothing could touch me. My father was my hero, big and scary, and I believed he would save me from the darkness. But now, as I walk through the halls, I'm certain he would allow me to be stolen if he could save himself.

I've learned the man I always thought a hero is nothing more than a selfish bastard.

That's what my mother called him, anyway.

The fighting started more the older I got. I'm not sure why.

Every night, Dad would be out with friends, he'd come home drunk, and he and Mom would be at each other's throats. Now, at sixteen, I've learned to focus on me, not them.

The fear that trickled through me the first night I heard them is now gone. I've since learned adults aren't perfect, even though they expect children to be. My father is nothing short of a bully, but my mother isn't any better.

She wants to be seen as perfect.

But she hides a series of secrets that I'm certain would hurt our whole family.

It's no secret she's not faithful to Dad. I overheard her on her cellphone a few times, talking to someone. A stranger. But I never can tell who it is. Perhaps one day I should steal her phone and try to figure out who she's talking to. Maybe then I can fix our family.

When I open the porch door, I feel it, warmth cascading over my body. The nightdress I'm wearing is tiny, hitting me under the butt, and barely covering my chest. The sleeveless material offers no comfort, but it's too hot to wear anything else.

I look out over the garden, trying to adjust my vision to the black that greets me. For a moment, I'm sure I see a figure moving in the trees, but as soon as it appeared, it's gone in the next second, and a cold shiver grips me as it slowly travels from the back of my neck to the base of my spine.

"The wolf and the hunter will always find you, little red," a voice comes from the darkness, causing me to yelp in surprise. *And that's when the thick fingers wrap around my neck and hold me in place.*

"No! No!" My eyes snap open and I find luminous

green staring back at me. Darius smirks as he hovers over my thrashing body.

"Boo," he murmurs along my mouth, the warmth of his breath fanning over my face, and I attempt to lift my knee to kick him in the crotch, but he's fast, grabbing my leg before I can make any contact.

"Get off me!"

He obeys without taunting. "What were you dreaming about?" he asks as he moves a tray from the desk to the bed. He sets it down, and I take in the mug of coffee, and a plate of toast with cheese melting into the bread.

The dream, or rather, the memory, messed with my mind, and I can't focus on when that was. It feels like the past, a long time ago, but it also feels eerily like the present. I recall my childhood with clarity, but there are moments that seem almost... missing.

Since the first night I heard my folks fighting, till the day Lycan took me, I had strange dreams in the Bardot house. As if I was always meant to be stolen by the hunter and taken by the wolf.

But I can't tell Darius that. I can't confess anything to this man. So, instead of explaining what happened, I answer, "Nothing."

"Didn't seem like nothing," he says, a dark brow arching as he regards me. When I don't respond, he doesn't push further, so I grab the coffee and gulp it down quickly. The heat scorching my tongue, but the caffeine offering me a sense of calm.

"Thank you," I say instead. "This is good." I hold up the mug which is almost empty.

He smiles then, and my heart lurches in my chest. Each time I look at him, he reminds me of my husband. The man who's wounded because of Darius. "I make a mean coffee."

"What are you going to do now that you know my grandmother isn't your mother?"

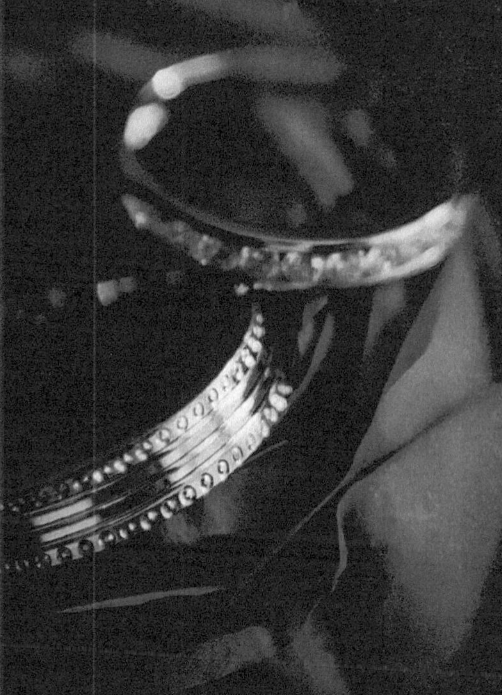

DARIUS

What am I going to do?

I've been so hellbent on revenge; I haven't thought about the *after*.

The way she looks at me makes me feel almost human. That's what Lycan saw, that's what made my brother fall for this girl. And that's what she is, too young for me and him, but she's here, trying to burrow herself in my mind.

"I have to head out for a bit," I tell her. "You'll stay right here while I'm gone. Howler will be right outside if you try any funny shit. And trust me..." I pin her with a stare. "They are under order to do whatever it takes to subdue you." Even though the thought of my men touching her sends rage through me, I can't help but smile when the fire sparks in her pretty eyes.

"I thought you were human," she spits, setting the mug down now that it's empty. She seemed to enjoy it. I make a mental note of how she likes her coffee before I open the door and step over the threshold.

"Never claimed to be, little one." I shut the door behind me, listening to the symphony of her screams from the other side. Howler comes walking up to me, a grin plastered on his face.

"Sounds like your girl is awake," he says, chuckling around the words.

Nodding, I glance over my shoulder at the thick wooden surface. Her hands will get sore eventually, and her throat can't deal with that kind of screaming for too long. "She's a fiery one."

"Let's go," he says, his tone turning serious. "They've got the Treasurer of the Serpents down in the basement. Luckily you took your girl out of there."

"She's not my girl," I bite out, frustration causing my fists to clench at the thought of not having her. Walking down the hall, I listen to the last few whimpers from Scarlett, and I crack my knuckles ensuring I'm ready to take on the bastard they brought in. The Serpents are a club of vile motherfuckers, and the member they brought in for me to talk to is our latest victim. A man who has a mile long list of crimes that would have made my skin crawl if I hadn't seen it before.

Outside, I find my men waiting. We make our way together toward the basement where I had Scarlett when she first arrived on the compound. Thinking about her has me glancing over my shoulder to find her at the bedroom window. Even from this distance, I can feel her anger.

I can't help but tip my fingers in a mock salute as I descend the steps into the darkness where I find William, better known as Billy, to his friends. He's bound to a chair, his mouth gagged with a thick cloth, but his eyes are wide as they take me in.

His muffled pleas fall on deaf ears as I focus on the metal table which holds the implements which I'm about to use on him. "Billy Boy," I greet, chuckling when he tries to mumble, but it's stifled by the gag. "Time for your reckoning."

The fear that skitters in his eyes has elation shooting through me. With having so many fucking emotions coil inside me since I took Scarlett, I need this. The violence and bloodshed. I reach for the cloth, ripping it from his mouth before I step closer toward him.

"Tell me something," I start, lifting the hammer I picked up from the table moments ago. "Did you enjoy those girls you took home after the party a few nights ago?" When my question hits home, his eyes are as wide as fucking dinner plates.

"W-w-what?" he stutters, but he can't deny it because we have proof. When I heard the rumors about this pig using his authority within the club to get teenagers into his car, or on his bike, we kept a close eye on him.

He hasn't slipped up before. But a few nights ago, a party at the edge of the local college campus attracted a few underage girls. The cops got there in time to shut it down, but with the Serpents hanging around, Billy Boy over here managed to pick up a couple of those partygoers and take them back to his place.

"I'm not stupid," I tell him, bringing the hammer down on his knuckles, earning me a howl of agony as the crack of bone echoes in the room. "I hear things. A lot of things."

"I-I didn't do a-anything," he mumbles, before I swing the hammer at his cheek, watching it cave in from the impact. It's small enough to ensure he's still able to speak, but if he was to survive this interrogation, which I'm sure he won't, he will live with a deformity for the rest of his life. And perhaps I should do that to him, to watch him suffer.

"You're telling me those two girls who sat at the police station last night were lying about you?" I tip my head to the side, setting the hammer down, which has relief flushing across Billy's face, but not before I pick up a pair of pliers which will come in handy. His expression, or shall I say half his expression, turns to pure dread when he sees what I'm holding.

"P-please?" he splutters blood, the crimson liquid dripping from his mouth, and a tooth falls from the left side of his lips.

"Shit, I must've gotten one of those pearly whites," I tell him, chuckling. "Now, you're going to tell me more about the job the Serpents are doing for the Cartel," I inform him, lifting the metal tool in my hand while waving it in front of his face.

The threat is clear.

I overheard the rumors about the Serpents stealing youngsters, but Billy didn't give them over to whoever he's working for. He made the mistake of passing out after raping both girls, and thankfully, they escaped.

My blood boiled when I heard their recollection of that night from our informant at the station. Which brings me here, to right the wrongs, to cleanse the sins of the devils. I've done some shit in my life, and some of it wasn't great, but never have I ever forced myself on anyone. I'll kill, I'll maim, but my victims have all deserved it, just like the man before me right now.

"I-I c-c-can't," he whimpers when I clamp his finger in the thick metal teeth. "P-please," he begs. "They'll kill me." I've seen grown men cry, most of them when I've had them in this chair, questioning them about some crime they've committed. And Billy is no different.

"I'll fucking kill you right now. How about that?" I challenge, squeezing the handle of the pliers until I hear the beautiful crack of the knuckle between the metal.

His cries are like music to my ears. I enjoy the torture, it allows me to focus, to realize that what I'm doing is good. I'm righting wrongs. I'm the fucking avenging angel and I enjoy the job.

"I-I can't..." His words falter into the silence as he

regards us. Six burly bastards ready to cut him to shreds because of his twisted mindset. "P-Please..."

"Pass me the gas canister," I order. Howler is the one to grab it, handing it to me with a grin on his face. The asshole loves violence, just like I do. It's in our blood, in our veins. We were born for this life, and even the knowledge of cops who are usually on our doorstep doesn't stop us.

But, if they could do their fucking job, like put shit like this away, then we wouldn't have to do what we are doing right now. Flicking the lighter in front of Billy's face, I watch the flames dance in his fear-filled eyes and I crack a smile.

I twist the cap on the gas, listening to the slosh of liquid escape when I tip the canister. He knows what's coming for him, and his eyes bulge with agonizing fear. It's a beautiful thing to hold someone's life in your hands. Knowing that at any moment, you could snuff them out like a light, and they'll never breathe again.

"Are you going to tell me who you're working for?" I ask again, halting my dousing of his body in the foul smelling liquid, knowing that he's going to break. He's a weakling. It's so clear when his lower lip trembles and the stench of his urine hits my nostrils when I bring the dancing flame closer to his face.

"F-f-father... L-L-Lorenzo," he mumbles, as tears stream from his eyes. "H-he's l-looking for g-g-girls." The moment he mutters the name, I nod, knowing Howler will be on the case, tracking down the bastard we need. I will bring down the organization, and I don't care who I kill to do it.

Without another warning, I bring the gas up and empty the clear liquid on him before flicking the lighter. The sizzle of flesh invades my ears, and the smell of burning skin assaults my nostrils. Justice is being served, and satisfaction courses through my veins.

The screams of a dying man is a sound I never tire of, the same way the moan of a woman is a melody I am addicted to. It's a need, a constant desire to listen, to have life in my hands and then to twist it into either pain or pleasure.

The moment Billy takes his final breath, I hand the gas canister to one of the other guys. I don't even notice who's standing behind me. I shove the lighter into my pocket, making my way out into the garden, needing fresh air.

When my gaze tracks the house, lifting to the second floor, I find her at the window, watching me. She looks beautiful as she stands there, her anger clear, her fear apparent, but her curiosity a fucking aphrodisiac.

Making my mind up, I hurry inside, taking the stairs two at a time, and when I reach my bedroom, I unlock the door, shoving it open. A gasp falls from Scarlett, but I don't pay her any attention. I lock the door and hang the key over my neck.

I can feel her gaze on me. She must smell the gas and death emanating from me like a fucking cologne. Shrugging off my cut, I tug the tee over my head and stop at the entrance to the bathroom.

"Care to join me?" I arch a brow over my shoulder at her.

"Fuck you, Darius!" Her words are spat with venom, but I don't miss how her gaze trails from my torn jeans up my torso before she locks her angry gaze on me.

Shrugging, I chuckle as I head into the room and push the door. I don't close it, leaving a gap just enough for her to peek through, because I'm convinced she will.

My mind flits back to the information we got from Billy. A fucking priest is stealing girls. Now all I need is to find the bastard and end him.

But it won't be a quick job. No, he deserves more than just a quick annihilation. He should get a torturous biblical killing. With a smile on my face, I step into the shower and turn on the taps. It doesn't take long for them to heat, and soon enough, steam fills the room.

The hot spray calms my tense shoulders. I'm lost in lathering the blood off my hands when I think back to the bedroom next door, remembering the woman who's livid at me for capturing her against her will, and I smile.

My hand grips my shaft, thick and hard from just her scent, and I stroke myself with one hand on the tiles to hold me steady. I don't look toward the door; my focus is on my need to find release. Because if I don't, I'll most certainly walk in there and fuck her into my mattress.

And that's when I feel her heated stare fueling the desire coursing through every fucking inch of me.

SCARLETT

His body is so different from Lycan's. There are more scars. Ink runs from his shoulders to his wrists, and his back is a canvas along with his chest. But he's as beautiful as his brother. I shouldn't be here, spying on him while he's in the shower, but my curiosity got the better of me. I'm almost certain he knows I'm looking. Still, I can't drag my gaze away from his big strong hand gripping the thickness of his erection as he strokes himself.

I wonder what he's thinking of. He's obviously just killed or tortured someone. *Does that turn him on?* His hand on the tiles slips, but he shifts it upward, and I can't stop watching his muscles bunch and tense as he finds pleasure.

My thighs squeeze together at the sight, and guilt churns in my stomach as I stare. The man is rugged. There's a violence in him that expels itself every now and then, something that calls to me, and I shake my head to clear my thoughts.

I can't do this.

My feet carry me swiftly to the bed where I settled cross-legged against the headboard. The door is still ajar, the promise of Darius naked and wet just a few meters away. That thought has me squirming on the bed once more, and I pray Lycan will be okay, that he'll wake up and save me.

But what would he save me from?

My own deceitful thoughts?

"Did you enjoy the view?" Darius smirks from the threshold of the bathroom. His hands holding onto the top of the doorframe, as he leans forward wearing only a towel. The dips and peaks of his body dripping wet, and I can't help but note the tattoos that adorn his body.

"I don't know what you're talking about," I respond, turning my attention to the window instead. Although the view outside is nothing like the one I'm trying my best to ignore.

He knows he has an effect on me, which is bad.

He moves into the room and it's as if his cologne is an entity—leather and wood. It fills my nostrils, the intoxicating warmth that it provides has me shivering. Not from temperature, but from the pure need to have him closer.

"Come on, little one," he coos as he stands at the foot end of the bed and I'm thankful he hasn't come closer. All I can do is pray he puts some clothes on, and quickly. "Tell me what filthy thoughts are dancing around in your mind right now." He tugs the towel, and my breath catches when I see the fluffy material on the carpet inches from where I'm sitting.

Shutting my eyes, I breathe deeply, trying to calm my racing heartbeat. "Just get dressed and leave me alone." My voice is a low whisper, but he heard me because he chuckles in response.

I hear the closet door click, and the ruffling of material as I exhale a deep breath that I've been holding since the moment his towel landed inches from me. When I hear his soft footfalls on the carpet, I peek through my lashes to find him dressed in a pair of gray sweatpants I didn't expect him to own, along with a t-shirt which hugs his muscled arms and torso.

"Little spies are meant to be spanked, little one," he tells me. "I think you need a good seeing to." Darius settles on the chair at the window, watching me as he twirls the key to the bedroom around his finger.

"Why are you being like this?" I question, trying to focus on the here and now and not that he knows I was watching him in the shower. "You don't have to act like a dick all the time."

He pushes to his feet so quickly, his hand wrapping around my throat in seconds, forcing a squeal of surprise from my lips. "I'm hurt, sweetheart," he says, his thumb circling my rapid pulse along the column of my neck. "Why would you call me a dick when all I've done is be nice to you?"

"Nice?" I spit the word, then laugh as he steals my breath with the tightening of his fingers. "You're far from nice." I croak my response as I glare at him, but I don't give in. I don't cower when he leans in closer, his mouth at my ear and his scent enveloping me.

"Was I nice when you were watching me jerk off in the shower?" he questions in a whisper, low and feral. "Did it make your little cunt wet when you saw my cock, little one?" His hand blocking any air that my lungs try to pull in, and for a moment, my vision gets blurry when Darius moves away just enough so I can see the satisfaction on his face. "Such a pretty doll," he coos, and my heartbeat thuds in my ears, echoing loudly as I claw at his hand.

I don't doubt he knows what he's doing, but fear overtakes the need to be brave, and I allow my tears to trickle from the corners of my eyes. Slowly, ever so fucking slowly, he eases his hold and I cough as my lungs suddenly fill with much needed air.

"Were you wet?" he asks again. "Because I can smell your sweet juices from here." There's confidence in his words. He knows I was. But he enjoys humiliating me by asking the questions.

"Fuck. You." Is my answer, which earns me a chuckle when he finally releases me. "I'm trying to get to know who you are. To learn how I can help you."

He turns away, his focus on the window, and for a moment, I wonder if I could tackle him and steal the key. But he's big. And there is no way I can fight him.

"The only way you can help me is by making sure your daddy pays me the money he owes." He settles back on the chair, resting one foot over the opposite knee. Those eyes, so familiar yet so strange lock on me. "And when your husband finally wakes up and comes for you, I'll make sure he knows how much you loved being my little captive."

"He won't believe you," I snap. "He knows I love him and I will not leave him for someone like you." He flinches at my words, but it's brief, only a split second of emotion mars his face before his mask returns, firmly in place.

"Someone like me?" he challenges. "That's interesting. Do you know that Lycan and I have very similar interests?" he asks then as he leans forward, his arms resting on his thighs as he looks me in the eye. "Because there are things you clearly don't know about my dear younger brother."

"He doesn't kill people," I spit angrily.

"Maybe he doesn't do it himself, but he has a team of men who work for him. Do you think he just dresses in those expensive suits because he wants to?" This time, Darius is on his feet. "The man I just killed moments ago, the man whose blood you saw on my clothes, was a rapist and a murderer. Would you like me to have saved him?"

My mouth falls open in shock at his confession. I saw the blood, but I didn't think he really killed someone. I don't know why, but mostly, I'm shocked he admitted to it. That was something I most definitely wasn't expecting.

"You... He... Are you serious?" I ask, still unsure of what else to say.

Darius chuckles, the sound reverberating through his chest. "Sweetheart, you're far too innocent for this world."

"I've seen and heard enough to make sure I don't believe everyone is good," I throw back. "But you, I can see goodness inside you, and you can't deny it." The challenge is there. The need to have him admit he feels something burns in my veins.

"I do bad things to bad people, it doesn't make me good," he bites out as he runs his fingers through his hair. He tugs at the strands, and I slowly move, needing to see the hunter that hides under the façade of a bad boy biker.

I'm on my feet, behind him, my hands trembling as I reach for him. The tension in his shoulders eases slightly as he stands still, allowing me to touch him. "You can't deny that this feels like something human."

Fear skitters through me when Darius suddenly spins on his heel, his glare locking on me. "Do you like dangerous men, little one?" he asks, dropping his voice an octave, making it vibrate in his throat, sending warmth racing through me. "You can't fix me." There's an edge to his words, and I want to poke at it, to push him further.

I keep my stare on him. "Nobody can be fixed. We're all broken in some way or another, but we can find ourselves in a better place." My voice is nothing more than a whisper filled with emotion I didn't expect to feel.

Darius's eyes flicker with pain. Heartbreak settles in those green orbs, and I can read every emotion dancing across his face as if he were an open book.

"We learn to live with our agony, we immerse ourselves in the discomfort we want to run from, and when we do that, we find happiness," I whisper earnestly, recalling my past. The demons that I've lived with. Not even Lycan knows the full truth about me. About why I enjoy what I do. "Forcing people who care out of your life is a coping mechanism." My bitter truth is Darius's. We share hurt, I'm almost sure of it.

The corner of his mouth quirks, his eyes blaze, and his hands find my hips, gripping me painfully, but possessively. "Did my brother teach you about pain, little one?" His dark brow lifts in question. "Because if he didn't, I would love to be the one to show you just how beautiful it can be." When I don't respond, something sparks in his eyes, and he nods. "You already know about it. Is that why you're not scared of us? You enjoy it." His realization is my silent confession. "You've lived through trauma."

And there it is.

But I don't respond. I don't agree and tell him about what I went through. Instead, I push away from him and ease myself back onto the mattress. Suddenly, I miss Lycan. My chest tightens at the thought of him in hospital. Hurt.

"He's alive. He'll be coming for you soon," Darius says, as if reading my mind. "But you need to tell him the truth, little one." He's right. But I can't. He won't love me if he knew. My captor heads for the door, but before he leaves, he glances over his shoulder at me. "Lycan is capable of a lot, and loving you is something he won't give up as easily as you think."

DARIUS

I need space.

I need to think.

She's seen me. The *me* I've hidden from everyone. Just her eyes locking on mine dug into my soul. As much as I try to hide the pain, Scarlett has seen right down to the depths of me. And if I'm honest, it fucking scares me.

When I walk into the living room, I spot a few guys with club whores on their laps, and Howler sitting at the bar watching the show. This is the life I was made to live in, not the one Scarlett *thinks* I should be in. She's reading too much into my actions. I don't want to hurt her, because if I do, Lycan won't help me. And for once in my life, I'll admit

I need his help.

I settle beside Howler, who's sipping a bourbon. The amber liquid almost filling his glass. "What's happening?" he asks but doesn't look at me. He knows I'm fighting a war within myself. This is one man who's known me for a long time. He can see past my bullshit, just like the woman upstairs.

"Hey, darlin'," one of the club whores, Kitty, sidles alongside me, her body pressed against mine. Heat courses through my veins, but when I take in her dark brown hair, I have to note it's not red. She's not Scarlett.

This is ridiculous.

Sliding my arm around her waist, I pull her closer between my thighs as I look over at Howler, who has his brow raised in question. The man is as intuitive as I am, and he knows me far too well to believe I'm into the woman I'm currently holding.

"You want some of this?" I question her, grabbing her hand and placing it on my crotch. Even though I'm not hard for her, a soft giggle falls from her lips. Most of the women who hang around the club are like this—too easy. I tug her wrist, practically dragging her out to the garages where all the bikes are parked. From here, I can glance up and see the bedroom window where the beautiful redhead is locked.

Leaning against the wall, I focus on the window while I push Kitty to her knees. She knows what to do, and as soon as my cock is in her hand, a hiss leaves my mouth. My eyes don't stray. I don't even look down at the woman with her lips now wrapped around my hardening shaft.

When I recognize the face watching from the window, I can't help but throb in Kitty's mouth. Her moans vibrate through me, but it's those silver eyes staring down at me that have me nearing my release.

The heat of the mouth what's swallowing my cock, and the wide-eyed glare from the woman who hates me, has my spine tingling. A satisfied smirk curls my lips because she can see what's going on down here. She can see the dark brown head bobbing back and forth in my crotch. My fingers tangle in the silky locks, and I wish with all I am that it was the scarlet waves of the woman upstairs.

Her name is perfection.

So is her smile.

And her body, that's purely sinful.

And I want her, I want her so bad it hurts.

At the window, Scarlett moves her hands over her chest, to her neck, and her finger slips between her plump pink lips, my cock jolts and my balls draw up as my release hits me like a fucking tidal wave knocking the breath from me.

I watch her slowly suck her finger before I empty jet after jet of hot seed down Kitty's throat. The moment I slip from the warm mouth that's swallowed every drop of cum, Scarlett disappears from the window, breaking the connection, leaving me empty and torn.

"Want me to spend the night?" Kitty asks, bringing my attention back to her instead of the fucking window. Her wide brown eyes shimmer with the promise of more where that came from, but I'm not into it and when she notices my expression, her smile falls. "You're a bastard," she bites out in anger before I have time to respond.

"I'm sure you can find someone to keep you company," I tell her before zipping my jeans and leaving her standing in the dim lighting of the garage. A decision is made. I'm going to have to get away from Scarlett. She's not good for me, and once her father's money clears in the offshore account, I'll give her back to Lycan.

Inside the house, I grab a beer and swallow it down until there's nothing left in the bottle. I can feel Howler's stare on me, and when I lock my gaze on his, there are questions dancing in his eyes.

"What?" I ask, sitting beside him on one of the bar stools.

He shakes his head. "You know, if I didn't know better, I would've said the girl upstairs has your head fucked." He lifts his drink to his lips as he regards me. But he says nothing more. I don't respond. I don't need to. He knows he's right, and if I said anything to dissuade him, he'll know I'm lying.

I don't lie to my brothers.

Turning to the prospect who's serving our drinks, I order another one before saying, "I think we need to find this Lorenzo fucker. I don't like the fact that he's dealing girls in our territory."

"Maybe it's time to go to Lycan, his team have—"

"Are you sure you want to go down that road?" I ask, meeting his gaze. "Because if they agree to help us, there'll be a lot more shit we need to answer for."

"Lycan's men are good. I can track shit, hack into machines, but they have men on the ground. We don't have those kinds of resources, Darius." *Fuck, he's right.* "I wouldn't say it if I didn't think it was a good idea."

I chuckle. "You say a lot of shit that isn't a good idea," I taunt.

"Fuck you," my best friend throws back and we both laugh.

Sipping my drink, I turn my attention to the men, to my men. They're good. They would do anything for me, for the club, but Howler is right, we need to get help. More men. "Any word on how he's doing?" I ask. I don't have to say his name because Howler knows who I'm talking about.

"Looks good, he'll recover. You didn't hit anything major."

I nod, thankful. I wanted to hurt my brother. But when I pulled the trigger, there was a part of me that knew I couldn't kill him. Not yet anyway.

He now knows Grace wants him dead. I let that little secret slip when I stood at the altar. She didn't look all too happy with me, and I'm waiting for her backlash because knowing how that bitch works, she'll be coming after me.

"I want us to get to Grace before she walks in here with

my name on a bullet." I glance at Howler, and he nods. We both know it's going to be a job to take her down. Mainly because it's Scarlett's grandmother, and it will hurt her, but she has to understand we have no choice. The woman is an evil bitch. But also, she has connections—police, politicians, even the fucking CIA is in her pocket, so we need to be very careful how we do this.

Hence the reason I'll wait for Lycan before acting out. He always used to tell me I was too reactive. I needed to plan. This time, I'm finally listening to his advice.

"She'll pay," Howler promises as the girls start dancing to the music that's blaring through the speakers. The guys are enjoying it, shouting and whistling, and I wonder briefly what's happened to me.

A couple of months ago, I would've loved this. Parties, drinking, the women, but right now, the consequences of what I've done weigh heavily on me. Guilt sluices through me at the thought of kidnapping Scarlett, shooting Lycan, and the thought of not being able to talk to him again hits me right in the chest.

This is Scarlett's doing.

She needled at me, asking me fucking questions, and now all I can think about is apologizing and making things right. It's not who I am. It never has been. Not with my mother, not with my father, but right now, all I want to do is make her pay for unlocking that box I'd kept hidden away for so long.

Pushing to my feet, I say, "I'm heading up. See you in the morning." I don't wait for Howler's response because I can only imagine it being a warning against what I'm about to do. And even if he had gotten it out, I may have just ignored him, anyway.

Outside the bedroom door, I grip the handle in a white-knuckle hold. I shouldn't do this. But I was never one for rules. I push it open and step inside to find Scarlett sitting on the bed, her arms wrapped around her legs, her chin resting on her knees.

In this position, she looks small, so fucking tiny and fragile. I want to wrap her in my arms and never make her cry. Confusion swirls in my gut. Want and need, overpowering the desire to destroy her.

"Did you enjoy the show?" I taunt, shutting the door behind me, my eyes keeping her pretty ones hostage as she looks me over. She trails me from head to toe, then meets my questioning stare once more.

"Did you do that on purpose?" she challenges, a small smile hinting at her lips, and I'm tempted to go over to her and steal it, to feel her softness against my hardness. But I don't. I refrain from even stepping closer to the bed where she's perched, because the moment I do, I'll lose all semblance of control that I'm grasping onto.

"Perhaps." Just the one word has her laughing out loud. "Were you wet, wishing it was your mouth bringing me pleasure?" Shrugging off the leather cut, I throw it onto the foot end of the bed. I make my way to the window, keeping my distance from her.

"I was wondering where my husband is. If he's okay. I thought about how much pleasure he brought me with his lips, tongue, and fingers. And then, I imagined him here, tasting me while I sucked his cock like she took yours in her mouth."

Even though she's attempting to anger me, to send my jealousy soaring, it doesn't work because the fire and desire dancing in her pretty eyes make it clear her words are almost a lie. I say *almost* because even though she may miss Lycan; she wants me. There's no doubt in my mind about it.

"I'm sure if you had us both you wouldn't survive the pleasure that we could bestow on you, little one." It's the truth. She's far too innocent to even imagine what Lycan and I could do to her. That is, if my brother would share.

And for a moment, I ponder the thought.

"He'll never share me with you," she informs me, tipping her chin in defiance, and I can't help but grin. She didn't say *she* doesn't want it, only that Lycan wouldn't allow it. But I know my brother better than she does.

"Get some rest," I order, trying to keep my voice calm as I settle into the armchair that overlooks the front garden. I'm not moving until she's asleep, and if she fights me on that, too bad because I'm watching over her tonight, and I'm going to enjoy it.

After a long while, Scarlett settles under the covers.

But her eyes are on me, watching and waiting. I lean back, relaxing as I rest my feet on the window seat. It's going to be a long night, and my little one better be in it for the long haul.

My phone vibrates in my pocket moments later, and I glance at Scarlett before pulling it from my pocket. She's finally asleep. At least it looks like it from where I'm sitting. A message on the screen has me grinning.

Time to get this game started.

LYCAN

When my eyes snap open, I find Kahn standing at the door talking to a couple of men dressed in black. I don't recognize them, which has me wondering if he's hired new guys. I try to shift, and my chest aches. Agonizing pain shoots through me the moment I scoot higher on the single bed.

Looking around the room, I notice it's one of the VIP suites at Crimson Falls General. I didn't think I would wake up from the shots Darius fired. The asshole hit me twice and took off after Scarlett.

"Kahn," I call out, causing him to spin on his heel. He tells the guys something more before they nod and leave. When he enters the room, shutting the door behind him, he looks at me with worry in his eyes. "Where is she?" Even as I ask, the answer is clear—Darius has her. If she was with Kahn, he would've probably brought her to the hospital, because she would've fought him tooth and nail to be here.

"They had a car waiting." He settles in the chair beside the bed. "I have my team scouring the vicinity because they couldn't have gotten far. We found the tracker we installed on his phone on the side of the highway about five miles down the road from the manor."

"Fuck," I curse, moving once more, only to have my breath stolen from me. "I need to get out of here."

"No, you need to stay right there. You almost fucking died," Kahn tells me earnestly. It's the first time I've ever seen him so concerned. Usually, he's stoic, calm even, but right now, the dark eyes of my right-hand man seem to burn with fear.

"How long have I been in here?"

"Four days," he informs me with no emotion, but the flickering of concern in his eyes makes me think there's more to it.

"If it didn't hurt so much, I would've told you to fuck off," I tell him, offering a smile, hoping he'll see that I'm okay. I haven't died, and I don't plan to anytime soon. I need to get to my wife. Finding her is my only focus right now.

"There's a house on the outskirts of Arizona where we

think they've gone. I just spoken to a couple of guys now, but what concerns me is that there's a funnel of women coming in from Mexico," Kahn informs me. "Lorenzo's name came up in a meeting I had with Alexei. He mentioned you told him he could come with us when we head to the convent. I've also asked Victor Cordero for his help."

"This thing sounds bigger than all of us," I remark, moving my legs in order to swing them over the edge of the bed. Pain shoots up my left side, and once again, I struggle to pull in air. Being injured is frustrating me, rather than offering me solace that I'm alive. "I want to be there when you go to the house."

"You're in no condition—"

"She's my fucking wife!" My voice booms through the room, bouncing off the walls, but Kahn stands his ground. For the years he's worked for me, he has never once answered back. He's never responded to me in any way other than, *yes sir*, when I asked something of him. For him to act like this, he must've been more than just concerned for his boss.

"I realize that, Lycan," he tells me, keeping his voice low. "but he won't kill her because he's asked for a ransom from Horatio."

"What?" This has me snapping my gaze to Kahn's dark eyes. "How much?"

"Fifty million," he tells me. "Which means he needs money, and he won't hurt her. Not until he has the cash. I have a team working with Horatio so when he does the transfer, we'll be ready to move on the house."

"Is it a compound? Because if it is, you know he won't be there alone." There is no doubt in my mind that Kahn has thought of everything, but the fear of losing Scarlett has me on edge. When I first met her, I didn't think she'd come to mean so much to me. I didn't expect my feelings for her to take a front seat to my own life.

But it has.

And now, I have to live with it.

"It must be, but I have fifteen men ready," Kahn assures me. "We will not fuck this up. If I had known Darius had his guys waiting, I would've countered them, but I missed that. This is on me."

Taking responsibility for something he couldn't have known is something Kahn has always done. Even when his sister was taken, he convinced himself it was his doing. Even though their folks were the ones who allowed Lorenzo to buy the young woman, Kahn has lived with the guilt of not being there to save her.

"Don't do that," I tell him. "It's on us all. I told her to run," I say as the memory of our wedding day returns with a violent vengeance. Knowing I sent her into the fucking woods on her own doesn't help the rage I'm feeling toward Darius.

"But I should've been there to catch her," Kahn says. He shakes his head before pulling out his phone to tap on the screen a few times before looking up at me. "She's at the house," he informs me. "Confirmation that Darius is on the compound."

"I want to be there." I attempt to push to my feet, and with a sigh, Kahn helps me to stand. The moment I tug the needle from my arm, the machines go crazy behind me. Seconds later, two nurses and a doctor come racing into the room.

"You're not cleared to leave yet," the doctor says, his tone filled with dread that I'd just freed myself from the drip. One of the nurses, a short brunette, nervously glances at the doctor, her trembling hands trying to fasten a bandage against the blood trickling from where the needle had pierced. "I can't allow you—"

"You're not *allowing* me to do anything," I inform him without stopping. At the cabinet, I grab my clothes and start dressing with the help of Kahn. Both nurses have quietened the machines, thankfully, because my fucking headache was slamming into my brain. "I'm leaving whether you like it or not. My wife has been kidnapped, and I'm going to find her."

When I lock my glare on the good old doctor, I can read the fear across his expression. "I–I've never had a patient walk out after two bullet wounds to the chest."

"Well, there's a first time for everything, doc," I grin, and I'm certain he's just pissed his pants. Kahn leaves the room for a short moment, returning with a wheelchair which I thankfully drop into.

"I need to check your vitals before you leave," Doc says, sounding a lot more confident than he was moments ago. The man doesn't realize just how much I don't give a fuck about me, but he's only doing his job, so I give a quick nod.

He does his job, making sure my heart rate and blood pressure are okay. He double checks my stitches, ensuring they're not torn after the way I got up and out of the hospital bed. With a long checklist of medication, and a thorough talking to, I'm allowed out of the building.

Even if they didn't want me to leave, I would've found a way out, and I'm certain they are aware of that. With Scarlett's life in danger, I'm not taking any chances.

In the town car, Kahn settles in the back with me while my driver, Hodges, takes us through the streets, heading back to the manor house.

I look at Kahn, who's busy on his phone. The sooner we get to this shit hole my brother's taken Scarlett to, the better. "What time are we leaving for Arizona?"

"Once we pack a bag for me and one for Scarlett, we'll head out. We also need to make sure we're all armed. I don't know what we're walking into. Not completely, and I didn't bring anything for you."

I nod. My focus is on the window as we pass through Crimson Falls. At one time, I loved this town. It was small enough for me to hide away from my life, but also close enough for me to monitor Grace because I don't fucking trust her.

I glance at Kahn and ask, "Did you get confirmation of Darius's claims about his mother?"

He nods. "Whatever document he had at the ceremony was bullshit. Grace isn't his mother. I'm not sure why he believed her, but the bloodwork we did after you were admitted to the hospital confirms you are brothers."

A nod once more, turning my attention to the window. If I've learned the truth about us being blood related, then he must've done a test too. His mind works the same way mine does, which means he knows he's not Scarlett's uncle. And that only makes anxiety twist in my gut.

Darius wouldn't hurt Scarlett. But that doesn't mean he wouldn't touch her, fuck her, or worse—make her want him as much as she wants me.

We have similar tastes sexually. When we were younger, we used to share our slaves, or submissives, and I've seen what my brother enjoys. Jealousy rears its head, my blood boiling at the thought of Scarlett being turned on by my brother.

By his words.

By his touch.

Darius enjoys humiliation, and something deep down inside me wonders if Scarlett does too. Her tastes run a lot darker than most women I've been with. And I'm certain if I'd pushed her, she would've allowed me to delve even deeper into her psyche.

And that's dangerous.

Because Darius won't stop. He won't allow her a safe word.

I think about the folder I had on Scarlett, which is still in my desk drawer. The information we found about her past, the night she was hurt, confirms she's using our sexual escapades as a way to deal with her trauma. When I tested her that night, chasing her through the forest, I thought she'd remember, that it'd push her to admit some drunk moron almost hurt her, but she didn't say a word.

But it didn't stop her from getting turned on when I pinned her down. When I took her, even though I didn't use violence, she wasn't triggered, which I can only assume is because she enjoyed the darkness before the event at the frat party.

It's one thing to have a kink, a fantasy, but it's another to enjoy it even after suffering a trauma like that. And that's what makes her interesting, what makes her so damn intriguing.

"We have to get to her now," I bite out through clenched teeth. I look to Kahn, whose gaze narrows on me. He can't read my mind, but I'm almost certain the jealousy coursing through me is painted across my face.

"We will. I promise you; she'll be okay." Even his assurance doesn't calm me down. Why would it? I've always been jealous of my brother, and this time, he's got something of mine. Something that means a hell of a lot more than some random woman I've been fucking for a few weeks.

The car weaves its way up the drive toward Shaw manor. The gates slide shut behind us as we near the monstrosity that is my home. Mine and Scarlett's home. Knowing she's not there waiting for me only makes me nervous.

The door opens and Gray walks out onto the tiled steps. The suitcase he's pushing is mine, and I can't help but grin. He's already packed for me. I love that old man. More than I ever did my father.

The thought of my father brings back memories of what I've lost in my life. I don't care what my brother does, but if he hurts Scarlett, I'll torture him for weeks before I end him. He's stolen from me, which needs to be rectified.

When he last took from me, I vowed to never let it happen again.

And now, it has.

This time though, I'll kill him.

I will spill my brother's blood and I won't think twice.

DARIUS

"He's on his way," Howler informs me with a grin. We planned this perfectly. Lycan is coming here, and soon enough, we'll come face to face. I want to tell him my plan. Once I learned my mother wasn't Grace Bardot, something struck within me. There's no shadow of a doubt that Lycan hates Horatio, which will leverage him on my side.

Taking that asshole's money was part of the plan.

The other part was breaking the bastard down, until he admits to the crimes his parents committed. The truth is they killed my father, and if Lycan will sit down and listen, I can show him the proof. For years I've been searching. Grace and her husband were nothing more than ruthless fucking criminals.

Yes, Grace may have loved my father once, but the moment she said 'I do' to someone else, she broke her promises to Dad and the Shaw name.

Lycan has to believe me, there's no other way. If we stand together for once, nothing will tear us apart. At least, that's what I hope.

"Make sure you keep tracking the car. The moment he's a couple of miles out, I want everything locked down. He has to request access." Even though I'm giving the order, my brother will have a team of men with him, and he'll be wanting his wife back.

"Will do," Howler informs me with a grin.

Although, taking Scarlett was a highlight. Feeling her tremble against me only brought back memories of when Lycan and I shared *her*. The one woman who broke me. No other female had ever come close enough to do what she did to us. Lycan never recovered, and neither did I.

Pushing from the chair, I head up the stairs toward my bedroom. The compound is my home, the place I found myself after leaving Crimson Falls behind for good. Having a beautiful woman here, even if she belongs to my brother, unnerves me.

Usually, when I'm with a woman for the night, I go to their place, not wanting someone to spend the night at mine. Even the club whores know that I don't kiss and cuddle afterward. Once the deed is done, you're out on your ass.

When I push my bedroom door open, Scarlett's asleep. Curled up on the mattress, the blanket haphazardly covers her body. Glimpses of flesh peek at me, and my cock thickens with need.

She's not blood.

But she is my sister-in-law.

However, I'm not one to follow rules.

I step into the room, inhaling deeply, and I realize she must have showered because she smells of my soap. The spicy scent mingling with her natural feminine fragrance, which doesn't ease the hardening of my dick.

I watch her sleep for a while. Her breathing is even, her dark red hair splaying across my pillows. The sight is foreign to me, but it's also alarmingly breathtaking. This woman is nothing more than a siren sent to lure me to my death. Because if I touch her, if I were to claim her with my mouth, my fingers, or my cock, Lycan would kill me.

I'm almost certain he's on his way with the cavalry to kill me. But what he doesn't know is that I didn't steal the pretty girl to hurt her, I took her to lure him out. To bring him into my space so I can be in control. I'm surprised my brother survived both gunshots, but I'm not shocked he's walked out of the hospital without permission from the doctors. It's just like Lycan to do what he pleases.

When I stepped into Shaw manor, it didn't feel like home.

Now that I'm here, the comfort of the familiar calms me somewhat.

Scarlett awakens with a start, her wide eyes locking on mine in surprise. She shuffles up the mattress, her back hitting the headboard as she tugs the blanket over her body to cover what I've already had a good look at.

"What are you doing, creeper?" she bites out, rage dripping from her pretty, plump lips. I can't help but grin at her fire. My brother chose well. Even though I'm sure he didn't plan for her to be like this when he had Horatio sign the contract, he's gotten lucky. Breaking her in the club would be a pleasure.

"I was enjoying the view," I tell her innocently with a shrug of my shoulder. I move around the bed and make my way to the window. The sun is slowly setting. She's slept most of the day away.

"Have you heard anything yet?" she asks, her voice breaking with worry over Lycan.

I don't turn to look at her, because seeing the affection she holds for him will only anger me. Jealousy is not a good look on anyone. And on me, it makes me violent. Come to think of it, everything makes me violent. "He's on his way here."

"What?" She's on her feet, her small, fragile body inches from mine, and her heat envelopes me. "What do you mean? How can he—?"

"Just what I said, little one. He's making his way here with his army of men. He's going to play the hero to save you," I inform her with a smirk, thinking of just how foolish he is. This is my territory; he doesn't know what could hurt him. Kahn has intel, that is clear, but he doesn't realize I have hidden landmines all around the compound. One wrong step, and you'll be in pieces just outside the property line.

Perhaps he does know.

Maybe he doesn't care.

Scarlett possibly means more to him than his life.

It's time to test my brother and see just how much this woman means to him.

"But you shot him. I mean, he should still be healing."

"He should," I agree, finally facing the beauty. "But my brother isn't one to follow the rules, little one."

"Then he takes after you," she throws back with a small smile, shocking the shit out of me. I didn't expect her to say that, or even acknowledge it. But that has my chest tightening when I think about giving her back to him.

"He does."

"Do you miss him? Do you miss having a family?" she asks then, stepping up beside me. Her wide eyes locking on the side of my face and it feels as if I'm being scorched. "Not the biker family you clearly have," she adds in a whisper.

I stare out of the window, watching the clouds move across the sky. The memory of having a brother feels foreign to me. It's been so long. My heart thuds against my ribs, reminding me once again that emotion is weakness.

"No." I turn suddenly, causing Scarlett to step back, almost tumbling to the floor, but my arm shoots out, wrapping around her slender waist as I pull her toward me.

Her mouth is inches from mine. It would be so easy to steal a kiss. To taste her lips and tangle my tongue with hers. My jeans tighten at the crotch when she gasps as I straighten, bringing her along with me.

Scarlett's hands land on my chest, her fingers burning me right through my t-shirt, as well as the leather cut I'm wearing. "I don't believe you."

"Do you like to taunt the predator, little one?" I question, keeping my face near hers, the hot breath that fans from her lips causing my hunger to rumble through me like an awakening volcano.

"I-I didn't mean... I just want to learn about you," she whispers, and her voice has a direct link to the desire coiling my gut. I want her. The hunger I have that's swirling through me is dangerous, and the longer I spend around her, the more I feel like letting go and stealing a taste.

It wouldn't take long to claim her.

I could do it right now.

"Nobody wants to know about me, sweetheart," I tell her honestly. With a twinge of regret, I release her. "It's better that you go back to your wolf and leave the hunter to fend for himself."

Suddenly, she reaches out a hand and cups my cheek. The softness of her touch has my body warming with need. "Why do you push people away?" Her whispered words fall over me and, like a wave crashing on the shore, it attacks me violently. I feel as if I'm being dragged down into the depths of the sea, where I've buried my feelings, where I've hidden the need and desire I long since wanted to feel.

"Because those who have come close enough have always been hurt. And I'd rather walk away than have anyone else in my life get hurt," I confess with a lump forming in my throat and the words as they escape feel like sandpaper scraping the truth from me.

Scarlett shakes her head. "That's no way to live," she whispers softly. The gentleness of the moment is broken when Howler shoves open the door. His eyes widen when he takes us in. He's never seen me act affectionately to anyone, not even the club whores who want my dick.

"They're close," he says, before tipping his head toward Scarlett and leaving us to finish whatever the fuck this is. I don't even know.

"I have to go." I turn, immediately feeling cold after putting distance between Scarlett and me, but it's for the best. We can't do this. I can't fucking do this because she's going to leave here with Lycan, and I'll be on my own once more.

She catches my arm before I walk out of the room, and the plea is shining in her pretty eyes. "Please don't hurt him." Her words are filled with worry, anxiety clear in her expression. A pretty girl in love with a beast.

"I promise you I won't. But I can't vow that he won't try to hurt me." It's the truth. My brother is coming here to get his girl, and what he does to get her may not be something she'll agree with.

"Let me go with you?" she asks, a question I consider

for a moment. "I won't run, let me talk to him, show him I'm fine." She gestures to her clothes, her body, no marks or scars. She's dressed in a pair of my sweats with a heavy black tee that makes her look like she's drowning in material and I can't help but grin.

"Like that?"

She glances at her appearance, then nods. "I don't have any other clothes since my wedding dress was ripped to shreds," she informs me, a bite in her clipped tone which has the corners of my mouth quirking at the fire that just never ceases within her.

"He's going to expect you to be hurt, to be crying and begging him to save you from the big bad hunter," I tell her with a grin of satisfaction curling my lips. This time, I turn to face her once more, my hands landing on her hips as I tug her closer. "What are you going to tell him, little one? Are you going to admit how much your body responds to my touch? Or are you going to tell him your lips ache to be claimed by mine?"

The air is heavy with promise, with threat, and the slight tremble from Scarlett's slight frame doesn't go unnoticed. I see her. I see everything she does, and this time, I'm not going to stop. Cupping her face in my hand, I hold her steady. My mouth finds hers in a slow, gentle kiss. Her breaths come out short, soft gasps of surprise when my tongue darts out and traces her full bottom lip.

"Is that what you're doing to tell him?" I whisper before I finally claim her mouth with mine, and I don't stop even when she tries to push me away. Her strength no match for me, but as our tongues dance, she gives up for a long moment and falls into the connection.

And when I pull away, her palm connects with my face.

"Don't ever do that again."

I arch a brow as I turn away. "Why? Because you liked it?" I walk away from her, leaving the door open knowing she'll follow. Time to welcome Lycan and tell him just how much his little princess is welcome in my home anytime.

SCARLETT

My body is still humming from the kiss. I can't believe I allowed it to happen. But the heat of his lips is still scorching mine as I walk behind him, following along like a lost puppy. Each door we pass is shut, and I wonder what's behind them. Probably bedrooms for the men in the club, but I don't want to see what goes on behind those wooden barriers.

Darius takes the stairs down to the foyer. For a moment, I wonder if I could make a run for it, but since Lycan is on his way, he'll save me. Somehow, he'll find a way to get us both out of here.

My anger hasn't abated. Darius still makes me want to

kill, but the memory of the kiss lingers in my mind. I don't know what's wrong with me. Even though the brothers aren't exactly twins, there are so many similarities between them. I put it down to that. Just missing my husband.

But it's a lie.

I saw Darius. I looked into his eyes and saw the human he keeps buried deep down, it's difficult to find him. He comes to a stop outside a set of double doors and pushes them open. When we step into a meeting room complete with a long boardroom table, I can't help but gasp at the sheer size of it.

There are twelve chairs surrounding the heavy wooden table. At the one end is a much larger chair, one with carvings in the back, which has the logo I've noticed on Darius's cut. The club's emblem—a skull with snakes slithering over it and blood dripping from both eye sockets. Under the logo is a banner with the chapter name—Devil's Cove.

"Where is he?" I ask the moment I notice it's only Darius's men in the room.

Those green eyes that match his brother's lands on me. "He'll be here soon," he tells me with a violent grin. "Sit." It's an order, which I obey quickly. I don't want to anger him after all. Even though every inch of my body is screaming at me to tell him to fuck off. I don't.

Settling into one of the empty seats, I take in each of the six men that surround the table. Each one of them is staring at me as if I am the main attraction in the room.

Gunshots ring off in the distance, and I fight the urge

to push to my feet when Darius pins me with a warning glare.

"Sounds like my brother is here," he chuckles. "Open the door," he orders one of the younger men who obeys him without question. Both Shaw brothers like to be in control, perhaps that's why they're always at odds with each other.

Moments later, four men, including Lycan and Kahn are brought into the house. Those familiar jade eyes find mine instantly, as if they're magnetized to my presence. The corner of his mouth tilts, and he offers me a slight nod in greeting.

"Wife." It's one word which holds all the weight of the world.

"Lycan," I gasp, pushing to my feet only to have a heavy hand hold me down. Inching back into my seat, I fist my hands, my fingers tingling with the need to touch him. To feel him alive and breathing. My heart thumps in my throat, threatening to choke me as he watches me with those mesmerizing eyes.

He glances at Darius as the men in leather release their hold on him. "Brother, you should've invited me for dinner if you wanted me to visit your home. Taking my wife prisoner is not the way to do it." Lycan's voice is cold, unfeeling, and filled with threatening ice even though he's outnumbered. But then again, he isn't a man who would walk into a situation without a plan. "Take your hand off her," he commands, straightening his spine as he glares at his brother.

A dark chuckle rumbles from beside me. "I don't know if she wants me to take my hand off her. Do you, little one?" I can feel the weight of Darius's stare on me, challenging me to refuse, to tell my husband we kissed. Or that he made my body react.

Lycan's stare flicks to mine, the realization that something happened skitters across the soft green that bores a hole right into my soul. "Scarlett." My name is nothing more than a plea, and my heart drops to my stomach when his face turns to solid steel. The mask he always wore when we first met is firmly in place, and I have a feeling I've just lost the man I've grown to love.

Kahn's gaze finds mine. He looks me over from head to waist where the table hides the rest of my body, taking in every inch, and when he finds no bruises visible to the naked eye, he turns to Darius. "My men are waiting."

"I'm sure they are. You're welcome to join them," Darius says right before a loud bang goes off in the distance, and we're all cowering in fright, except for Darius and his men. "You see, your plan to overthrow my club won't be as easy. Call them off, or more of them will be blown to bits." Darius chuckles as if killing is a joke.

"You fucker!" Lycan grits through clenched teeth, and I stare as his jaw ticks. Rage burns in his gaze, and I'm certain he would annihilate us all with a mere glance if he could.

"Call. Them. Off." The Shaw brother with all the power stands tall as his voice issues the command, and Kahn slowly but surely pulls out his cell phone and presses the screen a few times.

When Kahn nods at Darius, the man beside me says, "Good. Now let's get some drinks. I think it's time to celebrate my brother visiting."

"Cut the shit," Lycan bites out. "I'm not here to make a social call. I'm here to take my wife home," he grits, his eyes dancing with angry flames of defiance.

"Perhaps you should sit down, brother," Darius continues, as if Lycan said nothing at all. "We have a lot to discuss." He pulls out a chair, which has his men mimicking his actions, and Lycan slowly sinks into the seat opposite his brother. His gaze flicks to me every now and again, but even when he looks at me, something is missing. The fear he regarded me with when he first stepped inside is gone. And that's what scares me.

"I have a proposition for you," Darius says as he settles in beside me. The man who allowed me to talk to him earlier, to learn about his brokenness, is gone, and in his place is the VP of a motorcycle club making a business deal. A man who won't take no for an answer, and one that's hellbent on revenge.

"What makes you think I'll listen?"

Darius's hand lands on my thigh, causing me to jerk up, a gasp falling from my lips, and Lycan pushes to his feet. His hands flat on the smooth, shiny wooden surface of the long table that's keeping us apart.

"I think you should sit down, brother," Darius says. "If you don't listen to me, I'll have my guys escort Scarlett back to my bedroom where she spent the last few nights."

"Alone," I add quickly, keeping my focus on Lycan and ignoring the heat searing me at my side from the brother who stole a kiss while in the bedroom earlier. "Lycan," I call to him, causing him to finally look at me again. His name on my lips has his warmth returning, but only for a short moment before he slips the mask back on and glares at Darius.

"Speak, or I'll leave her here with you and you can deal with her bratty ass," he sneers, the anger in his tone causing tears to burn my eyelids.

"Horatio and Grace Bardot," Darius starts. "I want them ended; they can no longer rule over everyone's lives as if they hold our existence in their hands."

Howler sets a folder in front of Darius, who in turn pushes it toward his brother. "This is my contract. The terms are set out for you. You don't trust me, and I don't expect you to jump at this, but if we stand together, the way Shaw's were always meant to, we can win this war."

Lycan's dark brow raises as he regards Darius with surprise. "This war? This is a war you started, brother," he tells him. "When you took Scarlett, you took the very heart of me. I shouldn't be telling you just how much she means to me, but I can tell your affections are growing for her as well. Which means, something happened here. I don't need to know about it, but the moment I agree to anything, you will release Scarlett into my care, and you walk away. We will finish the Bardots, which is something I'd been planning for years—"

"But you never believed Grace had Dad killed," Darius confesses, exasperation clear in his tone. "The proof is in the folder." He pushes to his feet, a pair of strong hands loop under my arms and drag me from the chair. "Scarlett will wait in my bedroom while you ponder your decision."

The man holding me tries to carry me from the room, but Lycan's stare finds mine once more, a promise burning in those green gemstones—*I'll never leave you.* I don't know how I can read him so well, but I realize the mask he had in place wasn't for me, it was for his brother. A show of confidence and power.

"No." Lycan stands. Kahn beside him. Both men look like they're ready to take on the world. Perhaps they are. They seem like they're ready to fight for me. And my heart catapults into my throat.

My eyes burn once more, and this time, I allow Lycan to see my pain.

I blink the tears away, the salty emotion trickling down my cheek.

His hands fist at his sides. "She will stay where I can see her." His voice is dark, filled with poison. "Or I will walk out of here right now, my men will storm the gates, and I will kill you." He's so convinced of winning this war between him and Darius, even I feel confident that he can. Possibly.

"You don't have the—"

"You've known me my whole life, brother," Lycan assures. "Surely you'd know I wouldn't walk into a gunfight with a knife." This time, Lycan chuckles, the same demeaning one he gave me when I first tried escaping the Shaw mansion. He knows he's on top, and that's something I can't deny makes my body respond.

For a long, silent moment, they stare at each other. I'm almost certain Darius is about to pull a gun when he turns his body to face his brother fully. The tension in the air is thick with deadly intent. Two alphas in one room have far too much testosterone swirling around.

Then Darius nods. "Fine." He glances at me and points at the chair at the head of the table. "Sit." When I don't obey as quickly as he'd like, he shoves me into the seat, my ass hitting the leather, forcing a whoosh of breath from my lungs.

"If you so much as put another hand on her again, I will rip you limb from fucking limb," Lycan threatens, moving toward the chair where I'm currently being held prisoner. He reaches his brother, they're toe to toe, and if I thought there was violence in the air earlier, I had no fucking clue.

Darius lifts his hand from my shoulder, a smirk curling his lips as he challenges Lycan's strength. Lycan's still hurt. Still healing. He shouldn't be fighting a battle while he could relapse at any moment.

"Leave them be," Darius orders, and his men stand, the chairs screeching against the wooden paneled flooring, as they make their way out of the room. When it's only Kahn, Lycan, and I, I release a breath I've been holding since Darius and Lycan were inches from each other.

"Are you okay?" Lycan questions, his hands on my shoulders ground me to the moment, and I allow more tears to fall. "Did he hurt you?"

"No," I mumble. The guilt of kissing his brother eats away at me, and I want to confess, but I'm fearful of him leaving me with Darius. However, there is something else I don't want to acknowledge—my feelings for the older Shaw brother.

LYCAN

To say I'm angry would be an understatement. More like jealousy raging a war inside me. My brother and I have always vied for the same woman. It is just in our fucking genetics. But this time, I've laid a claim. There's a ring that weighs heavily on her finger, which means she's mine.

Seeing my woman, my fucking wife, be used as pawn doesn't sit well with me. If she's hurt, I'm the one to hurt her because with that she'll also find pleasure. But then, I also know how Darius enjoys the humiliation, and that Scarlett may find pleasure in it too. Even if she doesn't want to, her body and mind is synchronized to crave the darkness.

She said so herself.

"You should be in the hospital," she murmurs, her lips against mine as she speaks the words, and it sends heat coursing through me. She's right, but I don't tell her that, instead I stare at her. I can't stop looking at Scarlett Bardot.

How can I love the woman who's my enemy's daughter?

I'm not sure, but I do.

"I need to know what he did to you. I want the truth, little red," I whisper, my tongue darting out to tease her lips, to taste her flavor that I've missed. Even though it hasn't been that long, I still can't believe how my body missed hers.

"He kissed me, just before you arrived," she finally admits, a sigh tumbling from her lips. "I didn't mean to... I couldn't..." She shakes her head sadly, her eyes shimmering with tears, and I realize I don't want to see them fall. Seeing her upset makes my chest tighten in a strange way, which I've never experienced before.

"Don't," I tell her, cupping her face, holding her steady so she doesn't turn away from me. "Don't think about it. You're mine." I pull her closer, my lips claiming hers, hoping that with the kiss, I'll eliminate any doubt she's had about Darius taking advantage.

I knew he would.

And I'm going to kill him for even thinking he can break us apart. I'm not falling for his bullshit tricks anymore. "Tell me what he wanted from you, from me," I implore her. I could read the contract, but it will be filled with excuses as to why I should listen to him. Whereas Scarlett spoke to him, she's obviously learned about Darius, or he would never have taken the chance and kissed her.

"He is your blood," she finally confesses, but this is a truth I'm aware of, so I nod for her to continue. "He has proof that your father was murdered, not by who you think," she tells me, her voice falling to nothing more than a whisper. My heart constricts in my chest.

But she doesn't speak.

Tears form in her eyes once more, and when she blinks, they fall, trickling down her cheeks. She doesn't meet my gaze, and my lungs give out. For a moment, I think I'm dying because I have a feeling I know what she's going to say.

"The Bardots," I finish her thoughts for her. "Your grandmother, her husband. The man who she married." I won't refer to him as Scarlett's grandfather because he's nothing like the woman before me. But then again, neither is Grace. Perhaps only in her fiery personality. But other than that, Grace is nothing more than a two-faced pawn in a game she thought she could win.

"I'm sorry." Scarlett finally falls apart, and she does it in my arms as the door swings open and Darius walks in. His gaze lands on our embrace, and I can't help but smile. Satisfaction courses through me, but deep down, just for a moment, I wonder what it would feel like for her to have us both.

Would I be jealous, or would pride surge through me at seeing my wife take my brother?

"I'm guessing our little one has confessed the truth about her family," Darius says as he nears the table, settling in beside Scarlett. "What do you say, brother?" he asks, looking at me, and I can tell he's fighting *not* to look at my wife.

She's gotten under his skin. The tough exterior he portrays is nothing more than a façade. I see that, and so does he. For years I was convinced he hated me, but the truth of the matter is, Darius is the same teenage boy who ran away from home the moment he could.

He always hated the fact that there was a family business to run. He didn't want to walk in Dad's shoes, whereas I thought it was an honor. For a long time, we kept in touch, while I was becoming more like our father every day. Hell, we even had our fun at Heaven when it was nothing more than a one roomed club.

But then it happened.

The murder we never spoke about.

And the truth that hung over both our heads is what broke us apart.

"I'll do it." My words are confident, filled with the threat that the Bardots will pay for killing our father, and Scarlett shakes in my arms as she cries, but she doesn't release me.

"I never wanted it to come to this," Darius admits. "I wanted us to be the Shaw brothers." The regret in his tone is what stills me for a long moment as I regard my brother. It's been so long since we actually spent time together, since we spoke like adults.

Scarlett brought us together.

She mended my family.

While hers wrenched us apart.

The bedroom is lovely. Even though my brother's compound is nothing more than a house with bikers who lie around, fucking the whores who walk in here expecting a good time. He's built something from nothing.

Just like I did.

Scarlett's lying beside me, but she hasn't spoken since we came upstairs. When Darius escorted us to one of the many guest rooms, she glanced at a door at the end of the hall which I'm convinced is the bedroom he kept her in. His bedroom.

"Are you attracted to him?" I ask and I feel her still. My body cocoons hers, so there's no movement I won't notice. "I won't be mad at you."

"Did you really share women with him before?" she asks, lifting her head to look at me. Her fingertips still trail my chest, my stomach, and when she reaches the dips on my hips, she teases them, making sure my cock jolts with need.

"I did." I affirm, knowing she deserves the truth. "It was a long time ago. But he would enjoy being with you."

"You want to share me?" The shock is clear in her voice, her eyes wide as she regards me. But I don't answer. Instead, I watch her for a long moment. "Do you?"

"I'm not sure," I tell her honestly. "There's no doubt he

would and could make you feel good and perhaps having both of us will dull that fire for a time. I would love to see you taken and used, like you want," I whisper, allowing my hand to caress her shoulder, down her spine, causing a shiver to wrack through her. "He enjoys humiliation, he likes to see women bow for him, break under his touch."

I'm taunting her. She enjoys the darkness as much as I do. And perhaps, this would show her part of the world she's so new to. Maybe she'll see what's out there. The risk of her wanting him over me is there. It's always been that way when Darius and I have had the same woman.

A ring and a vow don't matter when it comes to the bitter truth of knowing that someone doesn't truly love you. Call it a test. I'm a bastard for even suggesting this. But I need to know where her head is at.

"Tell me, little red," I coo, tugging her up so she's straddling my now hard cock. Her heat against me, warming every inch of me. "Would you like to feel so full that you can't think straight?" I arch a dark brow at her, noting how her irises dilate at my words. "Can you imagine your body being so utterly used by two men, four hands, two thick cocks, that you can't breathe, can't think, can't even speak?" Her hips roll against me, undulating as she finds the friction she needs against my throbbing cock. "If you're going to do that, you better make sure my cock is deep in that little cunt of yours," I warn her, and she quickly moves to slip my erection inside her body. The heat of her pulsing around me, has my eyes rolling back.

It's been too long since I've been inside her.

"Why are you doing this?" she pleads, her body still moving, still turned on at the thought of being taken by both of us. "Why would you say these things? I love you," she tells me, her hands cupping my face, her eyes large, glassy as she regards me.

There's no doubt she loves me.

But she's struggling with the guilt of wanting Darius.

"Because I want to know if that love is enough to see us through this," I tell her earnestly, my voice scratchy as I confess, "Because I need to know that my obsessive need for you is matched by your possessive craving for me. To know I'm yours, that's all I want."

She stills all movement. My words have hit her hard. Her lower lip trembles as she watches my expression, which I keep guarded. I don't want her to see the fear that's coiling deep in my gut.

With all the other women, I've never once been concerned about them running off. Yes, it is the fear of not being good enough. I have to be better than Darius, this time because I actually love the woman in question.

This feeling, these emotions, are all new to me. And they scare the shit out of me. I never wanted this. I never wanted to feel so out of control, that I have to play games to make sure that someone wants me.

But with Scarlett, that fear is so real, it's debilitating.

"Do you want him?" I ask once more, gripping her hips as I move her back and forth. When she doesn't respond, I lift her up and buck my hips against her. Lifting my ass from the bed, I focus on the pleasure of her cunt and not the pain in my chest.

Her body tightens around me. My cock deep inside her, coaxing whimpers from her plump lips. I continue my assault, my mouth clamping down on one of her hardened nipples, my teeth grazing the flesh as I bite down.

A cry of pure pleasure breaks free from her mouth, and I steal it with my own. Our tongues dual as we kiss, it's violent, it's filled with passion I never once found with anyone else.

And when we both still with our releases, I realize she still hasn't answered me.

SCARLETT

When I wake up, Lycan is sitting on the bed with his back to me. His elbows resting on his knees as his head hangs down. I wonder what he's thinking, but I don't interrupt him. I don't speak.

He must know I'm awake, because I move, rolling over to really look at him. His body is perfectly beautiful. Thick corded muscles tense from whatever is racing through his mind. His shoulders wide, strong, a promise of a man who can look after himself and me.

My husband.

He fucked me again last night, and still the question hung between us like a heavy weight in the room. My answer non-existent, but I owe him the truth. I do. Never once have I wanted to lie to him, and this time will be no different. He is the man I love, and he needs to know that. I chose him. But then, his doubt is not unfounded.

"Yes."

He doesn't turn to look at me, but I notice how he stiffens at the whispered word that falls from my lips. His muscles in his back tense, and release, and I take in just how beautiful his smooth, tanned flesh is. There isn't a blemish in sight.

"One night." Is all he says before he stands and walks to the en-suite bathroom, leaving me alone in bed. My head hurts. My heart hurts. And my body thrums with the need to make him see just how much I love him.

He still doesn't believe me.

Even though I told him, honestly, how I felt. Even though I married him without being coerced. Can he not see the guilt I feel? Or is he ignoring the fact that I care for him so deeply that I didn't want to answer his question last night.

Stepping into the bathroom, I find him already under the warm spray. I join him, allowing my hands to trail over his strong back. Even though he's disappointed in the answer I gave, honesty is always the best path to follow.

I learned that by watching my parents. They were never honest with each other, and that's where they were wrong. They hurt each other with lies, and I don't want to be like them.

"I'm sorry."

Lycan spins at my words, and I gasp when his cock presses against my stomach. He's tall, and the thickness of him against my soft belly throbs as he pulls me closer. His strong hands grasping my hips in a vice-like hold.

Like this, he seems like a wild animal. One that's about to lay claim to his possession, which is me. And my blood heats at the thought. I want to be his, every part of me screams for him to take me. Never before have I craved such violence, such volatile possessiveness, but with Lycan, it makes me hungry for more.

"Never apologize for needing something, for craving it," he growls, the words feral and animalistic. "When you just admitted it, I wanted to fuck you so hard, you'd be bruised, I wanted to make you hurt, and scream, just loud enough for him to hear you."

Lycan's hands trail to my ass as he lifts me against him. My core at the tip of his cock, and slowly, ever so gently, he impales me on this erection. The thickness of him opening me, making me gasp as pleasure zips through every nerve ending in my body.

It's as if electricity has been shot straight into my veins, and I'm alive. He turns us until my back is flush against the cold tiles. The heat of the spray thrums against my chest as Lycan pulls out and slams back inside me, sending my pleasure into the abyss of darkness while he grips my throat with one hand and my thigh with the other.

It's a punishing hold. He steals my breath with a pulse

of his fingers, and I realize he can feel my erratic heartbeat as it thrums against his thumb. "You're mine, but I want you to find the most euphoric pleasure you can," he informs me as his lips tease mine. I want him to kiss me, but he doesn't. "He and I will take you, we will fuck you to within an inch of your life," he promises with a dark vow, "and when you come, it will be my eyes you look into, even though my brother will be fucking your pretty little ass," he grunts this time as he fucks me against the cold wall, sending shivers of pleasure and pain through me.

"Please, Lycan," I plead, as he slowly pulls out of me. He lowers me to my feet before spinning me around and bending me over.

"Palms on the wall," he orders, with a spank to my ass. Both cheeks zing when his large palm lands on the fleshy globes. And then he grips me, opening me to his gaze, and I can't stop from blushing when I realize what he's about to do.

His fingers taunt me, teasing the ring of muscle as he dips inside my body. He continues his ministrations, using my arousal to slick his fingers as he scissors me open until my knees are trembling. I shake as he teases me, the strange feeling sending both pleasure and pain through me. It's different, nothing like I've ever experienced, but it's what Lycan does to me. He takes me down new paths I never expected to enjoy. I do. I enjoy every moment with him, everything he does to my body, I find euphoria. He plays my body like a musical instrument, and he brings out a melody of pure ecstasy from me.

"Before he gets this," Lycan says, his voice low and menacing. "I'm going to fuck you hard." And then, slowly, ever so fucking slowly, he inches himself into my ass. I cry out as he sinks inside me, deeper and deeper. I claw against the slippery tiles as he claims me from behind. The pain zips up and down my spine, a promise of what's to come.

Lycan reaches around, his fingers taunting my clit as he thrusts into my ass. It's not gentle, but he's holding back. I realize he's grappling onto his restraint the same way I'm grasping onto the smooth tiles before me.

Once he's fully seated, he stills. His body looming over mine. "This is mine. Every fucking part of you, is mine. Your holes, those pretty fucking holes, are mine."

The truth in his words sends me soaring as he pinches the hardened nub between his fingers, and I scream his name, losing myself in the pain, in the pleasure, in Lycan's control over me.

I feel him pull out. I feel a splatter against my back. He lifts me gently, and I don't miss the wince on his face.

"Put me down, you're still hurt." I insist, but he cleans me under the shower before turning off the taps.

"If I want to hold my wife, I'll do it." He ignores any more debate about him in need of rest as he lifts me in his arms and carries me out into the now foggy bathroom. But the moment he tries to pick me up again, I step back, giving him a stare that he doesn't argue with. Once I'm wrapped in a towel, he embraces me for a long, silent moment before we move into the bedroom where he watches me climb on the mattress.

"Get some rest. I have a meeting with Darius," he informs me as I curl into the blankets. I don't care that my hair is still wet, all I need is to sleep. "And when I return, we'll play." There's a promise of something even more pleasurable in his tone, and I smile as he leaves me in bliss as my lashes flutter.

I don't know how I'm going to deal with them both, but if he is willing to let me, I'll most definitely try.

LYCAN

When I step into the living room, I find Darius staring out at the garden. He looks so much like our father. I wonder if he realizes. Even in a torn t-shirt and leather cut, he's got his coldness from the man who raised us to be emotionless, yet strong.

He turns his attention to me, offering a glimmer of a smile. "Brother."

"I thought we should talk," I tell him, hoping that this doesn't go down the fucking drain like every other time we've tried to be civil with each other. When I reach his chair, he rises. "And before we talk, I have something to say." My fist rears back and quickly makes contact with his jaw, sending him stumbling back. The chair he'd been sitting on falling on its side with a loud crash. When I see blood dripping from his lip, I smile. "Next time you go near my wife without my permission, it will be worse than that."

I pull out another chair and settle in, waiting for Darius to seat himself once more. A chuckle leaves his lips before he swipes away the blood with the back of his hand. Once he's sitting, he looks me over and nods. "Fair enough. I didn't expect you to come at me, but then again, I did get a taste before asking for your permission." He shakes his head. "Did you hit me because you're jealous, or because she admitted to wanting it?"

I don't even fucking know how to answer him. Yes, to both. But also, I don't blame her. She's new to this life, the same life I brought her into, and I cannot be angry with her. She needs to explore, to experiment. Hell, I did so much of both. I wasn't sure I'd ever settle down, or even have an inkling to settle down.

Yet here I am.

"Business first?" I say finally, needing to change the subject before Darius and I end up sprawled on the floor, ready to kill each other.

"The money I demanded from Horatio has cleared in the offshore account. But he doesn't need to know Scarlett is safe, not yet." A sly grin curls his lips, but then he turns serious. "Also, I want to bring down the Bardots, Grace specifically. She had our father killed when he wouldn't give up on their relationship. She forced him out, he married

Mom, and yet, after all those years, when Mom died, he went back to Grace who had her cunt of a husband kill him."

"And you have proof?"

"That's what I've been trying to show you for years." He lets out an exasperated sigh. But this is all fucking news to me. Yes, I knew my brother believed in something, in someone coming after our family, but he never had proof. I'm a man who doesn't take things at face value. I need it in black and white before I realize it's the truth.

"And I need your help," I tell him. Kahn mentioned the rumors that had been sifting through the underground that an informant of Lorenzo's was brought here, to this house. On our way to the compound, the call came through. That was the other reason I was ready to finally sit down and talk to Darius.

"Well, it seems we have no choice," he says, settling back as the door swings open and a beautiful young woman I'm certain is only here to get my brother's attention sidles in with a tray. The aroma of coffee, along with her sickly sweet fragrance wafts by as she sets the items down on the table and offers Darius a long look before leaving us.

Perhaps his world isn't too different from mine.

"Someone I should meet one day?" I challenge, taunting him because he's not a one-woman man. He never has been. Settling down is not something Darius would ever do. At least, that's what I think.

"No. Like you said, business," he says finally, before pouring two steaming mugs of java and sliding one over to me which I gratefully accept. Last night was long, after I made sure Scarlett remembered just who owned her, I fell asleep holding her.

"I have been helping Alexei Carnevali, one of the capos from New York. He's been looking into a string of girls disappearing. It led us to a convent on the outskirts of New Orleans. I'm not sure—"

"Father Lorenzo?" Darius arches a brow as he regards me, and I nod. He must've gotten the name from the bastard he brought here. "Just learned about him a couple of days ago. What's your connection other than Alex?"

My brother and Alex's twin, Atreo, spent many nights in my club before Darius left. They've been best friends for a long while, but Atreo is one of those men who kills first and asks questions later, which is why Alex is the one who took over their father's organization.

"Kahn's sister disappeared a few years ago." I sip my drink before I look at my brother. "She was fifteen." I note his jaw clenching and his fists tightening as he ponders my words. "He'll want in on this, and I promised him that. Carnevali just wants the girls freed. I didn't get into why. My guess is they have mafia princesses in their latest haul."

"Do we have a location?"

I nod. "Kahn has it. We were on our way here, wanting answers because we learned one of Lorenzo's men was brought to your compound. I needed to know you weren't involved."

"You think I would do this shit?" Darius is fuming, and

I don't blame him. If he brought that same thinking to me, I would've probably killed him.

"No, but I had to know why you had an informant here," I tell him, swallowing back the last of the strong liquid before refilling my mug. "So, can we put our differences aside and work together on this?"

It's been far too long since we could have a civil conversation. Where we could sit like this in one room without being at each other's throats, and I have to say, it feels good.

"Yes. Call your men, I'll get my guys, and we'll strategize. We have to do this properly."

"Careful, brother, you're starting to sound like me," I taunt. A smile plays at my lips as Darius pins me with a glare. But he knows I'm right. He's the one who acts first, I'm the one who plans.

"Once Lorenzo is taken care of and the girls are free, we go for the Bardots." Darius won't let it go. And after learning about what Grace did, I'm on board one hundred percent.

"Have you contacted Horatio?"

"I have," he tells me. "The money he transferred to me will set the club up for the next ten years. He needed to pay one way or another. This way, I get my club financial security which means a lot to me." There's pain in my brother's words, and I wonder if there's something he's not telling me. I should ask, force him to come clean about everything, but right now, our focus has to be on finishing this job for Alex, and for Kahn.

"You did all this for financial gain?"

He shrugs as if it means nothing, but I can see the truth shining in his stare. "I didn't think you'd help. To be honest, I thought you'd send me away like Dad did all those years ago."

Guilt settles in my gut like a poison. "I'm not Dad. I may have loved him, but I never wanted to *be* him." My assurance has Darius nodding. "Also, I'm not returning my wife to her father," I inform him. "If he thinks that's happening, he has to think again. I'm not cowing to the bastard; I don't give a shit what he says. She's mine now, the contract was signed."

"How did you get him to sign his daughter's life to you?" There's a smile gracing my brother's face as he regards me with pride for what I did. It's something he would've done. In the past, I would've been nicer about it, given Horatio the benefit of the doubt, but after seeing what he can do to women, to the submissives and slaves in my club, I knew I couldn't let him get away with it.

"I learned some secrets he'd rather I keep hidden," I tell Darius. "And because he fucked up, he agreed to give me his daughter. All for me to shut my mouth about his underhanded dealings, along with the abuse women suffered at his hand."

"Bastard." It's a whisper, but I heard it. Familiar eyes meet mine. "Ready to get this show on the road?"

"Definitely." Nodding, I push to my feet before pulling out my cell phone and hitting dial on Kahn's number. "Oh, and I hope you didn't kill too many of my men yesterday," I tell Darius before turning away and heading for the patio. The bombs that went off when we returned were heartbreaking, but then, I expected nothing less from Darius Shaw.

"Boss," Kahn answers.

"Have the men here in thirty minutes. Get them ready for a strategy session because we're heading to take down Lorenzo. I want everyone here."

"Consider it done," Kahn responds before hanging up, and I sit back, resting my left ankle over my right knee as I refill my coffee. I should go back up to Scarlett and let her know we're okay—me and her. But I need to consider my strategy. She wants to be with Darius and me, and I wonder if I give her one night, will it be enough?

It has to be because I can't share long term.

Not with her.

SCARLETT

With my back against the headboard, I sigh when Lycan doesn't return. Thankfully, they've brought clothes for me, and I was able to change into some comfortable shorts and a floppy sweater. Another thing Lycan brought along was my cell phone. Having my device back is a saving grace. I hit dial on Aelin's number and hope that she doesn't hate me. When she finally answers, she's out of breath, as if she's been running.

"What the hell, bitch?" she gasps through the speaker.

"I'm sorry I haven't been in touch. I've... I don't even know how to explain it." Looking around the room, I try to find the words to tell her what's been happening.

"Well, since the wedding that went horribly wrong, I've been worried about you. But Kahn told me you'll be okay, and he said not to worry."

"He did?" This is a shock to me because I didn't expect him to even know about Aelin. Well, I suppose being Lycan's right-hand man, he would know everything about me.

"Yes, I went to the hospital after the shooting to see if Lycan was okay. That's when I met Kahn," she informs me, but her voice is far too dreamy, which confirms she's got the hots for the man. "Anyway, he said you're with Darius?"

I sigh. "Yeah, I was. Lycan and Darius had this massive family feud for years, and he was trying to anger Lycan by taking me." I don't even know how the hell I'm supposed to live with the two brothers who turn me inside out. "I just needed to know you don't hate me for just disappearing."

"Fuck, girl, it's not your fault. I mean, if it weren't for Kahn sending me updates, I would've had a goddamned search party out. I heard your dad telling mine you'd been kidnapped, but they didn't seem all that perturbed. Why is that?"

I don't know what to tell her. There's so much I still don't know, so for now I reply, "I'm not sure. Lycan is working on finding out what's going on with my dad. I mean, he basically gave me to Lycan, but there's a lot more to the story."

"You mean he fucking sold you," she bites out, anger clear in her tone. Aelin knows a lot more than I ever did. Her dad works with criminals, and I'm sure she hears horror stories all the time. Mine may not be so strange to her as it is to me.

"I get that, but I haven't had the courage to see him yet, to talk to my father. I just don't know how I'm going to sit in the same room with him and listen to his excuses."

Aelin sighs. "I'd be fucking fuming, I tell you that," she says. "I miss you. I want my best friend back."

Her words hit my heart deep. The thought of not seeing her again breaks me, and my eyes fill with tears. It's not goodbye, but I do miss her. I guess I just miss having a friend who I can talk to about things.

"I have to go, but I'll call you again," I tell her, because I need to try and find Lycan. I need to figure this shit out before I can promise her that I'll be home soon.

"You better," she warns.

"Oh and don't you go falling in love with Kahn. He's a..." I want to say killer, or something like that, but I don't, because I don't know him well enough. I can't judge her feelings for Kahn when I'm in love with Lycan and attracted to Darius, who is a killer.

"Ha! You bet your ass I'll be making sure he knows just what I'm capable of," she teases, and I realize she's not talking about violence. It makes me smile. Perhaps she can soften the man who looks like he'll easily kill anyone with a snap of his fingers.

"Stay safe, girl," I tell her.

"You too." She hangs up before I can say anything more, and I blink back the tears. I want to be back in Crimson

Falls, I want her closer, and I'm going to have to talk my husband into my plans for a business. I'd love to have Aelin work with me. He wasn't so sure about me running my business when we first met, but things have changed. I've changed.

Sighing, I sit back and wait for Lycan to come back from his meeting.

Time for me and my husband to talk.

By the time Lycan returns it's dark out. I've just finished dinner alone in the room when the door slides open and my husband steps inside. His shirt is rumpled, his tie is undone, and he looks exhausted.

"Hi." I smile nervously, still unsure of what to say to him after my confession this morning. He glances at me, those usually desire-filled eyes are weary tonight. "You look tired. Do you need to sleep? How are your wounds?"

"I want you naked, in the shower, right now." Is all the response he offers. He doesn't smirk, grin, or even smile. I watch for a moment as he pulls the tie from his neck before throwing it on the bed. "Did I stutter?" This time, the glow of need dances in his stare and heat flushes from my cheeks, down my chest, all the way to my stomach, where desire coils like a sleeping serpent ready to attack.

I'm on my feet and racing for the bathroom without another word. And I can almost feel his smile as his gaze burns into my back. Pulling the nightdress that I'm wearing over my head, I turn on the taps. I slink out of my panties and step under the spray, a cold shiver trickling through me as the warming water hits my shoulders.

Lycan is angry, or jealous, or something, and I'm almost certain I'm in for a punishment after what I said this morning. When he took my ass for the first time, it hurt, but I craved it. I enjoyed every moment. Awareness skitters over my naked flesh, and I turn to find him watching me. His green eyes almost black with feral yearning.

"So beautiful," Lycan murmurs as he steps under the spray behind me. "You know," he starts, as his hands trail over my shoulders, down my arms, before he lifts my wrists and presses my palms to the cool tiles. "All this time, I thought you were a good girl." His words drip with malice and lust, and his hand connects with my ass in a loud clap, sending shivers of pleasure rippling through me. Another spank before he continues, "I thought you were innocent and sweet."

"Lycan—" His free hand which clamps down on my mouth muffles my response, silencing me to the assault. Another harsh swat only earns him a whimper, but it bounces off the glass walls as he continues his punishment of my ass.

"But instead of being a sweet submissive to me," he hisses in my ear, and more heat pools between my legs, my thighs clenching only to earn myself another swat, and another. I lose count after a while, my head spinning as my ass tingles with the burn of Lycan's forceful hand.

He uses his foot to push mine apart. I'm bent at the waist, holding onto slippery tiles. The same position I was in earlier this morning, but something tells me this isn't going to be the gentle, loving man from earlier.

His fingers dip between my folds, finding them slick with need as he taunts me in an unrelenting pace, dipping inside me, pulling out, before thrusting back into my entrance until my knees start shaking.

"Hold yourself up," Lycan warns, and I can practically feel his satisfaction from controlling my body with just his two fingers. "So wet for me," he remarks when he slides from my pussy up to my ass. The tightness of my body has a groan of pleasure rumbling in his throat as he teases me open. It's slow, deliberate, and without looking, I'm certain he's smiling.

Lycan enjoys this. It's where his demons come out to play. In the darkness, where he can control my pleasure, like I'm a puppet on a string. Once his fingers are deep inside me, he releases my mouth to taunt my pussy with two fingers. I'm open, filled, and bliss hits me when Lycan curls his fingers and gently massages my G spot, sending bright lights sparking behind my eyelids.

"If you make a noise, it will be my fucking name you scream," he warns me before his movements hasten. I'm so close. I'm standing on the edge of euphoria as his finger pump inside me, both holes filled with him. And I'm about to crash when suddenly, Lycan pulls from me and I'm left empty and whining with the need to come.

"Please, Lycan," I plead, glancing at him from over my shoulder. I can't help my heart from stuttering at just how handsome he is. Wet from the shower, his dark hair sticking to his forehead, and those eyes are pure, black desire.

"On your knees," he orders, his voice gruff, raspy with desire, and his thickness bounces in front of him, jutting out toward me. "Time for you to earn your orgasm," he informs me. I obey without debate. The water is warm on my back as I take him into my mouth. The saltiness of his arousal coating my tongue, and his fingers tangle in my long, wet strands.

A hiss of pleasure falls from his lips as I stare up, watching the man I love fall to pieces as he uses my mouth for his pleasure. My tongue licking along the underside of his thick cock as the tip of his erection hits the back of my throat, and I hum in pleasure. Knowing you can bring a man to the brink of madness with just your mouth is powering, a heady feeling I enjoy, which turns me on.

And watching a man as powerful and controlling as Lycan Shaw at my mercy, is a drug I'll never get tired of taking. A shot of adrenalin to my veins. He glances down, our eyes locked in a standoff. He's angry, I'm needy. It's an equation for disaster, but fuck, it feels good. I swallow him deeper, trying to make sure he can feel every inch of my warmth, the same way I feel every inch of him. The smooth, silky flesh, that's hard as steel.

Lycan's fingers tighten in my hair as I swallow around

the tip of him, breathing through my nose as I fight my gag reflex, and that's when I feel him throb. I reach for his balls. The heaviness in my hand feels good, and I slowly massage them, which only seems to turn him into the hungry wolf I know him to be.

Lycan fucks my mouth with abandon, and roars his release, loud and feral, and I swallow every drop of his seed. The jets of warmth coating my tongue before I hum my approval as I clean him, ignoring my own desire that's now at breaking point.

He helps me to my feet and cups my face in his hands. Lycan brings me close, our lips touching, before he whispers, "Such a dirty girl, now it's my turn." His smirk is pure sin when he spins me around and bends me over until I'm in the same position I was in earlier—feet spread, hands on the tiles.

My husband drops to his knees behind me and spreads me open to his heated stare before his mouth lands on my pussy from behind, sending shock waves of bliss through my veins. I cry out this time, and it is his name I call.

Lycan licks at me, tasting every inch from my clit all the way to my ass, and I can't stop the heat of embarrassment that warms my cheeks when he does that. Nobody has ever done something like this to me before.

He continues his ministrations with his mouth, before his tongue dips into my pussy, and he fucks me with it, over and over again, until my body is shaking my knees are about to give out. I'm so close, and I pray with all my might that he doesn't stop this time.

His big hands release me, only to spank my ass once, twice, before he dips three fingers inside me, as he sucks on my pussy. Wet noises from between my legs have my face burning once more, but the more he fucks me, the more my nervous energy abates, and I'm lost to the pleasure.

More spanks.

More licks.

Another finger.

And then everything goes black.

LYCAN

The clock ticks by, the red letters on the nightstand glare at me. Today is going to be a long one, but I can't sleep. I'm tense. With my wounds still healing, I should be resting, but lying around in bed isn't going to get shit done. Even when Kahn told me I should allow him to take over, I couldn't bring myself to agree.

Usually, he's the one I call when I need help. But this time, it's personal. More so than ever before. Knowing we're about to take down Lorenzo makes me anxious. I'm not sure what we'll find in that convent, and to be honest, I'm not sure I want to know. But we have to save those girls, which means doing the dirty work.

Most times, my men head out on a job and I stay at the office, but this time, I can't hide from it. I want to be there. I glance at my wife, the ring on her finger shimmers in the low light of the moon that's streaming through the cracked curtains. She looks like an angel lying in my arms, and I can't help but be proud of what I've achieved.

She's by far my most prized possession.

And as much as she wants to refuse the fact that she's a possession, I'll always think of our beginning that way. I did buy her, in a way, but nothing could prepare me for the months that came after. And nothing could ever prepare me for what our future will hold.

I doubt any day with this girl will be *normal*. And that's okay with me. Some might call me weak for falling in love, but I haven't been stronger. I would lay down my life for her time and again. And I would kill anyone who tried to take her from me, even my own brother.

Asshole.

I should've hit him twice yesterday, but when I saw blood trickle from the cut on his lip, the beast inside me eased up, put away his fangs, until I walked into the bedroom and found Scarlett in bed. I needed to feel her, taste her, and I also needed to shower off the day, so I killed two birds with one stone, so to speak.

And fuck, she tasted like heaven and hell, all wrapped up in a pretty, tanned package. Her arousal coated my tongue, and even now, the taste of her lingers. It's a flavor I doubt I'll ever get rid of, not that I would want to, anyway.

Her long, crimson hair fans over the white pillow, and her dark lashes flutter against her smooth cheeks. Her breathing is even, but I have a feeling my little red is awake.

"Are you being a creeper?" she whispers, her voice heavy with sleep, and I smile. I fucking smile at my girl. She doesn't open her eyes, but the softness of her words feathers over my chest.

"For you," I tell her. "Always."

A small smile graces those pretty lips, and as much as I want to wake her up fully, fuck her into oblivion, I shouldn't. We have a long day ahead of us, and the drive down to New Orleans is going to be tiring. Once there, we'll make our way to the hotel and make sure we're all in position before making our attack on the convent.

I'm not sure where Lorenzo will be, or even if he's at the church. But one way or another, we're saving those girls tomorrow.

It's going to be late by the time we get there, and I think it would be best if we plan our attack in the early hours of the morning when everyone is still asleep. I'm hoping it will have people slower to react, rather than while they're working, which will give them time to escape through the fence, or head to hiding spots we may not find.

I feel Scarlett's body relax once more and her breathing evens out. She's asleep. I settle back and close my eyes, praying sleep will steal me, even if it's for a couple of hours.

"It's so hot," Scarlett says from beside me.

Even in the air-conditioned car, the heat is stifling. "It is, but we'll be there soon."

We've been on the road for most of the day. To avoid driving in convoy, we each headed out at different times. Darius is in the car in front of us, while Kahn and the team will be coming through an hour later. At first, we wanted to all leave together, but it would be too conspicuous, and we need to fly under the radar until we walk through those church doors.

Alex is flying in, so he'll be waiting at the hotel for us, and I'm almost certain he's told his brother to be there too. Atreo runs on his own rules, much like my brother, so who knows if he'll show up. However, with the promise of blood being spilled, I don't doubt he'll be there.

I'm anxious.

I need this to go well. We have to get those girls out, kill Lorenzo, and find out if there are any others working for him. If we can get confessions from some of the girls, perhaps even names, it would be helpful. And most of all, I pray Kahn can find his sister.

"You're a good man," Scarlett says from beside me, causing me to glance down at her. "You are," she insists when I arch a brow at her.

"You see things through rose-colored glasses, little red," I tell her, but there is a smile playing at my lips, showing her that I love having her tell me how I wish I could be. Even though I don't agree with how she sees me. That's why

Darius's feelings for her had grown, she's alluring, magnetic.

"No, I don't." This time, she pouts, and my dick jolts with approval and seeing those plump lips purse. The memory of our shower last night springs into my mind and I can't stop the groan of need that rumbles in my chest.

"If you keep doing that, I'm going to fuck your mouth right here in the back of the car while our driver watches," I threaten, earning me a dick-jolting gasp. Her mouth falls open, but she quickly shuts it. "Don't act like you're shocked at my words. You should be used to them by now."

"Oh, I am, Mr. Shaw," she taunts in a low tone, while running her nail along the length of my tie, before dropping to my crotch where she teases my now hardening cock through the material. "I just didn't expect you to need release so quickly after last night," Scarlett whispers. The last two words are a breathy sigh, before I grip her hips and drag her over my lap to straddle me.

I make quick work of bunching up the long red dress to Scarlett's hips, and I push away her flimsy panties before dipping my fingers into her sopping cunt. "No more panties in the car on any of our future trips. They get in my way when I want to do this," I tell her while pumping two digits into her tight heat. The warmth of her pulses around me, and I need to be inside her.

Scarlett sees the need in my eyes and undoes my belt, tugs my zipper down, before she takes out my cock, and slowly lifts herself over my shaft. As she slinks down my cock, my eyes roll back in my head as pleasure zips through me like an electric current.

She whimpers, but I watch as she bites her lip to keep from making a noise. However, the driver can see exactly what's going on in the backseat because I didn't put the partition up. Knowing he can see my wife ride me only makes me harder. Gripping her hips, I move her faster as she grips my shoulders, her fingers digging into the material of my shirt as I lift my hips.

I fuck myself into her while she moans louder with every thrust of my hips. Her tits bounce in front of me, and I'm not going to last long. Reaching between us, I circle her clit, teasing the little nub which only forces her nails to dig into my shoulders, and if I wasn't wearing a shirt, I'd have claw marks down my chest as Scarlett mewls my name over and over again.

My own release hits me then, and I empty jet after jet of my seed inside my wife. And for a split second, I wonder what it would be like to see her pregnant. To see her swollen with my babies, and I force her down on my cock, fully seating myself inside her, until I'm spent and Scarlett collapses against me.

Perhaps once this is over, it's time to talk to my wife about giving me those heirs I'd like.

LYCAN

The room is filled to the brim with testosterone. I don't blame Scarlett for staying in the bedroom while we plan our attack. It's almost ten in the evening and everyone is here. Each and every man is ready to take down this bastard, and Kahn is leading the pack.

"He's everything vile you can think of. The devil incarnate. We have the cartel on the border. Victor Cordero has his men waiting, so if they try to escape, we have them locked down. The water is covered by my team, and the airport is being manned by the Italians." He pins a stare on Alex who offers a nod of agreement. "The roads are being watched by this chapter of The Kovenant MC."

Darius nods before stepping forward. "We also have men that will make their way around the walls of the church and convent, in case anyone finds a way out that we don't know about, they'll be caught."

"And I get the girls," Alex says.

"Have you told us why you're so adamant about them?" Darius asks the question I'm sure is on a lot of minds in this room. He never gave me a reason, only that he needed it done. When it comes to the mafia, I don't ask questions.

For a moment, Alex looks like he's about to walk out. The fear that flickers in his eyes makes me nervous. But then he responds, "They have three of the Don's daughters." And everyone in the room's mouth gapes in shock.

"Fuck." This comes from Darius, but he's only voicing what we're all thinking.

Alex settles in a chair, his hand grasping the tumbler of vodka in a fierce hold. "And one of them was meant to be my wife. Not that I want her, but she's young, innocent, and I need to save her. I don't play the hero, because I'm not, but for my Familia, I need to do this."

A lot of made men who are forced to marry women they didn't choose. And being a Capo, I'm certain Alex has rules he needs to follow, but if he refuses this girl, I'm not sure what that means for her future. Does she just get sent to another one of the other made men? That could be worse.

Even though Alex is still fairly young, some of them are in their fifties and sixties. I couldn't imagine Scarlett would be happy with someone so much older. But then again, who knows what people desire these days.

"Then it's settled." I break the silence. "We'll go in before sunrise, which will give us the element of surprise. Every man in position by three, no later. If this goes wrong, there will be innocent blood on your hands." I take a moment to look at each of the men, and every one of them nods with an expression of pure need for violence.

As they take their leave and head to bed for a few hours of shuteye. I make my way to the bedroom where Scarlett sits on the bed, Kindle in hand, and I wonder if she's reading one of those romance books she seems to love so much.

"I need some rest," I tell her.

Those silver eyes flick to mine. "I'm worried about you." Concern is etched on her face, and even though I should really be in bed for another couple of weeks, I can't stay here while my men go into war.

Because that's what this is, a war.

"I'm fine," I assure her as I undress. Shrugging off my shirt, along with my slacks, I slip under the covers before I pull her toward me, needing her warmth to quell the urge to kill. That will come. For now, I close my eyes and nuzzle my nose into Scarlett's hair.

She sighs, and I realize she's not happy. But I also know she understands this needs to be done. I have to be there. And I'm thankful when sleep steals me quickly.

It's still dark when I slip into the backseat of the car, along with Kahn and two of his men, Fletch and Amir. Both have been with us for years, and now that I'm out on a job with them, I can appreciate just how nerve-wracking it is because anything could go wrong.

I know this.

I've always known this.

But being on the front line is different.

The vehicle weaves its way through the empty streets. I didn't think it would be this quiet, especially for a city like New Orleans, but thankfully, we're under the cloak of darkness when he finally pulls up to the enormous building that's shadowed by night.

There aren't any stragglers around which is good. As we exit, my feet crunch on the hard ground. The gates of the convent are shut, but a couple of our guys, all dressed in black, make a move to slide it open, which it does, with a squeak.

We wait.

With bated breath, guns in hand, and masks covering our faces, we slip through the crack between the two ornate gates. The property looks even bigger up close. A garden that's filled with trees which offer great hiding places, but then again, if someone is trying to escape, it may not be so good.

There's a couple of benches under a few of the trees, and one closer to the entrance, where the large sign hangs, and I know what it says without needing to read it—St

Jude's Church & Convent.

We move quietly, but quickly toward the entrance. There are three from what we saw on the blueprints, and we station a few men at each. Kahn takes the lead, with Alex—who arrived a few hours ago—and I following behind him as he manages to get the heavy wooden door to slide open.

Silence greets us when we step into the dark space. From the sliver of the moon which illuminates the stained-glass windows, I can make out the pews lined from the back of the church to the front. Beside a metal rack of flickering candles is the pulpit, and to my left are a couple of confessional booths.

We each take an aisle, Kahn the center, Alex the left, and I take the right. As we make our way closer to the altar, I notice the crosses on the floor. When I reach another wooden door, this one smaller, I try the lock, which clicks open, leading me into an office space.

Using the flashlight, I move to the desk and shine a light on the top, where there are papers strewn haphazardly across the surface. It looks like random application forms with girl's names on them. Some have photos which make my stomach roll.

Leaving those, I head to the right of the room, where there's a filing cabinet. Two of the drawers are locked, causing frustration to burn through me. Luckily, the last one is open. Rifling through the tabs, I find names printed on each one, and my chest tightens when I find names with the letter B because staring back at me is a name I never expected to see in here—Bardot.

I'm not sure what it means, but I pull the file out and stuff it in the front of my hoodie. It seems the family my brother and I are trying to take down are linked with the church.

I head back out into the church to find Alex and Kahn waiting for me. "Let's go." I try to ignore their stares. We make our way out into the courtyard which forms a circle. This is where the convent is. The girl's rooms are meant to be surrounding this fountain, which has a statue of Mother Mary looking down at anyone who stands beneath the flowing water.

The other men slip into the courtyard from various directions, and with one final breath, we signal to move. And that's when all hell breaks loose. The doors are kicked in, screaming erupts from the young women who thought they would be in bed for the night.

Two men stumble out in sweatpants, and they're immediately taken by the Italians. Alex's men move quickly, and soon, most of the girls have been ushered through to the exit, with each man explaining why we're here and where they'll be taken.

I notice relief on their faces, but when I glance over at Kahn, the anxiety has his fists clenched, and his face is drawn with pure heartbreak. I go to him, knowing he won't want to talk, but just offering silent support.

We watch as the anti-climax of wanting to find Lorenzo settles over the men. The priests who were here are taken away, and something tells me there's more to all of this than meets the eye.

"Something's wrong." This comes from Kahn just as my phone rings.

I answer, "Darius."

"Get out of there, brother," the urgency in his voice has me already moving, tugging Kahn and signaling to Alex. I hit the speaker on my phone as we make our way through the courtyard, back into the church. "Howler picked up some weird vibration from underground. There are bombs planted beneath the church and fountain, they'll be detonated because of the raid."

I hang up before he can continue and shout to everyone, "Move out! Now!" Men race along with us as we head for the gates. "Move! Get the fuck out now!" We're nearing the gate when an explosion that sends us flying, hits the air, the smoke rising, filling my lungs as I go down, hitting the ground hard. Debris falls around me as I cover my head with my hands. In an attempt to crawl away, I scrape my hands and knees on the ground as more pieces of the building comes crashing down around us.

Panic settles in my gut, twisting and turning. I promised Scarlett I would come home to her and I'm not about to fucking break it. I focus on the men in front of me, on the gate, and that's when Darius steps in my view.

He holds out his hands and drags me up as I wrap an arm around his neck. This is the closest we've been to loving or affectionate since we were about sixteen. All the years after, have been filled with arguments and fighting.

"You saved my life," I tell him. "If I didn't know any better, I would think you loved me." Even in the darkness of what's just happened, I can't help but grin.

"Only saved you so you could gift me a night with your wife," he taunts as he drags my bleeding ass to the car, where I fall into the backseat. Pain shoots through every part of me, and my legs and arms feel like lead is weighing them down.

"Fuck you," I bite out, responding to his taunt about Scarlett. She's going to kill me when I walk into our room, broken and bleeding.

Alex and Kahn join us then. "Fucking bastard knew we would come," Kahn says, his teeth gritted, his hands fisting. There's a vein throbbing in his neck, and his throat works hard as he swallows. His frustration is at boiling point. Thankfully, none of us were hurt. At least, I fucking hope so. I don't know about the rest of the men.

Glancing between the two of them, I realize Kahn is angry, but first things first. "Were any others hurt in the explosion?"

"No," Alex is the one to respond. "They got out around the back, those who came with us are fine." He leans back, blood dripping from his forehead, and we all need to get checked out. Just in case.

"Hospital?" Darius asks, and I nod in response. He takes it upon himself to order the drivers around, telling some to take the girls to safety. The drive to the hospital is bumpy, at least it feels like that because I'm in agony. Perhaps I should've listened to Scarlett and stayed home, but then my men would've been hurt.

The bright lights of the emergency room burn my eyes as we're wheeled toward the waiting doctors. I hate these fuckers. It's their job to probe and prod, but right now, the only thing I want is my wife. To hold her, to tell her how much I love her. And to tell her that if she truly does want one night with Darius and me, she can have it.

There is one thing I need to talk to my brother about, and that's coming home. He needs to be back in Crimson Falls for our plan to take down Grace Bardot to work. The folder falls from my clutches when the doctor tells me to unzip my hoodie to check my breathing, and when I pick it up, I find a photo of Grace, along with an application form, this one is different to those of the girls they were selling.

This one it titled differently.

Sponsor.

SCARLETT

The moment he walks in, I see the scars. There are scrapes on his handsome face, and my gaze drinks in every inch of him within seconds of the door shutting. He sets something down on the desk which is positioned against the wall near the entrance, before he looks at me.

"Oh my god. Are you okay?" I rush toward Lycan, careful as I gently wrap my arms around his torso, ensuring my hold on him isn't tight enough to hurt. Even though he is bruised and battered, he seems to be okay because he's smiling at me. Relief washes over me like a tidal wave. Emotions hit me right in the chest and tears spring to my eyes. The burn on my lashes is enough to have me blinking and allowing them to fall.

He nods, but it's a concentrated movement, as if he's focused on not letting me see him in agony when it's so damn clear. "I'm fine, just a bit torn up."

"And the other guys?" I question before I have time to think. But I don't say Darius's name, even though I want to know if he's alive.

A slight grin on my husband's lips tells me he knows. "Darius and Kahn are fine, they're with Alex now." Relief washes over me at his admission. Both men are good, and they deserve to find their own form of happiness.

I can't hide how I feel, not with Lycan, because he can see right through me. And even now, as Lycan stares at me as if I were a precious gemstone, shining before him, but there's something bothering him. It's his eyes, those expressive jade orbs.

"What's wrong?" I ask, my brows furrowing in confusion as I watch him watch me.

Honesty has always been something I wanted. In our lives and in our relationship. I won't tolerate lies and hidden truths. Lycan leads me to the sofa where he settles in comfortably and pulls me in beside him.

He winces, and I can't stop the sigh when I think about him hurting again. "I found something in the church," he tells me, causing my heart to stutter. "I don't know what it means, but we need to go back to Crimson Falls, and we need to do that very fucking soon."

"What is it, Lycan? You're scaring me." And he is. I've

seen him take charge before. I've even seen him in that controlling, commanding way he has, but this is something different. Lycan pushes to his feet, moving slowly as he does so. His arm wrapping around his middle as he holds onto his ribs. He picks up the item he set down a few moments ago before joining me again.

Once he's managed to settle beside me, he hands me the manila folder. With trembling fingers, I flip it open and see my grandmother's name under the title of sponsor. But it makes no sense. She's given money to so many businesses over the years. This may not be anything to worry about.

"What is this?" I ask, my brows furrowing when I delve deeper into the documents, and my heart drops to my stomach. The job they went to earlier was the convent. When I learned about the details, I felt sick to my stomach. Lycan told me about the reason that place existed. It wasn't a sanctuary. The girls were stolen. This is where he found my grandmother's name.

"I'm sorry, little red," he whispers as his arm wraps around me. He pulls me into the crook of his body, and it doesn't escape me how well I fit there. "I'm not sure what this means yet," he tells me.

But I realize what it means. It's written in black and white.

There's no mistaking my grandmother's money funded the convent. And perhaps she was unaware of what was going on under the cloak of darkness. Maybe she was trying to help, but it makes no sense. *Why would she send money to a place like that?* All the way down in New Orleans. It's nowhere near Crimson Falls.

However, my grandmother's business in New York is somewhat of a secret. She's never spoken much about it, only that she has meetings with her board members every few months. She travels a lot, so there's no saying she didn't know about this. Or knew about the operation that was being disguised as a place for women to find solace and healing.

"I need to speak to her." I'm shaking. My hands tremble as I hand the folder back to Lycan because I can't look at it any longer. The thought of being lied to, of my family being part of something so horrific has bile racing up my throat, and I rush for the bathroom, making it just in time to hurl my dinner into the porcelain bowl.

My body convulses as tears trickle from my eyes. My chest aches. Lycan is at my side within seconds, holding my hair, his big, strong hand circling my back as he comforts me, and I take solace in the fact that this man loves me so deeply.

When I'm done puking my guts up, he helps me to my feet, and I brush my teeth in the sink before Lycan leads me to the bed. We settle under the covers, him on his back and me cocooned under his strong arm.

"I'm sorry," he says then, causing me to snap my gaze up toward him. "I'm sorry I can't explain why I found her details in that place. I wish I knew more. I'm sorry you're hurting." There's pain in those words, regret that seeps from his lips, and I press my mouth to his, needing to silence his apologies.

"This isn't on you," I tell him. "You can't protect me from everything in this world." It's a mere whisper, but he hears it.

Those green orbs lock with mine, hooking me and reeling me in. "I can damn well try," he confirms. "I'm your husband, and if I can't protect you, then my men will. I don't want you hurt, ever."

I nuzzle into his hold before I say, "Unless it's you hurting me?" I can't help but smile. My attempt at lightening the mood has him groaning. But I'm not sure if it's because of my words, or because he's in pain. "Do you want me to move?"

"No." He tightens his hold as he answers, and now I definitely can't shift away from him with his heavy arm wrapped around me protectively. "I don't want to let you go again," Lycan tells me easily, his voice rough with exhaustion, and I stay silent, hoping he'll get some rest.

We're all tired, and with the number of revelations that seem to be piling up, I'm not surprised. My family, his father, and the connection to that vile criminal, I have a feeling this is only the beginning.

"We'll leave in the afternoon," Lycan whispers before his breathing evens out, and I'm excited to go back to Crimson Falls, to the Shaw manor which is now partly mine. My ring shimmers when I trace my hand in circles over Lycan's chest as it rises and falls.

He's asleep within seconds, and I lie awake. His warmth cocooning me, but like I told him moments ago, he can't protect me from everything, no matter how much he tries. I wish he could. I do. But there comes a time in our lives when we need to keep each other safe.

We're equals, even though he is a dominant alpha male who wants to act like a caveman at times. But this is my family's lies that are coming to light, and I need to deal with this the only way I know how—by sitting them down and talking face to face. My parents and grandmother have a lot to answer for.

The contract my father signed comes to mind. He still hasn't answered for his transgressions and it's time he did. There are more things they need to explain, so many more, but we'll start off small and work our way up to the much more pressing matters, like how my grandmother could have killed Conall Shaw.

My heart hurts for the two men who have come to mean so much to me. My brother-in-law, who's so broken, so tortured, I'm not even sure he could have a normal life anymore. And my husband, whose need to control everything and everyone is now so much clearer. I thought he was just a domineering bastard, but he's more than that—he's a broken man who needs to know he won't lose anyone else that matters to him.

It makes sense. When you've had to say goodbye to everyone you love in your life, it's scary to think you would have to do it again. But he has to know I'm not going anywhere. If you had told me months ago that I'd be here, in this position, wanting to stay with Lycan, proud to be his wife, I would've told you you're lying.

I think about my life, and all the people who I thought were there to keep me safe. Instead, they lied to me, kept secrets from me, and sold me just to ensure their bullshit didn't come to light. That they didn't get found out for things they did.

Then I think of the only person who was there for me. Other than Lycan. And I realize how much I miss her. As soon as we get back, I need to see Aelin. I need someone to talk to that isn't a commanding, domineering man.

My lashes flutter against my cheeks as weariness finally comes knocking and with the thought of building a new life in my mind, I nuzzle deeper into Lycan's hold as I allow sleep to steal me.

LYCAN

I'm thankful to be back in Crimson Falls with my wife. The most surprising thing is that my brother is here too. I never thought I'd see the day where he walked into this house willingly. Yet here he is.

We're seated at the dining room table, the same one we sat at so many times before as kids. Growing up, we didn't think about the importance of spending time together. For us, we wanted to race out to be with our friends. Yes, we were close as brothers, closer than some, but right now, I feel like I've gained my family back.

Even though our father isn't here, I still feel his presence as we eat dinner. With Scarlett beside me, and

Darius opposite me, it feels like I'm finally home. I've spent so long in this house, especially when I first brought my girl here, but for the first time, I'm at ease.

I'm comfortable.

It's an emotion I've not allowed myself to feel for so long, it's jarring. I finish the last bite of steak before I settle back and pick up my drink. Watching the two people who mean the most to me in this world, I take a sip of vodka, a liquor I haven't had in years, and enjoy the bitter taste as I swallow it down.

"The first thing I want to do is settle this..." I start, thinking of the best words to use to describe what I want. I settle for, "...thing between us." I glance between Scarlett and Darius, noticing the blush that forms on my wife's cheeks.

My brother, on the other hand, looks like he's about to burst with excitement. I pondered this all the way back home. The thought of sharing her with anyone else doesn't sit well with me, but knowing my brother will give her what she needs allows me to consider it more and more.

I look at my wife. "You're new to this world of mine. And I haven't truly taken you like I want to, shown you what it entails." I smile when her cheeks darken to a soft rosy hue, and the image of her ass, her thighs, and her calves turning the same color has my dick thickening behind the zipper of my slacks. "I want you to experience it, just this once." I tack on the last three words to ensure there's no discussion.

"I don't know what to say," Scarlett responds, lifting her napkin to dab at the corners of her mouth as she finishes her meal. She's so fucking beautiful, at times it's difficult to look at her. To even fathom this woman is mine.

"We will come to an agreement, what you're not willing to try, and anything not on that list will be on the *yes* pile. It's free rein for us." I lift my glass and tip it toward Darius.

"Are you sure about this?" Darius asks as he watches me. I can tell he's worried about my choice to do this. But he doesn't need to be. I'm doing this for her.

"Scarlett hasn't experienced being a submissive to me yet. Yes, we've played, very little, but I've eased her into my life. I didn't want to throw her in the deep end. Mainly because the start of our relationship wasn't... conventional," I finally find the word to describe it.

"That's no lie," my wife sasses as she sips her wine. Her mouth crimson from the alcohol, and I can't stop the desire from burning through my veins as I watch her lick her lips. "I'm just surprised you're willing to do this, because you can be like a caveman at times."

"Keep up with that sass and I'll put you over my knee right here in front of Darius, as well as the staff and I'll spank your bare ass as they watch," I threaten, causing her mouth to fall open and a shocked gasp to free itself from her plump lips.

Darius chuckles. "Now that is something I'd love to see." When Scarlett pins him with a glare, he only laughs harder. "My brother doesn't fuck around when he threatens,

I would be careful if I were you."

My gorgeous woman folds her arms across her chest and tips her chin up in defiance. "Fine. I want to do it. So, let's do it." There's fire in her eyes, and I wonder just how much she'd be able to handle. The thought has my cock throbbing with the need to see her begging and pleading for mercy. Between Darius and me, she'll be nothing more than a whimpering mess of blissful female flesh.

"Are you sure?" I arch a brow, meeting her defiant gaze, which only seems to make my dick harder with each passing second. I want to be inside her, right here and fucking now. "Because once you agree, there's no going back."

"One night," Scarlett says with confidence, but I can read the hint of tension that's so clear in her voice. She purses her lips, and I smile.

"Then it's settled," I respond with a satisfied nod. I glance over at Darius, his gaze wide with shock. He didn't think I would agree to it. The thing about it is that my ring is on her finger. And even though it's only a scene, one night, I'm convinced she'll come back to me. Last night cemented her love and affection for me. While I was in pain, her need to care for me when she herself was hurting made it clear that there would be nothing that would take this woman away from me. I want to give her this, and to be honest, I'm going to enjoy it as well.

"And when do you propose we do this?" Darius asks as he watches me, still wary at my sudden change of heart to his request for one night with her.

We have a lot to do, I realize that. For one, we need to find out why Grace was funding Lorenzo's convent, and we also need to find the fucker. Kahn is working on tracking him, the bastard got away before we arrived, but when they managed to get into the building, they found proof that he'd been there, not long before we arrived.

The girls who have been questioned so far gave us a list of names, and I've agreed to allow Alex and Kahn to work together to end the organization. We know who they are, now all we need to do is find the kingpin.

This was always going to be Kahn's mission. He's still looking for his sister, and deep down, I pray that she's still alive. I'm not sure what condition he'll find her in, but if she's alive, we can get her help, therapy.

"Tomorrow night," I finally answer both Scarlett and Darius. "Once we've spoken to Grace, gotten some answers from her, we can come back here and have dinner. I have a feeling after talking to the old woman, we'll need to let off some steam."

"I want the police on standby," Darius says quietly before glancing at Scarlett, whose lip is wobbling. This must be difficult for her. Knowing your family has lied to you is one thing, but the proof we have of the money going into an account in Lorenzo's name is another.

I didn't want to believe it at first. But once Howler sent through the documents confirming payments, there was no longer a doubt in anyone's mind. Grace will pay. I'll make sure of it, but first, we need to talk to her, get answers for ourselves. The one thing I need to know is how she could've killed my father, or had him killed, when she loved him so dearly.

"She will be taken away, arrested, and I'll make sure she never sees the light of day again," I affirm with a nod before taking Scarlett's hand. "I'm sorry that you have to go through this."

My wife shakes her head, those silky crimson strands fall like a curtain, covering her face for a moment before she looks up at me. "She needs to pay for what she's done. And when my father arrives, he needs to answer for his transgressions as well." The confidence in her tone, and the conviction painted on her pretty face, make me proud to be her husband. She's so much stronger than I ever gave her credit for. At least in the beginning.

"Let's go up," I tell her, needing to be alone with her for a while, to hold her, give her the strength she needs in order for her to fall apart. Scarlett nods, and I push away from the table, offering Darius a nod in greeting before leading my wife to our bedroom.

The moment we step into the room, I pull her into my arms and allow her to break down. It's not easy, this is going to be one of the most difficult things she's ever had to do, but she'll get through it because I'll be beside her.

She shakes in my arms, her shoulders rising and falling as she cries. I could tell she needed this, it's partly my need to read everything that she's emanating, as a Dominant, but also, I've come to learn this woman inside and out. She can never hide anything from me, most of all her emotions.

"You'll be okay," I assure her confidently.

Slowly, she nods against my chest before looking up at me. Her wet lashes fluttering as she regards me. Those pretty silver eyes shimmering. "I will because I have you."

Shaking my head, I respond, "Not only that, but you're tough. On your own, you've got the strength to get through anything." She doesn't need me to hold her hand through life, because she can do things on her own. "You may be young, but you have an inner strength that can bring men to their knees. When we first met, I figured you were a spoiled little rich girl, but you're so much more, you're a woman. Fierce, resilient, and beautiful."

A small smile plays at her lips. "I'm glad you can finally see that," she sasses before I swat her ass hard with the palm of my hand. "Ouch!"

"That mouth will earn you a lot more than that," I warn her, but the smirk on my lips betrays just how much she controls me and my needs.

"Then show me, Mr. Shaw," she teases, and I lift her in my arms, planning to do just that and so much more tonight. Because tomorrow, we're going to walk into a fucking inferno.

SCARLETT

I'm nervous.

I didn't expect to feel like this. Anxious energy twists in my stomach, expelling everything I eat or drink. And that means I haven't eaten all morning. My grandmother is on her way, and I'm not sure I want to be here to have the conversation we need.

Last night Lycan held me, and I cried. I hadn't done so in such a long time; it was refreshing, freeing. His strong arms ensured I was safe, and it was as if his strength had grounded me. So, even though I was broken-hearted, I never felt as if I was alone.

I'd been focused on my future for most of my life.

My path had been set out for me, and I knew where I was headed. He walked in and my life veered in a different direction than I expected. But it's also been eye-opening.

I'm a new person.

A different woman.

All grown up and ready to take on the world as Mrs. Shaw.

Last night, at some point after I'd dried my tears, I decided I no longer wanted the Bardot name, so, as soon as we can, I'm changing it. The thought of being linked to my grandmother, and what she's done in the past, leaves unease in my gut.

I don't like it.

And I don't want it.

Slipping on my sneakers, I stand and make my way out of the bedroom I now share with Lycan. I still have my red riding hood themed room, which I can escape to if I feel the need. I haven't felt the need to yet. But it's only been a couple of days so far.

In the living room, I find Darius and Lycan talking with Kahn. They fall silent when I move closer, and each one of them glances at me. The need to tell them I'm not fragile overpowers my desire to roll my eyes.

"You do not have to hide things from me," I say, meeting my husband's gaze. "You know this." I settle in beside him, my arm instinctively wrapping around his neck as I take in the other two men.

"We may have a location for more of Lorenzo's clients,

so I'm making sure Darius and Lycan are okay with me taking the lead from here on out," Kahn informs me. Lycan told me about his sister, which only makes what my grandmother did so much more personal than if I didn't know anyone connected to the girls. It sounds strange, but it's true.

"We are," Darius says, along with Lycan's nod. "I think with your connection to this, it makes sense. But if you need help, don't hesitate to ask because my men wouldn't mind spilling some blood." There's a sinister grin on his face, and I'm sure he's included in that team of men who would like to have blood on their hands. He's done it before, and even though I should be scared, I'm not.

I'm proud of the men in my life because they're fighting for the greater good. Sometimes we have to do bad things to make sure the world turns. But when we do those bad things, they're done to bad people, which in a strangely fucked up way makes it okay.

"I think with the Italian's in on this job, along with your club, we can ensure these bastards never see the light of day again," Kahn says with a smile that belies what he's talking about. "Sorry." He looks at me, but I can't help but return the grin.

"Please, don't apologize," I tell him. "They deserve what's coming to them. And I certainly don't need to be handled with kid gloves."

He tips his fingers in a mock salute while offering me a smile. "I'll remember that, Mrs. Shaw," he responds, and the use of my married name sends heat skittering through me. It's the first time I've been acknowledged as Lycan's wife by someone other than my husband, and it feels good. Different, but good.

"Mr. Shaw," one of the men I recognize from the day Lycan came to rescue me from Darius, steps into the room. "There's a Mrs. Bardot here to see you."

My heart skips a beat, leaping into my throat, and I find it difficult to swallow past the fear. "Send her in here," I answer, pushing to my feet before I smooth down my hands over the jeans I'm wearing. My palms are sweaty, and my nerves are once more tingling with the need to run and hide. But this is something I need to do.

"Are you sure you're ready?" Lycan asks from behind me, his hand reaching for one of mine and I allow him to tangle his fingers through mine.

I nod slowly, but I offer him a reassuring smile before answering, "I am."

The door slides open, and my grandmother walks in. She's dressed in a white skirt suit, which is paired with a soft pink blouse underneath. Her dark hair is pulled tight against her head in a bun that's so precise, I'm almost sure she measured the width and height to make sure it's perfect.

"Scarlett," she greets, but doesn't acknowledge any of the men in the room. Her focus solely on me as she settles in a chair which I gesture to.

"Hello, Gran," I greet, my fingers trembling as my nerves get the better of me, but Lycan's strong, supportive squeeze of my hand gives me the strength I need. I should be angry, but I'm actually disappointed in her for what she's done.

"Hello, Grace," Lycan says, his hands finding my hips as he holds me gently, offering a reassuring squeeze before releasing me. "Would you like something to drink before we get into it?" He moves around me, standing in front of me, just enough to allow her to see the protective nature that's so natural to him. At least with me.

"I'd like you to tell me what I'm doing here so I can get back to my business," she says, her tone filled with ice and venom as she pins my husband with a glare. "I think this is rather inconvenient."

"Inconvenient?" I spit, attempting to step around Lycan whose hand shoots out to hold me back. His hand slips into mine, his fingers tangling with mine, and I allow him to subdue me for the moment. "Did you also think it was inconvenient when you decided to fund a criminal organization?"

"I don't know what you're talking about, girl," she says to me, her chin tipped in defiance as she regards me. The look in her eyes has my blood boiling. I want nothing to do with her. I want her to be locked away forever, but I need answers first.

"Does the name Father Lorenzo sound familiar?" I test, arching a brow, I watch as her face contorts from the cool, icy mask to emotion-filled guilt. But the moment it appears, it's gone in the next second and she schools her features once more.

"Can you get to the point? I know a lot—"

"Don't fucking lie to me," I spit, causing her to wince at my outburst. I shove the folder across the table, and it stops right in front of her. We've made copies of the documents. The originals are now with the authorities, and once Lycan gives them the signal, they'll arrive to take my grandmother away.

I watch as she picks up the manila folder and flicks it open. Her eyes widen for a moment before she lifts her gaze to me. "I can explain this."

"Really?" This comes from Kahn who's now on his feet glaring at her. He's shaking with rage, and I don't blame him. "Because my sister, who's been gone since she was sixteen, might not want an explanation. The girls we found in the convent will most definitely not want to hear your lies about why you were supporting this bastard." His voice has a violent edge to it, but he keeps his tone calm, and I'm in awe because I would've lost my cool.

"Scarlett," she addresses me, and just hearing her say my name has my body shaking with anger. "There were things that I had to do to ensure you had a life, a comfortable life."

"Don't fucking blame me for this," I hiss, rage fueling my words as I step past Lycan and toward my grandmother where she's seated in the chair. I place my hands on the arms of her seat, getting in her face, I continue, "Does he know?"

Her brows furrow at my question. "Who?"

"My father." I hold my breath. I'm not sure what I want her to say. If he does know, then would he have sent me to that place? I don't know. But he happily signed my life over to Lycan, so I wouldn't put it past Horatio Bardot to do something so sick and vile.

"He understood what we needed to do."

"I want you and him to rot in hell."

"Scarlett," grandmother gasps in surprise at my vicious words. "That's no way—"

"What? No way to talk to a criminal. Or to my grandmother who lied to me my whole life?" I push away, the chair sliding back an inch or two as I step into Lycan's hold. His strong hands grip my shoulders, and once more, I'm grounded in safety. "If I never see you again, it will be too soon. Don't try to contact me and never fucking come near me. You or my father."

This time she's on her feet, making her way toward me when suddenly Darius is in her face, his hand wrapping around her throat. "Did you kill my father?" The question is a low growl filled with pure hatred. I've seen Darius splattered with blood when he clearly murdered a man. I've imagined him killing someone, but I have never been more afraid of him than I am right now.

Grace Bardot is outmatched right now. It's the first time I've ever seen my grandmother falter. "What?"

"Tell me the fucking truth. Did you, and that bastard you married, kill my father?" he asks again, and with every moment that passes, Lycan's hold on my arms gets tighter. He's afraid, worried about what she'll say.

If she did, I don't doubt Darius will kill her. He would

squeeze his fingers, and her neck would snap with a crack. My stomach rolls at the thought of seeing someone die right in front of me. It's not the fact that it's my family, my blood, but more that I've never seen a dead body. Not even when my grandfather died.

I wasn't allowed to go into the viewing room where his corpse laid. My mother kept me sheltered all my life and I wonder if it's because of that, I'm scared of this moment.

"I... I loved him," Gran says, her voice croaky from not being able to breathe properly. Her face turns a bright red as she claws at Darius's hand. "H-h-he meant t-the world t-t-to me."

"That's not what I fucking asked you, bitch," Darius rumbles, the words a low, venomous whisper that drips with the threat of him holding her life in his hands. "If you don't answer me, I'll just torture you, over and over again until you find it in your fragile old mind to recall the moment Conall Shaw took his last breath."

Silent moments pass.

My lungs struggle as we wait for her answer.

The thrumming of my heart in my ears is loud as blood rushes through me. Anticipation coils in my stomach, and my hands tremble when I think about two boys, two young men losing their father because of my grandmother's inability to be honest.

"M-my h-h-husband didn't like him," she speaks finally, and it's as if my breath has been knocked from my lungs. She doesn't need to continue because what's she's already said makes it clear what happened. Darius releases her throat, and her hand flies up to massage the wrinkled skin as she locks her gaze on the older Shaw brother. "Randolf and Conall had an argument one night." She shakes her head, lowering her eyes to the ground before she speaks again. "I told Randolf to leave it be. He found the notes that Conall had written in the books in the library. I gave all but one back to Conall. I wanted so much to have one last memory of a time I was happy."

Silence hangs in the air when Gran falls silent. That explains why all the books were here in the Shaw library and I only found the one in my gran's home. I can't imagine why my grandfather would've gotten jealous over notes. But then again, I wouldn't like it if Lycan had memories of his exes.

But that still wouldn't push me to kill.

"I don't understand why he would've killed Conall," I speak up. "There's jealousy, and then there's what you're trying to say Gramps did. It doesn't add up."

She looks at me then. Her eyes locked on mine, and I notice how she doesn't veer from me. She doesn't look at Darius or Lycan. And something clicks in place in my mind. As if a puzzle piece just slides into place.

"You were pregnant," I whisper, realizing that my grandfather may have gotten angry, and possibly jealous, but to kill someone, there had to be more to the story. So much fucking more.

And when she nods, it's as if the room fills with ice.

LYCAN

No. No. No.

If Grace Bardot was pregnant all those years ago, just before Dad died, it would've meant that he had been with her not long after our mother died. He would've told me. We were close. Betrayal hits me hard as Grace confesses to learning about her pregnancy.

My hold on Scarlett tightens. I don't want her to think I'm angry, so I pull her closer. The softness and warmth of her keeps me somewhat calm. And if she weren't here, I would've lost my control, restraint would've been a thing of the past if my wife wasn't near me.

"I didn't want to tell him about it, but I had no choice.

He saw the test. He locked me in our bedroom and told me he was going to *sort it out* and when he came back, he was calm. There was still anger simmering in his eyes, and I knew something had happened."

"And you didn't ask him about Conall? I mean, our father was the love of your life for a long time. And the fact that you cheated with him means you still had feelings for him," I whisper as my mind tries to make sense of what could've happened.

"He told me he didn't want to raise another man's child." There's an edge to her voice when she says this, not the anger I expected, but guilt. Her gaze flicks to Darius, then back to me. "It was one of the most horrific nights I spent with the man I married."

"What happened?" Scarlett's voice is nothing more than a murmur, and I'm shocked Grace can even hear her. The fear in my wife's tone is clear, she doesn't want to know what had occurred that night, because we all have an inkling without Grace saying the words.

Scarlett shakes her head.

I want to step forward, to pull my wife away from the news she's about to receive and keep her safe from the atrocities that her family has done over the years. But no matter what I do, I realize I can't shelter her forever. She told me she's strong. But this is far beyond anything either of us imagined.

"I'm sorry, Scarlett," Grace says in a low whisper while I pull my cellphone from my pocket and hit dial on the number. Three rings, and I end the call. It's time to put a stop to this and keep my wife safe. "I didn't mean for you find out about this. I did things I'm not proud of and I accept my fate, but don't blame your father for this."

"Don't *blame* him?" My wife's voice turns loud, filled with shock that Grace can even request that of her. She shakes in my arms, her body trembling, and I can't imagine what it must be like to realize your family never truly loved you. "He fucking sold me! Do you even understand what that means?"

Grace tips her head as if she doesn't care. Her chin jutting out in defiance as she pins her granddaughter with a stare. "It doesn't look like you're too angry since you married him," she snips before tipping her chin in gesture to me. "I think you did rather well. Lycan is wealthy, can give you children, I'm sure. And when the time comes, you'll live a comfortable life without ever having to work again."

If anger were an entity, it would be beside my wife right now. I release her when she pulls free from me and stalks toward the old woman. I've seen her angry a few times, when I took her for the first time. When I saved her from the woods and brought her to my house. But those moments have nothing on this.

She gets in Grace's personal space, she's inches from her, before Scarlett speaks. "Don't you ever talk about me or my husband like that. I was pushed into this life, yes, but I made sure it was something I wanted. Do you even understand what it's like to have your choices taken away from you?"

When Grace doesn't answer, she merely watches her granddaughter, and for a moment, a split second, I'm sure I see pride in her eyes as she takes the younger woman in.

Scarlett continues, "You had a choice a long time ago, and you chose wrong. You could've righted those wrongs, but you didn't. You could've raised your son properly, but you didn't. I'm sorry to say, but you failed us, me, Dad, and even mom when she joined the family."

Grace nods slowly, and I can see the wheels turning in her head. She can't deny it anymore. And she most certainly cannot tell her granddaughter that she's in the right because she isn't.

"I know." Two words and it's almost as if Scarlett deflates. The breath is whooshed from her lungs, and I have to step in, pulling her toward me, wrapping my arms around her protectively. "I did things because I believed they were right. At the time. But now, looking back, I've made stupid choices. And I will pay for that. There is no doubt that I will, and I go willingly."

Even though Darius and I were at odds for a long time, we still did shit because we cared. There was anger, guilt, and rage that would flow from our words, and yes, he did shoot me, which we still need to hash out, but when I glance over at him, relief washes over me at him being here, by my side to take this family down for killing our father.

It doesn't take long for the doors to fly open after my call and the suits to walk in. They make a beeline for Grace.

Her gaze locks on mine. She knows I was the one who called them, and she doesn't put up a fight as they lead her out of the room.

Before she disappears from sight, she looks at me, then at Darius. "I'm sorry for my hand in what happened to your father. I should've stopped it, but I was weak. I never wanted to lose him or the baby, but fate had other plans."

It's time for Darius to step forward, and he quickly closes the distance. "Don't you ever think about him. Don't fucking shed a tear for him because you did this. Not your bastard of a husband, you." The anger in my brother's tone is chilling, and I'm certain if I left him to handle Grace Bardot, she'd be dead right now.

Second later, she's gone. Scarlett is still shaking as I wrap her in my arms. The dining room door closes, and I can't help but breathe a sigh of relief. Grace is in for hours of questioning, and when they're done, she'll be locked up, the key thrown away. It's what she deserves.

Darius glances at me, the knowing expression on his face that we've finally gotten justice for our father makes me smile. It's small, a mere quirk of the corners of my mouth, but it's enough for my brother.

Scarlett turns to me. Her eyes wide. "Is it over?" Her question has me taking her in my arms and nuzzling my nose into her fragrant hair. So sweet and so mine.

"Yes." It's the only thing I can voice, because I'm still shocked at the revelations that came to light today. I knew the proof Darius showed me was real, that it was the Bardots who killed Dad, so I'm not as shocked as I would've been if I didn't trust Darius.

"I'm sorry," Scarlett whispers, her hand cupping my cheek as she stares up at me. Before I can say anything, Darius is behind her, his hands on her hips and my inner beast roars with possessiveness. "I'm sorry." This she says when she looks at him.

She's so tiny between us. The thought of the past sitting behind us is calming. I turn my attention to Kahn, who's now moving around the table as he watches us, a smirk curling his lips, and I want to tell him it's not what he thinks, but I'd be lying.

I thought long and hard about it, and it's happening. Without a doubt it is because I recall the pleasure, the passion, and I can't deny us that.

"I'll be in the office. We'll sort out Lorenzo," Kahn informs me, still grinning as he arches a dark brow at me. He knows what's going to happen here tonight. I want to make Scarlett forget about her fucking grandmother.

We still have her parents to sort out. I want to ensure that Horatio knows exactly what he did to his little girl while being more concerned about his life than hers. And her mother, she's also in for it, because I'm going to let Darius loose on her. And I can't wait to see the aftermath of that.

Kahn leaves. It's only the three of us, like it will be for a long time to come. But for now, Scarlett will be ours to enjoy, and this evening, she'll learn what it's like to be loved by the two Shaw brothers.

I lift my gaze to his. A small, glimmer of a smile on his mouth. We know who killed our father, and I hope Darius and I can finally put the past behind us. I owe him an apology. I never believed him when he told me the MC didn't hurt Dad. It's my fault he had to live with the pain for so long. Away from our childhood home.

SCARLETT

My emotions are in turmoil.

Anger and sadness are at the forefront of my mind though. After hearing Gran's confession, I'm still reeling.

The sun shines down on my skin as I lie on the lounger in an attempt to read a book, but I can't focus. I wanted to relax, to try to forget everything that happened and focus on my future, but we haven't yet spoken to my mom and dad.

I have to.

I can't ignore the fact that my father paid money to Darius and signed my life over to Lycan. It's as if he doesn't care about me. It's almost as if I'm not his child, and anything that happened to me didn't faze him.

That thought hurts.

With Lycan and Darius gone to meet with Kahn, the house is quiet. The silence forcing my mind to whirl with images of my grandmother being taken away, with the wedding, the shooting, everything that happened over the past few months is slowly taking its toll, and I want to forget. Just for a night. Which brings my thoughts back to this evening and the promise Lycan offered Darius.

Both of them want me.

It's intoxicating knowing two powerful men want to be with me, at the same time. Even the few scenes I had with Lycan will not compare. I realize they won't. I'm so new to their world, and the thought of even just having them both touch me at the same time sends heat coursing through my veins.

Sighing, I set the book down and push to my feet. The warmth of the day will soon disappear, and I'm eager to learn what Kahn found out about the convent and Father Lorenzo. I pray he's got some answers and hopefully knows if his sister is alive and well. I can't imagine the pain of losing family you love and care about.

When I reach the bedroom, I find my phone vibrating on the nightstand. Picking it up, I swipe to answer the call.

"Little Red," Lycan's deep timber rumbles through the speaker, and my earlier thoughts about him and Darius's promise about tonight hits me full force. "I want you to prepare for tonight. I want you to have a long, hot bath.

There are some essential oils in the cabinet, relax, and try to clear your mind as much as you can. We'll be back in a couple of hours, and we'll both be ready to play."

"Yes, Lycan," I whisper, my thighs already squeezing together and the thoughts that are racing through my mind.

"Good girl." He hangs up before I can respond, and I'm left trembling in the middle of our bedroom. I head to the en suite to find the oils he mentioned and quickly plug the bath before turning on the hot tap and trickling some lavender oil into the water.

As the tub fills, I step into the warmth and sigh as relief washes over my muscles. I settle back, allowing my head to dip under the water, and everything around me goes silent. The world falls away, and I'm lost in the warmth, and the quiet of the water. It's serene under the surface, and I enjoy it for a long while until I need to take a breath.

I lather up with the liquid soap and take my time shaving. After about an hour of soaking, I get out and towel off. In the bedroom, I open the closet and take in each of the outfits Lycan purchased for me when I was first brought to the manor.

I choose a short, bright red dress which has a scoop neckline and non-existent back. It's beautiful and very sexy, and it will drive them both crazy. I can't help but smile at the thought as I take it into the room. Setting it on the bed, I moisturize with my rose-scented cream, dry my hair and straighten it until it's sleek down my back. I keep my make up natural, but dab some dark crimson lipstick on, which makes my lips look plump.

By the time I'm done, I check the time and realize I've been getting ready for two hours. I quickly slip my dress on and find a pair of black heels which have thin straps that wrap around my legs, all the way to my knees.

The hemline of my dress hits me on my upper thigh, and if I were to bend over, my black lace panties would be visible. The idea of teasing them makes heat pool at my core, and I'm pretty sure by the time we finish dinner, I'll be soaked with arousal in anticipation.

But that's what Lycan wants. He loves when I'm needy for him, and to be honest, it happens more often than not. Even when I hated him, I wanted him. It was unfair of my body to betray my mind, but I had no control.

I hear noise from outside the bedroom. Pulling the door open, I step out into the hallway, ready to take on whatever tonight will bring. As I walk down the hallway toward the staircase, my heart leaps into my throat, thudding wildly when I hear both Lycan and Darius's voices carry toward me.

The moment I step into their sight, I realize they've seen me because all conversation halts, and I swear I hear them pull in a breath of shock and desire. I turn, my hand on the smooth, dark wood railing as I take a few steps down. My fingertips brush along the wood, and even the cool surface doesn't calm my nerves.

"Little red," Lycan murmurs, his voice thick with lust, and when I lock my gaze on his, I practically burn up from the desire that burns in those green orbs.

"Shit." This comes from Darius, and his equally warm stare sizzles over my exposed flesh, and there is a lot of it, as he takes me in from head to toe and back again. Both men seem speechless as they stare at me and I take this opportunity to gracefully descend the staircase until I'm in the entrance foyer where they're frozen in time.

"Hi," I greet, walking up to Lycan and placing a soft kiss on his stubbled cheek which earns me a low growl of approval. I leave him, and move to Darius, who I offer the same kiss to. His beard is a bit longer than Lycan's, but the tingles that shoot through me from the almost innocent gesture is the same.

Lycan's hand grips my hip, and he's behind me in seconds. Darius takes a step closer to my front, ensuring I'm sandwiched between them. Heat courses through me, my blood like fiery lava as they hold on to me as if I were unbreakable.

Strong.

Fierce.

Unrelenting.

"You're a bad girl," Lycan coos as he presses his hardness against my ass. The thick shaft of his erection making me whimper and I push against him, rubbing myself shamelessly on his cock.

Darius's stare turns to fire as he leans in. I think he's going to kiss me, but instead, his mouth trails my cheek leaving goose bumps dotting over my flesh. He reaches my ear, his mouth hot against the sensitive lobe.

"You've got my dick so hard, it's painful. I bet that pretty mouth wouldn't mind relieving me of some tension," he says in a low order which Lycan hears because he's no longer hiding the fact that he wants me.

"Is that what you want, little red?" Lycan murmurs in my other ear and I swear I'm about to explode. My stomach coils with need, my core pulses with desire as lust shoots through every inch of me.

"I-I..." Words fail me when I feel two sets of hands trailing down my body, Lycan stops his exploration on my ass, while Darius's touch lingers on my shoulders, down my front until my nipples pebble against the flimsy material of my dress and against his palms. Finally finding my voice, I respond, "I do." And I can feel my husband's smile on my face when he presses a chaste kiss to my cheek.

"Good girl," he says, his voice more normal than it was seconds ago. "Let's have dinner and a glass of wine, and afterward, we'll have dessert." When he steps away from me, I can't help but shiver from the cold.

Darius's hands drop to mine as he takes them both and lifts them to his mouth. He presses soft kisses on my knuckles before he also releases me, and I follow them both into the dining room where we find the table set for three.

As we make our way to the place settings, I realize it's going to be a very long night. They're going to drag this out, ensure that anticipation kills me before I ever find the release I crave.

And that's going to drive me mad.

LYCAN

Today's meeting went well.

Kahn asked me to allow him to go with Alex when they found out Lorenzo was in Hawaii. He didn't need to ask my permission because this is his fight, but I granted his request anyway. Knowing he'll find some form of closure has calmed me.

I wanted him to find his sister. Nothing could ever compare to losing a loved one, someone so close to you. Especially with how young she was at the time of her kidnapping has vengeance ringing in my blood, so I can't imagine how he feels. He needs this, and I will never stop him from finding closure.

I pray she's still alive, but then again, knowing what those bastards are capable of when it comes to their prey, there's no telling what he'll find. But this is something he needs to do. With Grace now locked up, I'm thankful the only thing on my to do list this evening is to show my wife an evening of release.

We haven't spoken about Grace being taken, and we also haven't spoken about the truths that surfaced when we had her here, in this room, but that will come. I needed to ensure Kahn had his path set out before him, and now that I'm home, I'll make sure my wife can talk to me when she's ready.

The table looks amazing, the food smells incredible, and as I wait for Scarlett to settle into her chair, I can't help but feel happy for the first time in a long while. I didn't expect things to be so easy, but Grace walked away without a fight.

Acknowledging you're guilty, and finally having to pay for it makes you accept your fate. She chose wrong, that's what Scarlett told her, and when she looked at me, I saw it in her eyes—she knew she made the wrong choices in her life.

Even if she didn't want to marry my father, she could have stood up to her husband, the bastard who murdered him. But she chose to stay silent about what he had done. She went on with her life and we had to live with the pain of not knowing the truth.

"Are you okay?" Scarlett asks, as Darius and I seat

ourselves. "What happened at the meeting?" Those wide eyes I've come to love focuses on me, looking right through the worries racing through my mind, seeing my soul.

"Yes. Kahn and Alex will be going to pay Lorenzo a visit. For tonight, we don't talk about anything other than happy things, like our future," I tell her. "Tomorrow, when the sun rises again, we'll delve into the secrets and truths we learned today. Can you do that for me?" I ask her as I take her hand in mine.

A soft smile curves her lips, and she nods. "Of course," she answers. "I just wanted to make sure you're both okay." Those pretty eyes I'm addicted to slide between me and Darius. My own gaze trails over her sleek locks, those plump fucking lips, and down to her tits, which are barely contained in the skimpy dress she chose.

She's done it on purpose. My wife knows she's taunting us and she's enjoying the power she has over both of us. I've been hard since I saw her walk down those stairs, and if I know Darius, he's probably just as turned on.

"I'm all good, little one," he tells her confidently before popping his fork with a sliver of steak into his mouth. But even as he enjoys his dinner, his gaze never leaves Scarlett. I settle back in my chair and watch my wife eat her dinner.

I'm not hungry.

Not for what's on the plate in front of me, anyway.

She doesn't look up at me until she's scraping the last bits of her dinner onto the silver fork and slipping it into her mouth, and as she pulls the metal utensil from between those lips, my cock jolts and it's time to get this started.

It's been a while since I've played a scene, and with her, I haven't even delved into what I enjoy, what I want her to experience. But I've enjoyed the way we've slowly inched into the darkness, and tonight, she's going to be thrown into the deepest, darkest woods.

Let's hope my little red finds her way back to me.

I push my chair back and rise to my feet. Buttoning my jacket, I offer her a hand which she accepts with a shy smile. Her submissive nature is so intoxicating, and I offer a glance at Darius, who's noticed it as well.

He grabs her glass, and I lead her out of the dining room and down toward my office. We pass by that door because tonight is not about working. At the end of the hall, I unlock a dark mahogany door which slides open, and I allow Scarlett in first.

I follow behind, with Darius hot on my heels. He shuts us inside, and I flick the switch which illuminates the room in a soft silver light. The walls are painted as if we're in a forest, with thick trunks lined vertically from floor to ceiling.

The large windows overlook the garden, with the real woods just outside. This is the far end of the house, and you don't notice it from the outside because the glass wall is one way, you can see out, but nobody can see inside.

An enormous king-sized bed takes up the one side of the wall, while the toys and St Andrew's Cross take up the opposite side. All the while, you have a view of the greenery just beyond the windows.

I watch as Scarlett takes it all in. Before our wedding, I didn't have a chance to bring her in here. Even though we played at Heaven, it has nothing on this room. It's my sanctuary at home. I've always loved this space, and when I converted it into the playroom it is now, I felt at ease. It was always meant to be mine, and the fact that I can share it with her, makes it more special.

"This is incredible," she whispers, her fingers trailing over the wood of the St Andrew's Cross, her gaze taking in everything. She turns to face Darius and me. He's standing beside me, his gaze locked on her. Mine flicks between the two of them. There's no longer tension, it's only lust.

The emotion hangs in the air like a perfume, breathtaking and powerful. I glance at Darius, who looks at me for a second, and the time has come. This is something I didn't think I would be willing to do when he first asked, but now that we're here, I realize I want this, I need it.

Before we start playing, she'll need a safe word. Not that I think she'll use it, but that's non-negotiable. Both Darius and I won't do anything until we've made sure she understands she can call out for everything to stop the moment she feels uncomfortable.

She's been with me in a scene, but now that there are two of us, things can become more intense for her. There's no doubt they will, and my cock throbs at the thought of seeing her break. I wanted to hurt her before, to make her pay because I knew the Bardot family were bastards, but now that she's a Shaw, I want to hurt her with pleasure.

Flicking on the sound system, a soft melody escapes the speakers. Scarlett looks at me, awaiting an order. "Strip for us, little red," I command, attempting but failing to keep my voice even. Knowing what's about to happen has me anxious and anticipation has my blood turning hot, racing through my veins like a drug.

She moves to the song without question. I watch her spin around, and my little wife shocks the shit out of me when she spreads her legs, and trails her hands down those slender limbs, down to her fucking ankles and all I see are tiny panties that do nothing to hide her beautiful cunt and ass.

If I thought I was hard earlier, I'm now solid fucking steel. Darius's cough of shock and desire catches my attention. His eyes are wide as he takes in the show before us. Scarlett straightens as she slips the thin straps of her dress over her shoulders and the flimsy red material pools at her feel. My wife is standing before me and my brother in a pair of barely there lace panties and black heels which have straps wrapped around her calves.

Never in my life have I seen a woman so alluring, so fucking mind-altering, and so sexy she's got my cock weeping in my fucking slacks. I want to spank her ass for being a tease, but when I told her to get ready, I really wasn't expecting her to turn into a gorgeous siren like this.

It's more than I expected.

And I don't think I've ever been prouder of her coming

out of the shell I found her in. The music pumps through the speakers, and Scarlett dances, gyrating in front of us as she moves the discarded dress out of her way. She spins on her heels, locking her pretty steel eyes with ours, before she hooks her thumbs in her panties, and tugs them down, slow and steady, but before I can get a glimpse of her cunt, she turns again, her back to us, as she slips them down to her ankles and once again, both her delicious holes are bare for us to see.

My hand finds my crotch and I slowly stroke myself through the material of my slacks. My arousal seeps into my boxers, and if she continues this show, I'm going to come in my pants like a teenager.

"Stop." One word and Scarlett freezes. Her eyes on mine, her hands shaking as she stands naked, only in heels, in front of us. "Time to play."

SCARLETT

I'm not sure where my confidence came from, but when Lycan told me to strip, I did it, without question. I felt a sense of power watching both men practically salivate at my teasing. They're both so strong, powerful, and yet, seeing me like this, teasing and naked, they're nothing more than desire-filled predators.

I smile at Lycan, it's a shy one, but he gifts me one in return, his though is filled with a dark promise of what's to come. He steps closer to me, while Darius hangs back, allowing my husband to take the lead.

"You're beautiful," Lycan tells me earnestly as he cups my face and presses a soft kiss to my lips. It's a gentle gesture, one that will be the last until I am carried out of this room. "I want you to choose your safe word," he then says. "Remember it has to be something you'll think of while you're in subspace."

Nodding, I look into his eyes before responding, "My safe word is wolf." There's a glimmer of pride that dances in his gaze when I say it, because he knows what it means. I was about to be caught between the wolf and the hunter, and I'm choosing him. Even though we're taking this step into the unknown, at least that's what it is for me.

"Good girl," he praises before stepping back. He looks at his brother who nods, he heard. They both have to respect my decision, should I want to stop.

"Go over to the cross," Darius orders, his voice gruff with desire as he gestures toward the left wall. Without question, I obey because in here, in this scene, they're both my dominants tonight.

When I stop in front of the large apparatus, a shiver zips through me. My stomach flip-flops as I stare at the leather straps at either end of the long, wooden beams, and I realize I'm not going anywhere once I'm bound in those.

Darius takes the lead with this, dropping to a crouched position, he takes my one ankle and binds it with a resounding click of metal. He does the same with the other ankle, before rising slowly, and tying my wrists within the thick leather.

I'm facing them, my back against the cool, wooden surface of the cross. I'm open to them now, with only my shoes on, I'm exposed. Darius takes a step back, and Lycan walks over to the opposite wall to grab a crop. The black leather which will soon lick against my naked flesh.

He stops inches from me before leaning in, he whispers, "Are you ready, little red?"

"Yes, Sir," I mumble as nervous energy skitters through me, while butterflies awaken in my stomach, the flurry of wings taking over and soon I'm trembling.

"Don't be afraid," Lycan assures me. "This is all about your pleasure." Once he's spoken, he takes a step back, assessing me before bringing the soft leather down on my stomach with a swat which has a whimper tumbling from my lips.

"Beautiful," Darius murmurs as he shrugs off his leather cut and pulls the T-shirt from his body. The smooth, inked muscles of his torso pulse and tighten as he moves. I stare for a moment too long, not noticing the next swat on my pussy which sends heat coursing through me, and I yelp of surprise expels from my mouth.

Lycan hands Darius the toy before unbuttoning his shirt, slow and methodical, like he usually is, and he shrugs off the material with a whoosh as it falls to the floor. He's beautiful, tanned skin bared to me, free of any tattoos. They're polar opposites, but their desires match perfectly.

Darius swats me twice, once on my stomach, closer to my breasts, and another on my inner thigh which stings, but arousal pools between my legs. He continues with another two, and another, until I'm whimpering, and my pussy is dripping with desire.

"You look so pretty, little one," Darius says in a husky tone as he steps closer, pressing his lips against my smooth skin causing goose bumps to rise in the wake of warmth of his mouth. His tongue darts out as he licks at the now reddened patch of flesh, and the smirk that curls his lips makes me shiver. "Taste so good too," he murmurs against my trembling body.

I'm needy. I'm wet. And I want so much fucking more.

When he steps back, I shiver from the cold. I'm dotted in goose bumps when Lycan moves toward me, his hand trailing over my shoulders, sending warmth and shivers through me at the same time. The tender touch of this fingertips feather along my arms, and when he reaches my hips, he grips them tight. Pain trickles through me, but my arousal pools between my legs, and when Lycan's fingers dip into my core, he grins.

"Little Red is soaked," he murmurs as Darius steps closer to us, his body cocooning me from the left while Lycan stands on my right. Two fingers still inside me, he leans closer to trail the tip of his tongue over my neck, up to my cheek. "Your cunt is needy, baby girl," he tells me with a rough tone that skitters over my flesh.

"Please, Lycan," I moan as he crooks his fingers inside me, rubbing that spot that has sparks shooting through my veins, as if I were plugged into an electric current. I shake, my limbs trembling in their bindings with every tease and taunt of my husband's fingers.

Warm lips clasp around one of my hardened nipples and I cry out as pleasure takes hold of me. Darius sucks the bud into his warm mouth. Suddenly, a harsh slap contacts with my other breast as pleasure and pain mingle together in an erotic mixture sending me soaring. Another slap and another sting of my flesh, my tit bouncing with every attack, and my head falls back against the wood.

Teeth graze against my sensitive peak, and I soak Lycan's fingers and hand as my orgasm rips through me like a tidal wave and I cry out Lycan's name. My legs shake, my arms tremble, and I'm sure if I wasn't bound, I would have fallen over.

"Bad girl," Lycan grits as he kisses my lips, his teeth tugging the lower one harshly as he pulls his fingers from my pussy. "We didn't give you permission to come." Desire and danger glint in his green eyes, and I'm sure I'm in big trouble now.

Lycan leaves me whimpering as he heads for a chest of drawers. He pulls open the top drawer and I watch as he finds what he's looking for. He's about to torture me, I'm sure of it. Darius grins when he sees the vibrator in his brother's hand, and he moves to my breasts, sucking my nipples until they're aching.

He taunts and teases, slapping my chest with swats that have pleasure and pain heating my blood with desire. Lust warms my belly, and it feels like lava when Darius slaps my pussy once, twice, three times before I feel myself nearing the edge once more. But he knows he can read my body, and he steps back just before I leap over and find another release which I'm craving.

"If you come again without permission, you'll be punished," Lycan warns with a small smile on his lips, and I'm sure he wants to me to break the rules. He craves it just like I do.

Darius chuckles. "I think she likes to be punished." He grabs the crop while Lycan flicks on the vibrator which I realize is a magic wand and presses it to my throbbing clit. A cry of pure euphoria is ripped from my throat as the sensations send me soaring into an abyss of light and warmth.

He doesn't relent though. He keeps the wand on my core, teasing it up and down my slit until I'm crying. Tears stream down my cheeks, and I watch both men as Darius uses the crop on my stomach, breasts, and my inner thighs.

My brain is a mesh of pained pleasure. My mouth parted with gasps of pleas as they tumble free. I want more, but I can't take anymore. *How is this real?*

They don't relent until I'm practically hanging from the cuffs at my wrists. When I'm finally free of the vibrating tingles at my pussy, I open my eyes to find those of the wolf staring at me.

"Such a pretty girl," he tells me. "My wife is perfect." The smile on his face is bright, nothing like I've ever seen before. Lycan and Darius slowly remove the cuffs from my wrists, and I stumble into Lycan's arms, and he holds me to his naked chest.

He settles me on his lap on the dark wingback chair that faces the bed. I'm tired, but I'm still turned on. Lycan's hands move down my thighs, and he slides them open to ensure my legs hang over the armrests of the chair. I'm open, bared to Darius's heated stare.

"Only this once," my husband commands, his voice low and gravelly with desire as Darius drops to his knees. "You can worship her perfection."

And with that approval, Darius's mouth lands on my pussy with hungry fervor. His tongue laps at my core, causing my back to arch, and Lycan's mouth finds mine as his one hand trails up to my throat. He grips me harshly, possessively, there is no doubt he's enjoying this situation because his cock throbs behind me.

The warm mouth, the fingers stealing my breath, and Lycan's tongue stroking mine sends me into bliss. Suddenly, a slap lands on my thigh and I yelp into my husband's mouth. He's spanking me, and my nerves spark with electric need.

Behind my eyelids, all I see is white, black, and then nothing when the Darius moves away and a harsh swat lands on my hard clit causing me to cry out. Lycan steals the sound, and Darius's mouth is back. They alternate until my arousal is dripping down my body, my thighs are soaked, and Lycan's suit pants must be drenched.

I'm teetering on the edge, because each time I lean closer to my release, they both halt all movement. Lycan breaks the kiss, and my eyes snap open to find him looking down at me, a smile gracing his lips.

"Is my filthy girl needy?" he whispers along my cheek, sending waves of pleasure and desire coursing through every inch of me. Powerful hands brace my legs, Darius's mouth at my core teasing its way up and down my inner thighs, but never making contact where I need it most.

"Please, let me come?" I plead with a whimper as my hips lift toward Darius, but he only chuckles at my display of wanton lust. I glance down at him, finding those green eyes, so much like Lycan's, looking up at me. "Please?"

Even as I plead with him, it's pointless because he's not going to allow me an orgasm until Lycan's agreed. They're in charge, and they're making it known I'm theirs to toy with as much as they'd like.

My body trembles as I moan when Darius trails his fingertips over my pussy, the wetness drenching both digits that trail along my lips. "I think this bad little girl needs to play another little game. One that she'll enjoy," Lycan murmurs behind me as Darius lifts his fingers to his mouth, tasting my juices.

Darius rises, and settles in another wingback chair which he pulls over so he's facing us. "Want to play another game?" he questions from his seat, his gaze flicking to Lycan's as if seeking approval. When Lycan nods behind me, Darius meets my gaze once more.

"What kind of game?" I whisper, while my husband circles my clit slowly because he's enjoying just keeping me on the edge. He doesn't finger fuck me. He doesn't even push in slightly, he keeps his touch on the nub, ensuring I can't come.

"A little game of Red Riding Hood," Darius says, pushing to his feet, he sets his glass down on the cabinet before unbuckling his belt and pulling it through the loops. The heavy metal clinks as he loops it into a makeshift collar.

"Uhm." This time, it's my turn to be unsure. Before it was Darius, before his brother offered him the approval. "Okay." I'm not sure what the game entails, but with my arousal dripping from my core, and my nipples hard from the memories of what I've just experienced, I think I can handle it.

At least I hope I can.

"You'll have to wear a collar around your neck, or the belt around your middle, you decide," Lycan whispers in my ear. "Then, you'll be sent out into the garden, and you'll have to run and hide from us. Either the hunter or the wolf will have to find you."

I turn to my husband. "What happens if one or both of you finds me?" My voice is a nervous whisper, and Lycan grins because he knows I enjoyed our game of chase in the garden that one night. He knows this will bring me pleasure. That I'll fulfill a dark desire.

"If we told you, it would spoil the game." Lycan's words have my body shuddering, but my pussy pulses at the thought, and I nod slowly. "Good girl." He kisses me softly before pushing to his feet. He moves to the drawers and pulls out a collar with a little bell attached. "Collar or belt?"

For a moment, I ponder which would be easier to run with.

Finally, I smile before I say, "Collar."

My stomach tumbles with nervous energy when Lycan steps closer, clasping the make-shift collar around my neck. There's a small bell attached to the center, which makes a soft tinkling sound. I doubt you could hear it in the woods, but he seems convinced it's going to allow him to find me.

But what if Darius finds me first?

Lycan steps back once the collar is fastened and Darius hands me a pair of leggings and a tank top, which I slip on as they watch. Next, I'm given a deep crimson hoodie, which I can't help but smile at. When I tug the hood over my hair, I'm sure I look the part of Little Red that Lycan loves to refer to me as.

Those hungry gazes never stray from me, and it makes my blood burn hot with need. Knowing I enjoy the hunt and chase, I'm sure Lycan told Darius about it, and now that they're prepared to play this scene with me, I allow calmness to wash over me with deep breaths as I take them in.

Lycan hands me some socks, and my pair of sneakers I didn't even realize he had brought downstairs. Once I'm dressed, with the collar tinkling in the silence, their hungry gazes locked on me, I straighten, taking them both in from head to toe.

"I'm ready."

The curl of Lycan's lips has arousal pooling between my thighs, and I squeeze them together to quell the ache, but nothing can calm me down now. I'm hyper-sensitive, my skin prickles and awareness rushes over me. I'm about to play a game and I'm not sure how to win.

My hungry gaze trails my husband's movements as he walks toward the floor to ceiling patio doors leading out onto the garden. He slides one open, and steps aside. "Find your way to grandma's house before either of us catch you," he tells me. His wolfish, yet satisfied expression makes my heart thud faster.

He knows I'll get lost.

I realize I'll get lost.

But that's part of the excitement.

I take my first step outside, my breath catching as a cool breeze brushes over my body. My nipples harden against the soft material of my tank top, and I slip out into the garden. Glancing over my shoulder, I smile at Lycan, who's standing beside Darius as they watch me.

Then, I turn and race for the woods.

We all know the fairytale of Red Riding Hood, and we all know what happens in the end. But this isn't some made-up story. This is my life, and my husband, the wolf, is about to come find me.

As I race amongst the trees, I head right, in the direction of my grandmother's house, which I'm sure is empty now. I can't see anything. With the silver glow of the moon, I try to gauge how far I've gone, but the trees are too high, too thick for me to even see. I take a moment, coming to a stop against one of the thick trunks, to catch my breath, but also to look back. I make out the small glimmer of yellow, which is our bedroom light, but the moment I spot it, it's gone.

Blinking, I focus, but it's no longer there, and I wonder if Lycan turned off the lights to mess with me.

I'm still too close to the Shaw manor to make it to the Bardot home safely. So, I spin on my heel and start running once more. The deeper into the woods I go, the more disorienting it gets. But I think back to the night Lycan found me. It didn't take too long to get to his place from gran's, meaning the path can't be too long.

Only, there is no path.

A crack from behind me echoes amongst the trees, and a scream frees itself from my lips. I cringe, knowing they would've heard me. It's not meant to be a game of cat and mouse, but it's not the fairytale I grew up reading.

My lungs pull in air, which I expel in short spurts. My heart thrums a rhythm that makes my chest ache, and my thighs are starting to burn from the exertion. I'm not great with cardio, clearly, and this is seriously pushing my limits.

But I can't stop.

Another crack from somewhere to my left sends panic skittering down my spine as the cool air picks up, a breeze blowing through the leaves, causing them to rustle.

Suddenly, heavy footfalls bear down on me, and I push myself to run faster. Thankfully I'm wearing shoes, because the ground underfoot is hard, and each time I step on a fallen branch, or a stick, it cracks loudly.

Keeping my focus in front of me, I take a left, then a right, and when I come to a break in the trees, I'm almost certain I've found the house, but when I race closer, I notice it's only a small patch, and there are more trees ahead.

I'm back in the thick of it when suddenly, from my right, a pair of hands grab my hips, as if I weren't even moving. A scream is wrenched from my lips as I'm pulled against a hard body. The warmth cocoons me, and the hot breath of a man feathers itself over my neck, sending a shiver down my spine.

"Got you, little red." His voice sends a wave of calm over me, from the top of my head to the tips of my toes. "Did you think I would lose you to my brother?" he murmurs in my ear, the darkness that he usually reserves for us playing is clear in his tone.

"No," I squeak when he spins me around and pins me to the hard bark of the tree trunk. His body flush with mine as his hands roam my curves, tugging at the waistband of the leggings.

Footfalls make their way toward us, but Lycan doesn't stop until his fingers are inside me. He pumps them twice, sending heated pleasure pooling into his hand. His mouth claims mine as Darius comes up behind him. Lycan glances at his brother breaking the kiss. I can't see his expression in the dark, but I can only guess he's smirking.

I watch as Darius leans against a tree close by, watching as my husband fingers me harshly. He's in control, and he's not letting me go until I'm spent. A hiss of a zipper echoes in the dark, and I gasp when I see Darius's hand stroking his erection as he stares at us.

"My filthy girl over here likes to get wet for us," Lycan

comments, but his eyes are focused on me. With one harsh tug, the material of my leggings rips from my body, and I'm lifted against the tree. My legs wrap around Lycan, and I'm so wet, his cock slides easily into me.

I'm drenched.

"Keep those pretty eyes on him, little red," Lycan orders, his head gesturing to Darius, and I realize no matter how much I want to close my eyes and focus on the pleasure his cock is giving me, I need to keep my gaze trained on Darius as he strokes his cock to us.

He thrusts deep, hitting that spot inside me that tears a scream from my lungs, and my head falls back against the hard wood behind me. He doesn't waste time, he doesn't make love to me, he fucks me. His hips piston back and forth, his cock sliding all the way to the hilt as he takes me while Darius watches.

Our bodies sync as we connect on a primal level. Even with Darius here, it's Lycan who sends me soaring to another plane, and I can't catch my breath quick enough as he fucks me against the tree. The cool air causing me to shiver, but the heat of him, the warmth of his cock as it slides inside me, has me moaning loudly.

Nobody can hear me. Nobody can hear us.

"Come on my cock, little red," Lycan commands in a tone that's pure lust. My hands grip Lycan, my fingers digging into his shoulders as I hold onto him. I'm close to the edge, so fucking close. His mouth captures my neck as he suckles the flesh into his warmth, before he trails kisses to my ear and whispers, "show my brother how much your pretty cunt loves my dick."

And I detonate.

My body explodes, and I scream his name so loudly, it echoes against the trees. I convulse, my pussy pulsating around his thickness as he stills, and I feel him throb a few times and he comes with a growl against my neck. The warmth of him floods me, and I'm more than satiated. I glance over at Darius and my body warm with pleasure when I watch him find his own euphoria in the moment.

As Lycan slips from my body, he lets me to my feet and tucks himself in his slacks. He scoops me in his arms without warning, and I notice Darius has also righted himself. My leggings are torn, but with Lycan carrying me, I'm warm against his body.

They don't speak as we head through the woods. The wolf caught me. And my heart couldn't be happier. The men easily navigate the darkness, and not long after, we're in the garden again. Still, they don't speak, and I wonder silently what is about to happen. My body is exhausted. I'm ready to pass out from the number of orgasms and exertion I've been through, but I keep my eyes open.

"Time for something relaxing," Lycan coos in my ear with a gentle kiss to my cheek, and I'm thankful he said that because if I had to run anywhere right now, I'd be dead.

DARIUS

Bliss. Utter fucking bliss.

I've fucked women. I've come from jerking off and blow jobs, but the moment I shot my seed all over my hand, I realize I'd never felt pure euphoria than I did in the moment I saw Scarlett come.

The game was nothing more than an idea I threw out, wondering if Lycan would agree to it. He did. Much to my pleasure and his. And most importantly, to Scarlett's. I watch intently as they move, as he helps Scarlett to right herself.

Even in the darkness, the wolf finds his red, and that's how it was always meant to be. This may not be a fairy tale, instead, this is real life, but the story has to end with them finding each other again.

He carries here off into the woods, through the trees, and I smile. While I take a moment to breathe, to calm my erratic heartbeat, I wonder briefly if I will ever find that pure passion, raw lust, and the unrelenting love that simmers between Lycan and Scarlett.

I've never been one for emotion, especially when it came to sex. It was physical, why make it emotional, but with her, I felt something. But right now, I realize that she's opened up something in me, something I kept hidden for so long, and I want to finally have something more than just a one-night stand.

Perhaps the hunter isn't as heartless as he envisioned.

After a short moment, I follow them back to the house, and as we step into the warmth of the bedroom, Lycan sets Scarlett down beside me, while he goes to ensure the candles in the bathroom are set up for our shower. She doesn't realize it yet, but the party isn't over yet.

"You're exquisite," I tell her honestly. As much as I've enjoyed this time with her, soon, I'll have to leave. This may not be a home that's off bounds to me anymore, but it's not my home, it's not the place I feel most myself. "Tonight, wasn't just about sex, it was about giving you the power in this situation."

Scarlett gasps and her eyes widen. She didn't know I knew about what happened to her. But when I looked into the Bardots, Howler found out all her little secrets. That's why I told her I know more about her than she could ever imagine.

"How did you—"

"You need to tell him," I whisper, running my thumb along her cheek. "He needs to know. I hope that we've both given you the strength to realize it wasn't your fault. You're beautiful. You're strong. And you're going to be okay. My brother will always be there for you, no matter what. But remember, you'll always have a hunter in your corner as well. And I'll kill anyone who tries to hurt you." It's a promise, a vow, and I make it easily.

"Thank you," Scarlett murmurs, her lip trembling, and I watch for a moment as she swallows thickly. The tears that shimmer on her lashes make my chest tighten, but she blinks them back before looking directly at me. "I-I—"

"Shh, it's okay," I assure her.

"I don't know what to say about everything," she tells me, her voice raspy, and I cup her face gently. My thumb runs over the apple of her cheek, the soft, rosy hue that blooms at my touch makes me smile.

"There's no need to put anything into words. For once, just enjoy the feelings, the emotions, and the pleasure," I whisper. "And when it's all over, you'll feel renewed. Like a different person. And that's why we do what we do." I glance at Lycan as he walks back into the room, his eyes taking in the closeness of his wife and me. "That's why we enjoy the darkness."

"Because the truth is always hidden in the shadows,"

Lycan finishes for me.

I step back, and allow him to lift her into his arms, and I happily follow for the grand finale.

SCARLETT

I don't know how I'm still awake. Adrenalin courses through me, the need to show them I'm strong and can handle anything. I asked for this. I craved it, and I don't know if I can handle more orgasms, but for some reason, I'm ready to handle anything they throw at me.

"You were amazing tonight, little red," Lycan coos in my ear. The praise making my chest swell with pride, and my heart patters against my ribs. The need to please him seems to be ingrained in me. I want him to look at me with pride, with love and affection, and the way he's staring at me right now, calms the nervous energy I had about tonight.

He's not at all angry about the decision I made to agree

to this evening's events. With his arms holding me against him, I can feel his heart thrumming, and I lay my head against his chest, listening to the rhythm.

He walks me over to an en suite bathroom with a large shower that looks like it could fit ten of us. Darius turns the taps on, and I realize he's naked, his thick cock jutting from his waist, and a gasp falls from my lips at the sight. He steps under the spray while Lycan sets me on the counter to undo my shoes. Once I'm fully naked, he helps me step into the warmth, and I sigh in relief as the water massages my muscles. When Lycan steps inside as well before sliding the glass door closed, I'm sandwiched between them.

"Was that it?" I ask as weariness threatens to take hold of me, but I fight it back, and when my husband grins, I realize it was a stupid thing to question.

"Not by a long shot, little red," he assures me. They both wash me, four hands taunting and teasing me. Darius behind me, his hands on my ass, down my thighs, while Lycan washes my breasts and pussy. Once they're convinced that I'm clean, both rise and that's when Lycan lifts me against him. My legs wrap around his waist, and his cock nudges my entrance.

Slowly, ever so torturously slow, he sinks me down on his shaft. The thickness of him opening me, causing me to gasp as more pleasure heats my blood and my already aching pussy pulses around him. And that's when I feel it, Darius's fingers at my rear along with coolness which I'm sure is lube.

He taunts the tight hole, teasing it open until he has two fingers inside me. My breath comes in short gasps as he scissors me until he's happy. I hear the snap of a cap, and then a groan from Darius. His fingers disappear before his cock replaces them.

He pushes slowly, gently, his fingers gripping my hips as he thrusts into me. Lycan stills his movements as Darius enters me, and after long, sensual moments, I'm filled like I've never been before. My nails dig into Lycan's shoulders, and my head falls back onto Darius's chest.

He presses a gentle kiss to my cheek, before gruffly promising, "You're so fucking tight, I'm going to come in your tight ass, little one."

I'm between two strong men, and I'm lost in bliss as they start moving, slow, gentle, but I can tell from the tension in Lycan's shoulders, he's holding onto restraint. He thrusts into me, deep, hitting that spot he earlier stroked, and as Darius's cock throbs inside my ass, a moan of pure euphoria slips free.

My eyes flutter closed, and I focus on them both filling me. I've never been so lost to pleasure before. They move in sync, as if I was born for them to take like this, to own and worship. Soft lips trail over my breasts, to my nipples, and Lycan captures one in his mouth while Darius suckles on my earlobe. His teeth biting down as Lycan does the same to my hard bud, sending more electric shocks through me.

I claw at Lycan, his hands holding me up, while Darius's grips my hips so hard, I'm sure he's going to leave bruises, and I'm convinced this is something I won't ever forget. Their movements hasten as my body pulses around both thick erections inside me.

"That's my girl," Lycan coos when he feels my walls tighten. "I might allow you to come again," he whispers with a chuckle as he begins to fuck me faster, harder, and deeper. It's as if he was holding out on me, and now he's fully seated, while Darius claims my ass like a man possessed.

My lips part in soft mewls of bliss as I'm taken. I've never been so fully owned before. Yes, Lycan gives me what I need, he gives me everything I crave, but this is nothing like I ever expected. They fuck me harder, faster, and my body complies, opening and also tightening, giving them as much pleasure as they're gifting me.

I'm closing in on the precipice of pure euphoria, when Lycan releases his one hand from my butt, and Darius takes his place. For a moment, I try to open my eyes to see what he's doing, but the moment I do, he pinches my clit and orders, "Come for us." And my body detonates like a bomb has been set off.

I scream.

My body pulses and tightens.

"Good girl. Milk our cocks," Darius orders, and I don't know how, but my body knows what it's doing because seconds later, their grunts fill my ears as if on surround sound and their warmth fills me. Darius's cock throbs as his release jets inside me. Lycan's thick erection pulses inside my heat and I feel his seed coat me.

I scream some more when Lycan's teeth capture my nipple, and he bites down hard before suckling it into his mouth. And after what feels like days, I go limp. I don't remember anything after that. But when I open my eyes again, I'm in the bed in the playroom they brought me to. Both men are sitting on wingback chairs, watching me.

"The little one is awake," Darius remarks before sipping on a drink in his hand.

Lycan rises, making his way toward me as he settles on the mattress behind me, pulling me into his hold. It's still dark out, so I'm not sure how long I've been asleep, but it couldn't have been too long since it's still night.

"You're beautiful, perfect," Lycan coos, pressing butterfly kisses to my cheeks, neck, and my shoulders. I'm still naked, wrapped in soft silk sheets. Heat trickles over my flesh when Lycan's hand slips between my legs under the sheet and he strokes my mound gently.

"Thank you." I find my words to respond, and he smiles against my cheek. "How long was I asleep?"

"Only about an hour," he informs me. That must mean it's nearly one in the morning. I can't believe they're both still awake after what we did.

I glance at Darius, who's happily watching our display. Lycan's fingers taunt my cunt, causing arousal to coat both digits as they slip inside me. My hips instinctively move against his hand, needing the friction.

Lycan allows me to ride his fingers while Darius once again watches and strokes himself. This time, the lights are on and I can see him. His tattooed hands, glide along his thickness. It's a beautiful sight and one day he'll make some woman very happy.

His hand hastens its movements as the fingers inside me quicken as well. "You're going to come all over my fingers, and then you're going to sleep." Lycan's words aren't a request, they're an order, but I'm too far gone to respond, so all I do is nod. He teases and taunts, then dips his fingers in so deep, stroking my G spot until my vision blurs and Darius shoots ropes of his release all over his hand. The sight is so erotic, I cry out, gripping Lycan's hand against my pussy, holding him there as I ride out the waves of my release.

And as I feel him move, my lashes flutter, and I realize it's going to be a satisfied, dreamless sleep.

LYCAN

Last night has been playing on a loop in my mind since I opened my eyes this morning. Leaving Scarlett in bed was difficult, but I had to come down here and focus. Having her soft body against mine had me hard and wanting more, but she needs to rest. I pick up my mobile and scroll down to the number I need, hitting dial, I press the device to my ear and wait.

"What do you want?" His deep voice rumbles through the speakers, but I don't miss the hint of fear that trickles through each word, and I smile. The bastard needs to be afraid.

"You and your wife are requested to attend a dinner at

my place. We'd like to celebrate the nuptials you missed," I tell him. Even though our farce of a wedding didn't happen in front of the guests, I married Scarlett before our public wedding day.

"Your brother swindled me out of millions," he bites back. Horatio Bardot is nothing more than a waste of space, and I'm tempted to tell him that, but for the moment, I refrain.

"And you sold your daughter to me," I throw back, knowing it will piss him off. "I don't think you have a leg to stand on when it comes to morals, Horatio."

Leaning back in my chair, I grin when I see my office door opening and Scarlett padding into the room. She's dressed in one of my shirts. Her hair is a mess of red waves, and my cock throbs at the thought of her sucking my dick while her father is on the phone. I crook my finger, calling her over and she obeys like the good submissive she is.

"I don't think Marinda and I want to be in your home, not when you took our daughter as a wife when she is so fucking young." His voice is filled with sudden concern, but it's all bullshit. He doesn't actually care.

Scarlett wordlessly drops to her knees when I point to the carpet, her brows furrowed in confusion, but she doesn't question my actions. I unzip my slacks, and she makes quick work of getting my cock out.

"Suck me," I mouth, before speaking into the phone, "I would like it if you would attend the dinner. My wife and I are looking forward to your visit, and we would so like you to explain your actions."

Scarlett's lips wrap around the tip of my dick, sending pleasure zipping through my veins, and my lashes flutter closed in bliss at her warm and wet mouth. She doesn't yet realize who I'm talking to.

"I'll have to speak to Marinda, but I'm not admitting to shit while my wife is in the room." Anger laces his response, but I just smile because it doesn't matter what he *wants* it's what he will do because *my* wife deserves to learn about what a bastard her father is. Even though she knows what he did to supplicate her grandmother, she needs the whole truth.

"I think you shouldn't make excuses anymore, Horatio," I say as plump lips slide down my erection all the way to the base. Her eyes are on mine, wide with shock when she realizes I'm talking to her father.

She attempts to pull her mouth from my cock, but I tangle the fingers of my free hand in her long locks and hold her steady while shaking my head. Spit drips from her chin. Her pretty gray eyes tear up when I thrust up, causing a whimper to tumble from her lips, but it's muffled by my dick in her mouth.

"Fine. When did you want to do this dinner?" he finally responds, sighing in resignation because he knows between me and him, I'm the fucking alpha male.

"Tonight, be here at eight," I tell him before I hang up. Throwing my cell phone on the desk, I grip Scarlett's head and fuck her throat as she hums each time that I slide in deep, sending shock waves through my shaft. "Fuck, little red," I spit through clenched teeth as stars fucking burst behind my lids. My balls tighten, and my release hits me hard, and my wife obediently swallows every drop.

When I open my eyes, I watch her pop my cock from her plump, used mouth, and she licks the drops of my seed that coat her lips. "I can't believe you just did that," she tells me once she's recovered. "Were you really talking to my father?"

"Yes." I pull her to stand and push her over, forcing her to bend over my desk, her bare ass right in line with my hungry mouth. She isn't wearing any underwear which means she came down here knowing I would want to feast on that pretty little pussy. I enjoyed knowing I was using his little girl while he was talking to me. I slap her ass hard, causing a yelp to echo in the silent office. Gripping her ass cheeks, I open them and dip my tongue into her cunt from behind. I lick up and down until she's a sopping mess and my chin is glistening with her juices.

"Lycan." The way she moans my name turns me into a rabid fucking animal. I dip two fingers into her entrance, the tightness pulsing around them. As much as I want to fuck her, I'm convinced she would still be tender from last night.

"Shh, I'm having breakfast," I tell her before I lean in and tease both her holes with my tongue, while slowly fingering her. By the time she explodes on my tongue, I'm hard again. I stand her up. "Get on your knees for me," I order, my voice gruff with desire.

She does as I say. My fist wraps around my cock, and I stroke it quickly. I won't last long, not with Scarlett kneeling before me, her tongue stuck out, her mouth wide, waiting for my seed, and with that beautiful view, I shoot ropes of cum over her pretty face and mouth.

With a smile, she licks it all up, cleaning her face with her finger, as she sucks on the digit to get every drop into her pretty mouth. Once she's done, she rises gracefully and walks to the door.

"See you later, Sir," she coos with a seductive little smile before disappearing, leaving me hungry for so much more. I can't get enough of her. There isn't a moment in the day when I don't think about taking her, using her body for pleasure, and making her come on my fingers, tongue, and cock.

I'm a man lost to love and desire.

Because no matter how much I hurt her, I want to see her happy forever.

Now, all we have to deal with is tonight's dinner.

It's almost time for our guests to arrive. I shrug on my jacket as Scarlett walks out of the bathroom. She's draped in a champagne-colored floor length dress that makes my breath catch in my throat. There's never a moment where I don't think she's beautiful, but there's something about this dress that has me wondering if I should cancel the dinner and perhaps fly her to Heaven so I can show her off to every man in the club.

I realize the moment I take her back there, things will be different. There is one more thing we need to do when we get back to New York, a trip I haven't yet told her about. I need to have a chat with Yasmin. She's most likely going to try her bullshit with me and try to get into my good books, but I'm married, and that's not changing, unless Scarlett tells me to leave.

And even then, I may not obey.

"I think you need to put on something less distracting," I tell her as I pull her closer to me. My hands grip her hips, her body flush with mine. "Because tonight, all I'll be able to think about is fucking you on the dinner table while your parents watch."

"Stop being such a filthy animal," she accuses with a smile on her face, as she slides her delicate hands over my shoulders and loops them around my neck.

"You love it when I'm filthy," I counter, to which she cannot argue because I've seen how her pupils dilate with desire when I gift her my dirty words.

"Only when we're alone," she informs me before pressing a kiss to my mouth which I quickly deepen, my tongue dancing along hers, tasting the sweetness of my wife. When I finally pull away, her gaze is shimmering. "Thank you for being here tonight. I don't think I could do this without you."

"You'll never have to do anything without me again," I promise, and it's one I intend to keep. There's nothing that can tear me away from her. "Ready?"

Scarlett nods, and I realize she's nervous. I can read her like a book, and tonight is most definitely not going to be easy on her. With the number of secrets that have been spilled over the past few weeks, I doubt anything can shock me anymore, but as we make our way down to the dining room to wait on our guests, I wonder if tonight will illuminate more hidden truths.

SCARLETT

I've only had a couple of sips of my drink when the doorbell goes, and I see one of the staff making his way to the door to open it. Even from here, I can hear my father's voice, deep and commanding, something he and Lycan have in common.

Only, when Lycan gifts me his commands, it's filled with affection. My mother's voice bounces through to where I'm standing, her carefree laugh is something I didn't miss. She never called once to check on me. Even after I got my phone back from my grandmother's home the night of the gala dinner. Something I thought would come naturally didn't come at all.

"Darling," she greets with a wave of her hands when she enters the dining room. Draped in a black dress that sweeps along the floor, she looks ever the public figure, but she's nothing like the person she portrays in company. "I've missed you."

"Have you?" I challenge, stepping back when she tries to lean in for a kiss. I don't want it and don't need it. My anger has a hold of me, and the fake smiles and words are no longer something I will put up with. Her face falls when she takes me in.

"Of course, darling," she responds. Her mouth gapes in surprise when I don't make a move to give her air kisses either. "Now that you're married you want to act like an adult?" Her tone takes on a cold, unfeeling grit that makes me even angrier than I was moments ago.

"I've been an adult for a long while. You just didn't notice because you were too busy making sure everyone else loved you, not at all bothered that your daughter felt like a stranger." I don't know where my words come from, but they fall free as I look at the woman I don't know. I'm nothing like her. She's nothing more than the person who gave birth to me, she's not, and never will be a mother.

"Don't talk to your mother like that, Scarlett," my dad says, or shall I call him a sperm donor because that's what he is.

"Oh look, the man who sold me the first chance he got just so he didn't have to go to jail," I bite out through gritted teeth. This was a mistake. I want to run and hide, but Lycan's hand on my lower back steadies and grounds me. His touch is warm, strong, and I take a long, deep breath.

"Good evening," Lycan greets, not wavering under the clear scrutiny of my father. "I think we need a few drinks in here. Don't you?" His tone is light, but it's laced with a threat they clearly notice because my dad's face turns to ice.

"We do." This comes from my mother, because of course she'll need alcohol to get through a dinner with me. I'm used to it. I've grown up with her either drunk on expensive wine, or with her head in the clouds from the Valium she loves to swallow.

Lycan moves around me toward the cabinet where the tumblers and bottles of alcohol sit. "What would you like, Marinda?" he questions, keeping his tone calm, while I'm anything but relaxed.

"White wine, please, Mr. Shaw," she answers, and I see Lycan's shoulders tighten at the way she says his last name. I'm also certain my mother knows that grandad is guilty of killing Conall Shaw. There's no way she wouldn't know.

Lycan returns with a white wine and a tumbler with a double shot of whiskey for my dad. "Still enjoy the vodka, Horatio? I don't have any, but I'm sure scotch will do." My husband grins when he hands my father the glass, and there's something in the look Dad gives him that's filled with warning.

"Thank you, Mr. Shaw," my mother says.

"Call me Lycan, please," he tells her before joining me again, his hand finding its place at the base of my spine. "I'm not my father, he was Mr. Shaw," he says with a hint of pain in the words he speaks.

And that's when I see it. The guilt written on my father's face. He does know. Seconds pass before he schools his features, and he's once more the man in the ice mask. The dining room door opens, and I'm met with Darius's grin.

"Sorry I'm late," he says as he enters, dressed in a black suit, white button up, and a tie which is the color of blood. I've only ever seen him all dressed up like this at my wedding that didn't happen, but now, I can't help but smile at seeing him all cleaned up.

My father turns to see who's entered, and his rage explodes. "You fucking bastard!" Dad pushes away from the table where he'd been standing, his face bright red from anger as he pins Darius with a glare so fierce, but the man in the line of fire is not at all perturbed.

"Mr. Bardot," he greets, a smirk gracing his handsome face. My brother-in-law. The man who took me last night, with my husband, and made me feel things I hadn't felt before. He saunters into the room with all the grace of a predator ready to devour its prey. "Good to see you."

"You stole my fucking money," Dad grits, spewing his anger. His teeth clench, his jaw ticks, and I'm shocked he hasn't broken it. "And you stole my daughter!" He throws his hatred toward Lycan.

Darius shakes his head slowly as he regards the older man. "It's funny you should say so," he says. "Because there's something I wanted to talk to you about. I heard you've become a regular at Heaven, where there are girls your daughter's age."

The accusation hangs in the air, and my mother sucks in a shocked breath. "What are you talking about?" she asks, stepping in front of Darius, but the interest in her eyes says more about her than it does about the concern she's trying to portray. She wants Darius. My stomach roils. She's standing next to her husband, and the desire is clear on her face.

I can't judge though. I was with both men last night. *But that was different.* Was it? My mind is awash with guilt and shame as I consider what I did. Lycan's warm breath is on my ear. "Don't you dare question yourself," he whispers, as if he were reading my thoughts. There are times I wonder if he can. Perhaps he has a superpower, not only to make me feel powerful and strong, but also to delve into my thoughts and pull out those negative ones, only to replace them with positive.

"I... I mean..." When I turn to him, he's shaking his head at me.

"Don't." The warning is clear. "We'll talk about this later." His promise is one I believe, because if I've learned anything about my husband, it's that he's not someone who leaves things unfinished.

"Don't you fucking threaten me." Dad's voice cuts through my thoughts. I turn my attention to him, finding him pointing a finger at Darius, his face inches away from the younger man. "I will—"

"You won't do shit to me," Darius interrupts with an easy smile. The calmness he exudes is what I usually see with Lycan, and I wonder if he's keeping his cool because I'm here. Surely he hates my dad, and knowing Darius, that would lead to my father being tortured, and possibly killed. Not that he doesn't deserve it.

"And why not?" Dad's challenge has Darius chuckling.

"Because you know that all those filthy little secrets you've been hiding will be spilled, and your daughter over there will learn about what a lying, cheating bastard you are. Or are you not bothered with her since you sold her off to a Shaw? You know, your mother was a sucker for the Shaw name."

Dad rears his fist, but Darius is faster, catching the attack without flinching.

"Don't you speak about my mother."

"Or shall we talk about your murderous father?" There's another challenge that drips from the question.

Dad's resolve falters, and it only confirms that he knows. He knew about Lycan and Darius's father. "That wasn't—"

"You know your father is a murderer, don't you, Horatio?" The corner of Darius's mouth tilts in satisfaction, knowing he has Dad on the ledge.

There's no way he can deny it now, and finally, Dad surrenders and lowers his head. "I thought so. When she told me, I didn't know what to do. I was already in too deep. My name was linked to things I didn't want anyone to find out about."

"What are you saying?" my mother questions, stepping up beside my father who looks like a defeated man. As if he walked into a war that he thought he could win but got annihilated in the process. "Horatio?"

When Dad turns to Mom, I can see the guilt written all over his face. "I didn't make the best decisions. There are things that I hid from you to keep you safe. I couldn't let you get caught up in the grave that I've dug for myself."

"I don't understand." Mom shakes her head, and for a moment, I feel sorry for her. I want so much to go to him, to tell them I don't know if I can ever forgive him, but then he glances at me.

"I signed your hand in marriage to Lycan because I knew he'd keep you safe."

"From you?" I ask, arching a brow, folding my arms across my chest, as if to keep any lies away. But the barrier won't hide my heart from the pain. "Or from Gran's lies? What is that you were trying to save me from?" This time, I take a step closer, my stomach coiling as unease settles in my gut. I've learned so much about my family, I'm not sure anything else can hurt as much as learning my grandfather was a monster, and my grandmother hid it from us.

"I'm an addict. I do things." He shakes his head, and for a long moment, I hold my breath. "When I first walked into Heaven, Lycan gave me a place to live out fantasies I couldn't tell your mother about."

Everything around me stills. The air gets thick with

something I can't quite put my finger on. Not guilt, but understanding. I've hidden my desires for such a long time. I feel his words right down to my soul.

"But I got out of hand," Dad admits slowly, softly, as if he's afraid I'll kill him with my bare hands. And for a moment, I feel like I can, like I will. "I got to a point where I was drenched in sadistic tendencies that I took it too far."

My mouth falls open. Mom's face is a picture of disbelief, and Lycan's hands grip my shoulders, holding me up. His warmth behind me, offering me shelter from what my father is saying.

"I-I don't... I don't understand," I tell him, but deep down, I do. It's in between the lines, in between the words he's just uttered. I know what he's trying to say, but I don't want to believe it. If he utters those words, it will make it true, and I don't want to believe my father is capable of murder.

"Horatio," Mom's voice cuts through the beating of my heart. It's deafening. A lump in my throat makes it difficult to swallow. My father did something. He did the unthinkable. Just like his father.

Is this something that runs in the family?

Violence.

Chaos.

Destruction.

"I'm sorry, Marinda. I didn't mean to, it just happened. An accident. I lost control," Dad admits, shaking his head.

"The girl," mom says. "The one with the long blonde

hair," she continues, looking at my father as if she doesn't truly know who he is. Does she? Do I?

He nods slowly, but he doesn't look her in the eye. "Lycan banned me from Heaven, he told me he would make sure it went away, that the family will be looked after, if I signed over our daughter's hand to him because I lost a bet with Miles," Dad says, mentioning a man he works with.

"I don't understand," I whisper, and he looks at me as the guilt slowly eats away at him.

"If Lycan didn't marry you by your twenty-first birthday, Miles was going to take you as his. But Lycan stepped in just before he banned Miles and I from the club. He told me if I were to ever do anything like that, go to any club that offered scenes, or playrooms, if I even stepped out of line, he would kill me himself and he would kill Miles. Lycan wanted to keep Scarlett safe from me, from my friends. And I agreed."

Spinning on my heel, I meet the green eyes of the man I've loved since the moment he took me. He saved me from my father, and he saved me from the bastard who wanted to marry me because of a lost bet, and he also saved me from myself.

Lycan showed me what love is. He allowed me to delve into my desires, to live out my fantasies in a safe place. And he offered me my own heaven. Beside him.

"You really did save me," I whisper once more, disbelief lacing every word.

He doesn't respond, merely nods. His hands don't leave

me. They remain glued to my curves. It's as if he can't let me go, even if he wanted to. "Why didn't you tell me all of this before?"

This time, he does respond, "Because I needed your father to tell you the truth."

And that's when I realize, unlike my grandmother, I made the right choice.

LYCAN

Horatio Bardot has always been a no-good bastard. But seeing him whimper about his transgressions makes me angry. The pretty gray eyes that are currently locked on me calm me somewhat, because if she wasn't here, I'd probably do something I'd later regret. And that's not who I am. I regret nothing in my life. Taking Scarlett wasn't part of my plan, I didn't set out to steal or buy her from her father.

The contract was a choice, the right one it seems. I needed her safe, away from Miles, who is old enough to be her father, and the lying, cheating asshole who is actually her blood. Both men are sadistic in their tendencies, and even though I've given her pain, it's always come with pleasure.

"I tried to make sure you saw your twenty-first birthday, and I made sure Miles couldn't come for you later on. He's not a good man, not even by a long shot," I tell her, knowing she's already come to terms with being my wife, but this has solidified her feelings. I knew there was a small inkling of doubt in her mind. I could see it in her eyes.

"Thank you," she tells me, a soft, calm whisper. When she turns around again to face her father, she steps closer to him, and instinct tells me to keep hold of her, but I don't. I allow her to take a stand for what she needs. My girl is strong. She can handle herself; she's proven that time and again.

When she reaches him, she stops, right in front of the man who bargained her life away. The bitter truth is, she's better off, and I'm proud to have her bear the Shaw name. Scarlett shocks me when she grips his shoulders, lifting onto her tip toes, and gifts her father a kiss on either cheek.

There's symbolism in the action.

Also known as the Kiss of Judas if I recall correctly. My mind flits through information I've garnered over the years, and even though I'm not religious, I can't deny my wife has finally realized she's free of her deceitful father.

"Goodbye, Dad," she says, her tone serious. Her voice doesn't break, it doesn't even crack as she steps back, releasing him from her hold, and that's when she nods at Darius. She knew my brother would take the lead because I wouldn't.

I've already saved her.

He's her soldier, while I'm her king.

My queen sidles up beside me, her body slinking under my arm and she relaxes instantly. We watch as Darius grabs Horatio, pushing him to his knees. Marinda's face is a picture of heartbreak as she steps closer to her husband and slaps him harshly across the face. Her anger is palpable, an entity that hangs heavily between them. The room is stifling, and I'm tempted to open the door just to allow fresh air inside.

"You're a bastard, Horatio," Marinda tells him. "All these years, I've stood by you, kept the secret about your lying father, because I thought you were better. And you could've been, but you made the wrong choice."

Those words ring in my mind. Scarlett said the same thing to her grandmother. It seems the Bardot blood line is cursed. It's not the love between Scarlett and me that brought about the curse, it's the choices of a mother and son.

Darius slides his blade from the back of his suit pants, and I have to stifle a chuckle. My brother always keeps a weapon on him, no matter where he is. I guess this time is no different.

"Shall I tell you about a little something I believe in called an eye for an eye?" he questions, gripping Horatio by the hairline, tugging his head back, and slipping the sleek steel against the column of his neck.

"I deserve it," the older man whispers, but it's loud enough for us all to hear. "I don't deny it any longer. Please, do it because I can't live with myself. Now that my daughter knows what I've done, I can't live with her hating me."

"Do you think you deserve the mercy of death?" Darius tips his head to the side, his eyes blazing with pure malice, and Scarlett shivers as she watches her hunter ready to kill for her. "Your daughter is now my family. She's a Shaw," he tells Horatio. "If you truly think you can slip from his life easily, then you're sorely fucking mistaken, because what you're actually going to do is pay. For the rest of your fucking life," Darius promises. I'm not sure what he has in store for the man on his knees, but I can only assume it's not something good.

We watch as the knife slides across his neck, not deep enough to kill, just enough as a warning. The wince on Horatio's face is clear. He doesn't cry out though, his face contorts, his mouth falls open as the trickle of crimson slides slowly down his neck. And then Darius tugs the knife away, releasing his hold on Horatio.

He pulls out his phone and taps on the screen. We wait. Silence once again hangs in the air, threatening and foreboding. And then the dining room doors slide open and a few of the Kovenant saunter in.

"Take him to Atreo. I'm certain the mafia will know how to deal with trash," Darius orders, and this time, I do chuckle.

Alexei's brother is Darius's other half, both ready to kill and torture at a moment's notice.

He looks to Marinda. "You going to follow him?"

She glances over her shoulder at Scarlett.

I'm not sure what my wife wants to do. Her mother was mostly innocent in all this, but she still kept secrets. Even though she wasn't responsible for her husband's actions, I don't trust her. She needs to leave my home, my wife, and my family. But I'll allow her daughter to grace her with that news.

"Will you sit with me, to talk?" she asks, turning to face her daughter. Hope dances in her eyes, her expression is one filled with the need to come closer, but she doesn't. I'm not sure if she's fearful of me or Scarlett, but she doesn't shift an inch. But she waits, and I'm almost sure she's holding her breath, waiting on the answer.

Scarlett glances at me for a moment, and I offer a nod of support. It's her choice, not mine. But whatever she decides, I'll stand by her side. I can't deny her the chance to learn about her mother, I mean truly get to know the woman, but it has to be her who makes the decision.

"We can talk," Scarlett says when she turns her attention back to her mother. "But I can't say I'll ever forgive you." Her voice is strong, confident, filled with conviction, and my chest swells with pride.

"I can live with that." Marinda nods, and a hint of a smile graces her lips.

"I want to know what happens to him," Scarlett says suddenly, and I realize she's looking at Darius. "I need to know exactly what is done to him, and if he's alive afterward."

"Of course," he says with a smile. "You'll be the first to know."

I take this moment to step forward, making my way to Marinda, and I stop inches from her. "Let me make something very clear to you," I start, before fisting my hands to calm down, and continue, "This opportunity you have with my wife, is what she graces you with. If you decide to fuck it up, I won't think twice to get my brother involved and let me tell you, he does enjoy torture. If you so much as make Scarlett cry, I will come for you. The time you spend in our home, Scarlett and I are allowing you, is a privilege, because you don't deserve it."

I take a deep breath, my body is taut with anger, with the rage I felt when I learned about what Grace and Randolf did to my father. It wasn't Marinda's fault, but she was an accomplice.

I lock my glare on hers so she can see the rage swirling in my eyes. "So, don't for one second take this for granted. Am I understood?"

"Yes, of course. I just want a moment to talk with her, just to try and explain. I was wrong. My husband made bad choices, and I followed him. There's no excuse, and I kept those secrets of theirs as well, I'm as guilty as they are, but I've always loved my daughter even if I couldn't show it like I should've."

"The moment Scarlett tells you to leave, you'll be escorted from this property," I inform her before stepping back. She nods, and I turn to my wife, taking her hand in mine. "I'll give you some privacy."

"Thank you," she mouths with a small, grateful smile,

and I press a kiss to her lips before Darius and I leave. I don't close the door, because I still don't trust Marinda. And if Scarlett needs me, I'll be in there within seconds.

"Time for a drink, brother," Darius says as he follows me into the connected living room so we're not too far from Scarlett.

"Time for you to apologize for fucking shooting me," I bite back, and he chuckles.

SCARLETT

My mother.

I watch her as she settles on the chair on the patio. Anger doesn't cover what I feel for her. I'm not sure I can explain it. All my life I wanted someone to show me that I'm worth more than what I can offer them. The only person who's given me that is him—the wolf in a tailored suit— Lycan Shaw.

I settle opposite her, needing to be as far away, but also as close as I can be to her. She watches me for a long time. Her gaze flitting between me and the garden. Her nervous energy makes me anxious, and I wonder what she's about to tell me. Probably something I don't want to know.

"For a long time, I thought I had struck it lucky. There were times I looked at your father and convinced myself he was a good man," she speaks, her voice soft, but I can hear her. "I wanted nothing more than to be someone."

When she lowers her head, I take in her hunched back, her slumped shoulders, and I wonder how a woman who was always so obsessed with what everyone thought of her has come to this. Perhaps it makes me cold, but I feel nothing. There's no sadness, not even an inkling of pity.

"When he told me what he had done," she starts again, her voice raw, and that's when I notice her crying. In all the years, I've never seen this woman shed her emotions. Even when they used to fight, she never allowed herself to show weakness. Because that's what crying is, at least, what she believes.

When I was younger, she taught me to be hardened to the world. She explained how when you're weak, people take advantage of you, but now that I'm learning more about her, I realize, she wasn't offering advice from naivety, she was speaking from experience.

"I wanted to be a woman who could show the world I made it. Coming from nothing, I learned early on that there are those who only care about what they can see. Which is why I was always so hard on you."

"One thing is for sure, mother, you made sure I wasn't the same as you," I inform her. "No man will treat me the way dad treated you."

"You think a man like Lycan Shaw can give you

happiness? Love?" This time, when she looks at me, I see the doubt swirling in her eyes. "He has money, he can buy you anything your heart desires, but there will never be connection."

Her words make me laugh out loud. The muscles in my body tense and tighten as anger warms my stomach. "My husband has given me more in the few months I've known him than yours has in the years you've been married." My words are confident, fierce, and my fingers tremble to smash something.

"You truly love him," she murmurs, her eyes wide as she takes me in.

Looking at her, I nod. "I do. And he loves me, more than you or anyone else can ever imagine. He's swallowed down his own needs, shoving them in a box in order for me to explore who I am as a person." I don't tell her more than that, because she doesn't need to know. All she needs to hear is that I love the man who's probably giving his brother an earful because of our wedding day.

"I wanted what was best for you."

"So, you allowed Father to sell me to someone? To lose me in a bet while he was drunk and partying with girls who were my age?" The disgust is clear in my tone, and it makes her wince. I should care that I just hurt her, but I don't. I push to my feet as her hands shoot out to grab onto mine.

"Don't go yet," she pleads with me, the tears dancing on her lashes as she regards me. The touch of her fingers on mine has me wanting to rip myself away and tell her to leave, but I swallow down the anger, and I don't move.

"Give me a reason to feel anything for you but pity?" I ask, even though nothing is currently flickering through me. Nothing but the need to escape from her, from the lies of the Bardot family. If I'm going to make a name for myself, to finally have a family filled with love, I need to walk away.

"I love you," she says, and it is one of the very few times those words have ever left my mother's mouth. I don't remember a time she didn't say it loud enough for everyone to hear, to ensure all her socialite friends cooed about how sweet she was to me.

"It's all pretense," I tell her. "Everything you've ever done or said has been for the benefit of those around you. Are you saying this now because you know Dad has no more money? That the moment I go to the police and tell them what he did you'll be left in the gutter?"

Once again, my mother winces at my words. I could forgive her, well, I could voice my forgiveness, but for a long while, I don't think I can. Yes, in my heart I've let go of the torment that's hurting me. As I look into her eyes, I silently forgive her for what she put me through, but I do it for me. To allow myself to move on.

"Do you even know what happened to me when I was at school?" I bite out, rage consuming me as I look at the woman who was meant to be there for me. The person I was supposed to be able to talk to when I needed advice, love, support.

From the look on her face, she clearly has no clue.

"I came home before summer break; I was two weeks early, and you didn't give a shit about why the school sent me home." My voice is nothing more than a low hiss. I'm shaking as I rip my hands from her grasp and fist them at my sides.

"I thought you said—"

"I didn't say anything because you weren't even home for me to talk to," I bite out, interrupting her because I need her to know this before she leaves here today. "I was assaulted, forced into a bedroom with two frat guys, who tore my clothes and pinned me down making sure I begged for them to free me. And you know what happened?" Spinning to face her fully, I hiss, "I came home praying you'd come to my aid, to talk to me and see your daughter hurting, but all I got was your usual claims of fun with your friends. Lunches and dinners, tennis matches and country club cocktails."

"I-I... Why didn't you sit me down?"

"Don't make this about what I should've done. The dean said he'd contacted both you and dad, but neither of you responded." This time, the tears that had been burning slip past my lashes, and I allow them to. "I lost all my control that night. I lost a part of me. But I learned how to deal with it. Over time, I'm thankful they didn't get as far as they wanted to. It could've been so much worse." Even at my confession, she doesn't come to me, she doesn't even attempt to hold me.

You cannot walk forward in life while holding onto

your past hurts. It will hinder you, hold you back while you try to make your way to a better future. And I won't allow her to hold me back anymore. I'm done being a pawn in their game.

"My life is my own now. I'm healed." As I say this, she twists her hands in her lap. "I've moved on, I'm creating my own family, one filled with truth, with honesty, and with love."

She blinks, a single tear trickling down her cheek. Slowly, she nods as if coming to terms with what I'm saying. She hardened me so much, and what I've been through, had ensured I could take care of myself. No amount of begging and pleading from her will make me falter in my decision.

I'm strong now.

This is the woman she created.

"This conversation is over. I'd like you to leave." I keep my voice clear, confident, and my chin raised. "I don't want to hear from you again. I no longer have a family linked to the Bardots. With Grace in prison," I tell her, using my grandmother's name to ensure she realizes I'm washing my hands of the Bardots. "And with your husband paying for his sins in other ways, I'm going to let you go as well."

"Scarlett, please—"

"When I needed a mother, you weren't there. What I got instead was a coach, a socialite trainer who taught me how to smile when I hated everyone, to lie when I needed something, and to dress up my pain with pretty fabrics and expensive jewels."

She shakes her head swiftly, her mouth opening, but words not escaping. She can't deny it because she knows it, the bitter truth. Nothing I'm saying is a lie and my mother, the woman who is an expert on lies realizes it's done.

She pushes to her feet, her hands trembling as they hang at her sides. Those eyes, so like mine, look through me. She's an empty vessel, one my father took advantage of, but as much as he's to blame, she is too. Even though she showed me how to be strong, she never took her own advice.

"Goodbye, Scarlett," she says finally, lowering her head before turning and walking back into the house. I watch her go. Once she disappears from view, I let out the breath I've been holding.

For a long while I stand in silence. My mind replaying the events of the day. I was so scared to face them, my parents, but now that it's done, I feel a sense of unease. As if nothing is done. Perhaps it's because my father went so easily. He gave up without a fight. Yes, he knew they outmatched him with both Lycan and Darius, but I've known him my whole life, and he has never given in to anything so quickly.

And that's when I hear the shots echoing through the house.

LYCAN

It wasn't even the moment of impact. I heard a rustle outside the door, and I knew. Call it instinct, but my feet carried me faster than I anticipated. Pushing Darius to the floor, landing beside him, shots ringing out around us.

I don't know who is shooting. But the bullets travel through the office door. Whoever is on the other side has a tussle, and suddenly, the door cracks and splinters as a body flies over the threshold, landing with a loud thud on the floor.

My lungs struggle to pull in air as deep voices come from the hallway, and men dressed in leather come bounding into my office. The smell of alcohol from mine and Darius's drinks sting my nose as I push to my feet to find Horatio lying on the remains of the door.

His body slumps in a manner that confirms he's out cold. Lifting my gaze, I find a couple of the Kovenant members staring at me. "Sorry, man," one of them, I think his name is Howler or something like that, says. "Bastard managed to get free from the prospects that were watching him."

Nodding, I step closer to Horatio, taking him in. His wrinkles more prominent with his face contorted in pain. His chest rising and falling. Honestly, I don't care if he is or not.

"Get this bastard off my property. Make sure he doesn't make a run for it," I order, taking the lead, and I'm surprised Darius allows it. Suddenly, my wife races into the room, her pretty gray eyes wide with shock as she takes in the mess.

"What happened?" Her voice is a soft gasp that has a direct link to my cock. "Uhm... Why is he—?"

"Your dad tried to make his way back in here, to kill me I guess." I shrug it off as she steps into my arms and wraps herself around me. She doesn't notice the looks she gets from the rest of the men as they lift her father from the broken door and carry him out. "Bastard needs to pay for a new door," I mumble before pressing my lips to the top of her head. Her silky hair smells like a spring morning, fresh and floral. Her fragrance has always been something I notice about her, it's as if it enters a room before she does.

"My mother is gone," she whispers into my jacket,

and I glance at Darius, who nods. I watch him take out his cell phone and tap out something before looking at me. A smirk gracing his expression. He must have sent someone to make sure Marinda doesn't try to disappear. I need to know where she is at all times. With my wife choosing to allow her mother to leave, I want to make sure Scarlett is safe.

"Are you happy about that?" I ask softly, running my knuckles over the smooth skin of her cheek. The warmth she radiates is nothing like I've experienced before. Nobody has ever made me weak and strong in equal measure like she does.

"Sort of," she admits with a shrug. "I just needed to hear her side of the story. The thing about it is, she always taught me to be strong, to never allow anyone to walk all over me and yet, she let my father do just that to her."

"But even so, she must still love you in her own way. Parents aren't perfect," I tell her gently because my father wasn't. My mother was her own person, she didn't allow my father to dominate her or tell her what to do. She was a strong woman. Even when she died, she looked like she was sleeping.

"I realize that, but it's just that all these years I craved her love. I wanted her to *see* me, to allow me into her heart, but she never did. I lived my life alone because my parents were more concerned with what they appeared to be to their friends. They didn't love like parents should love."

My chest tightens at her words. She hasn't had a good relationship with her folks, and that makes me sad. I don't like seeing her cry, not when it's from sorrow. When those pretty eyes fill with emotion, I want it to be from pure pleasure.

"When we have kids, I'm going to be a good mother," Scarlett says suddenly, her wide gaze on mine. I have thought about kids before, a few times. But never realized I would have the opportunity to be a father.

"Well, I wouldn't mind being an uncle," Darius interrupts, causing me to glare at him over my shoulder. I wanted to ask her about her dreams for the future, but now that my brother spoke, the moment is gone.

"I thought you had some place to be," I bite out, frustration clear in my tone. Arching a brow, I pin him with a glare.

His chuckle only rankles me more. He does it on purpose, there's no doubt he does, but it doesn't stop my annoyance from building. "I do actually." He nods as he makes his way to where we're standing. He takes Scarlett from me, and for a moment, I want to hold on to her, but he's only saying goodbye. "I'll be seeing you soon, little one," he tells her before pressing a chaste kiss to her forehead. "Be good for him."

"I'm always good," Scarlett responds with a sly smile that she knows will get her a spanking later. But when she slides under my arm, hers wrapping around my waist, I'm calm once more and the jealousy that's bubbling in my gut settles.

"I'll see you soon," Darius tells me, holding out his

hand, he grins. I accept his gesture, and we shake on it. I didn't think we'd ever get to this place again. But since we're here now, I feel like we will finally be able to move on from the past.

"Soon. When we're back in New York, I'll let you know," I tell him.

Once Darius leaves, it's just me, Scarlett, and my broken office door. I look down at her, taking in her face. A work of art, that's what my wife is. "So, tell me more about these kids we're having," I tease, allowing my hands to trail down to her ass. I lift her against me, and she instinctively wraps her slender legs around my waist.

"I was thinking we should have two kids, a boy and a girl," she says, a smile brightening her expression. A look I want to see on her forever.

"Oh?" I tip my head to the side as I regard her. "You do realize you can't order them like that. Life has funny ways of not giving you what you want."

"Did you want me?"

I think about how to word this, so she understands. "No. I didn't want you, I needed you. Life didn't give me what I wanted, which was a life alone, with a woman who just had to give me heirs. Instead, it gave me a woman I truly love who will bear my children and give me a family. Something I never realized I wanted."

This time, Scarlett's smile is so bright I'm blinded by her beauty. "Well, aren't you just a poetic man when you need to be. A romantic if ever I saw one." She taps my nose as she teases me, and her ass hits the desk before she can say anything more.

"I'll show you romantic," I growl, lowering my mouth to her neck, suckling on the silky flesh, biting down hard. I'll leave a mark, and that makes me smile against her throat.

"Lycan—"

"Since you want two, I think we should start practicing now." My hands are already at her thighs as I say this, and I'm about to teach my wife what happens when she wants romance.

DARIUS

Time is of the essence.

Since walking out of the Shaw manor, leaving Crimson Falls, I've settled into a newfound life. Yes, I'm still a biker. I still run the MC, but the anger that had plagued me for so long is gone. I talk to my brother almost every day and we've come to an agreement that if he needs men on his side, the club will be there.

With Kahn heading off soon to find Lorenzo, the bastard who took his sister, I promised I'd help. They had a decoy in Hawaii, thinking he was there, but it was nothing more than a ruse. Nothing angers me more than what happens in the underground. What people don't see is the filth that infiltrates cities, walking amongst them. And generally, they're dressed in designer suits.

I click on the email from Alex confirming the location of the bastard we're looking for. He's flown out of JFK and will be landing in Italy soon. When Kahn told me about this job, I asked him to let me help. And my blood is already at boiling point after reading the case files.

I don't take shit from most people. But when I see criminals getting away with the vile acts that they do, it only spurs me on to do something about it. Since the law doesn't give a shit, or they're too stuck up their own asses to even find pieces of shit like this, I've taken it upon myself to walk in, kill, maim, and torture, until all of them have paid.

Scrolling through the details of my flight, I quickly send a text to Lycan, letting him know I won't be there for Christmas. I'll be in Europe, enjoying myself as I get messy with blood on my hands and some pretty ass Italian women on my dick. I know he'll only chuckle at that because my brother wants me to find someone.

He hasn't said it in so many words, but since he and Scarlett have started trying for kids, he's become softer, less of the cold-hearted bastard I came to know. He's still an asshole, but with her, he's different.

It's not that I don't want a family. Or even a few kids running around. It's just that I'm so lost to this world, the violence and torture, the revenge that I seek is no longer for my family, but to help those who can't help themselves. I'm not sure I want to raise children in the club.

And leaving the club means walking away from everything I've ever known. At least for a long time. I spent most of my adult life with these guys, and the thought of just leaving them doesn't sit well with me.

Perhaps I need to find a woman who can put up with my crazy ass, as well as the rest of my brothers. And that's not going to be an easy feat by any means. They're a lot to handle. Even Scarlett was afraid of them to a certain extent. And I don't blame her. When I saw one of my brothers trying his luck with her, I knew he had to go. I may do a lot of shit, but forcing a woman is against my very fucking soul. Needless to say, the bastard has been buried where nobody can find his body.

She doesn't know that, and she doesn't need to know. My phone beeps with an incoming message. A couple of guys who have been keeping tabs on Horatio and Marinda it seems. My eyes scan the message about Scarlett's father and the breath is knocked from my lungs.

Fuck.

Horatio Bardot committed suicide last night in a hotel room. Police are investigating the scene and will confirm if this was a murder and if there are any suspects.

I don't reply. They don't need to. As long as they've seen I read the message. Setting the phone down, I wonder if I should tell Lycan now, or do I leave it until it hits the news. He'll know that I knew beforehand. And he'll most definitely want to tell Scarlett before she learns from someone else.

I hit forward and type out a caption, letting him know. All updates come directly to me, and I vet them before sending them on. Once I hit send, I lock my phone, grab my keys and wallet. Time to get to the airstrip before they leave without me.

Making my way through the house, I notice a few of the brothers in the bar, a couple in the lounge, and when I step outside, I find Howler talking to some pretty bird. She's tall, possibly about five foot eight, but that's in the heels she's wearing. He doesn't look happy.

Her long blonde hair hangs to the middle of her back, and she looks about nineteen. Fuck, her tits are almost tumbling from the tank top she's wearing. Thankfully she's wearing jeans, or my dick would be standing to attention if she had her ass out. Even so, with those tight ass cheeks in the denim, I can't deny she's hot.

"But Dad," she whines, and my breath is knocked from my lungs when I realize she is Howler's fucking daughter. Jesus Christ. "Why can't I go to the party? Mom only dropped me here so you could let me stay with you for a while."

"Get inside and change. Put your tits away," he grunts, and the girl sighs when she makes her way past me, I get a whiff of vanilla which does nothing to calm my thickening erection.

Too young.

She's too fucking young, Darius.

She glances my way, big, bright blue eyes locking on mine. Her plump, pink lips shimmer with gloss, and her rosy cheeks darken when her gaze roves over me. *I am so fucked.*

Once she's gone, I take a deep breath and face my best friend. "What was that about?"

"Fuckin' ex-wife lumps me with a newly turned nineteen-year-old," he grumbles, and I hold back my smile at my guess at her age. But still, I remind myself, *she's too fucking young.* "It okay if she stays here a while?"

"Yeah, you know my home is your home," I tell him, while my mind starts running through scenarios that I doubt he wants to hear.

"Thanks, man." He slaps me on the shoulder in a show of camaraderie, but if I were to be honest about my thoughts, he'd probably knock me the fuck out. I would if I were him. Before I can answer, he asks, "You headed out now?"

"Yeah. Not sure when I'll be back. I'll need you to watch the club," I tell him. "Also, she can stay as long as she wants." I gesture with my head toward the door where his far too young for me, daughter just walked through.

"Thanks, man. Anything you need while you're away, just call."

I nod. "See you soon." Before he can say anything more, I head to my Harley and swing a leg over. I pick up my helmet, but before I slip it on, my gaze flicks to the house, and on the second floor, at the window which is at the staircase, is a pretty blonde girl watching me.

I'm so fucked.

Time to get away from here.

A few weeks of hunting and killing in Europe will sort me out.

At least, that's what I tell myself as I pull away and head to the waiting plane.

SCARLETT

Lycan saunters into the office where I'm perched on the couch, reading my Kindle. The latest romance novel from my favorite author released and I'm already four chapters in. But when I look up at my husband, all those romantic thoughts dissipate.

"What's wrong?" I ask, pushing to my feet as he closes the distance between us.

He settles on the sofa, pulling me into his lap, and I wonder what has happened. From the expression on his face, it looks like he's gotten some bad news. And that is never good.

"Darius has been in contact," he starts, and my chest

tightens. Lycan said that his brother had been keeping tabs on my folks, making sure they both behave. Because of reasons I don't want to know, torturing my dad with what we know about him is better than sending him to prison. Although, I think that was something Darius enjoyed more than Lycan.

"Tell me?" I plead, looking at my husband, taking in his expression, which is deadly serious, I pull in a deep breath and hold it.

"You dad committed suicide last night," he finally says, and my lungs expel the breath I'd been holding onto. "We're not sure if it was murder made to look like he took his own life or not, but there's an investigation into it."

My mouth opens, but I find no words. My heart slowly cracks at the thought of my father taking his life. But not in sadness, more that I didn't get a chance to have a normal relationship with him. He's a bad man. He's done deplorable things, and my heart aches because I feel cheated that my family is so broken.

Lycan's thumbs swipe at my cheeks, and I realize he's wiping tears away. "I'm sorry, little red," he tells me. The seriousness in his eyes tells me he knows exactly how I feel. And he does to a certain extent. He lost his father as well as his mother, but at least he had a close relationship with Conall Shaw.

"Is it wrong that I don't feel sad for him, but sad for me instead?" I ask, my voice raspy with emotion as I blink away more tears that seem to be coming more frequently. It's as if the floodgates have opened and I can't close them again.

Lycan's arms cocoon me. He holds me tight, keeping me close to his chest, and I can hear his heart beating in a steady rhythm. The calmness of his demeanor grounds me, and even though I let my emotions run free for the first time in a long while, especially for my family, I'm safe right here.

When I first came to Lycan's home, I didn't think I could ever love him. There was so much anger inside me, but now I realize it wasn't him I was angry at, it was my father. He was the one who put me in a situation where I could've easily been in danger. I'm thankful Lycan stepped in. I don't know what would've happened to me if he hadn't, and that's the worst part. My father didn't care as long as he got away with what he did.

My life meant nothing to the man who created me, and that's what hurts the most. Parents are meant to keep you safe and protect you, and yet, the man holding me now is the one who did all that and more.

I don't know how long we sit in the silence of the office. But as darkness takes hold of the room, I realize it must've been hours because when I finally open my eyes, it's nighttime. At least, it's dark out.

"What time is it?" I ask, lifting my head from Lycan's shoulder to find him watching me. His gaze intense, warm, yet filled with love and affection.

"Almost seven," he tells me before pressing his lips to my forehead. "You needed rest, and I wanted to hold you."

His voice is rough with emotion, and I wonder how I got so lucky.

"So, you spent the afternoon watching me sleep?" I ask, a small smile playing on my lips, and he nods. "Most people would say that's strange."

"I never once claimed to be normal, little red," he tells me before suddenly standing, holding me tighter as a squeal falls from my lips. He carries me through the house until we reach the kitchen. When Lycan sets me down on the countertop, my stomach growls.

"I'm hungry," I tell him, causing him to chuckle. It's obvious that's the problem, since the silence is shattered by my rumbling stomach.

"I'm guessing my girl wants something quickly, so a sandwich will have to do," he informs me, and I sit there, my legs dangling from the counter as he moves about the kitchen. I haven't ever seen him cook and watching him just making a sandwich is definitely one of the hottest things I've ever witnessed.

Silence hangs over us for a long moment. There's been something weighing on my mind. The one thing I haven't yet told Lycan about me—what happened at college. Even though I told my mother some of it, I didn't admit the whole truth, not to her. But Lycan would understand, at least, I hope he will.

"Will you tell me something," he says as he works, interrupting my inner thoughts. He slices the bread, and I watch him add the spread before grabbing some cheese and tomato, layering it perfectly. He then continues to heat the cooker and places a pan on the stove.

"What would you like to know?" I smile, taking in the way he builds the layers of cheesy goodness. The heat of the cooker warms me, as he sets the sandwich in, and the sizzle starts.

"When you were studying," he starts, but he doesn't have to continue because my secret is something he already knows about. Perhaps not the whole truth, but what I've kept hidden for so long, is about to come out. "Something happened."

Two words cause my breath to catch. Lycan doesn't say anything more as he picks up a plate after shutting off the pan. "My kind of grilled cheese," he explains, but he doesn't look at me. "I can't be your father, or give you those years back, but I can show you the affection I feel for you now. I can look after you and care for you." He sounds almost sad, as if he would do it if he could, and my chest aches with emotion.

"I know, Lycan. I know that because you've already given me so much." When he finally turns around to face me, he's offering me the plate with a steaming grilled sandwich with cheese melting from the corners. The scent makes my stomach rumble once more, causing him to laugh out loud.

"Eat." An order. One I don't argue with because I'm famished.

He watches me for a long while, a smile on his face as I moan at the deliciousness of my sandwich. It's such a simple thing, but it's definitely one I'm enjoying. Once I'm done, Lycan takes the plate from me and sets it on the counter.

"I had just turned eighteen when I went to my first frat party," I start. I finished school a year earlier than everyone else and managed to get into college with my father's connections. "I was young and stupid, but also, I wasn't. I've read the stories of girls who got hurt, who got..." Shaking my head, I drop my gaze, the guilt and shame of what happened still haunts me. It's like a phantom pain that just doesn't seem to go away.

"You got drunk?" Lycan urges gently as he watches me.

I shake my head. "No. I was actually still sober. A little buzzed, but sober." When I finally lift my gaze to meet his, I continue, "These two guys danced with me for most of the night, and I felt powerful, in control, until I wasn't."

"And nobody helped you?" I can hear the rage burning in his words. The question drenched in pure anger at the fact that I was alone, and none of the students bothered to come to my aid.

"They were all pretty wasted. I mean," I whisper now, feeling the burden of what happened. "I was alone with them in this room. One pinned me to the wall, the other stuck his fingers under my skirt, inside my panties."

With every word I mutter, I watch as Lycan's rage takes over and the wolf bares its teeth. I'm sure if those boys walked in here now, they'd be mauled by my husband.

"I wasn't... They didn't get any further than their fingers. They didn't rape me," I finally utter the words.

"But..." I swallow past the lump in my throat. "Fear and adrenalin had spiked through me, at least, that's what I tell myself because I... I..."

"You were wet, turned on," Lycan finishes for me, and I shamefully nod. "I don't want you to ever feel ashamed to tell me something." His voice is low, rough with emotion. "What happened to you was reprehensible. But how you deal with it, in your mind, in your heart, that's how you cope. If you want to talk to someone, a professional, I'll go with you, or not. But I never want you to feel as if this is your fault for enjoying a fantasy, or a kink."

"I think..." Sighing, I rub my hands over my face, trying to come up with a reason for it. There's no doubt I felt broken, betrayed by my own body. The helpless feeling, along with the way they touched me flicked a switch inside me, and now I'm delving even deeper into the darkness.

"Anything we do, every moment we're in a scene, or each time I touch you, if you feel you need to stop, if you have to walk away, tell me." The honesty in Lycan's gaze heals my shattered heart, not completely, but the way he's looking at me with so much love and affection, makes me wonder if my beliefs all these years, were a lie. "I love you, Scarlett Bardot, and I'll do anything for you." There's no lie in his admission. He would do anything for me.

"Deep down, I don't think it's wrong, with you, but with them..." My words falter once more, but Lycan steps closer. He doesn't touch me, not yet, but he does offer strength even from inches away.

I meet those green eyes that are currently regarding me with breathtaking emotion. He's always stolen my moans and whimpers, but right now, he's stealing my thoughts.

"With you it's right."

"Then don't question it. Most people deny themselves pleasure because they listen to what society tells them. You're not hurting anyone. You're not hurting me. And if I were to ever cross a line, you have to tell me."

Shaking my head, I speak, "You wouldn't, but if I ever felt the need to stop our play, I will. I just spent years feeling guilty for getting turned on."

"You shouldn't feel that way," Lycan tells me. "For years I thought being domineering over a woman was abuse, until I learned there are ways to enjoy yourself without hurting anyone. Safe spaces."

A small smile cracks my lips, and I nod. "Okay." My stomach growls even louder, causing Lycan to chuckle. "I guess I should eat."

He nods. Leaving me on the counter, I watch as he creates a fresh sandwich, and hands it to me once it's steaming. Lycan watches me eat, and once I'm done, he takes the plate and places it in the dishwasher before closing the distance between us.

His hands grip my thighs as he pulls me closer, stepping between my spread legs. His mouth at mine, inches from me, as he whispers, "Now it's time for my dinner." And the low, huskiness of his tone tells me he's probably not having what I just did.

With a squeal, I wrap my legs around his waist, and my arms twine around his neck as he lifts me once more and makes his way out of the kitchen. We head up the stairs to our bedroom, which I've asked him about redecorating, so it actually looks like *our* room, not just his.

When my ass bounces on the mattress, I realize I'm in for a long night. One that will make me forget about my heartache, and have me feeling like I'm completely, and utterly claimed and possessed by my own prince charming, even if he is a rabid wolf.

LYCAN

One month later

It's time to put the past to bed. It has been for a long time, but now that I'm readying myself to be a father, I can't continue to allow history to walk in and fuck up my family. Walking into Heaven, I take in the clientele, all dressed to the nines, and each person looking as if they'd entered their own personal sanctuary.

I find the woman I'm looking for at the bar. I figured that's where she'd be. In the corner, slinking away one of her signature martinis, the familiar eyes that I held so dear years ago glance up to find me.

"Lycan," she murmurs seductively. And if it weren't for Scarlett giving me all I need, being my wife, a mother to my unborn children, I would have considered Yasmine. But I found love. I found happiness, and my need for the woman before me is no longer there. It's as if my little red extinguished a flame, and I'm thankful for it.

"Yasmine," I greet her. "I was looking for you."

"Oh?" She arches a brow, her gaze taking me in from head to toe. "It's good to see you without that flimsy little girl you were parading around."

Anger surges through me, but I swallow it down. I slip my hand in my pocket and pull out the gift my brother left me after he shot me. When Kahn found the truck, he told me Darius had left a hint as to what he wanted. The small, square photos were taken on a disposable. Even though Yasmine denied being with my brother when I first questioned her all those years ago, Darius had filmed their escapades. The photos are snapshots he'd printed out from those videos, which I'm almost fucking certain he still has.

I don't know if it was his way of apologizing for all the shit he'd caused, but now, I'm thankful he gave them to me. I drop them on the counter in front of her, and I watch as Yasmine's face turns into a mixture of anger, shame, and guilt.

"Lycan, I can explain," she starts, dropping to her heels from the bar stool, following me when I turn away from her. My feet carry me to one of the VIP booths, and I settle on the velvet sofa.

"There's no need to explain," I murmur before lifting me hand, and signaling to one of the waiters to bring me a bourbon. When I look at Yasmine again, I smile. But it's not a friendly gesture, it's one of pity. "I'm done playing your games. This run around you enjoy so much, it's over. It has been for a while; I just didn't have the time to come here and speak to you."

"But Lycan, we were good together." Her pleas fall on deaf ears. "Are you doing this because of that little girl?" she spits, and even though I'm tempted to grip her throat and throw her out of my club, I wait for it. And the payoff doesn't come too much later when my drink is set on the table.

"That *little girl* is his wife," Scarlett hisses, her voice poison, her gaze venom as she pins it on Yasmine. "And like my husband told you, whatever you think you had with him..." My little red leans in, getting in Yasmine's face before she hammers the final nail. "Is over."

I can't deny, my dick is hard, and I'm tempted to bend my wife over this table and fuck her in front of every man and woman in this club, but for now, I pick up my crystal tumbler, and sip my drink.

It doesn't take long for Yasmine to push to her feet, offering me one last glance, she spins on her heels and storms out of my club. I'm convinced it will be the last time we see her. And I'm more than happy about that.

My wife slides into my lap and giggles the moment she feels my cock hard against my zipper. "Did me baring my teeth turn you on?" she quizzes me, a sly grin on her face as her hand teases me under the table.

She elicits a groan from deep in my chest, and my palm itches to spank her hard. But for now, I allow her to play. Because the moment I get her in the VIP room, she's going to pay for it.

SCARLETT

Six months later

The evening has settled with a chilly wind which sweeps along the paved driveway of our home in Crimson Falls. This is my home now. My forever. I chose to stay here instead of New York because for now, I want our twins to be born in a place where I found happiness, love, and the man who's coming home to me from a few days away.

My gaze tracks the man I love as he makes his way from the sleek, custom-built, charcoal Jaguar F-type SUV toward me on the threshold of our home. Dressed in a jet-black suit, matching tie, and a crisp white shirt that looks like he's just shrugged it on, he looks ever the man who runs the world.

His dark hair is longer now, and it's currently styled

messily atop his head, which has my fingers tingling to run through the strands to feel the silkiness. His stubble is longer, darker, making him seem even more dangerous than he usually does.

The rain has abated for the moment, but there's a slight trickle of drizzle which falls on him, making him shimmer, as if he's stalking toward me through the mist. A small smile captures his mouth, tilting the corners up, and my stomach tumbles. It could be the twins growing inside me, or it could just me Lycan Shaw's effect on me. Who knows?

When he finally reaches me, he pulls me into his arms, and I fit snugly against him because my stomach is huge. He doesn't say anything, he merely cups my face, and his mouth steals mine in a soft, gentle kiss. There are times he's like a rabid animal, and at others, he's a man needing love.

When he finally breaks the kiss, I'm breathless, my lips wet, and I'm sure my eyes are glazed. I'm needy. Being pregnant has left me turned on more often than not. My husband doesn't mind and takes full advantage.

"I missed you," he murmurs against my mouth, and I capture his lips in another soft kiss before pulling away.

"I've made dinner." Lacing my fingers with his, I tug him inside. I've set up a special dinner tonight because I have news for him. He's been helping me to set up a business. At first, I didn't know how I'd work because I would soon be a mother, but now, with my home office set up, I'll be able to work remotely, and if I need to get into the city, I could go for the day, and we'll have a nanny stay for the time I'm away.

I've already hired Aelin to work for me. She'll be my eyes and ears while I'm here, and she was more than willing to travel out to Crimson Falls when I needed her. Knowing I'm going to be a mom, she's excited to finally be a make-shift aunt. We're not blood, but I learned that family isn't always those you're born with, it's those you choose.

When we reach the dining room, Lycan stops, staring at the elegant place settings, the wine — non-alcoholic for me — and even the candles. I stop at the head of the table, and gesture for my husband to sit, he does so only after regarding me with narrowed eyes.

"What is going on here? What are we celebrating?" he asks as I settle in beside him.

I pick up my glass and hold it there. "I've finalized the details for my media start-up," I tell him. "And I've spoken to Aelin, she's willing to do the running around for the first year or two. I will, if I need to, take the twins with me, but she said she's more than capable of helping me every step of the way."

His smile brightens the darkness that's always on his face. There's something handsome about it, about the danger he exudes. And it has me needy for him twenty-four seven. But the way he's looking at me right now has my stomach tumbling.

"I'm proud of you," he tells me, his voice gentle, deep and commanding. "You've grown a lot since the moment we met. You've become more yourself than you were then.

Stronger, feistier," he says, a smile tilting his lips seductively. "And I've gotten you a gift, to show you just how proud I am of you."

Lycan reaches into his pocket. His eyes locked on mine, holding me hostage as he hands me a set of keys. There's a little heart-shaped locket on it, and attached to the silver keyring, is a card which shimmers under the candlelight.

On the front is my name, Scarlett Shaw, with my job title below, CEO – S. Shaw Media. The lettering done in gold, against the black background of the card makes the wording pop. Running along the bottom of the business card is my cell phone number, along with an email address and website.

"This..." Words fail me as I try to fathom what he's done. "Where do the keys go?" I flick my gaze between my husband and the gift in my hand.

"They're offices in the Shaw building in New York, top floor beside mine." There's a hint of satisfaction on his handsome face. One that makes every inch of my body burn with the need to kiss him, to climb into his lap and forget about dinner.

"You got me offices even though I won't be there?"

"We'll visit before you give birth, and the twins will be able to travel afterward, so there's no need for you *not* to go to the office." He takes my hand in his. "I wanted you to have the career you always dreamed of, but I couldn't have you too far from me, so you'll have to live with working next door to your husband." He winks, and my heart catapults wildly in my chest.

This man.

"I think I can deal with that," I tease, but I'm already moving, sliding into his lap, into his arms, and my lips find his easily as I enjoy the softness of his mouth against mine. This is my life, my future, and I doubt I could be happier. "Oh!"

Lycan's eyes widen in fear and shock when I cry out, but it's only a kick against my stomach. Taking his hand, I place it on my swollen belly, allowing him to feel the movement which has pride shining in those perfectly gentle green eyes.

The eyes I fell in love with. And the eyes I want to look into every day for the rest of my life. "Am I dreaming?" I ask, laying my head on his shoulder.

"No. This is the fairy tale you've been dreaming of all your life, little red," he taunts, pressing soft kisses to my cheeks, mouth, ear. He even tugs at my long hair as I nestle into his warmth.

"Mmm, I don't think Red Riding Hood actually marries the wolf," I tell him, as I recall the ending of the story.

"Well, don't you think it's time to rewrite the story?" Lycan whispers along my cheek. His lips grasp my ear, and he bites down hard on the sensitive lobe, sending heat coursing through my body, pooling between my thighs.

"I think that sounds like a good idea, Mr. Shaw," I tell him, turning to look at the man I love. "Now, you better eat your dinner before it gets cold." I move to shift from his lap, but he holds me tighter. His arms a vise around my waist.

"How about I get dessert first?" he taunts in a low growl. "The wolf always gets what he wants, and right now, he's fucking starving, for his pretty little red." He doesn't wait for my answer before he lifts me onto the table, the place setting clattering against the smooth wooden surface.

I don't have time to think as his hands explore my thighs, my yoga leggings are tight against me, and the heat coming from my pussy has him growling when his fingers taunt me through the thin, flimsy material.

"My little red is all wet, soaking her panties for me," Lycan murmurs as he looks up at me through dark lashes, a predator ready to devour his prey. I'm about to respond when his hands grip the material, and rip the gusset, opening me to his fiery stare. He shoves my panties to the side, and his mouth latches onto my clit, sending me reeling as I lean back on my elbows, watching him lick and lave at my entrance.

His tongue dances along my slit, flicking my hardened nub as he teases me into submission. My legs tremble when he inserts two fingers inside me, and he taunts my opening, sliding in and out slowly. He doesn't touch my G spot, merely teases until I'm a trembling, soaking mess. My arousal drips from my body, his fingers coated with it, the slickness allowing him to slip a third finger in and I'm lost to the pleasure.

I cry out when his free hand slaps my mound. The trickle of pained pleasure sends me to the edge. I'm so close, so needy for my orgasm, I can't think straight. He swats my pussy again, and again, until I'm flying over the edge in a screaming cry, calling his name.

My whole body shaking as I open my eyes to find him smiling at me, his mouth wet with my juices, his tongue darting out to lick at his lips. "Now that's what I call a delicious fucking meal."

LYCAN

Four years later

Giggles and my wife's sweet voice filter through my office window as they play out in the garden. The twins are going to be three, and with them racing around the property already, we've had a fence built around the edge of the property line to ensure they don't venture into the woods. But Scarlett knows there's a small gate just waiting for us to escape through if we want to play out there.

While watching them, I think back to how this all started, how it almost all ended, and what it's like now. I didn't expect her to take a hold of me and never let go. When we met, she seemed too young, but when she opened her mouth that night, I was blown away by just how grown up she truly was.

Having her under my roof changed things. For both of us. I'm not sure it would've been the same had I agreed to allow her to live with her parents until we wed. But I'm glad I stepped up the moment I heard about her father's deal. The bastard would've given her to a vile piece of shit who would've truly hurt her.

I asked Darius to keep an eye on Miles, even though he's no longer a threat, I always like to know where my enemies are. Darius has The Kovenant MC keeping close tabs on him, watching his every move. He's turned into a hermit they tell me.

My thoughts flit back to the conversation I had with my brother.

Setting the tumbler on the table, I focus on Darius. I've put this conversation off long enough, but now that we're alone, he needs to come clean. I have to know why my brother shot me just to take Scarlett.

"To new beginnings. And making sure history doesn't repeat itself," I lift my drink, watching as my brother clinks his glass with mine.

"Jealousy was always something I'd struggled with. Even as the older brother, it always felt like dad favored you. I mean, you were the one set to take over Shaw Industries, so I got that, but my gut didn't. Those feelings don't just disappear when you tell them to."

"So, you shot me?" I arch a brow in question, knowing that's

not the reason. There has to be more. "I mean, if you wanted money, you didn't have to kill me and take my wife."

Perhaps I'm toying with the hunter here, but I need to know.

Darius's gaze lifts to mine and he shakes his head. "I've lived my life in awe of you, Lycan. How much control you had wasn't because you were born that way, you learned it. When I saw you moving on without me, learning that I may actually not be your brother, it led to anger. You know I'm one to shoot first, ask questions later," he tells me, honesty lacing his words. I can see the pain he holds, even under all the layers of violence and cockiness, he's still the broken teenager who wants what his brother had—Dad's attention.

"To be honest," I start, "having father's attention wasn't something I wanted. Yes, I am business minded, but only because he made me that way."

"But you always did everything with him, while they left me to fend for myself."

"We were hardly poor," I throw back, annoyance taking hold of me.

Darius sighs. "I know. I mean... He never once looked at me as if I was his. At least it never felt that way, and I wondered if he hated me because I wasn't Grace's." He sips the alcohol, and I don't take my eyes off him. I can't imagine what it would feel like not knowing who you are.

"So, why my wedding day?"

"I wanted to take everything from you, I felt as if everything was taken from me."

"So, you wanted me to suffer like you did," I say with an

understanding nod. I get it. I do. Lifting my glass, I tip it toward him. "This is our fresh start."

"You're not going to shoot me?" This time, he arches a brow at me, and I chuckle. "I mean, I can take it if you want to."

"Oh, I know you can. But you see, where you're the impulsive one, I'm the level-headed one. This is why we work so well together when we're on the same page."

He shrugs. "I guess so." This time, he smiles. "I won't stay in Crimson Falls," he informs me, but I knew this. He's not cut out to live in a small town. My brother loves the city, and that's where he belongs. Hell, sometimes I wonder if I should stay in New York. But then I remember Scarlett, she should be the one to choose where we end up.

Perhaps, once she's opened her business, she'll choose the Big Apple instead of Crimson Falls. I'll do anything for her. And she knows it. I smile at my brother, happy to finally have some semblance of a family. It's been a long time coming. Far too long.

"To the Shaws," Darius says, and we clink our glasses to that. Scarlett and our children will bear the Shaw name, and maybe one day when they're older, my wife can tell them about the Bardots. But until then, we'll make sure it's nothing more than a distant memory.

I never believed in fairy tales and true love. It was a myth I was happy to allow to pass me by. My life had been filled with work, with scenes at Heaven which if I even try to recall now, don't even come close to what I've found — happiness.

There were days I thought about myself as a father and almost laughed it off. I couldn't do it. I glance out the window to find the kids settled on a blanket while Scarlett pours them some juice. And I smile. At least, I thought I couldn't be a dad.

I watch them for a long while, and when I finally rise from my desk, I realize I'm smiling. I do that a lot lately. At first, Scarlett pointed it out, telling me that something had changed in me. Granted, I am still the bastard she loves, but with Kadence and Kailee running around, I've softened. Not entirely, because I still put Scarlett through her paces, and she enjoys every moment of my domineering self. But there are times she'll smile wistfully at me.

She glances up to the window where I'm now standing and gives me a wave. The kids follow suit, excitedly jumping up and down on the grass as they wave both hands in the air. I respond with one of my own, and the shrieks of giggles that filter toward me have me chuckling.

My perfect family.

We do have to get ready though because Darius is on his way, and both girls will be excited to see their uncle. I think it's the leather cut and rumbling of the motorcycle that always has them squealing.

He's also softened. His usually grim features will relax when he sees them, and he'll give them a smile I haven't seen on my brother before. At least, not for a long time. Not since we were kids. It's good to see him change before my very eyes. The man he became is less of a violent rogue, and more like a family man. My thoughts flick to his love life, and I wonder if he'll ever find someone who will lock him down and give him a family of his own.

He's great with Kadence and Kailee, so I believe he'll be a great father. He just needs to realize there is more to life than killing and revenge. I suppose, running a motorcycle club has its responsibilities, and he has to portray a certain persona. But there comes a time in everyone's life where they have to change. Where they have to really think about what's important.

I turn and make my way down the hall toward the back door, which leads me out into the sunshine. The garden looks magnificent with the flowers blooming, the grass is a stunning, bright green. With summer being here, we've spent a lot of time outdoors. Scarlett's company is doing well and watching her grow into a businesswoman fills me with pride.

"Are my beautiful princesses behaving?" I question, as I close the distance between us.

"Yes, dad!" They both answer at the same time, giggles filtering to me, and I chuckle. They race up to me, and I quickly scoop them up in my arms. Scarlett pushes to her feet, coming toward me to kiss me, and we get a chorus of *ewww* from the girls.

This is the life.

This is happiness.

This is our happily ever after.

Looking for more?

Check out my website for a list of all my books:
www.danirene.com/books

ACKNOWLEDGMENTS

The conclusion was emotional. Writing both books was such an adventure, I didn't want to leave Crimson Falls. But, for now, we will leave Lycan and his Little Red to their HEA. If you're already wanting more from this world, I promise, you won't have to wait too long, because I've already planned the next book, but who it's about is a surprise ;)

Thank you to my editor, Brian, from Illuminate Author Services for fitting me in last minute. Your insight and suggestions made the story shine, and I'm so happy to have the opportunity to work with you.

To the team at Greys Promo, you ladies ROCK! Thank

you so much for everything you did to keep me in line and on deadline.

To my ADULT, Caroline for putting up with my bullshit. And for ensuring I'm on time for everything I would be late to if it weren't for you.

To my BEAUTY, Carolina, for helping me with the group, and for being so sweet when I forget everything I'm meant to do.

The Street Team, you ladies work your ass off to get my name out there, thank you. From the bottom of my little black heart, THANK YOU!

My Deviants!! I love my group, and you ladies make it so amazing to pop in every day when I need an escape from the world. Thank you!!

To my fellow authors who are there with advice, support, and just a general pick me up. Thank you. It means more to me than you know. Thank you for sharing my work with your readers, and giving me a friendship that is second to none.

To the bloggers, you ladies read, read, read, support, post, review, and you do it with a smile. Thank you!! We wouldn't be here if it weren't for you, so keep what you're doing, we appreciate you! #AllBlogsMatter!

Lastly, to the readers, thank YOU! It's because of you I'm able to put out book after book. Giving you what you ask for, and hopefully making you excited about the next book. Thank you for your reviews, keeping them SPOILER

FREE ;) But most of all, thank you for buying our books. For your support, love, and encouragement.

Mad love, D x

FIND ME ONLINE

My exclusive reader group gets news on all up and coming releases, sales, and a chance at early ARC copy giveaways! Join us, we don't bite... hard ;)

Dani's Deviants
https://www.facebook.com/groups/danisdeviants/

Or sign up for my newsletter and get an exclusive novella not available for purchase anywhere!

Sign Up Now!
https://bit.ly/DaniVIPs

ABOUT DANI

Dani is a USA Today Bestselling Author of seductive and deviant romance.

Her books range from the dark to emotional, but every hero is alpha, and each heroine is strong-willed, bringing the men down to their knees.

She now lives in the UK, after moving from Cape Town, with her better half who does all the cooking while she writes all the words.

When she's not writing, she can be found binge-watching

the latest TV series, or working on graphic design. She has a healthy addiction to reading, tattoos, coffee, and ice cream.

www.danirene.com
info@danirene.com

BookBub: http://bit.ly/DaniBookBub
Facebook: http://bit.ly/DaniFBPage
Instagram: http://bit.ly/DaniIG
Goodreads: http://bit.ly/DaniGoodreads
Amazon: http://bit.ly/DaniAmazon
TikTok: http://bit.ly/Dani-TT